She's running out of time
to hook up with the
immortal of her dreams.

"Pia Thomason just might be my favorite heroine ever . . . an entrancing story, and a very good escape."

—*The Romance Reader*

"I completely loved *Zen and the Art of Vampires*! . . . The chemistry between Pia and Kristoff sizzles all the way through the novel. . . . I don't think I can wait for the next Dark Ones installment! Please hurry, Katie!"

—*Romance Junkies*

"Steamy."   —*Booklist*

The Last of the Red-Hot Vampires

"MacAlister's fast-paced romp is a delight with all its quirky twists and turns, which even include a murder mystery."   —*Booklist*

"A wild, zany romantic fantasy. . . . Paranormal romance readers will enjoy this madcap tale of the logical physicist who finds love."   —The Best Reviews

"A fascinating paranormal read that will captivate you."

—Romance Reviews Today

"A pleasurable afternoon of reading."

—*The Romance Reader*

"The sexy humor, wild secondary characters, and outlandish events make her novels pure escapist pleasure!"

—*Romantic Times*

Praise for Katie MacAlister's
Silver Dragons Novel
Me and My Shadow

"Just like always, MacAlister delivers the fun, even in the drama. The characters are engaging [and] quick, and [they] inhabit a universe that only a genius can imagine. The dialogue is witty, Jim the demon dog is hilarious, and the scenery is beautiful."

—Romance Reader at Heart

"The writing was wonderful."
—The Romance Readers Connection

"A fabulous urban fantasy.... The story line is fast-paced from the onset and never slows down.... Fans will enjoy visiting the chaotic charming world of Ms. MacAlister, where the unbelievable becomes believable."
—*Midwest Book Review*

"Laugh-out-loud funny . . . a whimsical, upbeat humor-filled paranormal romance . . . delightful."
—Romance Junkies

Praise for Katie MacAlister's
Aisling Grey, Guardian, Novels
Holy Smokes

"[A] comedic, hot, paranormal caper."   —*Booklist*

"A wonderfully amusing relationship drama . . . a laugh-out-loud tale."   —*Midwest Book Review*

Light My Fire

"Crazy paranormal high jinks, delightful characters, and simmering romance."   —*Booklist*

"A nonstop thrill ride full of sarcastic wit, verve, and action right to the end."   —A Romance Review

Fire Me Up

"[A] wickedly witty, wildly inventive, and fiendishly fun adventure in the paranormal world."   —*Booklist*

"Who knows where she will take us next . . . a fascinating and fun writer."   —The Best Reviews

You Slay Me

"Smart, sexy, and laugh-out-loud funny!"
—Christine Feehan

"Amusing romantic fantasy.... Fans will appreciate this warm humorous tale that slays readers with laughter."
—The Best Reviews

IN THE COMPANY OF VAMPIRES

A Dark Ones Novel

Katie MacAlister

A SIGNET BOOK

SIGNET
Published by New American Library, a division of
Penguin Group (USA) Inc., 375 Hudson Street,
New York, New York 10014, USA
Penguin Group (Canada), 90 Eglinton Avenue East, Suite 700, Toronto,
Ontario M4P 2Y3, Canada (a division of Pearson Penguin Canada Inc.)
Penguin Books Ltd., 80 Strand, London WC2R 0RL, England
Penguin Ireland, 25 St. Stephen's Green, Dublin 2,
Ireland (a division of Penguin Books Ltd.)
Penguin Group (Australia), 250 Camberwell Road, Camberwell, Victoria 3124,
Australia (a division of Pearson Australia Group Pty. Ltd.)
Penguin Books India Pvt. Ltd., 11 Community Centre, Panchsheel Park,
New Delhi - 110 017, India
Penguin Group (NZ), 67 Apollo Drive, Rosedale, North Shore 0632,
New Zealand (a division of Pearson New Zealand Ltd.)
Penguin Books (South Africa) (Pty.) Ltd., 24 Sturdee Avenue,
Rosebank, Johannesburg 2196, South Africa

Penguin Books Ltd., Registered Offices:
80 Strand, London WC2R 0RL, England

First published by Signet, an imprint of New American Library,
a division of Penguin Group (USA) Inc.

First Printing, November 2010
10 9 8 7 6 5 4 3 2 1

This book owes its existence to all the fans who sent me e-mails demanding the further adventures of Ben and Fran, more Viking ghosts, and another shower scene with Ben. It is to those readers that I gratefully dedicate *In the Company of Vampires*.

Prologue

Fran, the wind whispered.

My mother's voice was just as distant as the wind. "Honestly, Fran, I have no idea what you thought you were doing—"

I tuned her out to listen as hard as I could for the elusive sound that flirted on the edges of my awareness.

Fran.

It was Ben. I knew it was Ben, and he needed my help. Desperately. I ran into the darkness to find him, the nightmare re-creating an event that somewhere in my brain I recognized had actually happened, but this version of it was twisted by both the passing of time and my own tormented emotions.

The moon was out, but its illumination did not reach through the dense forest. I dodged skeletal branches of trees as they tried to snatch at my hair and clothing. *I'm coming, Ben! I will save you!*

Too . . . late . . .

Desperation filled me, both mine at the need to find him, to help him, and that which he was pouring into me: the knowledge that I wouldn't be there in time.

Sobs of pure frustration caught in my throat as I battled my way through the eerily grabbing tree branches until at last I saw a dark shape slumped up against a dead tree.

Ben!

He wore the tattered remains of a leather jacket, his shirt completely gone, his face, arms, and torso stained dark with a crisscross pattern of blood oozing up from deep slashes. As I ran toward him, his body slumped to the side. *Too . . . late . . .*

I screamed in wordless horror as he died in front of me, the sound echoing in my head until I woke, drenched with sweat, from the nightmare.

"Nightmare again?" came a sleepy voice from the other side of the room.

I swallowed back the fear that clutched my throat. "Yes. Sorry I woke you."

" 'Sokay. Just stress. G'back to sleep."

"I will, thanks."

I turned my pillow over to the cool side, my heart as sick as my stomach. It wasn't just the stress of my job that had given me the nightmare. I was having them more and more frequently, making me all that more desperate to escape my life.

I lay back down, and prayed for dreamless sleep.

Chapter 1

"And I said to her, Look, you don't own me, okay? Yes, we have incredibly hot sex, but there's more to a relationship than just that. And she said that she just wanted to be with me, and couldn't live without me, and all sorts of things like that. Don't get me wrong. It's nice to have your girlfriend want you and all, but there's such a thing as stifling someone! There are times when I think you're so lucky, Fran. You have no idea what it's like to be in a relationship that's doomed from the very start."

I stared blankly at the sidewalk, my heart contracting at Geoff's words. She was a remarkably pretty girl despite her masculine name (she said her parents didn't believe in conforming to traditional gender roles), with shoulder-length black hair and cute freckles. Although we'd been roomies for almost a year, I was still a bit startled by her lack of awareness.

"You tell your boyfriend you want some space, and poof! He gives you space. You see him, what, once a year? And the rest of the time he leaves you alone to do whatever you want. Now that's a mature relationship.

Do you have a couple of bucks I can borrow? I don't get paid until Friday."

"He's not really my boyfriend." I reached into my jeans pocket for my Starbucks card, handing it to her as she stopped at the walk-up latte window and ordered a latte and an Americano.

"Thanks, Fran. You're a doll. What were we talking about? Oh, your boyfriend. You're so lucky with him."

"He's just a guy I know. Used to know."

"Your setup is perfect," Geoff said with blithe disregard. "He's in Europe, and you're here, doing your own thing. No one on your back all the time, telling you what to do. No one demanding that you stop what you're doing to pay attention to her. No one pressuring you with drama queen scenes, saying she will die if you're not right there for her. I envy you, Fran. I really do."

I accepted the latte she handed me, following as she led the way down the street toward the old redbrick building where we shared a third-floor apartment, each step causing my soul to cry a little more. I ached to tell her the truth, but had decided when I first met her that she would never understand. Her feet were too firmly planted in the everyday world. How could I explain that my former boyfriend was a vampire?

"I told Carmen that I needed a little space, too, but you know what she did? Started cutting herself." Geoff's cell phone burbled. She pulled it out as she continued to talk. "Like I don't have enough of my own emotional issues that I have to deal with hers, too? Do you have any idea what a stress it is to be bisexual these days? My therapist says I'm just asking for trouble, but what does she know? Oh, great, it's the drama queen again. This is like the fiftieth time she's texted me today. I had to turn off my phone in surgery because she wouldn't stop sending me messages, and Dr. Abbot said she was going to end up pulling some poor dog's tooth instead of cleaning it if my phone made her jump just one more time."

I murmured something noncommittal.

We stopped in front of the residents' door at the side of the building. The first floor was taken up by a bookstore, one of my favorite places to spend time. "My hands are full, Fran. Can you get your keys?"

I set my latte on the large metal mailbox that was attached to the building and hunted through the backpack I used as a bag for my keys, my fingers groping blindly in its depths.

"I tell you, if I could, I'd trade Carmen for your Brent any day."

"Ben," I corrected, his name bringing another little zap of pain to my chest. "He's not mine. You can have him."

"He's like the ideal man, leaving you alone except for when you want him. If I was into guys as much as girls—and I'm not because some men are okay, but most of them have way too many issues for me—then I'd definitely give you a run for your money with him. But I'm not, so you don't have to worry."

"That's reassuring," I murmured, the tiniest of smiles making an appearance as I pulled out a couple of paperbacks in order to grope around the bottom of my backpack. If there was one thing I knew about Ben, it was that he wasn't looking for another woman.

At least I didn't think he was. I frowned, thinking about the last time I'd spoken to him. It was the last and biggest in a series of arguments, and he'd sounded so distant and cold. . . .

"I'm loyal that way. It's one of the reasons why we're such good roomies. Because seriously, there are some weirdos out there you can get stuck with. And you're just as normal as they come." She glanced toward my hands. "Well, almost as normal as they come. But you know, hey, everyone has their little quirks, right? And I can definitely put up with you being a tiny bit paranoid about germs and insisting on wearing latex gloves all the time. It doesn't bother me at all. It's probably good, actually, given all the colds and flus that go around nowadays, and if you want to look like a goth by wearing black lace gloves over the latex ones . . . Well, that's no big deal, either. My last roomie was into that Lolita crap, and you looking a bit gothy is a big improvement on that, let me tell you! Although you don't really look goth anymore since you cut your hair and dyed it auburn—"

I frowned harder into the blackness of my bag, still not finding my keys, so frustrated by that fact, it took me a few seconds to realize that Geoff wasn't talking anymore. I looked around, my eyes opening in surprise as a large man in black overalls shoved Geoff into a van.

"Goddess!" I yelled, dropping my backpack to run toward them. "Stop that! Help! Someone help! My friend is being kidnapped!"

"Mmrph!" Geoff said, the man's hand over her mouth. Her eyes were filled with panic as she struggled. A second man was in the back of the van, grabbing her legs as she tried to kick the first guy.

"Help!" I screamed again, but the street, normally filled with shoppers, was strangely devoid of anyone else. It was up to me to save Geoff. Without thinking, I leaped forward as the driver of the van gunned the engine, throwing myself into the back of the van on top of Geoff and the first man, who was in the process of slamming shut the door.

"Let go of her," I growled, curling my fingers into a fist the way Ben had showed me all those years ago. "Or you're going to be really, really sorry!"

"You'll be the one who is sorry," the man said in a heavy Scandinavian accent, his eyes holding a red light that warned me he wasn't a common, average kidnapper. "The master seeks this one. Begone."

Before I could land the punch I was about to make, the man threw his weight against me, sending me flying backward. Frantic to keep from falling, I grabbed at him, but it did little good. All I got was a necklace the man had been wearing before I tumbled out of the van, hitting the street hard enough to knock me silly for a few seconds. When I looked up, trying desperately to clear my vision, the street was empty.

"The master," I repeated, getting painfully to my feet and hobbling over to the sidewalk. I'd heard someone refer to the master five years ago. "Oh, no, it couldn't be him. What on earth does he want with Geoff? It's me he swore to get revenge against!"

I looked down at the necklace in my hand. Because of my gloves, I couldn't feel anything other than the weight of the gold chain. I should have called the police and reported an abduction. I should have screamed until someone came to help me. I should have let someone with power get Geoff back. I should have . . .

"Bloody boiling bullfrogs!" I snarled, ripping off one of my black lace gloves and the thin latex glove beneath it, taking a deep breath. If it really was who I thought it was behind the kidnapping, the police wouldn't be able to help at all, which meant it was up to me to find out who was behind the abduction of Geoff.

The second my bare hand touched the chain, my head was filled with images, a variety of faces that I didn't recognize, a confusing jumble of women in old-fashioned outfits with bodices and long skirts, of men riding horses across a coastline, waving swords and yelling at the top of their lungs, and of a big structure burning while screams ripped into the night.

"And if that doesn't say Loki at work a millennium ago, then I don't know what does," I growled a minute later, stuffing the necklace into my pocket as I pulled on my gloves again, hurrying down the road to a busy cross street. I hesitated at the bus stop, knowing time was of the essence. If the emotions I'd felt on the kidnapper's necklace was right—and I had no reason to doubt my psychometric abilities—then he and his buddies were planning on hustling Geoff to the airport in a few hours. I had little time to make it to the warehouse they were using before she was out of my reach.

"This situation calls for a little splurging. After all, if you can't spend a little mad money when your roomie is kidnapped, when can you?" I muttered to myself as I hunted down a cab. I finally found one and gave the driver instructions on where to go. "I don't know the address, but I do know it's on Knowles Street. Big warehouse with the picture of a penguin painted on the side."

"Sounds like the old Icy Treats place," she said, punching in a couple of buttons on her laptop before pulling out into traffic. "Shouldn't take us long to get there."

Fifteen minutes later we pulled up a half block away. I looked at the warehouse, worried that we were too late, but no, there was the nose of a black van just barely visible from behind an industrial-sized trash bin. I glanced back at the cab, gnawing on my lower lip for a second. "Um . . . how much would it cost for you to wait here for me?"

"How long will you be?" the driver asked me. She had bright yellow hair—not blond, actual yellow—and so many piercings on her head I couldn't count them all.

"I don't know. Maybe ten minutes?"

She named a figure. "But you'll have to pay me what you owe me now. I'm not allowed to let customers leave without paying."

I flinched at the amount she mentioned, but gave a mental shrug as I pulled out some cash, thrusting it toward her. "Wait for me. I'll be as quick as I can."

"Ten minutes. After that, I leave," she said, getting out of her cab to lean a hip against it. "I need a smoke anyway."

I nodded and hurried behind the trash bin, peering around it in the very best James Bond "sneaking up on kidnappers" manner. No one was in the van, and although the warehouse had windows, they were boarded up. I prayed they had no sort of high-tech security system as I dashed to a small door along the wall, pausing to snatch up a big piece of metal pipe that was lying near the trash bin. I weighed it for a couple of seconds, trying to decide if I could actually bring myself to use it, but the memory of the stark horror in Geoff's eyes had me clutching it tight. "You are going to be one sorry god if she's hurt," I snarled under my breath.

The door creaked a little when I opened it a few inches, making me flinch and hold my breath, but no sound emerged from the warehouse, and nothing met my gaze as I peeked in. Sending a little prayer to the god and goddess my mother always swore would always protect me, I slid inside, braced for an outcry or attack.

The warehouse was mostly empty, a huge old building filled with a whole lot of black, and a few faint rus-

tling noises that I took to be rodents. I wasn't particularly
afraid of rats and mice, finding the two-legged variety
much more worrisome. But the relative quiet of the
warehouse worried me. Was I too late? Had the men
taken Geoff off in another car?

The faintest murmur of male voices had me stiffen-
ing as I turned to the right, where the vaguely black
shape of a staircase loomed. I gripped my piece of pipe
and started up the stairs, blindly feeling my way up each
step, moving slowly and carefully so as not to alert anyone to my presence.

By the time I neared the top of the stairs, the sounds
of voices were much clearer. I flattened myself against
the steps and eased up my head to see how many of
them there were. In a small oval pool of bluish white
light, three men stood around another person, who had
been tied to a chair.

Three against one. Not very good odds. But I wasn't
about to let Loki take my roomie. With another deep
breath, I lifted my pipe and flung myself up the last couple of stairs, yelling a one-word spell of protection that
my mother had insisted I learn. *"Salvatio!"*

The first man dropped before I even realized that I
had swung my pipe at his head.

"Oh my god!" Geoff screamed as I stood stunned for
a second, staring down at the man lying at my feet.
"That was awesome!"

The two other men clearly couldn't believe it, either,
because they stared at their fallen buddy for a couple of
seconds before turning identical expressions of surprise
on me.

That didn't last long. The one who had shoved me
out of the van yelled something in a Nordic language
and ran for me.

"I can't believe I'm doing this," I told him as I swung my pipe and sidestepped him, the pipe connecting with the back of his head with a metallic clang that made my stomach turn over. "I'm not at all a brave person. I don't beat people up. Ever. Well, okay, maybe a demon or two, but they aren't real people."

"The master will have your life for this," the third guy said as he slammed me up against a wall.

"Get him! Smash him! Beat his brains in!" Geoff chanted from her chair, the scrape of wood against the floor audible as she chair-hopped over to us.

"Eep," I managed to squeak out, trying to crack the man on the head with my pipe, but he had wised up after watching his two buddies drop and held my arm straight out at my side. His fingers started to tighten around my neck, causing black splotches to dance in front of my face. "Tell your master that he can't have Geoff. If he wants to get tough, he'll have to face me, and the last time he did that, it didn't end well for him."

The man stopped strangling me for a second, a look of confusion filling his eyes. "Who are you?" he asked.

The chair screeched against the floor.

I twisted my body, bringing my knee up to nail the guy in the noogies, biting his arm at the same time. He cursed profanely, dropping to his knees as I raised my pipe high over my head. "My name is Francesca Ghetti, the keeper of the Vikingahärta, and Loki's worst nightmare!"

"You go, Fran!" Geoff cheered as I stood over the kidnapper.

Her words brought some sanity back to me. I was panting, the blood rushing in my ears, my heart beating wildly. I looked down on the man for a second, toying

with the thought of braining him, too, but instead I just
stomped on his foot hard enough to make him yelp, and
jumped over his halfhearted attempt to grab me.

"There's an X-Acto knife over there," Geoff said,
nodding toward a rickety table half hidden by shadows.
"I've been watching it for the last ten minutes, trying to
figure out how I could get to it. Oh no, you don't, Buster
Brown."

As I snatched up the knife, Geoff kicked at the kidnapper, who was just getting to his feet. He howled as
she hit him dead center in his groin.

"Oh, that has to hurt," I murmured as I bent over
her, cutting through the nylon cord that bound her to
the chair. "Poor guy isn't going to have kids after this."

"Poor guy? Are you insane? He's a kidnapper! You
sure you don't want to smash his brains in?" Geoff
asked when her bonds fell to the ground. She rubbed
her wrists, glaring down at the writhing man. One of
the others started to moan and move his arms and legs.

"I'm sure. Let's get out of here before the other two
wake up."

"Okay, but you know, no one would blame you for
roughing them up a little. . . ."

We made it outside before the groin man started
down the stairs (hunched over quite a bit). I didn't stop
to explain to Geoff, just grabbed her arm and hauled
her after me to where the cabby was just getting back in
her car. "Take us to 1021 Woodline Avenue," I told the
cabby, shoving Geoff in the car. I glanced back at the
warehouse, adding, "And hurry, please."

The door to the warehouse was flung open, and two
men staggered out. I was relieved to see that I hadn't
done any permanent damage to them, and hoped the
third wasn't seriously hurt. The cabby eyed them for a

moment, then met my gaze in the rearview mirror. "You in some sort of trouble?"

"No. Someone else is going to be, though," I said grimly.

"Gotcha." She gunned the engine and pulled a very illegal U-turn, the shouts of the guys faintly following us as we zipped down the road.

I leaned back against the seat, letting go of my breath.

"You want to tell me what all that was about?" Geoff asked, examining her wrists.

"Er . . . not really."

"They thought I was you, you know," she said, eyeing me carefully.

"They what?"

She nodded. "They called me Francesca. I guess it's because I copied your haircut before you cut yours. They said the master wanted to see you, and they were going to take me to him. What the hell is going on, Fran? Who were those goons? And why would they want to kidnap you to take you to some bondage dude? Or wait—*was* it a kidnapping?"

"Bondage dude?" I asked, confused how she leaped from Loki to that.

"Master, remember? What else is that if not bondage?" She eyed me again. "You know, I had no idea you were into that sort of thing. I'm not, myself, but I have friends who run a little club in town—"

I held up my hand to stop her. "I'm not into bondage. The master in this instance isn't into bondage, either. At least I don't think he is. He's an old man. A really old man." Like a couple of thousand years, at least. "He's . . . uh . . ."

She raised an eyebrow as I thought frantically of

what to tell her. Almost a year of living with her had made me very well aware that she freaked out at anything even remotely supernatural. There was no way she wouldn't do the same if I told her the old Norse gods were alive and well and after revenge.

At least one of them was.

"He's what?" she asked, prodding me.

"He's . . ." My shoulders slumped. "He's into bondage."

"I knew it! I knew there was more to you than just a germ fetish! So this was what, a fantasy setup? Wow, that's really wild. I'll give you Mistress Dominica's number later, if you like, although if you have your own connection, you probably won't care too much. Are you a bottom or a top?"

I blinked at her. "Eh . . ."

"Bottom. I knew it. I'm a top, myself, but as I told you when I moved in, you don't have to worry that I'm going to try to seduce you." She smiled at the cabdriver's startled glance in the mirror. "I have to give it to you guys—that was a hell of a kidnapping fantasy. I guess I won't be siccing Daddy's lawyers on the guys if they were your friends, although I have to say I thought they were a bit rough, especially when that one guy slammed you up against the wall. Unless, of course, you like that." She gave me a considering look.

I smiled feebly, and spent the remainder of the ride wondering why the vengeful Norse god Loki would pick now to pop back up in my life.

Chapter 2

"Any luck?"

"No. It's gone. Everything but my wallet, which I took with me to pay the cab." I slumped down on my bed and thought seriously about crying, except I wasn't a crying sort of person. It just made me stuffy and hot. "My cell phone, my books, my keys, all gone. The worst part is, it's my own fault—I should have taken the backpack with me, not left it lying next to the door. It all happened so quickly that I just grabbed my money and went after you."

"Sorry that your fantasy went so bad, Fran," Geoff said as she patted me on the shoulder. "I think you ought to tell your bondage dude to reimburse you for your stuff, though, since he botched the whole thing."

I stifled a smile at the idea of demanding money from Loki. "Um . . . yeah."

"Well, once you tell him that you cut and colored your hair, I'm sure it won't happen again. And who knows? Maybe next year I'll go back to being blond, although I have to say I like the ebony look. It's so dramatic and Vampira and all."

My gaze shot to her, but she was bustling around the tiny kitchen in the apartment we shared.

"About next year . . ." I bit my lip, watching as she plugged in an electric teakettle. "I know I said I'd be here at least a couple of years, but I've decided it's time to move on. I accepted an IT job at my dad's office. I'll be starting there just as soon as I wrap up the Web site launch project for the vet hospital."

"You're moving?" Geoff looked surprised, but not in the least bit distressed, which relieved my mind considerably. I figured it wouldn't be hard for her to find a roomie in a university town.

"To California, yes." I rubbed my fingers over the material of my jeans, my hands a bit hot under the two layers of gloves. Ever since that last fight with Ben almost a year ago, I had been growing steadily more unhappy and restless. "I've been thinking about this for a while, and I think change is what I need right now. A change in employment, a change of life, a change in . . ."

My gaze fell to the tiny chest of drawers that butted up against the foot of my bed. I knew well that Geoff had noticed when I removed the picture of Ben that used to sit on top of it. It resided hidden in my underwear drawer, the sight of it bringing me too much pain. It lashed me now as the memory of an angry voice echoed in my head.

"I don't know what more you want from me, Fran! You asked for time apart, and I gave you time apart. You wanted to go to school, and I've followed every rule you set down, only seeing you once a year. Now you don't even want that?"

"It's not that I don't want to see you," I had tried to explain, but it had been difficult doing it over the phone.

Part of me ached with the need to see him, but I knew I had to make a stand. I had to take back my own life. "I just want some time, Ben."

"You've had time! It's been four years since you left GothFaire. Fran, you're my Beloved, the other half to my being. I need you. I can't exist without you. You are the only one who can redeem me. Why can't you understand that?"

And that was the point where I exploded on him. "I do understand it. I just reject the whole idea of Beloveds! I don't want to be your soul mate because I have to, Ben! I don't want to be bound to you just because of some quirk of fate. I want to make my own choices, make my own life, pick my own man! I want to know that the man I choose to spend my life with is right for me not because it was written into some grand plan, but because our hearts say we should be together. Is that so wrong?"

"How do you know that our hearts aren't saying that?" he argued.

"Do you love me, Ben? Can you tell me, right here, right now, that you love me beyond all reason?"

"You are my Beloved," he said in a low, angry voice. "I cannot help but honor and cherish you."

His words pierced my heart like little shards of ice. "You *can't help but cherish me*. That's exactly what I'm talking about, Ben. Neither one of us had a choice in this relationship—you got stuck with me without any say in the matter, too. One minute we had two separate lives. The next we were tangled up together without either one of us wanting it. It just *was*. But that's not good enough. Not any longer, it isn't."

Silence followed my tirade, a silence so filled with pain it almost made me relent. "You don't want me."

I took a deep, shaky breath. "I want to make my own

choices. I don't want to be handed a man and be told I have to bind my life to his simply because of a sympathetic link between us. I want to fall in love, not be told I must love. I want to make my own fate, not accept what life has dealt."

Ben's voice was flat and lifeless, as cold as the arctic wind. "It will be as you wish. Good-bye, Fran."

I closed my eyes tight as I remembered the pain of hearing him speak those words, knowing they would be the last ones I'd hear from him. The year that had passed since that call had been filled with anguish over my decision. Had I been right to sever the relationship with Ben? Was he suffering because of it, or had he, too, been set free to make his own choices. At one time, when I was a naive sixteen, I had fancied myself in love with him. But even then I hadn't wanted to be pushed into the irreversible commitment demanded as a Beloved without knowing my own mind first.

"Is it so much to ask to want to have a say in my own life?" I asked sadly, wiping at a tear that had sneaked out of the corner of my eye.

"No. But sometimes life doesn't work that way." Geoff held out a mug to me. "Sometimes life is messy and confusing and makes you cry, and you have to work like hell to get things straightened out. You going to see your boyfriend?" I started to protest, but she continued. "Oh, I know, you claim he's not your boyfriend, but you don't keep a man's picture in your undies if he doesn't still mean something to you."

"He's . . . it's . . . no. I made my decision. I'm sure he's happier for it."

"I sure hope so, because you've been miserable as hell." She pulled open the top drawer and extracted Ben from my panties. "I gotta admit he's yummy," she said, eyeing the picture. "You said he's even better in person?"

"Yes." My gaze was drawn to the picture, even though I'd stared at it so often it was permanently etched into my memory. Ben's face was half in shadow in the picture, a little smile curling those delectable lips that I remembered with much fondness, but even with his face partially in shadow, I could see the warmth in his gold and brown eyes, see the stubbornness in his jaw, see the black as sin hair that he pulled back into a ponytail. Just looking at him made my body tingle and my heart thump uncomfortably.

"I'm surprised you left him," Geoff said softly, her gaze now on me.

I made an effort to pull my mind back from the deep well of pain that surged up whenever I thought of him. "I had to. He wanted a commitment that I wasn't ready to make. And everyone wanted me to make it, too. Well, everyone but my mother, who told me I needed to get out of the relationship because it wasn't healthy."

Geoff rolled her eyes. "Heard that. Have the T-shirt. My last girlfriend, she makes Carmen look like Miss Free and Easy. I finally had to get a restraining order against her because she started stalking me. It was really creepy. I don't blame you for leaving Brad when you did, because seventeen can be such a wacky time, but are you sure you don't want to see him? I mean, you're all grown up now. Maybe things will be different."

"No. Nothing will be different." I'd still be his Beloved. We'd still be bound together because of that odd quirk of fate, and not because we wanted to be together.

"Well, good luck to you. I'd be scared stiff to move in with my dad. He's so rigid. He still thinks I'm twelve."

I grimaced. "My father isn't much different, but it'll only be for a couple of weeks until I get a place of my own. My mother isn't going to be happy, though. She thinks my dad is the devil incarnate, and she really can't stand her replacement."

"Yeah, my mother hates the current Mrs. Widden, too. I just wish Dad would get past his trophy wife stage and settle down to one."

"Well, there's nothing my mother can do to stop me. Except maybe a spell or two," I added under my breath.

"Except what?"

"Nothing." I scooted back on the bed, mentally counting down the days. Two weeks and I'd be done with the big Web site launch project that I'd been working on for the last three months, and I could leave Oregon and step into a new life.

Why did that thought seem so bleak?

"Doesn't it just figure," Geoff said with an exaggerated sigh, pulling out her phone when it indicated she had another message. "I finally find a normal roommate, and you're dumping me."

"I'm sorry about leaving you in the lurch."

She waved away my apology, tucking the phone into her pocket. "It's your life, and you have a right to live it the way you want. Damn, she's having another hissy. So much for relaxing. I'd better go see what bee is up Queen Carmen's butt this time. See ya."

"Later," I said, mentally rehearsing the conversation I was going to have with my mother. A sudden itchiness had me twitching slightly. Maybe I should tell her now, rather than wait until I was in California. "It's not like it's going to be one simple conversation," I murmured as I put Ben's picture back into the drawer. "I might as well start my martyrdom sooner than later."

I reached for my cell phone, remembering after a few seconds that it was lost with the backpack. "Bullfrogs! I'll just have to wait until Geoff gets back."

I used the time to trot downstairs to check if my backpack had been turned in to the bookstore (it hadn't), finally using their phone to call the police and report it stolen. I suffered through a lecture about leaving valuables out in the open, then headed back up the stairs to the apartment, wondering how my life had suddenly become so chaotic.

"Goddess!"

I stared openmouthed at the man who turned from the small ancient refrigerator that squatted next to the TV, a chicken drumstick in his hand. He was tall, had shoulder-length bleached blond hair, and blue eyes that had seen more history than I could possibly imagine. "Eirik? Eirik Redblood?"

"Goddess Fran! We are so happy to see you again! You have grown bigger!" A second man popped out of the tiny bathroom, wiping his hands on his linen tunic. He was bigger than the first, large and imposing, with a long brown beard that was split down the middle and braided.

"Isleif? What—?"

"She is pleased to see us," a voice said behind me. I spun around and stared with continued stupor at the third man. He, too, was tall and muscular, but his hair was walnut, and he had a short goatee and mustache that gave him a roguish look. "Finnvid."

"Aye, she is pleased," Eirik the Viking ghost said, frowning as Finnvid captured my hand and pressed his all-too-real lips to my knuckles. "Do not slobber on the goddess, Finnvid. It is unseemly."

"Sorry." Finnvid's brown eyes twinkled at me with an expression I remembered well.

"What are you guys doing here?" I asked, trying frantically to wrap my mind around the fact that three Viking ghosts—*my* three Viking ghosts—were standing here in my apartment. "Aren't you supposed to be in Valhalla? Didn't Gunn and her Valkyries take you there? I distinctly remember her taking you away."

"We have returned," Isleif said simply.

"Freya has sent us to you to beg your help," Eirik said, waving the piece of chicken at me.

"Freya wants my help? The goddess Freya?" I asked, remembering a very pissed-off, very beautiful woman.

"Yes. Frigga—that's Odin's wife—she asked Freya to take care of Loki, and since he keeps trying to sell her to the dwarves, she finally had enough and sent us to help you banish him to the Akashic Plain."

My mouth was hanging wide open in prime fly-catching position. I blinked at Eirik a couple of times, wondering if I'd suddenly gone insane. I reached out and touched his chest. He, like the other Vikings, wore a combination of fur, leather, and wool clothing. Each man had a sword strapped to his back, and a dagger and ax on his hips.

Eirik's eyes lit with interest as my hand touched his chest. "You wish to rut at last, goddess?"

"No!" I snatched my hand back from him, remembering well his desire to do things that I had only ever considered doing with Ben. "No, I do not wish to . . . er . . . rut with you."

"Ah, that would be because you rut with the Dark One. He is here?" The three men looked around.

"No, Ben's in Europe."

"Europe?" Isleif pursed his lips and lowered his large body gingerly onto Geoff's overstuffed beanbag chair.

"You have had a quarrel with your man? We will give you advice."

"No, no, that's not at all necessary," I said quickly, all too familiar with their sort of relationship advice.

"Advice," Finnvid agreed, nodding. He shoved Isleif upright when the latter tipped over backward, having evidently not realized there was no back to the beanbag chair. "We are excellent in advice. I, myself, have had five wives. Eirik has had two, and Isleif has been married to the same woman for over a thousand years."

Isleif smiled smugly.

"We are experts on women," Eirik said, taking my hand. "You will tell us about this quarrel, and we will tell you what you have done wrong."

"Honestly, guys, it's all good. Ben and I . . . er . . . we aren't really a couple anymore. He stayed in Europe when I came home to go to college. Now I work for a Web development company." I fought back a little bit of panic at the thought of the three Vikings, well-meaning as they were, giving me endless advice regarding Ben.

"You aren't a couple of what?" Finnvid asked.

"Nothing. It doesn't matter. Tell me about this thing with Freya. Why does she want Loki banned? And how on earth does she expect me to do anything about it?"

"You are the goddess Fran, bearer of the Viking-ahärta," Eirik said, releasing my hand when I tugged firmly. "Freya knows you have the power to defeat Loki, since you have done so in the past."

"I didn't defeat him, per se," I said, mentally going over the events almost five years in the past. "We kind of hit a deadlock. And as for the Vikingahärta . . . I don't have it."

The three Vikings goggled at me. Eirik dropped his

piece of chicken. "You don't?" he asked, absently wiping his fingers on his wool tunic.

"No. It's in Europe. I left it with Imogen."

"Imogen," Finnvid drawled, a wicked smile coming to his face. "How I have missed her."

"Uh-huh." I gave him a look that told him I wasn't buying it. His smile grew broader. "She's keeping it safe for me. I didn't feel it was right to bring it with me when I went to college, and I haven't seen Imogen since I left Europe."

"Then you must retrieve it from her," Eirik said, picking up the chicken and blowing on it. He must have seen my face because he added, "Five-second rule."

I gawked at him. "You know about the five-second rule?"

He shrugged. "Odin has many televisions. Sometimes he lets us watch *MythBusters*. There was a show about the five-second rule."

I held up my hands, having too many difficulties trying to picture a bunch of Viking ghosts sitting around watching TV. "Let's get back to Loki, shall we? Freya sent you to me to help get rid of him?"

"Aye. She was impressed with how bravely we fought against him before," Isleif said. He suddenly brightened as he turned to the other two men. "We can pillage a McDonald's again!"

"McDonald's!" Finnvid and Eirik exclaimed in unison, their faces filled with delight.

"Oh, for the love of the birds in the trees . . . you guys know the rules! No pillaging!"

Finnvid patted me on the shoulder. "You need not get yourself roused with anger, goddess Fran. Freya gave Eirik much gold to spend while we aid you."

Eirik pulled out a credit card. "We have weasel gold."

"That's Visa Gold, not weasel . . . Oh, never mind. Just be sure you use that and don't pillage anything." I took a deep breath. "I don't know why Freya thinks I can banish Loki, and frankly, the aborted kidnapping of Geoff notwithstanding, I'd rather be left in peace."

"Goddess Freya wishes you to banish Loki as soon as you can," Isleif told me, struggling to get out of the beanbag chair. Eirik and Finnvid were rummaging around in the fridge, murmuring softly to themselves over my yogurts and Geoff's leftover take-out chicken. I gave Isleif my hand, planted my feet firmly, and did my best not to topple over when he managed to get to his feet. "He is scaring away the dolphins."

I was getting a little tired of all the goggling and gawking, but there was nothing else I could do at such a bizarre statement. "Huh?"

"He scares away the dolphins. Is that chicken I smell? Excellent. I am very hungry. I will eat a whole one myself."

"What dolphins?" I asked, tugging on the sleeve of the linen shirt he wore beneath his wool tunic.

"The ones at Asgard." He frowned as Finnvid handed him a lemon crème yogurt. "There is no more chicken?"

"Eirik is eating it."

"The goddess will get us more," Eirik answered around a mouthful of fried chicken breast, little crumbs flying from his mouth.

"The goddess will do no such thing. You boys can feed yourselves."

"She is right. We have the weasel gold," Finnvid said, sucking on a wing.

"Low-fat? I do not want low-fat," Isleif declared,

examining the yogurt. "I need fat to maintain my strength."

"You have *dolphins* in Valhalla?" I asked Eirik.

"No. We have fighting and blood and ale wenches in Valhalla," he corrected. "The dolphins are in Asgard."

"But I thought—" I stopped, confused.

"Valhalla is part of Asgard. Some years ago, Odin moved it to the Bahamas because Frigga wished to swim with the dolphins."

"Your Nordic heaven place is in the Bahamas?" I asked, incredulous.

"I just said so. Loki scares the dolphins away. Frigga is most angry with him, and tried to have him banished from Asgard, but Odin refused. He said that Loki lost much standing with the other members of the Aesir when you defeated him, and it would be cruel to take Asgard from him."

"I didn't defeat him. It was a deadlock."

Eirik shrugged, cracking the chicken bones and sucking on the ends. "That is not what the gods think. Loki has been stomping around Asgard muttering about revenge for the last few years. Frigga demanded Freya's help, and she turned to us, charging us with aiding you to do the job. That is why she gave us solid forms—to help you."

I sank bonelessly onto my bed. Eirik sat next to me, still sucking on the chicken bone. "I wish I could help, but I don't know what I can do. I don't have the Viking-ahärta, and even if I did, Loki probably wouldn't let himself be banished with it."

"We will come up with a plan," Isleif said, frowning as Finnvid sucked down a container of yogurt in one slurp. "We will need equipment, however. The weasel gold will get us that."

"I will need a laptop," Finnvid said, wiping his mouth. "I left mine in Valhalla."

"We will all need new spears and shields. And the goddess will need a ladies' beheading ax, since she did not get one the last time we went shopping for her," Eirik said, nodding toward me.

"Oh, no, not again," I moaned, wanting to curl up into a little ball.

"I will need a new bow, since Birta, my wife, broke mine over my head when I tried to shoot her cats."

I stared at him in abject horror.

"I thought they were sick and needed to be put out of their misery," he said quickly, looking offended. "I was trying to help them, but Birta didn't see it that way. And in the end, it turned out to be balls of hair that were distressing them."

"I think I like your wife," I said, giving him a long, hard look. "A lot."

He grinned suddenly. "She would approve of you, too, goddess."

"That's nice, but in truth, neither here nor there." I got off the bed and folded my hands as I faced the three Vikings. "There's no way I'm going to get out of this, is there?"

"No," Eirik said. "Why would you want to?"

I sighed. "Right. Since Loki brought this fight to me by nabbing Geoff, then I guess I don't have any choice but to take care of him. I will do what I can to help you guys—or rather, let you help me—but I need a couple of weeks first to wrap up a big work project. Once that is done, then I can get the Vikingahärta from Imogen and we'll go from there, okay? In the meantime, it was wonderful to see you again, and if you check back with me two weeks from now, I'll be able to tell you when we leave."

They looked confused. "Check back with you?" Finnvid asked.

"We must stay with you," Eirik said, shaking his head. "We have given our oath to Freya to aid you."

Panic hit me hard and hot. "You can't stay with me! I only have this little apartment, and I share it with another woman! There's no room for you here, not to mention the distraction you'd be!"

"We are not leaving you until we have banished Loki," Eirik said with a firmness that made my stomach clench up. The other two Vikings nodded.

"But what am I going to tell Geoff—"

As if her name was an invocation, the door opened and Geoff walked in, freezing when she took in the sight of three large men in Viking wear. "Uh . . ."

"Oh, bullfrogs!" I swore, plopping down onto my bed as I dropped my head onto my hands.

Chapter 3

"Your bondage group *really* gets into their personas," Geoff marveled as I wondered what I could do to escape the hell my life had suddenly become. "Wow. Those are some inventive outfits. Kind of like Ren Faire meets Mistress Sadista. Most of the bondage ensembles I've seen have just consisted of a hood and banana hammock, and maybe some chest restraints. But your group is really . . . interesting. I really like the weapons."

"Bondage!" Eirik said in an outraged tone. "We are not slaves! We are the masters of slaves!"

Geoff sidled over to me and said in a whisper, "Seriously, three tops to one bottom? You don't want to go there."

"That's not what she means," I told Eirik before turning back to Geoff with a speculative glance. "How much money would it take for you to leave for two weeks?"

"Leave? Here?" Rather than looking angry, she looked intrigued. "Why? Oh my god, you're going to have some sort of bondage group orgy, aren't you?"

"No orgy!" I said quickly, frowning as Finnvid's expression turned hopeful. "And they're not part of my bondage group."

"We will be happy to have an orgy if you wish, goddess," Eirik offered.

"If they're not part of your bondage group, then who are they?" Geoff asked, and I had to admit that was a reasonable question.

"We are Vikings, sons of Valhalla, and we have come to help the goddess Fran banish the trickster Loki to the Akasha," Eirik answered before I could think of an answer.

"Ah. Actors," she said, enlightenment dawning in her eyes as she nodded. She peeled off the other T-shirt she wore and grabbed a bath towel. "I didn't know you were doing the drama thing this semester, but knock yourselves out. I'm going to take a shower."

I waited until the door closed before turning on the three Viking ghosts. "You guys cannot stay here."

Finnvid and Eirik had been whispering together while Isleif raided the now mostly empty refrigerator.

"Ah, so that is the bondage," Eirik said after Finnvid stopped talking. Both men looked at me with raised eyebrows. "I have heard of women who enjoy rough bed sport. I had no idea you did."

"I don't. I don't like any bed sport, rough or otherwise."

Their eyes grew round. "You are celibate?"

"No! That is, Ben and I never . . . Oh, it doesn't matter. I like bed sport well enough, but don't have anyone to do it with, okay?"

Isleif returned with a piece of celery, which he dipped into the remaining package of yogurt, crunching loudly as he asked, "The goddess seeks bed-sport advice now?"

"No! For the love of the goddess above, no more advice, please." I took a deep breath. "Look, I know you guys mean well, and I appreciate that. I really do. But the whole subject of my nonexistent intimate relations with Ben is no longer open to discussion."

"Nonexistent . . ." Surprise danced on Eirik's face. "The Dark One has not bedded you?"

The two other Vikings stared at me as if I was the eighth wonder of the world.

"No, he hasn't, not that it's anyone's business," I said meaningfully.

"Perhaps he is unsure of how to proceed," Isleif commented around a mouthful of celery. "It is the Dark One who needs our advice."

I wanted to beat my head on the wall, but knew that would only leave me with a headache. "Okay, new rules: no more discussion of bedding, bed sport, or anything related to that."

"You are a virgin," Finnvid said in a soothing voice, taking me by the shoulders and leading me over to the bed, where he sat down next to me. "You do not know what you are saying."

"Aye, virgins are often confused," Eirik agreed.

"I'm not a virgin!" The second the words left my lips I swore silently to myself. All three Vikings pursed their respective lips. "Not that it's anyone's business. Just forget I blurted that out, all right?"

"You want us to forget you're a virgin?" Eirik asked.

"Yes," I answered. "Can we please move off the subject of sex, or lack thereof?"

"We wish to help you, virgin," Finnvid argued.

I glared at him. "That is totally inappropriate. You are not to call me virgin!"

"My apologies. Virgin *goddess*. You will listen to our most excellent advice. We are older and wiser, and have pleasured many women. We know what is what, and if your Dark One is confused, we will guide him in his time of need."

"No one listens to me," I said, breaking down and gently banging my head on the wall. "I say no talk about sex, and still they go on. Why, why, why?"

"Bed sport is good," Eirik said complacently. "We enjoy it."

"A lot," Finnvid added.

"It is not quite as good as spending a day fighting outside of Valhalla, knowing there is endless ale waiting for us upon our return, but it is almost as good as that," Isleif said.

"Aye, the fighting is best of all," Eirik said, nodding. "Although I would put the bed sport before the ale. Ale is satisfying, but good bed sport is vital."

"Bed sport with an ale wench is the best of all," Finnvid said with a wolfish grin.

"Oh, aye, that's so," Eirik agreed.

"Can we please change the subject?" I begged. "Like to what I'm going to do with you all?"

"Assuming bed sport is out—" Eirik said.

The scowl I shot him should have turned him into Viking dust.

"—then we will escort you to the Vikingahärta, and make our plans for the capture and banishment of Loki."

"No, see, that's not going to work because I'm not going to be able to leave for two weeks."

"Why not now?" Finnvid asked. "Freya will not be happy if you wait when you did not have to."

"No," I said firmly. If there was one thing I'd learned

from my past experience with the Vikings, it's that they'd run all over your good intentions if you let them. "I said I would try to help you, and I will, but on my terms. Loki's goons know now that Geoff isn't me, so I don't have to worry that they'll grab her again, so really, there's no pressing reason why I should leave before my vet hospital Web site project is done. I wouldn't feel at all right leaving it, even if Joann at work is aching to have me gone so she can take over the project and put all sorts of Flash elements into it. We'll just have to find a place for you guys to stay until I'm ready to go."

"That would leave us time for much bartering with the weasel gold," Isleif told the others. "We could get new clothing. Freya said we must blend in with the mortals if we are to walk amongst them."

"Shopping is an excellent idea," I said, pulling out a phone book. "Let me just find you guys a hotel you can stay at, and then I'll show you where the mall is, okay?"

It took the rest of the day, and the last of my patience, but at last I herded my small band of Vikings out to a hotel that was six blocks away. The receptionist didn't look like she wanted to let them stay there, but when I told her in a whisper that they were rehearsing for a movie, she got all excited and gave them a suite. I prayed Freya's credit card held up to that and the shopping spree the Vikings were about to embark on when I left them.

A feeling of unease grew in my belly until I returned back to my apartment. Geoff was chatting with her girlfriend, so I puttered around online, searching the apartment listings in the town in which my father lived, hoping something reasonably priced would magically open up. By the time Geoff was done talking, the worried feeling had grown to consume my thoughts.

"Geoff, I hate to ask you, but would you mind if I used your phone to call my mother? I'll pay you for it since it's an international call."

"Doesn't matter. I've got free everything on my phone," she said, tossing me her cell phone. "Dad gets it through his business."

"That's nice of him. I won't let my mother go on and on, though. I'd hate to use up all your minutes. I just want to tell her I'll be going to see her in a couple of weeks." I wouldn't say anything about the Vikings, though. Mom still had not-very-nice things to say about the last time I ran into them. I sat back on my now rumpled bed and punched in my mother's phone number. "I just hope you don't mind hearing my mom scream when she hears I am going to work for my father . . . Hi, Mom? Oh. It's her voice mail." I waited until her little speech was over and left a message telling her I'd call back later.

The next two days passed with relative normalcy. Eirik left a note on my door saying he had a cell phone, and that if I needed him, to call. He and the other Vikings had decided to take advantage of my stubbornness and had gone out to the coast to do whatever Vikings did in the ocean. Sailed around, probably. So long as they weren't pillaging anything, I figured it couldn't hurt.

But when I couldn't reach my mother for a third day in a row, the worry that had continued to gnaw at my gut turned into a raging torrent of concern.

"I think something's wrong," I told my dad over the phone that night. "She's never gone incommunicado like this. You're sure she didn't e-mail you?"

"I haven't spoken to your mother in over a year, not since she sold her house and sent some old boxes of mementos to me," he answered. "I think you're worrying about nothing, Fran. Your mother is perfectly capable of taking care of herself. I speak from experience, if you recall."

I smiled at the dry note in his voice. When my parents were in the act of splitting up, Mom had been very inventive in her spells. Most of it, he tolerated, like being forced to walk backward, an unnatural growth of hair out of his ears, and even the appearance of a black rain cloud that followed him for two entire weeks. But when she smote him with a spell that left him incapable of pronouncing the letter *s*, he moved out for good.

"I know, but this is different."

"Why not call that friend of yours who's with the Faire?" he asked, his voice distracted.

"Imogen? I think I'm going to have to. I hate to because . . . well, just because. But it's call her or Peter, the head of the Faire, and I don't have his number. If you hear from Mom, let me know, okay?"

"Will do. I'll see you in a few weeks, yes?"

"Yes." I grimaced into the phone and hung up. Taking a job at my father's Internet-based company hadn't been a priority for my life, but I desperately needed to do something to turn my life around. "That's all well and fine, but where on earth is my mother?"

"Maybe she's got a girlfriend, and went off for a wild weekend with her," Geoff suggested, looking up from her book.

"Mom doesn't swing that way."

"That you know of. Maybe she does but she's afraid to tell you, and that's why she's not answering her voice mail."

I thought about that for a few minutes, finally shaking my head. "She's pretty white bread, Geoff. She didn't even like me dating a vam—" My lips closed around the word.

"A what?"

"Nothing. I guess there's nothing for it but to try Imogen, if you're sure you don't mind me using your phone again."

"Knock yourself out. I've got to write a letter to my nana. She doesn't do e-mails, and her ninety-ninth birthday is next week."

"Thanks." I stared at her cell phone in my hand, my stomach tight with the thought of talking to Imogen.

"Something wrong?" Geoff asked.

I made a face. "Not really. It's just that Imogen and I were really close friends. Ben is her brother, and when I decided to leave the Faire and go to college . . . Well, it was kind of ugly."

"Ugly how?"

I was silent for a moment, the memories all but swamping me with grief.

"How can you be so selfish?" Imogen had asked me nearly five years before, tears trembling in her blue eyes, her face mirroring the pain I felt in my heart. "You know what you have to do. Stop fighting your destiny and just do it!"

"Is it so wrong to want some time to just be myself before I have to become an extension of Ben?" I stormed back at her.

"You should be happy to be his Beloved! How can you say you love him, and yet refuse to do what's right?"

I had turned on my heel and walked out of her trailer at that. Three days later I left GothFaire and Europe.

The memory of that time was fresh even now. "Ugly in that Imogen felt I was betraying Ben by refusing to tie myself to him."

"You were only seventeen, right?"

I nodded.

"Man. Talk about pressure," Geoff said, her face filled with sympathy. "Just because you didn't want to date her brother?"

"It goes a bit deeper than that," I admitted. "There was . . . Ben and I had a . . . for lack of a better word, a sort of chemistry thing going on. Everyone said we were meant for each other, and I was expected to fall in with him whether or not I wanted to. Only my mother was on my side." I choked to a stop.

"It was the right thing to do," Geoff said softly.

"I know. I had to have some time to think about things, and at first, Ben was okay with that. But later . . . well. No sense beating that particular dead horse. It's Imogen I'm worried about now. If she's still angry with me, she might hang up before I can explain what's going on." I picked up the phone to dial a well-remembered number.

A man's voice answered Imogen's phone. For one brief mind-constricting moment I thought it was Ben, but the accent was wrong. Ben spoke with a slight accent that I found out was Czech; this man sounded German. "Hallo?"

"Hi. Is Imogen there?" I ordered my heart to start beating again.

"Ya. Who is?"

"My name is Fran. She . . . uh . . . knows me from a few years ago."

A brief muffled conversation was held before the phone was handed over, and a familiar lilting voice greeted me. "Fran? Can this really be you?"

"Yes, it's me. Hi, Imogen. It sounds incredibly lame to say long time no talk, but . . . well, it's been a long time."

Geoff gave me a thumbs-up, and gathered up a duffel bag filled with laundry, mouthing she'd be back shortly.

"It has been forever," Imogen said, her voice rich with sorrow and regret that made my eyes burn painfully. "Oh, Fran, I have missed you so much. Can you ever forgive me for trying to force you and Benedikt together? I was so angry, but then I realized that you were right—you needed to have time to grow up and be who you were meant to be. I just wanted so much for you and Benedikt to be happy together—"

"I know you did. And I really wish it could have worked out. But before we get all maudlin, I'm trying to locate my mom. Is she there?"

"Here with me? No, she went to Heidelberg for the weekend to do some shopping."

I frowned at my feet. "But it's Tuesday. Shouldn't she have been back by now?"

"Yes, she should be back . . . one moment. Günter, my love, would you mind terribly going out and seeing if Miranda is about? You remember her, don't you? She's the Wiccan who has those lovely good luck charms I bought for you. Günter is checking, Fran. Now, you must tell me how you are, and what you have been doing, and oh, everything. I wanted to talk to you so many years ago, but Benedikt said we must give you space, which just sounded silly to me, because we are best friends, are we not? But he insisted, and so I abided by his desire, and let you grow up. You have grown up, haven't you?"

I laughed at the wistful note in her voice. "Yes, I'm a big girl now. Well, bigger, which is pretty awkward, considering I'm six feet tall and built like a—"

"Brick oven," she finished, snorting a little. "Are you still worried about your appearance? I've told you many times that you are a lovely girl—woman—and just because you're not petite like Miranda doesn't mean that men don't find you attractive. Not that it matters what any of them think except Benedikt, but still, it's nice to know one is admired, is it not?"

"Er . . . yeah." A sense of horror filled me. Had Ben not told her that I'd broken off with him?

"And so you will be returning to us soon? Benedikt says that you have completed your education and that you are working making Web sites."

The horror grew. "He knows what I'm doing? I hadn't realized he was keeping track."

"He has abided by the rules you set down for him," she answered softly. "He has not contacted you outside of the designated periods you allowed, has he?"

"No." I didn't want to tell her, but honesty compelled me to make sure she understood the truth of what had happened between us. "I just wasn't aware that he knew what was going on in my life. Imogen—"

"You are his Beloved," she interrupted. I ground my teeth. Why could no one ever look past that fact? "You *are* life to him. It has not been easy for him to do as you asked, but he is a man of much honor."

My shoulders slumped. "Has he . . . I haven't talked to him in a while. Has he been okay this past year?"

"He misses you, naturally. But yes, other than that, he has been very busy."

A smidgen of relief filled me. Although I knew it was the melodramatic imaginings of my deranged mind, I had wondered if Ben had suffered because of my decision. That he hadn't was proof I had made the right choice.

So why didn't I feel better?

Before I could think of anything to say, I heard a male voice in the background.

"How very odd," Imogen said after a moment. "Miranda doesn't appear to have returned from Heidelberg."

"Son of a pus bucket," I swore, the fear that gripped me driving away the misery about Ben. Had Loki gone after my mother once he had failed to grab me? "Where are you, exactly? I mean, what town?"

"Brustwarze."

"I beg your pardon?" Did she just say breast warts at me?

"Brustwarze. It means nipple."

"You're in a town named for nipples?"

"Yes. It's near Heidelberg."

Oh goddess, it was true—it had to be true. Who else would want to kidnap my mother but Loki, who had sworn vengeance on me the last time we'd met?

Well, that was pretty much all she wrote. I couldn't sit here and let Loki do who-knew-what to my mother. I had to save her. I had to go to Germany, go back to the GothFaire.

Ben. Was he there? He frequently visited his sister. Would I be able to cope having to see him again?

Did I have any choice?

"I hate it when life does this to me," I snarled, shocking Imogen.

"I beg your pardon?"

"It's nothing important. I'm catching the first plane I can to Germany."

"What?" she almost shrieked. "You're coming out here? Now?"

"My mother's missing, and I have a nasty feeling I

know who's behind it," I said, logging into a travel Web site. I punched up flights to Germany, bile rolling around in my stomach. I didn't want to go, but there was no one else who could tackle Loki. Besides, it was my responsibility. Loki had threatened vengeance against me because of actions I took, no one else. It was only right I should be the one to face his wrath.

St. Fran the martyr. What a depressing thought.

"But, Fran, I'm sure your mother is fine, just fine. Maybe she told Peter she was going to be away for longer and he didn't mention it to anyone."

"You can check on that, but I doubt it. It's not like my mother to ignore her cell phone. Looks like I can be out there in about twelve hours, if I get cracking. It'll eat up a big chunk of my new apartment money, but that can't be helped."

"Twelve hours . . . oh, but Fran! What about Benedikt?"

"He's there?" Excitement shimmied down my arms before I told my Inner Fran to get with the plan. I was *not* excited about the thought of seeing Ben again.

"Yes, but, Fran, I think you should—"

"I know, I should have a long talk with him. And maybe I will. But right now, I have to find my mother." My gaze fell on the clock. "Crap. Gotta get moving or I won't make the airport in time. See you when I get there."

"But, Fran!" Imogen sputtered something, but I didn't have time to argue with her. I said good-bye, hung up, then quickly punched in Eirik's cell phone number, trying to calm my wildly excited nerves. Part of me was panicking at the thought of Loki having my mother, the other was focused on the idea that I would see Ben in just a few hours. I hadn't seen him in almost five years.

Would he make a scene when I showed up at the Faire? Would he try to persuade me that I was meant to spend the rest of my life with him?

"This is Eirik Redblood, Viking warlord, left hand of the goddess Freya, and right hand of the virgin goddess Fran."

"Oh, for the love of . . ." I took a deep breath, deciding to hold off the argument about the Vikings' latest name for me. "Hi, Eirik. It's Fran. How fast can you guys get to the airport?"

Silence answered that question for the count of five. "We are going after Loki?"

"You're darned tooting we are. He's taken my mother, and no one—*no one*—messes with my family!"

The sound of murmuring answered that, followed immediately by ear-piercing Viking battle cries. "Command us, virgin goddess!" Eirik declared happily.

"I don't have enough money to get you guys tickets, so you'll have to use your weasel money to buy them." I gave him information on the flight I had booked myself. "Oh, man, passports—"

"We have them. The goddess Freya had them made up, and gave them to us with the weasel gold."

"Excellent. I hope you boys are all geared up and ready to kick some serious booty!"

"Our enemies will fall!" I heard Finnvid yelling in the background. "We will not fail you, virgin goddess Fran!"

"We will cleave his head from his shoulders!" Isleif growled.

"Normally I'd say I'm not up to cleaving anything, but at this moment . . ." My eyes narrowed as I thought of all the things I wanted to do to Loki. "At this moment, I might just take a swing at him myself."

The Vikings cheered, and promised to meet me at the airport in time for the flight to Germany.

Geoff came back just as I was stuffing clothing into my suitcase. "What's going on? I thought you said you were staying for a couple more weeks?"

"That was before my mom was kidnapped." I smiled grimly at her look of stupefaction. "If he's so much as touched her, I'm going to open the biggest can of Viking-ahärta whoop-ass Loki's ever seen!"

Chapter 4

"To yo ta ho," a man told us as we stepped off the train at the tiny little town of Brustwarze. He was dressed in a horned helmet, metal breastplate, leather pleated skirt, and had two long blond braids. He also held a trident.

"What in the name of a three-legged toad is going on?" I asked as I stared in confusion at the mass of people streaming onto the train. Over half of them were dressed in bizarre costumes, everything ranging from mermaids to guys wearing big shields and long, dramatic capes.

Finnvid, who had been studying a sign on the wall of the train station, said, "It says there is a competition being held for the next week to decide which town will become the new home to Wagner's operas. The mayor has directed everyone in the town to participate, showing the town's worthiness."

"What is opera?" Isleif asked, dodging a woman in a long marigold medieval gown who almost poked out his eye with her gigantic spiky headdress, complete with glittery veil, as she wheeled twins in a baby stroller.

Both babies wore tiny little winged helmets. One had on a pair of Groucho glasses, as well.

"You remember—we saw it on Odin's television. Opera is women singing high enough to suck up your stones right into your body."

"That's not opera," Eirik said with a dismissive gesture. "That's *America's Favorite Idol*. Odin loves that show," he added to me in an aside.

"Er . . . okay. Town competition or not, we have to get to where the GothFaire is parked. Finnvid, you seem to speak German—can you ask where they are?"

Twenty minutes later we managed to pull Finnvid away from two young women evidently dressed as medieval dairy maids, both of whom seemed to be encouraging him to do wholly inappropriate things in public.

"They told me I could pretend they were cows and moisturize their udders," Finnvid protested as I dragged him by the ear over to where Eirik and Isleif stood. His hands were covered in honeysuckle-scented body lotion.

"No woman in her right mind would ever refer to her breasts as udders," I grumbled, releasing his ear as I stopped in front of the taxi Eirik had snagged. "Rub that lotion into your arms or something so you don't get it everywhere."

"Well, that is what I thought the word meant," he said somewhat ruefully as he complied with my demand.

"I just bet. Did you find out where the GothFaire is?"

"Aye, virgin goddess. It's about twenty minutes to the north of town." He held out a piece of paper. "They wrote it down for me."

"That looks like a phone number," I pointed out.

He grinned and turned the paper over. On it were two words. "They also gave me their phone number."

"Do they have friends?" Eirik asked as I hustled them to the taxi.

"You guys can pick up dates later. Right now I need you to focus on finding my mother." I leaned forward to show the address to the driver, who was dressed in a pretty gauzy gold gown, with matching blond braids, and a flowery wreath on her head. The face that turned to squint at the address had a goatee and mustache.

"Er . . ." I blinked at him a couple of times. He nodded and said something that I assumed meant he knew where that was. At least I hoped that's what he said.

Half an hour later I paid off the Wagnerian cross-dressing driver and stood looking at the large open field before us. It must have been a grazing pasture, because it was perfectly flat, surrounded by low stone fences on three sides and a modern wooden fence that ran parallel to the road. The big double gates were open, and tire marks on one side of the field indicated that it was used for parking. But it was the colorful flutter of bright cloth that caught and held my eye.

"GothFaire," I said, drinking in the sight. Somewhere in that collection of trailers and tents, Ben was sleeping. He usually stayed with Imogen unless she had a boyfriend with her, which it sounded like she did, and that meant he could be anywhere, most likely holed up with one of his friends at the Faire.

"Eirik, I will need to use your iPhone later, to call Sabeine and Siglinde," Finnvid said, examining the paper that he'd retrieved from me. "They said the day's competition would be over by sundown."

"Quiet. The virgin goddess is having a moment,"

Eirik said in a hushed voice, nodding toward me before suddenly looking thoughtful. "Did they say I could moisturize their udders as well?"

"Aye, there's plenty there for both of us," Finnvid answered with a knowing leer.

I gazed at the Faire, unable to keep from remembering the year and a half I'd spent there, remembering the good times with Ben . . .

"Good. I like a woman with large—" He made squeezy motions at his chest.

. . . Remembering Ben's kisses, and the way his eye color changed, and how he seemed to like me in the gypsyesque outfit that I wore when reading palms, the one he said made him want to kiss me senseless.

"You can have Siglinde, then. She was bigger than her sister."

I smoothed down my blouse and wondered if Ben thought I was large in the breast department, then told myself it didn't matter what he thought, and that I really needed to stop thinking about him and focus on what was important.

"You examined them?" Eirik asked, looking somewhat put out.

My skin began to tingle, all of me, as if just being in the same town as Ben had electrified the air, especially my breasts, which badly wanted his attention. I stopped that thought dead in its tracks, glaring at the Vikings. Damn their talk of breasts.

"Of course. That's the first thing I do with a woman I'm considering for bed sport. What sort of moment is the goddess having?"

"One that has been invaded by the mental image of you two oiling up those buxom ladies," I said with a little glare at the two of them. "Do you have any idea how difficult it is to indulge in soul-searching insight with people yammering away about breasts?"

Isleif looked righteous. "I did not yammer, virgin goddess."

"Oooh, oil." Finnvid's eyes went a bit glazed.

"Stop that. We have things to do," I said, frowning at his twitching fingers.

"But oiled breasts . . ."

"No breasts for you!" I ordered, feeling a bit like the Breast Nazi. "Can we move past that subject?"

"Aye, we can. Our apologies, virgin goddess." Eirik narrowed his eyes on me. "Are you finished having your moment?"

"Yes, thank you. It's over. Come on, let's see who's— What in the name of all that is bright and glittery is that?"

We all turned to face the road. I had been aware of the faint sound of singing, assuming someone at the Faire had the radio on. But the volume was growing, and at last I realized that the noise was coming from the road, where a group of about ten young men clad in ragged cloth pants, bits of wool wrapped around their feet with leather thongs, and torn tunics jogged past us, singing as they went.

"This is Tuesday, yes?" Finnvid said, pulling out a pamphlet. He looked at his watch. "Ah. The schedule says they are the Brustwarze High School Athletic Pilgrim's Chorus."

We watched the track team as they sang their way past us. I applauded politely. A couple of them managed a bow in midjog before they continued off into the distance.

"What was I saying?" I asked Isleif once they were far enough away that we could speak without shouting.

"Something about seeing someone?" he asked.

"Ah! Yes, we will see who's awake at this time of the morning." And then I would find out where Ben was, so I could brace myself for what I knew would be a somewhat emotional meeting.

We marched across the large open field until we were up to the ticket booth, sitting on the fringe of the Faire.

"It looks just the same as it did before," Isleif commented, eyeing the long U shape that was created by a big tent at one end and two rows of vendors and Faire performers.

I stopped for a moment, the sense of déjà vu so great it was almost as if the last five years had never happened. "It certainly does," I mused. "There's the aura photography booth. There's Desdemona's personal time travel tent. That's where Tallulah talks to the dead. And there's my mother's booth."

I walked over to the small canvas and wood tent that served as booths for the Faire folk, familiar with every inch of the structure. They were easily set up and taken down, each with brightly painted designs. Mom as the resident Wiccan offered to counsel people who wanted to get in touch with the goddess and god, provided products like do-it-yourself love potion kits, and benign spells and potions that she felt made the world a better place. The flap to the tent was laced down now, concealing the long table that was no doubt set up behind it with rows of tiny bottles of happiness, understanding, generosity, luck, and even forgiveness.

A little pain contracted around my heart at the thought of the years I had spent helping her dry the herbs and flowers that had gone into her potions and spell kits. Once I would have given anything to have a normal mother, but now I just wanted her back, with all of her irritating, irrational ways.

"We'll find her," Eirik said, obviously reading the distress on my face as I touched the bright red and orange tent. The other Vikings murmured their agreement. "We will force Loki to give her back."

"I know we will, and thanks, guys. I really do appreciate your help with this. Well, I suppose I should find Imogen and see if there is any news of Mom." Now that there was nothing but a short distance between Ben and me, my palms were suddenly sweaty. I had to stand firm. I had made my choices, and I would stick to them, no matter how annoying my breasts were in their demand to be placed in Ben's hands. And mouth.

I moaned slightly at the thought of his mouth on my flesh.

"Virgin goddess?" Eirik asked. "Is all well?"

"Yes." My voice came out hoarse. I cleared it. If Ben was staying with Imogen, then the sooner I got a meeting with him out of the way, the better it would be for everyone. "Perfectly fine. This way."

We moved off past a group of people standing in front of the aura photography booth. It wasn't yet noon, and the Faire wasn't due to open for another two hours, but I remembered from my time working the palm reading booth that there were always a few early folk who liked to stroll around and eyeball the various offerings.

A big blond man with a very square jaw strode by, calling something in German to the clutch of people. They answered and moved off, evidently having seen the wisdom of waiting until the Faire opened. The blond man started to turn around, then paused, casting a glance back toward me. His step faltered. "Fran? Is that you?"

I smiled and ruffled my now short hair. "Hi, Kurt. Er . . . Karl. No, Kurt?"

"Kurt is right," he said and laughed, and before I could say anything else, he embraced me in a bear hug that just about squeezed the breath out of my lungs. "You are back now? You are done with your schooling?"

"I'm done with college, yes, but I'm not here to stay. My mother hasn't returned, has she?"

His eyebrows rose. "I haven't seen her in a few days. Is something wrong?"

"Possibly."

His eyes slid past me to the Vikings. They bugged out a bit (his eyes, not the Vikings). "Those are . . . those are . . ."

"Those are the Vikings that I inadvertently raised almost five years ago in Sweden, yes." I smiled at his look of shock. "You have to forgive their choice of clothing. They were in Valhalla until a couple of days ago, and they went a little nuts at the outlet mall."

Eirik brushed his hand down his navy blue muscle tee and adjusted his white-framed sunglasses. I squinted a little as the sunlight glared off the brilliant yellow of his tight clam diggers, white belt, and matching white shoes. "You do not like our new clothes, virgin goddess? I noticed you did not comment about them at the airport, where others were clearly envious of them."

I bit my lip for a moment. "Your clothes are just fine."

"A woman on the plane told me she had never seen anything like them before," Isleif said with obvious pride, grabbing either side of his neon blue–and–white-striped plus four pants and pulling them out to maximum fluffiness. He wore a scarlet angora sweater that he had decided was too hot, so he pulled off the sleeves and cut a strip from the bottom, leaving him with his arms and belly button exposed.

Kurt gurgled a little. We both turned to look at Finnvid. He wore what I had assumed was a swimmer's full-length body suit, the tight spandex clinging to his body like a second skin, leaving little, if anything, to the imagination. Luckily, he had also donned a black and white polka-dot knee-length knit coat, and a black fedora that he wore tipped at a rakish angle.

I sighed and smiled at Kurt. "The Vikings have been sent to help me with a little situation. They won't cause any problems with the customers. Right, gentlemen?"

"We have sworn to not slay anyone you do not authorize us to slay," Eirik said with a frown. "Although I dislike you binding us to such an oath, virgin goddess. It makes us feel helpless."

"You guys are anything but helpless, and you know it. Is Imogen up yet, do you know?"

Kurt blinked. "I don't know. I haven't seen her this morning. Did he say *virgin* goddess?"

"No, he didn't," I said loudly, narrowing my eyes at each and every one of the Vikings. They grinned at me, the rats. "She knows I was coming, so I'll just go say hi and get my Vikingahärta from her." And get the meeting with Ben out of the way.

Inner Fran could not help but wonder if he missed me.

I hurried toward the gold and white trailer decorated with scarlet hands and runes that was Imogen's home when she was traveling with the GothFaire, ignoring both Inner Fran and my suddenly rapidly beating heart.

Kurt called something after us, but I was suddenly frantic to see Ben. Imogen! Not Ben, but Imogen! I didn't want to see Ben at all. In fact, I'd pay good money to have someone haul him away so I wouldn't accidentally run into him.

Inner Fran told me it was the purest folly to lie to oneself. I gritted my teeth and told her to go do something rude to herself. As we walked to Imogen's trailer, I stopped and turned to the Vikings. "Uh . . . guys, would you give me a few minutes alone with Be . . . er . . . Imogen?"

Eirik looked suspicious. "If you command it, virgin goddess. What should we do while we are waiting for you?"

"It would be really helpful if you could scout around the area and see if there are any signs Loki was here."

His suspicion turned darker. "We are not scouts! Vikings do not scout! We are above such things!"

"Well . . . what do you do?" I asked.

"We pillage," he answered quickly. "We plunder."

"We kill," added Finnvid. "A lot."

"Don't forget drinking. We drink a lot, as well."

The other two nodded.

"It's too early to drink, I don't want anyone killed, there will be no pillaging, and since I know one or the other of you is bound to add this to your list, no oiling of breasts, either. At least not out in public. What you do in private is thankfully your own business." I filled my expression with as much pathos as I could pack into it. "But if you don't want to look around for signs of Loki, and where he might have gone, I'll have to find someone else to do it."

Eirik's nostrils flared. "We were assigned by the goddess Freya to aid you! You will have no others. If you desire us to scout . . ." He shuddered. "Then we will lower ourselves to scouting."

"Think of it as being Viking ninjas." I leaned in and lowered my voice to a conspiratorial level. "Stealthy and covert."

"Stealthy," Finnvid said thoughtfully.

"Covert?" Eirik glanced at the others. "Have we ever been covert?"

Isleif shook his head. "No, but I watched a movie about ninjas. They were most deadly and feared by all. Just like us. We will be ninjas, virgin goddess. *Viking* ninjas."

"The best kind," Eirik agreed.

"Sounds good. You go be stealthy, covert Viking ninjas"—really, I deserve an award for being able to say that without so much as one titter or a twitch of my lips—"and I'll meet you guys back here in a couple of hours, okay? You remember which trailer is my mom's?"

They nodded.

"We must go shopping again," Isleif commented as they headed off. "The ninjas in the movie had special armor. We will need the same."

"Aye." Eirik's voice drifted back to me. "We will find the local ninja store, and use the weasel gold to buy everything they have. . . ."

"Heaven help the local shops," I murmured before eyeing Imogen's trailer and taking a deep breath.

I was ready. I knew this day would have to come sometime. I lifted my chin and reminded myself that my mother needed me to be strong, and by the goddess, strong is what I would be.

Chapter 5

No sound answered my tap on Imogen's door. I waited a moment before opening it just a smidgen, enough to poke my head in to see if Imogen was up. The long living area was devoid of anyone. Perhaps she and her Günter were out getting morning coffee and breakfast.

"Best thing is to just wait for her," I said, ignoring the fact that my stomach did a few excited backflips as I entered the trailer. "Ben is not here, stomach, and Imogen has a boyfriend. Stop being so excited. Ben won't be up and about until it's dark."

Unless, of course, Imogen's boyfriend wasn't staying with her. Which meant . . . I glanced down the narrow passage to the door that marked Imogen's bedroom. It was quiet, very quiet, the sound of quiet that comes when no one else is around. Perhaps I should just double-check to make sure no one was in Imogen's bedroom. Just a quick peek to ease my mind and calm my unduly excited stomach.

Would Ben be happy to see me? Would he think I'd changed in the last few years? I touched a hand to my short auburn hair. When he last saw me, it had been in a pageboy, and black as night. Would he like the new color and style?

"Stop it. It doesn't matter what he thinks," I told myself before I put my hand on the door. "You are here to find your mother and nothing else. Certainly not to see the pushiest vampire ever made. Get to it, Fran."

I opened the door the bare minimum amount needed to slide through, so no sunlight could sneak in and harm any vampires who might be sleeping therein.

The room was dark and warm. A muffled grunt came from the bed.

"Ben?" My heart beat wildly, and my stomach did flip-flops. It *was* him! He was right there in front of me. I should leave. I should run away as fast as I could. I should put him from my mind and heart.

I groped my way along the bed to sit on one end of it, pulling off both sets of gloves before reaching out to find him. My hand touched bare flesh.

A light clicked on at the exact moment that I realized the man wasn't Ben. I snatched back my hand as two surprised hazel eyes met mine. *"Was ist es?"*

"Er . . . hi. You're not Ben."

The man pulled the blanket up over his naked chest. "Who?"

"Ben. Benedikt. Are you Günter, by any chance?" I asked, hastily getting off the bed and backing toward the door, my face redder than a baboon's butt.

"Ja. You are Imogen friend?"

"Yes, I'm Fran. I'm sorry to disturb you. I thought you would be out with Imogen. And then I thought you were Ben, but clearly you're not. Where is she?"

"He?"

"No, she, not he. You know, the word 'she.' 'She' is female; 'he' is male."

He blinked at me. "In trailer," he said, waving a hand toward the window. "Tattoo trailer."

"Oh. Okay. Thanks. Sorry again about waking you up. Nice meeting you." I slipped out of the room, closing the door behind me, leaning against it for a moment while I covered my burning cheeks with my hands. "Just when I think you can't be a bigger idiot, you top yourself. Nice job, Fran."

I all but ran down the line of trailers until I reached one with familiar artwork. I never had much to do with Gavon, who did tattoos and custom piercings at the Faire, mostly because he struck me as somewhat creepy, but I had a faint memory of Imogen being friends with him.

I knocked on the door, mentally writing an apology to Imogen for barging in on her boyfriend, when the door opened. A woman stood in the doorway. I stared at her bare legs, stared at her thigh-length silk robe, stared at a pretty face topped with a cloud of soft, curly hair. This was not Imogen.

"Yes?"

I gawked at her for a minute. I'd always thought Gavon was gay . . . Maybe I'd been wrong, and this was his girlfriend? "Is Imogen here?"

"Imogen? No. Her brother is." She continued to stand there, looking me over with narrowed blue eyes. I suddenly felt every inch my six-foot, built-like-a-linebacker self, not to mention the wrinkled T-shirt and pair of jeans I wore.

"Ben's . . . here?" I groaned to myself. Somehow in the conversation with Günter, we'd crossed our lines regarding pronouns. "Right here?"

"Yes. You wish to see him?"

No. I absolutely did not want to see him. I had not

gone through the hell of the last year for nothing. I had
made a decision, and I was going to stand by it.

"Yes, please," I heard someone say, and realized with
horror that it was me.

I knew I should have turned around and left. I had to
find Imogen, and then make a plan to locate my mother.
But despite the desperate need to know she was okay,
my feet refused to leave. After all, my brain pointed
out, I would be much less distracted once a meeting
with Ben was done.

"He was sleeping when I left him," the woman said in
a voice with a faint French accent. "Why do you want to
see him?"

My heart shattered. Just like that, it was whole one
moment, then in a billion pieces the next. Poof! Dust.
Not that it had any right to shatter, but you try reasoning to a heart. It's impossible. "You're not Gavon's girlfriend, are you?"

"Gavon? No. I took over his business. I am Naomi,
the tattoo artist. I am Benedikt's girlfriend. And you
are . . . ?"

"Fran Ghetti." Pain seared my soul with such inten-
sity I had to clutch the side of the trailer to keep from
keeling over at her feet. Stupid, stupid Fran! You broke
up with him; you can't be shocked now because he got
over you.

"Ah, the *former* girlfriend." Her look scalded me up
and down with enough heat to peel off at least three layers of skin.

I gave her a long look that by rights should have left
her hair smoking. "If he's sleeping, I won't disturb
him."

"Benedikt is mine, now. Did he not tell you? Poor
little American. Did you believe that he still wants you?

Desires you? He does not even think about you. He thinks only of me."

Her voice turned suddenly syrupy and sickeningly sweet. It was just what I needed, because her words pulled me out of what threatened to be a massive well of self-pity, and into the land made up of me turning her into a wart-encrusted cockroach. "There's nothing *little* about me, chicky. Now, if you don't mind, I'd like to talk to Ben."

She made an annoyed sound, but stood aside. I climbed the steps and edged past her, hardly able to catch my breath, so fast was my heart beating. I couldn't believe it, couldn't believe the proof that was before me. Ben had moved on. He had really moved on. While I'd been spending miserable nights telling myself that I'd gotten just what I wanted, Ben, the bastard, had just blithely gone on with his life.

I glanced over my shoulder at Naomi. She smiled a slow "Ben is my lover because he's so over you" smile. "He's in my bed. He was so exhausted after our night together, he went right to sleep."

I gritted my teeth, my fingernails digging into my palms even through the two layers of gloves I'd replaced. I toyed with the idea of turning her into a toad or bug, but spells had been my mother's forte, not mine. The only power I ever wielded came from the Vikingahärta. With much reluctance, I pushed away the thought that I could get it from Imogen's trailer, then turn both the she-devil and Ben into what they deserved.

I turned back toward the door. With every step, the pain in my heart morphed into anger, a fury so hot I thought I would spontaneously combust by the time I flung open the door.

"Nrrf?" a voice said from the bed, then yelped as

sunlight streamed in around me. "What the hell are you doing, Naomi?"

The man who rolled over onto his back and sat up, his short hair mussed, his eyes confused and sleepy, brought me to a halt.

"I just came to tell you that I was here, and I never want to see you again. Not that I had planned on doing that, because I thought Günter was saying Imogen was in this trailer, not you, but as long as we're both here, it's as good a time as any to get a few things off my chest. So I will. I never want to see you again, you two-timing, cheating rat bastard."

His eyes widened as they focused on me. "Fran?"

I stared at him for a moment, pain and anger roiling around inside me. "I'm so glad to know I was right about freeing us both. I'm delighted to see that it took you absolutely no time to find a replacement for me. I'm nigh on ecstatic that I meant so little to you that you couldn't wait to screw the first girl you could find!" I ripped off the ring I still wore on my middle finger and threw it at his head. "I'm so happy I could bloody well burst into a Broadway show tune!"

"Francesca—"

"I told her, but she wouldn't listen to me," Naomi said from the doorway, her smile gloating and so evil I wanted to smite her as she'd never been smited. She strolled past me, then sat on the edge of the bed next to Ben, putting a proprietorial hand on his chest. "Now do you see, little American? He is mine, not yours. Aren't you, lover? Why don't you tell her? She clearly needs to hear the words."

I saw red as she leaned forward and pressed her lips against his mouth. Ben's eyes were the color of honey oak, and filled with an expression I couldn't read.

"Yes, *lover*, why don't you tell me?" My voice came out croaked and hoarse.

His lips tightened. "I'm sorry. I was going to tell you what was happening. I just . . . I didn't expect you to come to Europe yet."

Naomi nibbled on his ear, cooing softly into it. I stared at him for a few seconds, not believing what I was seeing, not understanding the words he spoke. I had left him, I had told him I didn't want to be his Beloved, and yet somehow, I had remained true to his memory. I hadn't dated, hadn't been interested in other men, I hadn't even *seen* other men. I had left him, and he had done just what I had wanted him to do—he had gotten on with his life.

While I remained in limbo, bound to a man who now didn't want me.

Anguish overrode my anger and I choked on the bile of my own hypocrisy. I spun around and ran blindly from the room, the mocking laughter of Naomi following after me.

I dashed past Kurt, who was emerging from a car with two lattes in his hands. I ignored his surprised greeting as I ran straight to a familiar navy blue trailer decorated with gold stars and moons. Just as I was fumbling in my pocket for the key I'd brought with me, the door opened and Eirik started out.

"Ah, virgin goddess. We were just leaving off our things before we go to the ninja store. Finnvid was concerned someone would pillage our laptops. We will— What is the matter?"

"Nothing," I said, pushing past him into the trailer, tears spilling down my cheeks.

"You are crying," he said, frowning as he followed me. Isleif emerged from the tiny bathroom, pausing next to Finnvid as I yanked open a cupboard and snatched up a couple of tissues.

"It doesn't matter. It's just something personal," I said, trying to stop the tears, but it was as useless as trying to quell the pain that wrapped around my heart.

The three men exchanged looks. "It is the Dark One, is it not?" Eirik asked, putting his hand on my arm to gently steer me toward one of two curved club chairs that sat at a tiny table.

"Yes. But it doesn't matter, as I said. That's all over now."

"All over? You are his Beloved," Finnvid said, looking confused. "You cannot cease to be that."

"No? You might tell Ben that, because he's gone and found himself a new girlfriend. Probably a new Beloved, for all I know." The last couple of words were a bit shaky, but I managed to speak them without wailing, which I thought was pretty good, considering everything.

All three men shook their heads. "Dark Ones have one Beloved. He cannot change them. Everyone knows that," Isleif said, sitting down opposite me.

"Please, don't start on that again. I am not a victim of fate; I make my own way. And besides, it's clearly not true because Ben at this very moment is shacked up with a French—" I bit back the word I wanted to say. "He's shacked up with a woman who told me he was hers now. And he agreed."

"Then he will die," Eirik said simply, reaching for his hip. He swore when he remembered he'd had to leave his sword back in Oregon.

"Aye. He will," Finnvid said, looking around the trailer. He picked up a small red object. "What is this?"

"Fire extinguisher," I said, sniffling into the tissue, making a heroic effort to get hold of myself.

"Would it kill an immortal?"

"No."

"Ah. What is this? It looks like a stone grinder." He pulled an old-fashioned egg beater from the drawer below the tiny microwave.

"That's an egg beater. It wouldn't be effective on stones at all."

Finnvid's lips quirked. "It would on a man's stones, I'm willing to bet." He spun the handle around vigorously a couple of times.

Isleif crossed his legs. "You cannot kill a Dark One by grinding his stones."

"No, but we can make sure he doesn't rut with anyone but the virgin goddess," Finnvid answered.

"True."

"Look, I appreciate this, but no one is going to kill Ben, or grind his stones. I'm a big girl now, remember?" I gave a loud, wet sniff. "He's moved on, and I've taken steps to do the same, so now I'll just get down to it. Besides, there are more important things I should be doing. I have to find my mom. I have to beat the living daylights out of Loki." I have to figure out how I'm supposed to go on living with the thought of Ben with another woman.

Never once during the last year had I pictured Ben actually hooking up with another woman. I bowed my head, sick at heart over my idiocy. I had given him his freedom; I couldn't now berate him for taking it.

"What about this?" Finnvid pulled a piece of frozen meat from the minuscule freezer section of the refrigerator.

"That's the wrong kind of stake for a vampire," I told him.

"Not if we hone a sharp edge to it," Eirik said thoughtfully, taking the slab of meat from Finnvid. He ran his finger around one edge of the package. "If we got it sharp enough, could we cut off his head?"

Isleif rose to consult with them. "No. But it could be used to pierce his heart."

I debated the folly of trying to point out the unlikelihood of them using a piece of frozen steak to murder Ben, but decided that both my wounded ego and my sanity deserved a little break. "Knock yourselves out," I told them. "Once I have a few minutes to pull myself together, I'm going to go find Peter and see if he knows anything about my mother. Why don't you guys go into town, like we planned. We can rendezvous later tonight."

"Yes," Eirik said, giving his buddies a look filled with portent. "We will do as you suggest, virgin goddess Fran."

"Don't kill anyone in the meantime," I warned them as Finnvid and Isleif filed past me, the latter pausing to give me a fatherly pat on the shoulder.

"Your daughter Anna," I couldn't help but ask. "The one who you told me about when you guys were giving me dating advice—did she ever get married?"

Isleif looked surprised at the question. "Yes, three times."

"Did she ever . . . Did her husband ever . . ." I couldn't put into words what I wanted to ask. It just hurt too much.

His smile was filled with pride. "Aye, the first, Bruni. She caught him one morning rutting with a sheep. She was so furious, she struck him down with a hoe. You take her actions to heart, virgin goddess. She did not suffer a fool, and neither should you."

I gawked at him. "Your daughter killed her husband because he had sex with a sheep?"

"No, not because of *that*," Isleif snorted. "Bruni used her best gown when he made the sheep a dress."

"I remember that dress," Finnvid said thoughtfully. "She looked very nice in it."

"Anna?" I asked.

"No, the sheep."

"Which dress?" Eirik asked, his brow wrinkled. "The red or the gold?"

"Oh, the red. The gold was all wrong for the sheep. Made her look too bulky."

"Aye, the red was best," Eirik agreed. "She had a pleasant face, that sheep."

"I like bulk on a woman," Isleif commented. "But I agree the gold dress did not flatter the sheep. Now blue, that would have been nice."

I shook my head, amazed that we were having this discussion. But then, I frequently felt like that when I talked with the Vikings. "I know things were different then, but I just can't believe that your son-in-law had sex with a sheep."

"It was a ewe," Isleif said, just as if that made it all right. "It wasn't a ram."

"Does that make any difference?" I asked.

"It would to the ram," Eirik said sagely.

The others nodded.

"I never thought I'd have to say this, but bestiality has officially been added to the list of things we don't discuss, okay?"

"If you wish," Eirik said and shrugged. "Although Isleif has many amusing tales about—"

"I don't want to hear them!" I said loudly.

To my annoyance, he patted me on the shoulder as if

I was upset about nothing. "You rest for a bit, virgin goddess. When you need us, we will be here."

"Well, I can try, but I suspect there are going to be a few mental images I'll have a hard time getting rid of," I muttered as the Vikings left.

The silence that followed their departure was almost overpowering. I looked around the trailer, desperate for something to do, noting absently that Mom had a new coffeemaker, and a laptop. Davide, her fat black and white cat, wasn't there, but I didn't expect him to be if she had gone away for the weekend. Likely one of the Faire people had taken over cat-watching duty while she was gone. I made a mental note to find out who, and retrieve him.

"He might hate me, but at least he'll be some company for my bleak, unbearable life," I said, my voice echoing slightly in the trailer. It was the sound of it that brought me to my knees in a ball of abject misery, the horrible reality of the situation piercing me to my very soul. For the first time in a year, I admitted that I had made the biggest mistake of my life. The fact that Ben and everyone else expected me to just accept what fate had thrown at us still rankled, but it had been my choice, and no other's, to end the relationship.

And now that I realized just what I'd lost, it was too late.

I cried out the tale of my broken heart to no one, and when I was done, I lay hiccupping on the floor, wondering what I was going to do with the shattered remains of my life.

"Go on without him," I said in a voice that was as empty as my heart.

Chapter 6

It took me a bit to gather myself and get cleaned up so no one would know I had indulged in a major fit of crying, but an hour after we arrived at the Faire, I walked slowly down the steps of the trailer inhabited by Peter Sauber and his son, Soren, the latter of whom was attending the University of Marburg. "It's just not like her to do this," I reiterated to Peter as he accompanied me. "It has to mean that Loki has her. Especially after the attempt to kidnap me back home. Loki clearly went after Mom when he couldn't get me."

Peter rubbed his face, leaving me with a momentary guilty twinge about having woken him up. Peter was the main act magician, in addition to being co-owner of the Faire with his sister, Absinthe. Most of his act was big, flashy illusions, like turning his horse Bruno into a member of the audience, but every now and again he indulged himself in an act of real magic, the kind that left you with goose bumps. "It is possible, although why would he do that?"

"Revenge against me, I suppose."

Peter made a *tch* noise in the back of his throat. "If he wanted that, he would have done so years ago."

I frowned, thinking about that. I had to agree that Loki had had many opportunities to strike at me, as he had promised. Why would he take Mom now and not earlier? "I'm not sure what to say, Peter. If Loki didn't take her, then where is she?"

He shrugged. "That I do not know. She was seeing that Frenchman, so perhaps she went away with him instead of going to Heidelberg."

"What Frenchman?"

"The one she met in Brussels. He sells some sort of farm equipment. Did she not tell you about him?"

"Not a peep." Once, back when I assumed my future was secure with Ben, I had hoped that she'd find someone with whom she could share her life. Now the thought just made me feel ostracized, as if everyone had paired up but me. "Do you know his name?"

Peter gave me the little information he knew about the man, which I wrote down in a little notebook. "I guess I could talk to the police about this guy, just in case he, and not Loki, has abducted her."

"Will that not be very extreme?" he asked, worry filling his eyes. "What if she has gone away for a romantic weekend?"

"A romantic weekend is one thing, but five days without telling anyone?" I shook my head. "Not at all like my mom."

"Perhaps she left some note or sign of where she's gone?" he suggested.

I stared at him for a second. "You know, that's not a bad thought. Let's both of us go have a look around her trailer."

"Both of us?" He looked sleepy, but came along

when I tugged him toward the trailer. "I don't know what I can do to help."

"You dated Mom for a bit, didn't you?"

He looked a bit abashed. "Just for a few months. We . . . it wasn't meant to be."

"That's okay, Peter," I said, laughing at his expression. "I don't mind that you guys were dating. I'm sad it didn't work out, but you don't have to be uncomfortable with me on that account. Now, where to start?"

We had entered the trailer and stood looking around it. "Bedroom?" Peter suggested.

"Good idea." We both toddled back to it, making a quick search of the dresser pressed against one wall. There was just clothing in it, no big note saying where she'd gone, or even a love note from an admirer. More reassuringly, there were no signs of a struggle, so if Loki did take her, she hadn't fought him.

I sat on the bed and thought for a few minutes. Peter went out into the living area and poked around in the drawers and cupboards out there, but I knew they wouldn't have anything important. I mulled over where I would leave any references to a weekend trip, and after another few minutes' thought, reached under the bed and pulled out a small metal box with a combination lock.

"What is that?" Peter asked as he returned to the bedroom. "I found nothing out there. Not even a notepad."

"I'm not surprised. This is mom's lockbox. She keeps things in it like her passport. I can't imagine why she'd put anything in here about her weekend trip, but it can't hurt to look." I spun the dial to register my birth date, my mother's standard password, and sorted through the contents. As I suspected, it contained a few legal documents, a picture of the two of us together when I was about eight, her passport and various stamped visas, a credit card, three necklaces in silk bags, and a couple of stiff pieces of yellow paper.

"Well, that was no help," I said as I replaced everything, absently unfolding the paper.

"What are those?" Peter asked.

"Nothing. Just birth certificates. Mom's. Mine." I tossed the first two aside and glanced at the other one. "This must be a copy of mine that she got when she thought she lost the original. Well, this has been a lesson in frustration. . . ." I stopped and looked back at the last paper. Something about it had registered on my brain as being not quite right.

"This isn't my birth certificate." I frowned at it as I read the name of the child. "Petra Valentine de Marco. Who on earth is that?"

"A friend of your mother's?" Peter asked, looking in the tiny wardrobe that held Mom's dresses.

"Why would she have someone else's birth . . . green grass and salamanders!" I raised my gaze to Peter. "My mom's name is on this."

"It is?" He sat next to me and looked as I handed it to him.

"Right there. Where it says mother's name." I pointed. "That's her name. Miranda Benson."

"Is it your birth certificate? With a different name? Sometimes parents change the names of their babies. Perhaps this was your original name and they changed it."

"Alphonse de Marco. That's not my father's name." Chills ran down my arms as I realized what it was I was seeing. The birth date of the baby was almost ten years earlier than mine. "Goddess above! My mom had a baby before me. I have a sister."

Peter looked suitably shocked. "I don't believe I've ever heard her mention another daughter."

I studied the birth certificate. "She was only sixteen when she had this baby. And it doesn't say they were married. Stars and stripes forever. I'm just . . . I don't know what I am. Flabbergasted, I guess. I never had the slightest idea I wasn't her only child. Why didn't she tell me?"

He took the birth certificate from me and tucked it away in the box with the other two. "I think, perhaps, this has nothing to do with your mother's weekend in Heidelberg."

"Even if she was sixteen, and it doesn't look like she was married to this guy, did she think I'd judge her for that? I have a half sister out there who I didn't even know existed." The idea was so strange, I had a hard time processing it. I won't deny there wasn't a bit of hurt with the realization that my mother kept something so important from me, but I was more confused than anything else.

"Fran."

"Hmm?" I realized what he said. "Oh. Yeah, you're right. This is something I'll have to talk to her about once I find her. It's just . . . I never knew. I don't understand why she would hide this from me. And speaking of that, just where is this Petra person?"

"Perhaps she did not survive?" Peter said, his expression sympathetic as he patted my arm. "I think we've pried enough. You will talk to your mother about this later, yes?"

"She must have been ashamed, but . . ." I couldn't

imagine my mother being ashamed of having a baby, even an illegitimate one. "Yeah, I guess it's not really of vital importance right now. I'll have to visit the police, though, since there was nothing in the trailer to show us where she's gone. I'll drop in on them and see what they have to say."

"If you insist. How long will you be with us?" He walked with me to the trailer door. "That sounded rude, didn't it? I didn't mean it that way. It's just that your mother's booth was always very popular, and if you were going to be around for a while . . ."

"I don't know how long I'll be here," I said carefully. "My plans have kind of changed."

"Ah?" He gave me a long look, then nodded. "Naomi."

"Yes." I examined my gloves, biting down hard on my lip to keep the tears from burning in my eyes again.

"It was a mistake to hire her, but we were short-handed, and Benedikt swore she would fit in well."

"Ben got her the job?" I asked, the tiny little atoms of my heart crumbling even further.

Peter looked embarrassed, his gaze dropping as he fidgeted with the doorknob. "I had no idea that he . . . that they . . ."

"It's all right." I dredged up a ghost of a smile. "It's likely I'll be around for a bit, so I can run Mom's booth while I'm here if you like. Although I really can only sell the things she already has made up—I can't make any more."

"No, no, of course not. But you know the things to say to customers, and you are familiar with Miranda's stock. It would be a great help. The opera contest that is going on in town has brought in a tremendous number of people to the area, and the Faire, and I hate to waste the opportunity. I don't like to ask you to tie up your evenings, but perhaps if you could see to her booth every other night? I will pay you, naturally."

He looked so hopeful, I agreed, but declined the offer of payment.

"She would want her booth open." My throat closed for a moment on a painful lump. "I just need to know Mom's okay. If Loki hurt her—"

Peter patted my arm when I couldn't finish the sentence. "She is strong."

"I know, but she can still be hurt."

"Not easily." He looked thoughtfully at me for a moment before adding slowly, "I would not suggest this in normal circumstances, because Absinthe does not like it to be known, but she might be able to help you."

"Absinthe?" I swallowed the painful lump of tears in my throat and tried to figure out how a mind reader could help me. "You mean like find out who's taken Mom?"

"No. She would need a subject for that. She has lately started studying with a diviner."

"A who now?"

"Diviner. They see things, you know? Tiny things, little bits of a bigger picture, Absinthe says. I don't really understand it too well, but she has learned much in the last three years."

"And she could tell me where Mom is!" I said, hope filling me. "I could kiss you, Peter! What a brilliant idea!"

"No, no, do not kiss me yet. I am not that brilliant. Absinthe is not learned enough to locate your mother, but she might be able to see if she has been . . ." His voice trailed off.

"Harmed," I said, filling in the word he clearly didn't want to say.

He nodded.

"I'll take it."

"It isn't much, and I can't guarantee that Absinthe will be able to tell you anything—"

"I'll take it," I repeated. "Is she here now?"

"Yes. I believe I saw Kurt about this morning."

I hesitated for a few seconds. Part of me wanted to run to Absinthe and beg her to tell me how my mother was. But even as that thought ran through my brain, the word "beg" reverberated with ominous portent. Absinthe was someone who viewed every interaction on a credit and debit scale. Asking her to divine my mother's state of health, and possibly location, would mean I placed myself in debt to her. And Absinthe had very inventive ways of making people pay their debts.

"Would you like me to ask Absinthe for you?" Peter asked, knowing his sister well enough to see my dilemma.

"No." I straightened my shoulders. "I appreciate the offer, though. I'll just go see if she's awake."

She was. She was also in a pretty foul mood, sitting in a garish orange and green chair in a pink track suit that matched her hair, sipping a latte and glaring at me with red-rimmed eyes. Kurt puttered in the background, which left me wondering if Absinthe had settled down to just one of the brothers.

"So you want me to divine for you, eh?" Her eyes narrowed as she raked me over with a look that snapped with irritation. "The so-sensitive Fran needs my help, does she?"

I held on to my temper, keeping a firm smile on my

lips. "Yes, I do. I would be very grateful for it, as a matter of fact. I'm worried about my mother."

She made a *tsk* sound, sliding Kurt a glance from the corner of her eyes before leaning forward, both hands on the table that sat between us. "And what payment do you have to offer?"

"Well, I have a little set aside for emergencies," I said slowly, wondering what was the going rate for an apprentice diviner's services.

"It is not money I wish," she said, waving her hand. I was surprised to see that her nails were bitten. In the past, Absinthe had seemed to me to be a very with-it woman, almost scary in the control she exercised on others. But control freaks did not bite their nails, and the proof that she was, after all, human helped me to relax. "What I want is you."

"I beg your pardon!"

"Not sexually," she said, her lip curling in disgust. "Why would I want you when I have Kurt and Karl? No, it is your services I desire."

I had a feeling my touchy-feely abilities were going to enter into the negotiations. "When and where and for how long?" I asked, settling back to haggle over the details.

"I do not know. But it will be a debt of honor, you understand? I will do this thing for you now, and you will owe me."

I was vaguely uncomfortable at the idea of such a debt hanging over my head, but the thought of my mother in pain made that concern pale. "Deal. Can you tell me where she is?"

She shrugged, and rose to dig around in a drawer under the couch. "I do not know until I try. Kurt, the incense. No, not that one, the clarity incense."

I watched with interest as Absinthe and Kurt set up the round table for divination purposes. Absinthe laid a scarlet red and gold cloth on the table, smoothing it out before placing on it a long incense holder shaped like a dragon. My nose wrinkled at the sharp acidic tang of the incense—a blend that had a lot of rosemary in it—but to my surprise she didn't bring out a crystal ball or even a scrying bowl. She just sat at the table, her fingers tracing the gold embroidered design on the cloth, her eyes unfocused.

"What is it you seek to know?" she asked after a few minutes.

"How my mother is. If she's hurt or scared or . . . worse."

"She is happy."

I felt my jaw sag at that. *"Happy?"*

"She is wrapped in love. She is happy where she is at."

Dear goddess, had Loki done something bizarre to my mother, like make her fall in love with him? "Where is she? Is she near here?"

Absinthe studied the cloth for the count of five before shaking her head. "I cannot see that. I sense only that she is happy where she is."

"Is she with a man? Does he have red hair? Is he a Norse god?"

"I cannot see who else is with her, although I sense the presence of another person. Only faint glimpses are available to me . . . No, I see a shadow of someone. The person hands Miranda a glass of wine. She blows a kiss in return."

"Holy hobgoblins." Peter was right! She had run off with a man! My *mother*!

I blinked wildly at the thought as I tried to wrap my brain around it.

Absinthe looked up from the table as she sank back into the chair. "I cannot hold the connection anymore. It is gone."

"I see. Well . . . thank you," I said, getting to my feet.

Her pencil-thin eyebrows rose. "You do not look pleased to know your mother is well and happy."

"I am pleased. Relieved, too, since I had imagined the worst. But this is just so . . . unexpected. It's not like her to take off without telling anyone."

She shrugged. "She is getting old. She sees a man and he wants her, and she knows she cannot play coy. So she runs away with him. There is nothing unexpected in that at all."

I bit my tongue in order to refrain from telling her that my mother simply did not act that way. It was obvious that she did. But it still went against her personality.

Inner Fran pointed out that the same thing could be said about her hiding the existence of my half sister.

I thanked Absinthe again, nodding when she reminded me that I was in her debt, and quickly escaped from the overpowering rosemary-scented trailer. Although the burden of rescuing my mother from a dangerous situation had been lifted, curiosity wasn't going to let me leave things alone. I was going to have to find her, if for no other reason than to see who it was who would tear her away from her beloved GothFaire.

It took me a while to walk into town, long enough that I mulled over the strange fact that there were facets to my mother I'd never known existed. By the time I worked through that and set it aside to be worried over later, made a mental note to take down the number of the local cab company, considered—and ultimately rejected—the idea of setting the police on Mom's trail, I was hot, melancholy, and possessed of no fewer than seven flyers directing me to various events that were intended to show the competition judges that Brustwarze was the best candidate.

"Thank you. I already have a bunch of flyers," I told the man in a long white robe and knee-length white beard who tried to press yet another flyer on me. I waved my handful at him.

"Mine is better," he said, taking my handful and tossing them into the trash before shoving his piece of glossy paper into my hands. "You take. Party tonight. Will be fun."

I was about to tell him I would be busy looking for my mother, but before I could do so, he stepped out into the street, right in front of three women on bikes who had on long streaming green wigs and grayish brown gowns with sleeves that would have touched the ground had they not been knotted up. One of the women yelled at the man and made a rude gesture. I grabbed him and pulled him back onto the sidewalk as he shook his fist at them.

"You have to watch where you're going," I told him.

"Valkyries. Is everywhere," he grumbled, straightening his robe and beard, which had been tugged askew. "You go," he repeated to me, nodding to the flyer, then headed off to tackle the next unwary person.

"Valkyries, huh?" I looked at the women as they rode away from me, a memory making me smile. I had once seen real Valkyries, and they were nothing like the robed, long-haired women depicted here.

The Vikings were nowhere in evidence, so I wandered around the town for a bit, aimless and restless. The sunlight was starting to fade, and my stomach was rumbling despite the fact that my heart had been smashed to smithereens, when suddenly the pain that I'd kept at bay for the last couple of hours lanced me with a sharpness that took away my breath. I wanted to crumple into a little ball and just let the world wash past me, but if there's one thing I've learned, it's that life doesn't let you off so easy.

Evening commuters rushed past me in varying costumes, everything from briefcase-toting knights in chain mail to begowned and bewigged women (and some men) adorned with breastplates, backpacks, and cloth shopping bags filled with the makings for dinner.

I'd never felt so alone in my life. For one moment, for one tiny little moment, I unguarded my mind and reached out to see if Ben was there, but before I could find him, I withdrew. What if he was with Naomi at that moment? What if he was feeding from her, or worse? Dark Ones and their Beloveds shared a unique mental bond that sometimes allowed more than just the sharing of thoughts—and I knew for a fact that had I let him, I would feel both Ben's emotions at that moment and the sensations of whatever he was doing.

"I won't let this destroy me," I swore to myself as I turned into the flow of traffic and let it carry me along to the center square in town, where I had earlier seen several cafés. My stomach growled loudly at the thought.

Hungry?

"Sorry. I haven't eaten all day—" I stopped as soon as I realized that the voice that spoke wasn't from the man walking nearest me. *No. I will not do this.*

Francesca, don't shut—

I closed my mind against him, against the agony of hearing his velvety voice in my brain after so many years. I stood with my arms wrapped around myself for a few minutes, struggling to keep from crying, fighting to keep control. Just as I did so, a voice pierced my awareness.

"Virgin goddess!"

I looked up to see Finnvid standing next to an outdoor café table. He waved and yelled again, "Virgin goddess! Isleif is getting our ale, and Eirik is using the privy, but he will return soon, unless his guts are bound up again. If that is the case, then he may need to purge his arse. You will have ale with us?"

Several pairs of heads swiveled from Finnvid to me. I tried to smile. I think it came out pretty bad because the people averted their gazes quickly.

"I swear," I muttered under my breath as I made my way over to the Vikings. "One of these days, I'm going to beg Freya to take them back. . . . Hello, Finnvid. I'm pretty sure people would be grateful if you didn't yell details about constipation while you're at a café."

He looked curious as I pulled out one of the white metal chairs that sat around a table littered with shopping bags. "Why? Do your guts not get bound up occasionally?"

"Item number—what are we up to now, fifteen thousand?—on the 'things we don't discuss' list is constipation, unless there is a pressing medical reason to do so. What in the name of the goddess's ten little toes have you been buying?"

"Many things." He patted a couple of the bags with satisfaction. "Ninja things."

"Yeah? Like what?" I tried to peek in one of the

white plastic carrier bags, but he slapped my hands away.

"Eirik said we are not to talk to you about it. But we did bring you an offering." He rustled around in the bags, muttering to himself as Isleif returned with three gigantic beer steins filled to the brim with frothy ale.

"Why aren't you supposed to talk to me about what you bought?" I asked, suspicion making me suddenly very wary.

"Virgin goddess!" Isleif shoved aside some of the bags in order to set down the steins. "Eirik is empty-ing his bowels. You would like ale? I will get one for you."

"No, thank you. I think I'd be comatose if I drank that much," I answered, eyeing the massive steins. I swear they were just pitchers shaped like traditional beer steins. "I wouldn't mind some food, but before that, I'd like to know just what it is you bought that Eirik doesn't want you to talk about."

Isleif said something that sounded very rude and punched Finnvid in the arm as the latter was taking a swig of beer. "Do you have no brains? You do not tell the virgin goddess that we are not to talk about the weapons! You know how she is about them!"

"What weapons?" I reached for a bag, but both Finnvid and Isleif pulled them back out of my reach. "Something other than the knives we agreed you could buy here, even though you're not going to be able to take them back to the U.S.?"

"You agreed—we did not. We told you that no Vi-king would be caught dead without a sword and ax! It is like being naked." Isleif plumped down in a chair with a disgruntled look.

"Worse," Finnvid said. "If you are naked with a

sword and ax, you can still kill. I have done so many times."

"In many ways, I prefer to fight naked, like the berserkers. The blood does not stain your armor that way," Isleif said and nodded.

"Aye, that is true. I can't tell you the number of times I'd return home after a successful pillage, and my wife would complain about having to clean the caked blood and brains from my tunic."

The people nearest us rose suddenly, tossed a few coins on the table, and hurried off. I sighed to myself and wondered which was worse—Ben's betrayal, or time spent with the Vikings.

"Virgin goddess!" Eirik's voice was naturally deep, but I hadn't realized until he bellowed it across the outdoor café area just how carrying it was. "You have found us!"

I ignored the curious looks of the people who hadn't heard the other two Vikings earlier. "Yes, I have."

"There is Eirik," Finnvid said happily. "Are your bowels running again?"

"Aye, they are. I had to use three handfuls of leaves they moved with such vigor."

The people on the other side of Finnvid scurried off with bowed heads and expressions of horror.

"I've had those sessions in the privy," Isleif said, obviously settling back to indulge in a few scatological anecdotes.

Before he could do so, I raised a hand. "Stop. The moving of bowels is also on the list of things we don't talk about."

He stared at me for a moment in utter bewilderment, and was clearly going to ask why, when Finnvid said,

"My fourth wife forbid me to talk about shite. Perhaps the virgin goddess is like her."

I closed my eyes. To my left, I heard the noise of chairs scraping and people leaving hurriedly. I prayed the café owner was not watching.

"I knew a woman like that, as well," Eirik said, sitting next to me. "She liked me to write her name in the snow, though."

"What weapons did you buy?" I said, giving great deliberation to the words.

Eirik shot a glare at Finnvid.

"Why do you look such at me?" Finnvid answered the look, pulling his bags a little closer. "It could have been Isleif who told her about the Walther P38s."

"Walthers?" I searched my memory. I wasn't too hip on weapons, but those sounded familiar. "Aren't those guns? You bought guns?"

"We needed them. We saw Nori."

"You saw Nori. We did not," Isleif said, pouring about half the ale down his throat. He belched so loud I swear my hair fluttered.

The people behind him left. Quickly.

"You think I would mistake Nori? I am not so foolish." Eirik turned from the Vikings to reassure me. "It was Nori."

"Who's Nori? And why do you need a gun just because he's here? I thought we agreed knives would be perfectly fine."

"You agreed," Eirik said. "You forbade us to pillage swords or axes, so we got crossbows instead."

"You got crossbows *and* Walther P38s?" I took a deep breath in order to better lecture them, but before I could, Isleif interrupted.

"The Walthers *are* crossbows," he said kindly, as if explaining something to an idiot.

"They are?"

"Aye." All three Vikings nodded, and smacked their lips loudly as they downed their beer. "The man at the ninja shop told us they were very effective in stopping attackers. We will find a bowyer later to get the bolts for them."

"You need not worry, virgin goddess," Eirik added, patting my hand. "We will protect you from Loki's son."

"Nori?" I asked, relief swamping me when I realized they didn't understand about the ammunition needed by modern guns.

"Aye. He is tricky like his father. I saw him leaving the train station a few hours ago. If Nori is here, he is up to no good."

I frowned at the table as I mulled over a new thought. Could it be Loki's son who swept my mother off her feet to some love nest, goddess only knew where? Or was it a coincidence that Nori was in town? I explained to the Vikings what Absinthe had seen in her vision.

"I don't know what to think. It's all so confusing." I rubbed my forehead. "Maybe we should talk to Nori, just to be on the safe side."

"We will search for him tonight," Eirik said, putting on his white-framed sunglasses even though it was dark enough that streetlamps were starting to flicker on. "You will go back to the Faire?"

"Yes, I have to go back to the Faire." I would not think about Ben. I would not allow the misery that was now my life to spread to others. "If you get tired and want somewhere to sleep, you can use the chairs and my bed in my mom's trailer. I'll sleep in her bed."

They agreed to this plan, and since my appetite had gone at the memories I would not allow, I stood up to leave.

"You forgot to give her the offering," Isleif said, pointing to a bag at Finnvid's feet.

"Aye, give the virgin goddess the offering we have brought for her," Eirik said.

Finnvid dug through the bags until he held in his hands a shiny gold metal helm, crowned on either side with curved plastic horns. I stared at it for a moment before turning my gaze on the three delighted faces that beamed at me. "You got me a horned helmet?"

"Is it not splendid?" Finnvid asked, admiring it. "The man at the shop said that it is a Viking helm, although we have never seen one like it before, so it must be a ninja Viking helm. We thought you would like it, since you are our virgin goddess."

With reverence, he placed the helm on my head. I bit my lower lip, not wanting to hurt their feelings when they were so very pleased with their present. I started to take it off, saying, "I will treasure it always."

"You are removing it?" Isleif asked, his expression a little hurt.

"Well . . . it's so very pretty, and shiny, and . . . horny. I wouldn't want someone to steal it from me if I were to wear it out on the street. Maybe you could give me the bag and I could carry it back to the Faire in that."

"Ah," Eirik said, nodding. "That is smart thinking. It is a most attractive ninja Viking helm. Many people will want it."

I didn't point out that just about everyone was wearing them. "Exactly. So I'll just tuck it away safe and sound in this bag, and that way no one will know I have it."

"Until you get to the Faire," Eirik prompted me. "Then you will wear it. It will be safe at the Faire."

"Er . . . yes. I will be safe wearing it there." I heaved a mental sigh, but pointed out to myself that as easily distracted as they were, I probably wouldn't have to wear it more than once or twice before they forgot about it.

They escorted me to a cab, promising to pass along word about Nori should they find him again. I returned to the Faire with a heart filled with anguish, an empty stomach, and a historically inaccurate horned Viking helm.

Somehow, that just seemed to sum up my life.

Chapter 7

"The little kindness is five euros, the bigger one is ten, and the do-it-yourself love charm kit is twenty-five."

"Oh, love charm is good, yes? We will take it," one of the two young women who stood before me said in a charming German accent.

I handed over the box and took her money. "Forgive my ignorance, but who are you dressed as?"

The woman smoothed a hand down her floor-length black dress and matching belted waist cincher, pulling down from the top of her head a silver metal mask. "I am a death eater!"

"So you are. Er . . . isn't that from Harry Potter? Not a Wagnerian opera?"

"Yes," she said, pushing the mask up before waving to her friend. "Sabeine is Hermione."

"And a very good Hermione you are," I told her, handing over the change and admiring her Hogwarts robes. "Enjoy your love charms."

The two women left, excitedly discussing whether to visit the wizard's sanctum first or the aura photography booth. I eyed the table in front of me, mentally adding

up the stock on it and the boxes of extras I'd found earlier. I had assumed that the items would last several
days, but Peter hadn't been kidding when he'd said that
the town's opera competition was sending the Faire lots
of customers—center aisle was a solid mass of bodies,
and I had done a roaring trade in just the hour we'd
been open. I'd kept so busy I hadn't had time to do more
than twitch whenever a man of Ben's general build and
color walked past.

"Fran!" A petite woman with long, curly blond hair
and brilliant blue eyes darted around a small clutch of
people and ran toward me. "It is you! I am so pleased to
see you, but there is something I must tell you about
Benedikt before you see him—"

"Too late." I smiled when she froze just as she was
about to hug me, the delicate lines of her face unmov-
ing. "Hello, Imogen. It's been a long time."

"Yes, it has," she said absently, her gaze searching
my face. "You have seen Benedikt?"

"Yes." I set down the bottles of kindness, idly checking the lid on the tester my mother kept to show people
how the potion worked. "I've seen him. And Naomi.
Ben seemed surprised to see me. You didn't tell him
that I was coming?"

"No, I thought the surprise of seeing you might do
him some good. Sort of a shock therapy, you know. Oh,
Fran." Remorse filled her eyes as she hugged me, waves
of sympathy rolling off her. "I am so sorry. Benedikt
is . . . I do not know what has happened to him. I have
tried to talk to him about his decision. I have tried, you
must believe me. But he will not listen to me. He will
not speak with me. He avoids me, he will not even let
me feed him anymore. It is as if he is bewitched by
that . . . that . . ." She spat out a word I didn't recognize,

but assumed it wasn't something I'd ever be saying. "But it is very hard to bespell a Dark One, and Naomi does not have that sort of power, so it cannot be that. My dearest Fran, I do not know what to say to you. I have let you down. I fear Benedikt is lost to us."

She hugged me again, and I patted her back, smiling a little at the fact that she was the one who needed comforting. "It's okay, Imogen. You don't have to cry. If Ben is lost to us, it's my fault, not yours."

"That, I do not believe," she said, pulling a lace handkerchief from her sleeve. Imogen was the only person I knew who liked nothing more than to spend a night clubbing, but who still used handkerchiefs. She'd told me once that she had seen a lot of things come and go over the more than three hundred years she had lived, but handkerchiefs were a constant in her life. "You are his Beloved! How he can spurn you this way is beyond my understanding. There has never been a Dark One who has done so. No, I tell a lie. There was one, a Frenchman, but that is an entirely different situation. He has a woman he took as his Beloved in the other's place."

"Just when you think your heart can't break any more," I said wryly, the pain that lanced through me at her words now a familiar sensation.

"Oh, Fran, no! I did not mean that!" She took my hands, her fingers tight on me, tight enough that I winced at the glass tester bottle I still held as it dug into my palm. "That Naomi, she is not the one for Benedikt. He could not have replaced you with her in his affections. He could not!"

It sounded like she was trying to convince herself of that more than me.

"It doesn't really matter anymore," I said, and would have bared my soul to her, but at that moment, the tattered remains of my heart clumped together just in order to fling itself around inside my chest. Imogen turned and swore under her breath as she looked with me to where a couple was strolling past the booth. My fingernails dug through my gloves into my palms. Naomi, catching sight of us, pulled Ben to a stop, and with deliberately slow motions reached up to first brush back a bit of hair off his forehead, then stroked her hand down his chest, wiggling her hips into his as she gazed up at him. "Benedikt, would you like something from the little witch's booth? You don't need a love potion, but perhaps something else? She looks like she could use the money."

Ben's eyes were black as midnight as he looked over the top of Naomi's head to me. I forced my face to adopt a placid, unruffled expression that I prayed conveyed no interest whatsoever in the fact that Naomi practically had her hands down his pants right there in front of everyone. He shook his head.

"What's that?" Naomi cooed. "You don't want anything you see? Nothing whatsoever?"

"Oh!" Imogen said, outraged by the show Naomi was putting on. "Benedikt, I insist that you stop this! You don't know what you're doing!"

Ben's jaw flexed. He shook his head again.

Naomi laughed and tossed back her hair before she put both hands on his butt and licked his chin. "On the contrary, he knows exactly what he's doing. Darling, you are *sure* there's nothing the witch has to offer that you want?"

"No," he answered, the word piercing me like an arrow. "There's nothing there I want."

"I thought not," Naomi said with a smile at him as she stroked his chest.

"That . . . that . . . oh! I'm not going to stand for this!" Imogen said, starting forward, her hands fisted.

"Why bother?" I said loud enough that my voice carried over the drone of the people packed in the main aisle. I held Ben's gaze, proud that I could speak without so much as a tremor in my voice. I was angry now, both at myself and at him. While I had been the one who had broken things off, I had never flaunted myself with another man in front of Ben. I'd never told him how much I was looking forward to dating other men. I'd never allowed another man to fondle me in front of him.

No, Inner Fran said bluntly. *You just let the man believe you didn't want him.*

I closed my eyes for a moment against the guilt that swamped me, fighting it and the pain until I could speak. "Don't bother, Imogen. People have the right to make their own choices. Ben has made his."

Imogen spun around to stare openmouthed at me. "You're not going to tell Benedikt what you think of this?"

"I believe I made myself quite clear the last time we spoke." I kept my eyes on Ben despite the pain of it all. It was a suitable penance. "I hope he knows that I'm . . ." I couldn't say the word. I just couldn't. My fingernails dug even further into my palms. ". . . happy he's found someone."

Naomi turned a self-satisfied smirk on me as she rubbed her butt against Ben's hip. "How very sweet. Come, lover. You can help me with the piercings tonight."

By the stars that lit up the night, I was going to keep my expression from showing Ben just how devastated I was or I was going to die trying. As Naomi walked past, pulling Ben by his arm, my fingers tightened until the vial of happiness broke, sending hot little spikes of pain into my flesh.

"Son of a basket weaver," I swore, opening my hand to find blood seeping through the gloves. Ben, almost beyond the booth, froze for a moment and glanced back at me, but Naomi jerked his arm, and with one last unreadable look, he followed.

"Did you cut yourself?" Imogen exclaimed, hurrying over to pick tiny little fragments of glass from my hand.

I laughed. I couldn't help myself. The oddest emotions were swirling around inside of me—fury and pain in a tight little core, all coated with happiness from the introduction of the potion into my bloodstream. "Yes, I did. Isn't it glorious? Look! I'm bleeding all over the place! Ben has broken my heart, left me for another woman, and destroyed my entire life. It's all so wonderful, I could dance!"

And I did, severely hampering Imogen's attempts to peel off my gloves in order to see how badly injured I was. It took a combination of her, Peter, and Kurt before they could get me to sit still long enough to clean up my hand. Three hours later I was still a bit giggly, although two pots of strong coffee and a measure of my own despair that would have dropped an elephant had helped work through most of the artificial happiness.

"You're sure you'll be all right by yourself?" Imogen asked as she hesitated in the door of my mother's trailer. "I worry about you being alone. Perhaps you could stay with me. Günter would not mind, I'm sure."

I had no doubt he'd mind very much, but I wasn't about to say that. "I'll be just fine here, thanks."

Imogen frowned. "Speaking of him, I wonder where

he is? I haven't seen him since this morning. I shall go look for him. You get some sleep, dear Fran. And about Benedikt . . ."

Her expression said it all. I smiled wearily and waved her off before staggering to bed, where I lay tossing and turning for another couple of hours. I'd just fallen asleep when the weight of someone sitting on the edge of the bed had me grumbling, "Please, whichever one of you it is, not tonight. I'm really not up to randy Vikings."

"I'm delighted to hear that. How about a randy Dark One?"

I rolled over and clicked on the light, my eyes already narrowed into a glare directed at the man who sat next to me, looking perfectly normal, perfectly ordinary, just as if he had a right to sit there and be so sexy, it made me want to rip off all his clothing and lick every inch of him. "You slimy, scummy strings of spit! How dare you come in here? How dare you sit there with your shirt open so I can see your chest? Get out! Go back to your precious Beloved."

"I am with my precious Beloved," he said calmly, trying to take my hand.

"Ow! Stop that, you're hurting me," I snapped, pulling my hand back. He shifted his grip to my wrist, slowly uncurling my fingers to reveal the bandages Imogen and Peter had applied.

"You did cut yourself. I thought so."

"Take your hands off me, you slimy, scummy—"

"Strings of spit, yes, I know. Nice alliteration, by the way. Stop fighting me, Francesca. I wish to see your injury. I won't hurt you."

I stopped struggling with him at that, not because he had ordered me to do so, but because the sight of his head bent over my hand as he gently removed the bandages made a sob of misery catch painfully in my throat. "Why are you here?" I asked, my voice sounding thick with unshed tears.

His fingertips softly caressed the lacerations on my palm and fingers, causing no pain but generating a heat that seemed to spread up my arm. "I had to come. I couldn't stand the look in your eyes."

"Oh, you couldn't? How thoughtful of you. I wonder that you didn't think of that the second you jumped Naomi's bones. How long was that after I broke things off, Ben? A month? A week? A couple of minutes?"

He looked at me with an unreadable expression. "Are you finished?"

"Yes. But only because . . ." My gaze dropped to where he was still holding my hand. A lump in my throat ached. "Only because I told you to go find someone else."

"I don't recall you ever saying that."

"Not in so many words. But it's usually what a breakup means." Anguish caught on the lump in my throat, and I looked up at him, tears burning in my eyes. "I never so much as looked at another man."

"I know."

I stared at him in confusion as he brushed away one errant tear with his thumb. "How do you know?"

He was silent for the count of five. "You are my Beloved, Francesca. No, do not get your hackles up. I'm not going to debate the wisdom of that, or the fact that you are bound to me without your consent. I am simply saying that you are my Beloved, and as such, I am responsible for your welfare. I know that you have seen no other men because I was told so."

The meaning of his words sank in. "You had someone watching me? Like a private detective?"

"I asked a friend to make sure you were in no danger," he said carefully.

"And that friend just happened to report on my dating habits? Or lack thereof?" I couldn't decide if I was furious at such a high-handed manner or touched. Both, I decided.

"Naturally, he was interested in the people in your life. That would include any romantic or sexual partners, had there been any."

I couldn't believe I was hearing this. My emotions had been through such extremes, I just didn't think I could feel any more pain.

I was wrong. "I'm sure that suitably flattered your ego to know that no other man could live up to your standards. Just out of curiosity, how long have you and Naomi been together?"

His eyes darkened. "Six months."

"Happy anniversary. Now get the bloody hand grenades out of my room."

"Bloody hand grenades?" One corner of his mouth quirked up as he looked at me. "You still don't swear."

"No, I don't, and give me back my hand." I tried again to pull it back. His fingers held firmly to my wrist.

"Not until you touch me."

I goggled at him. I outright goggled. "You think I'm going to give you a hand job? Are you delusional? Insane? Have such an inflated ego you think you can get away with any amount of crap?"

The other side of his mouth quirked up. I told my Inner Fran to stop noticing his mouth, and remember that it had only taken him six months to replace me. "I was going to suggest my chest, but if you wish to touch me elsewhere, I would not object. Francesca, I did not betray you. I realize you believe I did, but appearances are misleading. Touch me."

"No." I jerked my hand back, staring in surprise at my fingers. There were faint red marks on them, but the cuts from the glass vial had healed over. There was no pain, only a little sense of tightness when I wiggled my fingers. "You healed my hand."

"Of course. You are my Beloved."

"Stop staying that," I snapped, glaring at him again.

"Touch me, Francesca."

"Since when did you start calling me that instead of Fran?" I snarled, holding my hand tight against my chest when he reached for it again.

He brushed a strand of hair back from my temple. I wanted simultaneously to leap on him and strangle him. "It seemed fitting when I saw you standing like an avenging angel at the foot of Naomi's bed. I realized then that you aren't the Fran I remember. Now you're a woman, one who I fervently desire to know better."

"I was a woman when I met you!"

"No." His hand dropped to my lips, his thumb brushing across my lower lip. "You were sixteen, just budding, but your petals were not yet unfurled."

I batted away his hand. "You leave my petals and bud out of this!"

He laughed, the sound of it triggering memories so sweet it brought tears of purest pain to my eyes. "Ah, Francesca, what would I do without you?"

"Evidently fall in with the first blond hussy you can find," I said, shoving him off the bed. "Go away, Ben. I gave you your freedom. I don't want you here. I don't want you in my life. Just go away and—"

He sighed even as I was talking, and before I could stop him, he sat on the edge of the bed again and took my bare hand, placing it between his shirt and chest, right over his heart. Ben had always been the only person other than my mother who I could touch without being swamped by thoughts and emotions. He had some sort of an ability to dampen them, to shield me so that I wasn't overwhelmed. He shielded me now as my fingers lay against his skin, slowly merging his mind with mine. I didn't want to see what was in there, didn't want to feel his emotions for Naomi, but even as I tried to pull back, some horrible masochistic part of me had me looking deep into the darkness that raged within Ben.

My gaze met his. "You haven't betrayed me."

"No, I haven't."

I stared at him in incomprehension. "But . . . I broke things off. I told you I didn't want to be with you any more."

"That's what you *said*. But what I *heard* was a plea for two things: time to finish finding out who you were, and romance."

"Romance?"

"You said you wanted to fall in love, not be told you were in love. I realize now that what is perfectly natural to me—finding a Beloved and being bound to her—was overwhelming to you, and made you feel as if you had no choice in the matter."

"I didn't. You and Imogen and everyone said I had to save your soul—"

He stopped me with a touch of his finger across my lips. "We were wrong. We didn't take into account the fact that you were so young, or, for that matter, your temperament. You never were one to take being led well."

"No, I wasn't. I still don't like it."

"When you railed at me, declaring that you would

make your own life, that you would not allow fate to rule you, I knew that you needed both more time and for me to court you."

I gave a grim, mirthless laugh. "That's a very antiquated notion, Ben. People don't court anymore. They meet at online dating places, and run background checks, and get married and divorced."

He shrugged. "It doesn't matter. I'm concerned with you, not other people."

"I'm confused. You didn't betray what we had, but you're with Naomi? Are you . . . are you in love with her and hiding that fact from me?"

"Do you think I am?"

"Of course I do. You told me in front of her that you didn't want me. Why would you say that if it wasn't true? Why were you with Naomi if you really want me?"

He leaned forward, his mouth brushing against mine. "I can't tell you why."

"What?" I jerked back. "What sort of an answer is that?"

"The secrets I keep from you are not mine, Francesca. I can't tell them to you without first receiving permission to do so."

I put my other hand on his chest, intending to push him away from me, but with both hands touching his skin, I could feel to the tiniest iota the depths of his emotions. I closed my eyes against the despair and anguish a thousand times more horrible than what I had felt at his betrayal. His pain was so deep it seared through his being, from which he had no escape. He was tormented and tortured, his heart empty, his future bleak, and all because the one woman who could save him had abandoned him, left him alone, refused him. . . .

"Not refused," I said, opening my eyes, tears scalding my face as I bit back a sob. For the first time since I had met him, he had wholly opened his thoughts and emotions to me, and the experience left me reeling. He hadn't moved on with his life. He was the one who was betrayed, the one who was left to live in perpetual torment while I blithely went off to find myself, believing he'd be just fine on his own.

"Oh, Ben," I said on another sob, and he was there, surrounding me, warm and wonderful and everything I wanted in the world. "I'm so sorry. I've been wholly selfish. But no one seemed to understand how frustrating it was to be told I had to accept you, had to redeem your soul, had to spend the rest of my life bound to you without regard to anything I might want. Not even you understood."

"No," he agreed. "I didn't until that last call. Then I knew that you truly felt trapped by our bond. So I gave you what you wanted—time by yourself, without restrictions. I knew that in your frame of mind, you would not hesitate to rush out and do everything you'd felt unable to do before. And you did—you changed your hair, you left school and moved out on your own. You got a job that was a far cry from your history degree. I expected you to start dating. You didn't. In fact, it seemed to my friend that you almost had an aversion to other men, refusing even what must be commonplace associations with them. That surprised and pleased me. It led me to believe that the situation wasn't as hopeless as I first thought."

I looked up into the eyes that I knew so well, now a warm oak color, the tiny little flecks of black and gold making his eyes shine. *Why, Ben, why?*

He knew exactly what I was asking. I sensed his withdrawal, the secrets he kept from me. *I can't tell you. I wish I could.*

You told me once you couldn't lie to me, that by being your Beloved, I held some sort of amazing power over you. You said you'd let me kill you, if that's what I truly wanted.

And so I would, but I have oaths I must honor, Fran. I don't like it any more than you do, and I assumed that since you weren't ready to talk to me, that I would have time to take care of this situation before I would begin broaching the subject of courting you. A tiny little frown appeared between his brows, and without thinking, I smoothed it away. *Why did you return now?*

"I thought Loki had kidnapped my mother, but Absinthe says she's in love, and just off on a love spree. I don't know what to think, but I'm going to find out just what's going on," I said, feeling as dull as my words sounded. "How can I trust you if you can't be honest with me, Ben?"

"You know what is in my heart. You've felt it," he pointed out. "Can you not trust me to do what I must?"

I pulled my hands from him, my own heart somewhat pieced back together, but aching and bruised still. "I think it's possible for a man to want to be with more than one woman at a time."

"A man, perhaps. But I am not a mortal man. There is only one woman for me, and you are that woman."

Part of me wanted to hear that, but the other part wondered if it was his heart speaking, or the Dark One who simply recognized his salvation. "Ben—"

"I know. You're not ready to hear that. I apologize. I just don't want you thinking that I am indifferent to you."

"And Naomi?" I couldn't help but ask.

"The situation with Naomi is . . ." He bit off the words as if he'd said too much.

I watched his face for a moment, not needing to touch him to feel his regret. Idly, I looked down to my fingers, touching the now almost faded marks, trying to make sense of what he said, and of emotions so confused and tangled I wondered if I'd ever straighten them out. "You're not going to leave her, are you?"

He opened his mouth to speak, but closed it again, his face hard and angular.

Having my answer, I touched the hair that swept back from his forehead to the nape of his neck. Ben's hair had always been gorgeous, and now, worn about four inches long, brushed back and curling slightly on the ends, it made me want to run my fingers through its silky lengths. "You cut your hair."

His gaze went to my head, a little smile on his lips. "So have you."

"I liked yours better the way it used to be, when it touched your shoulders. I've always thought long hair on men was sexy."

He slid his fingers along the back of my neck, pulling me forward until his mouth brushed mine again. "I prefer yours longer, as well. Tell me you understand, Francesca."

"Well . . . I don't understand, Ben. I just don't." I hadn't intended to kiss him. I really hadn't. But I had wanted to for so long, the need just overwhelmed me. "I think I want to kiss you, though."

Passion flared in his eyes. His hands slid around my waist as he leaned into me. "What word will you say this time?"

I nipped his lower lip, sucking it into my mouth to

take away the sting. "Do I still need kissing lessons so badly that I have to say words like 'Mississippi' against your mouth?"

"Absolutely not," he growled, his fingers digging into my hips. I tipped my head up, my fingers in his hair, whispering against his lips just before I kissed him, really kissed him, relishing the slightly spicy taste of his mouth with a pleasure I felt down to my bones.

Ben had a unique scent that never failed to make me tingle; it wasn't the chemical smell of a cologne, but something that came from within him, a scent that reminded me of frankincense mingled with leather, touched with the sharp tang that I remembered from a trip into an alpine forest. He smelled wild and untamed and dangerous, and I knew down to the very last atom that made up my body I would never get enough of it. Of him.

"Did you mean it?" he murmured against my mouth when I let him have his tongue back.

"Oh, yes." The lust-filled haze in my mind cleared slightly and I realized I had no idea what he was talking about. "Did I mean what?"

He chuckled, a sound that had its origins deep in his chest. I was seated sideways on his lap, my side pressed against his torso, allowing me to feel the rumble of it in my suddenly sensitized breast. "Did you really miss me?"

I pulled away from the lure of his mouth, noting absently that his eyes turned to burnished oak when I kissed him. "Yes. Every night since we broke up, I've wondered what you were doing, and whether you missed me." I paused, watching the little gold bits in his eyes glitter. "About this courting . . . I don't know that it's going to be the answer. What if you woo me and it doesn't work? What if we don't fall madly in love? What if we're just the way we were, a vampire and his Beloved, and nothing more?"

"Then we will deal with that. If you wish to be free of me, then you will," he said simply, and I felt a little piece of the ice shard that had pierced my heart melt away.

"You can't very well date me and Naomi at the same time. It goes without saying that I don't share."

He said nothing, but tilted up my chin and took possession of my mouth in a way that made the kiss I'd initiated seem tame by comparison. The taste of him triggered so many memories of the past, and so many fantasies that followed in the long years without him. His tongue was as hot and bossy as I remembered, and I reveled in the scent and feel and taste of him. For a few seconds, I let everything else fall aside, glorying simply in the sensation of having him in my arms.

A pulsing red hunger rose in him, urging him to take what he needed, to fulfill the most primal part of him. I sucked his lower lip for a moment, releasing it to turn my head slightly, saying, "You're hungry."

He moaned as his lips caressed my neck, burning me with both the touch and the desire that spilled over from him.

"Go ahead, Ben. I may not be sure of a future with you, but at least I can feed you."

His fingers were tight on my arm as his kisses burned even hotter on my flesh until his mouth was pressed against a pulse point. My heart thumped so loud I swear everyone in the Faire would hear it.

Feed, Ben.

Teeth stung across my skin for a moment, and I braced myself for his bite. With a profane snarl, he shoved himself back from me, stalking to the door, leaning his forehead on it as his shoulders heaved.

I stared at him first in surprise, then mortification. He didn't want to drink my blood?

"I want to," he said, his voice rough and tight. "Dear god, Fran, how can you believe I want anything but to Join with you once and for all? That's all that's filled my mind for the last five years. But I can't. Not now. Not while . . ."

Hurt and confusion twisted around my heart. I looked at Ben, his head down as he faced the door, his body language reading anger and frustration. "Imogen told me once that if you fed from me, you wouldn't be able to take blood from her or anyone else, that all blood but mine would be poisonous to you. You don't want to drink from me because then you wouldn't be able to feed from Naomi. Is that it, Ben? You'd rather feed from her than from me?"

His shoulders slumped. "I can honestly say that now that I've seen you again, I want you more than I've wanted anything in all the centuries of my life." He turned around, his face showing a little of the agony that leached into the room from within him. "But I can't feed from you. Not yet. Please try to understand."

I looked at him, this man who I hadn't wanted, who bossed me around, and drove me insane with both desire and an almost overwhelming urge to walk away once again from the pain he'd caused me. He had crushed my heart. He said he wanted me, but didn't want to be with me. He craved my blood and the bond it would bring, but refused it nonetheless.

I should have told him I couldn't trust someone who kept secrets from me.

I should have told him to hit the road.

I should have thrown him out of my life once and for all.

"What do you want me to do?" was all I asked.

"Trust me." He stood there watching me with eyes that were now the color of mahogany, so handsome it almost hurt, everything I ever wanted in a man, everything I had ever dreamed about, as dark as sin, and twice as dangerous.

He didn't love me. I had asked him, and bound to tell me the truth as he was, he hadn't said he did. Could I trust him, given that we might have no future together? What if we simply ended up together, my chemical makeup reacting to his, two people who were physically meant to be together, but lacking the emotional bond that I knew I could not live without?

He had given me time when I needed it; surely I could return the favor. Hadn't I gained enough insight into myself in the last twenty-four hours to grant him what he asked? I pulled up the blankets. "Good night, Ben."

He said nothing, just gave me a look that left me tingling to the tips of my toes, and left.

I lay awake in the darkness for a long time after that, thinking about what he said, half asleep, rousing only for a few minutes when the low rumble of masculine voices outside the door woke me. I kept still and silent as the door was opened just a smidgen, allowing a thin finger of light to spill across the edge of the bed.

"Is the goddess—" I heard Isleif ask.

"Still a virgin," Eirik answered in a satisfied tone, carefully closing the door. "She has not been touched by the Dark One."

Was that a prophecy, or merely wishful thinking?

Chapter 8

I didn't see Ben at all the following morning, but I didn't expect to, given that sunlight was not his friend. Instead I spent a fruitless six hours with the Vikings as we searched the town of Brustwarze for signs of either Loki or the man the Vikings claimed was his son.

"You're sure you saw him yesterday?" I asked them as we stopped for a quick lunch at an out-of-the-way café.

"I am sure it was Nori," Eirik said with a stubborn set to his chin.

"But you didn't see him later on, after I went back to the Faire?"

"No." He scowled at the waiter who brought our food, the latter hurrying away quickly when Eirik fingered his (still thankfully ammo-less) Walther P38. "We searched most diligently until it was time for our rape."

I blinked at the word, thinking I must have misheard. "Your *what*?"

"Our rape. We went to a rape last night." Eirik's expression lightened when the waiter hastily brought him another mammoth stein of beer. "The music was loud and horrible. There were bright lights and much ale. We enjoyed it greatly, did we not?"

"You went to a . . . Oh dear goddess, you mean a *rave*, not a rape."

Eirik shrugged. "It was good, no matter what you call it. There were many women. Finnvid rutted with five of them."

My jaw sagged as I looked in horror at Finnvid, who smiled smugly and cocked a jaunty eyebrow at Eirik. "You had sex with *five* women in the same night?" I finally managed to ask in a stunned whisper.

"Aye. Not at the same time, of course."

"Of course," I said, shaking my head at the mental image that rose.

"Finnvid has always been more in favor of quantity rather than quality," Eirik said, draining his gallon of ale. "I prefer women who desire a man more for his skill at planting than the size of his plow."

"As do I," Isleif said and nodded.

Both men looked at Finnvid, who smiled at me. "Can I help it if women love me for my rod, virgin goddess?"

"I suppose not, although you know, women today pretty much go with the whole idea of size doesn't really matter."

"Of course it matters," Finnvid said, scoffing, and before I could change the subject, he rolled down the top half of the swimmer's body suit that he wore and looked with pride at his groin. "Look upon my rod and tell me that it wouldn't please any woman."

I swear my eyes just about bugged out as my gaze, drawn against my will, took in all that there was to see. Quickly I rallied my wits and looked away, but not before I dredged up a memory of a time Ben was in the shower, and in a mentally sharing mood. I was somewhat relieved to note that he had nothing about which to feel insignificant, and changed the subject with a rapidity that I suspected fooled no one. "Put yourself back in your pants, Finnvid, before you get arrested. Right, so let's go over the game plan for this afternoon. We searched north and west of the town this morning, so if we split up into two groups, we can cover the south and east sides. Then after that, we can . . ."

I stopped, realizing that the expressions the three Vikings wore matched my own dismal mood.

"What is it you wish us to do?" Isleif prompted.

I shook my head, staring glumly down at my plate of sausage. "We're not going to find him by searching, are we?"

"No," Eirik answered. "Loki is the trickster, virgin goddess. His son is the same and will not so easily be found. You must use cunning and wiles to bring Loki forth."

"Then why did you let me spend half the day searching the town?" I asked, exasperated, and immediately contrite because I was snapping at Eirik. "I'm sorry. I have no right to be mad at you."

"You wished to search the town, so we searched the town," he said, making an indifferent gesture. "It is not for us to contradict you."

"You want me to use the valknut, don't you?" I asked, unhappiness filling my stomach. I pushed away my plate, absently noting that a few days spent with the Vikings might just lessen my resemblance to a linebacker.

"Aye, it would be best."

"I'll have to get it from Imogen." I slumped against the back of the chair. "I guess I have no other choice. I had hoped that we could find some trace of my mother or Loki without it, but I guess you were right when you said I'd have to use it."

"It is your Vikingahärta," Isleif said, stroking the long braids of his beard. "Why do you not wish to use it?"

I was silent a moment, trying to put into words the feeling that the Vikingahärta brought me. "When I used it before to summon Loki, he swore revenge against me. I didn't realize that because the Vikingahärta had been his, and was imbued with his powers, using it left me vulnerable to him."

"Ah," Eirik said, enlightenment dawning in his pale blue eyes. "You are worried about what curse he will lay upon you if you use it again."

I flinched at the word "curse." Those were nothing to mess around with.

"You have nothing to worry about," Finnvid said, puffing himself up. "We will protect you from the god Loki."

"Aye," both Eirik and Isleif said.

I was touched by their devotion. "Thanks. It means a lot to me that you're willing to stand by me when I need you. I guess I'd better stop wasting everyone's time and go get it. If you guys are done, we can go back to the Faire."

"You go back," Eirik said, waving an airy hand. "We must locate a bowyer. The man at the ninja shop said that he thought there was one in Munich. We will take the train there to locate the Walther cross bolts."

I was about to tell them it was a waste of time, but figured a little trip would be a good way to get them out of my hair. It wasn't the Vikings I needed to help me use the Vikingahärta. . . . It was an ebony-headed vampire who I knew would keep me safe while I was forcing

Loki into either giving up my mother—assuming it was he or his son who had seduced her—or banishing him so that I could focus on finding my mother's love nest.

We agreed to meet up the next morning, and after I made sure they remembered the rules regarding pillaging and other forms of violence, I took a cab back to the Faire.

Imogen wasn't in her trailer when I arrived to ask her for my Vikingahärta. I did a quick check for her in the common area, but didn't see her there, either. I chatted briefly with some of the people I remembered from my time at the Faire, spending a little time with a Gypsy medium named Tallulah who both intimidated me and left me wishing that I had just a smidgen of her self-possession.

"I'm so sorry to hear about Wennie's passing," I said as I left her trailer after a quick cup of tea. "But I do appreciate you taking in Davide for Mom. I'd be happy to take charge of him again if you're tired of his fussy ways."

The cat in question sat on the top step of the trailer, his tail wrapped around his feet, giving me the most jaded look a cat could give.

"Not at all. He is a comfort to me," Tallulah said, her hand making a little fluttering motion. For the first time I noticed tiny little age spots on the graceful hands. Other than that, she looked the same, her black hair with its white stripe lending dignity to an austere countenance that misled the casual observer to believe she was a hard, emotionless woman. "Sir Edward tells me I should look for a new dog, but I do not feel myself able to do that."

"I've never known Sir Edward to be wrong, but I know how you feel. When I was fourteen, my old Lab died, and it took me years to get over her. In fact, it wasn't until I got Tesla that I even thought about having a pet. Not that you can call a horse a pet."

She smiled, and the faint air of mystery that always wrapped around her changed slightly. I had heard once that she was some sort of Romany royalty, and I could well believe it. The fact that she spent her nights contacting dead relatives of Faire patrons, and had a boyfriend who was a ghost, just added to the whole package. "How is Tesla?"

"Doing well, according to Mikaela. He had a little hoof problem, but they got that cleared up quickly. I hope to go see him soon. I've missed him."

"As I'm sure he has you. Do not forget him in your quest for justice," she said, making me blink in surprise.

"Uh . . ." She closed the door to her trailer, leaving me with a question on my tongue. "I just really hate it when people do that to me." I sighed, and headed across the Faire encampment to the trailer that housed Peter. Just as I got there, he and Imogen strolled from the direction of the cars.

"Are you certain?" Imogen asked him as I stopped in front of them, casting me a quick smile before turning back to Peter.

"I did not see him, but Karl did, and yes, I asked him. He's certain."

"Something wrong?" I asked, noting the frown on Imogen's face. She normally didn't frown, feeling it encouraged wrinkles to run amok.

"Karl says a lich has been seen around the Faire," Imogen said, still frowning as she looked over my shoulder. "Around my trailer."

"A what now?"

"Lich. I have no idea what interest one would have in me. Moravians pose no danger to liches, and I have not met a necromancer of late."

"Have you met with any Ilargi?" Peter asked. "Or vespilloes? Both of those work with liches."

"No, not at all. I would know an Ilargi." Imogen looked aghast at the idea.

"Well, I will have the security doubled up, just in case," Peter said, and hurried off to consult with Kurt and Karl, in charge of keeping everyone at the Faire safe.

"What's an Ilargi? And for that matter, a vespillo?"

"They both have dealings with liches."

"Do they, indeed. I hate to sound ignorant, but what's a lich, other than something that sounds like it should be in my dad's old Dungeons and Dragons book?"

"Come. I feel the need for some tea." I followed her back to her trailer, sitting at the tiny table as she bustled around the kitchen area, plugging in the electric tea-kettle and pulling out a plate of pastries that she set before me. "Let me just check if Günter is back."

She returned from the bedroom just as I was licking the last of the raspberry jam off my fingers. "That's odd."

"What is?"

She stood in a pose of indecision for a moment before slowly sitting down across from me. "He still isn't back. I was sure he would be back today. He said nothing about going away for a length of time."

"Your boyfriend is gone, too?"

"So it would seem," she said slowly, then shook off her abstraction and claimed a piece of baklava. "A lich is a servant of a necromancer, or Ilargi."

I sighed and collected the crumbs off my shirt to lay on the plate. "And what's a necromancer?"

"Someone who raises liches."

I started laughing. "I feel like I'm in the middle of an Abbot and Costello movie."

She looked startled by my laughter, pinning me back with a long look that left me with the uncomfortable feeling she was seeing straight down to my soul. "You are not distraught."

"On the contrary, I'm worried about where my mother has got to, and who her Lothario is."

"Yes, that is true, but you are not in pain as you were yesterday. Then your aura was a dark, muddy gray. Now it is . . ." She considered me again. "Now it is indigo. What has happened to bring insight to you, Fran?"

I made a little pyramid of the crumbs, kept my gaze on them for a few seconds, then gave her a quick rundown of my talk with her brother.

A slow smile spread across her face as I finished. "You must love him very much to forgive his actions with the evil one."

I shrugged one shoulder. "I don't know exactly what I feel, other than I'm willing to give us another chance."

"This is good. You will not give up on him. You will destroy that she-devil Naomi."

"Maybe not outright destroy, although I have to admit the temptation is pretty strong." I laughed again. "And no, I'm not giving up on Ben. Not unless we find out that things . . . Well, we'll let that go for now. For some bizarre reason that he feels he can't explain, he's pretending to be in love with Naomi. I don't like it. I don't like him keeping things from me. And I really don't like her. But he asked me to trust him, and I'm trying to do that."

"Ah, my dear friend, I cannot tell you how happy that has made me," she said, tears shining in her eyes as she leaned across the table to hug me. "Benedikt has suffered so much these last few years waiting for you. I am happy to know that it was not in vain."

"Gee, thanks," I said, wondering if it was any use trying to explain to her my emotions concerning Ben, eventually deciding that where he was concerned, she really only heard what she wanted to hear. I hurried on at the distraught look on her face. "No, don't apologize. I'm just teasing you. I'm well aware that Ben suffered a lot more than I could have imagined he would. I'm sorry for it, but there's nothing I can do to change the past. I need to focus on the present. Which brings me to the inevitable: Can I have the Vikingahärta? I don't want to use it, but I don't see any other way to find my mother."

She nodded and got to her feet, heading toward the bedroom. "I expected you would want it. I had Peter take it out of the safe for you yesterday. I'll fetch it."

"How long have you and Günter been together?" I called after her, successfully resisting the temptation of an orange ginger scone. "He seemed nice, the little bit I talked to him."

Imogen appeared in the open doorway to her bedroom, her eyes wide. "Fran."

"Hmm?"

"It's gone."

"What is?" A horrible thought struck me, sending goose bumps down my arm as I leaped to my feet. "Not the Vikingahärta?"

"Yes. I put it on the nightstand, but it is not there."

I hurried after her as she returned to the room. "Maybe it fell under the bed?"

We searched there, in the closet, the dresser, and finally tore the sheets and blankets off the bed, just on the chance the small scarlet velvet case had gotten caught in a blanket. There was nothing, not so much as a scrap of velvet.

"Bullfrogs!" I swore as I sank onto the edge of the bed, my stomach an icy leaden weight at the thought of the lost Vikingahärta. "Holy cow, Imogen. What am I going to do?"

"I don't know where it could be," she answered, shaking a pillow in hopes of feeling the small hard box. "It was right here, I swear that to you, Fran. I put it right there, right next to the lamp."

"Was it there this morning?" I asked, swallowing back a sudden rise of bile. If I didn't have the Vikingahärta, how was I going to force Loki to tell me if he seduced my mother, let alone banish him?

"I don't know," she repeated, clearly miserable. "Günter didn't come back yesterday, and I . . . Well, I'm afraid I was in town most of the night, looking for him in the clubs."

The thread of pain in her voice penetrated my own sense of desolation. I gave her hand a little squeeze. "You can't possibly believe he left you for another woman? Imogen, you're gorgeous and funny and sweet, and a man would have to be stark raving mad to want someone else over you."

"Perhaps," she said mournfully, tears filling her eyes. "But the fact remains that he has left me without a single word."

Something tickled the back of my brain. I sat very still for a moment and tried to let my thoughts dwell on nothing, as my mother taught me to do whenever I sought to concentrate on something. For once, it worked, and as the tickle blossomed into a full idea, I stared in growing horror at Imogen.

"What is it?" she asked, dabbing at her nose with a handkerchief. "Why are you looking at me that way?"

"What if he didn't leave you as you think? What if he's missing?"

Her honey blond brows pulled together. "I don't understand the difference."

"A whole lot of things have gone missing of late," I said, a little chill running up my back. I ticked the items off on my fingers. "First, I lost my backpack with my keys and cell phone. That could have been stolen by someone passing by the house, but what if someone else took it?"

"Who?"

"Then my mother went missing," I continued. "Then the Vikingahärta, and now Günter."

"It seems very coincidental to me," Imogen said doubtfully.

"Yes, I agree, it seems that way, but what if we're meant to think that? Remember Loki's oath of revenge, Imogen."

She pursed her lips. "He would take from you that which meant the most to you."

"Which I thought at first was my mother, but . . ." I stopped, not wanting to put into words what I was thinking.

"But that's not what you love the most," she said softly.

"I don't know if it is or not. I love my mom. But . . ."

"But there is Ben, and your feelings for him must supersede all others." She patted my wrist. "I understand.

But does that mean that Loki is behind everything? And if he is, why would he whisk away your mother on a romantic whim when it is Benedikt who means the world to you?"

"I don't know." I slumped onto my side, curling into a fetal ball of depression. "And I'm not likely to find out without the Vikingahärta. Oh, goddess of the endless night. Imogen, what am I going to do?"

She tapped a long finger on her chin for a few seconds. "You're going to find the Vikingahärta."

"How? We don't know if someone stole it, or if it's lost, or even if Loki summoned it to him, or something impossible like that."

"I wonder . . ."

I uncurled myself and looked at her. "You wonder what?"

"The lich who was seen around here yesterday." She continued to look thoughtful. "I wonder if he could have been sent to take it."

"Sent? Are liches some sort of minion or something?"

"Not really." She suddenly smiled and sat down next to me. "I'm sorry, Fran. I forget you have a limited experience with the Otherworld. A lich is a being who was once dead, but who has been raised and returned to life."

"A zombie? A zombie took my Vikingahärta?"

"No, not a revenant. A lich is raised by a necromancer, you understand. Those are powerful mages who utilize both dark and arcane sources of power, and by the act of raising, they sometimes imbue magic into the lich."

"Oh, lovely. Magical zombies have stolen my valknut." I wanted to laugh again, but had a nasty suspicion it would have a hysterical tinge to it.

"It won't be easy finding the lich," she mused. "If they are raised by a master necromancer, they are almost indistinguishable from a mortal. Except for their eyes."

"What's wrong with their eyes?" I had an image of bloody eye sockets and dangling optic nerves.

"They are black."

"Big gaping black holes, you mean?"

"Black as in the irises are the same color as the pupils. All liches have black eyes. Well, most do. I have heard there is an exception, but that doesn't concern us."

"Oh? What's the exception?"

"Dragons."

I stared at her for the count of eight, then said, "Moving on."

"Yes, I think that's best. Well. We shall have to find the lich, I believe, and he will tell us who sent him to steal the Vikingahärta." She got to her feet and started changing her clothes into a black leather cat suit.

"I suppose we could," I said slowly, not convinced that the lich was the answer to the problem. "Although I can't help but wonder about Mom. I never thought I'd say this, but if she's just off on a romantic fling with a normal guy, then fine. But if Loki has seduced her somehow, is she safe?"

"Why wouldn't she be?" Imogen gave me an impatient frown. "You're not thinking, Fran. It must be jet-lag. If Loki seduced your mother just so he could harm her, then he would have done so by now. Either he's seduced her in order to use her as bait to draw you in, or she's off with a mortal. Either way, she is most likely unhurt and in love, as Absinthe told you."

"I guess so. Back to the lich . . . we don't know for

certain that he took it. Forgive me, Imogen, but maybe Günter . . . ?"

She shook her head. "I wouldn't think it likely. If Günter wanted to steal the Vikingahärta, why send a lich?"

She had me there. "Good point. Where do we start?"

"Go change your clothes. Wear something tough. Leather is best, if you have it."

"Er . . . will jeans do?"

"If that is all you have. Wear something you don't mind getting dirty. I will meet you at my car in"—she consulted her watch—"half an hour."

Seeing no other option, I agreed, saluted her, and headed off for my mother's trailer.

I had just stepped into the darkened trailer when a big black shadow rushed me, smothering me in a cloying, sickening smell that sent me sliding into a dense abyss of nothingness.

Chapter 9

Sounds, thick and heavy, like they were wrapped up in thunder, rumbled in the distance, slowly, ever so slowly sharpening until I realized I was hearing two men talking.

"—you told me not to hurt her doing it, so I used chloroform," one man said.

"Where the hell did you get chloroform?"

I frowned to myself. I knew that voice. It resonated within me. Through the dense fog in my brain, an image rose.

Ben! It was Ben.

Francesca?

The floor beneath me rocked. I cracked an eye open to see what was going on, and found myself held in Ben's arms. "You got your cross back," was the first thing I said, touching the Celtic cross he wore.

He smiled, his eyes so beautiful, so warm and sexy I just wanted to lick them.

That sounds uncomfortable, but I appreciate the sentiment. You're still a bit drugged, aren't you?

"Drugged? Hrr?"

"Let's sit you up. Maybe that will help."

The world wobbled around quite a bit but finally settled into a familiar orientation, and after a few minutes to clear my head, I had enough wits to realize I was sitting on the ground, leaning against a smooth boulder, Ben squatting on one side of me while another man knelt on the other. Two camping lanterns sat next to them, casting a thin white-blue light around us. It was dusk, the sky a deep indigo, with just a smidgen of the moon starting to come up.

"Hello," the man said, smiling broadly when I looked at him. He had kind of a singsong accent, something I hadn't heard before. It sounded almost English, but wasn't quite. It was a nice voice—not as intriguing as Ben's, but nice. The rest of him wasn't bad, either. He had a squared chin with a little cleft in it, very pale blue eyes, like polar ice, and reddish blond hair that made me think of the word "russet."

"Hi. Are you the one who put a bag over my head and drugged me?"

"Yes." He grimaced a little. "Well, it was a blanket, but yes, that was me."

"Ah. Gotcha." I made a fist and slammed it into his nose.

He fell over backward with a squawk. Ben, who quickly righted me when I tipped over from the momentum of punching the man, laughed loudly. "I told you she wouldn't take kindly to that sort of treatment."

The man sat up, gingerly feeling his nose, his eyes crossing as he tried to look at it. "Next time I'll take your word for that. I'm sorry if you're feeling any after-effects of the chloroform, Fran. I assumed that since you were a Beloved, you wouldn't suffer any of the normal unpleasantries that mortals might."

"Well, I'm not a Beloved, so don't do it again. Who are you?" I asked, taking advantage of my wobbliness to lean into Ben.

"Benedikt's blood brother. And I'm delighted to meet you at last. He talked about nothing else for so long, I was beginning to think he was mad. But now I see why he did so."

"You're . . . uh . . . Daffy?" I asked, racking my brain for his name.

Ben laughed even harder as the other man pulled a face. "David Kneath, actually."

"I'm sorry." I rubbed my forehead. "I could have sworn Ben wrote me an e-mail about you and your name was Daffy. I must be punchier than I thought."

"It's spelled Daffyd, but pronounced 'dav-ith' actually. I'm Welsh, you see."

I didn't see what that had to do with anything, but nodded.

"If it makes it easier, just call me David. Most people do."

"Thanks. Would you mind terribly me asking why you kidnapped and drugged me? And where we are? And what you're doing here?" The last question was asked of Ben.

"I told you that the secrets I had were not mine to share. They're David's," Ben answered, his voice seeming to skitter along my skin. I shivered and rubbed my arm, trying to pull my mind from all sorts of thoughts about Ben so I could focus on what was important.

You're going to make it difficult for me to court you if you think those sorts of thoughts.

I told you the idea of courting is outdated. I don't want some grand, epic love story sort of saga, Ben. I just want . . .

You want to fall in love with me.

Yes. No. Both. I just want to know if I want to be with you because I'm in love with you, or just programmed to be with you.

I understand. But it's still going to make it difficult for me to restrain myself from making love to you if you think about doing all those things you're thinking about doing with your tongue.

I'm a modern woman, Ben. I can actually have sex without being head over heels in love with a man.

His eyebrows rose.

That didn't quite come out the way I hoped it would, I admitted, feeling pretty trashy. *I just meant that I like you well enough to have sex without formally declaring that yes indeedy, you are Mr. Right Forever. And while we're on the subject, stop eavesdropping on my smutty thoughts about you.*

I can't help it. You're sharing them with me.

No, I'm not. I have made very sure to keep secret all those fantasies about licking you, and nibbling on your chest, and touching your . . . Gah! Now you're putting thoughts into my head!

He chuckled.

David shot him a startled look.

"My apologies. Continue, David."

"Benedikt told me that you'd come here to Join with him, but the work he's doing for me has interfered with that," David said slowly, his face suddenly grim.

You told him that?

I thought it was best.

Well, you can just straighten him out on the subject! I will if it becomes important.

David sat down next to me, his elbows on his knees as he looked out into the gathering night. "There are not enough ways to apologize for messing up what should have been something wonderful between you, so instead of even trying, I'm going to explain to you what's going on." He glanced over at Ben. "People's lives are at stake, Fran, so I'm going to ask you not to repeat anything we say here."

"Of course I won't, not if it's that important." *He looks sad, Ben.*

There has been much tragedy in his life the last few years.

Is he the reason you disappeared those couple of times?

Yes.

"Benedikt has been assisting me the past six years to uncover who is behind the disappearances of my pride members. It took us until this year to finally pinpoint the group we believed was behind it all, and Benedikt, in an attempt to infiltrate the Agrippans, connected with Naomi. He got her a job at the Faire, since he knew that would give him a cover to travel with her."

"Wait a second. Did you say pride members? Like gay pride?"

David looked from me to Ben. "You didn't tell her?"

"Tell me what?"

Ben shook his head. "No. You swore me to secrecy, if you recall."

"Tell me what?"

"That's right, I did. Do you want to tell her, or shall I?"

"Someone better tell me, before Mr. Punchy Hand gets annoyed," I said with a narrow-eyed look that I split between them.

"David is a therion," Ben said, just like that explained everything.

"Bully for him. What's a therion?"

David laughed and stood up. "I think in this case, seeing is believing."

My eyes widened as his body did an odd sort of shimmer, rippling and twisting until it turned into a sandy cinnamon-colored lion, an honest-to-Pete lion, complete with big brown mane, pale light blue eyes, and what I assumed were exceptionally big teeth.

"Goddess above," I said, my eyes almost bugging out at the sight of the lion as it turned and faced me. "That's a . . . that's a . . ."

"A lion, yes," David said as the lion form shimmered back into that of a man. A naked man.

Stop ogling him.

I'm not. But . . . holy crickets. He's naked.

You are ogling. I wish for it to stop.

I'm trying, I'm trying. Oh man! My eyes widened further as David nonchalantly bent to retrieve his pants.

If you wish to ogle someone, you may ogle me.

Yeah? Think Naomi would let me?

He was silent, but I could feel his irritation.

David buttoned up his shirt and gave me a rueful smile as he sat down again. "A therion is a shape-shifter with two primary forms. One of mine happens to be that of an Asiatic lion."

"You're like a werewolf, but with a lion instead of a wolf?" I asked, then craned my head to look behind me, where the moon was beginning to clear the horizon. "Is it a full moon?"

"Therions can shift at will, Francesca," Ben said, taking my hand and rubbing his fingers across mine. It

was a possessive move that I knew had its origins in the
eye candy David had provided. I smiled to myself. "The
myth about the full moon is a human fiction, nothing
more."

"Oh." I looked back at David, my mind struggling to
cope with the fact that he was a lion. "I thought . . . This
is really stupid, I know, but I have to ask . . ."

"You thought vampires and werewolves hated each
other?" David grinned at Ben. "That's a fallacy, too.
For one, the therions who favor wolf forms tend to be a
very tight-knit group, and don't mingle much with out-
siders. For another, therions have no reason to dislike
Dark Ones."

"I'm glad to hear that. So, people in your . . . er . . .
pride are disappearing, too?"

"Too?" Ben asked.

"There are a lot of things disappearing around me
lately," I told him. "My mother and the Vikingahärta,
to name two. And Imogen's boyfriend."

"That's no great loss," Ben said in a tight voice.

*I just bet Imogen loves it when you give her boy-
friends a hard time.*

If she had better taste in men, I wouldn't have to.

Spoken like an overprotective brother.

"These disappearances have been going on for years,
so I'm afraid they're not related to yours," David said,
rubbing his face wearily.

"All right, but what does Naomi have to do with anything? And why is Ben letting her touch him and slobber on him and think she's his girlfriend?"

Jealous much, sweetheart?

*Perhaps. Or perhaps I just don't like seeing a friend
hooked up with someone who's not good for him.*

That gave him something to think about, I noted

with satisfaction. Until, that is, it struck me that he didn't protest being called a friend. And then I realized that I had better take some responsibility for what I wanted, and not dump it all on him. I couldn't think of anything worse than to realize I had fallen in love with him, only to find out he didn't reciprocate the emotion.

Okay. I will admit that I'm the teensiest bit jealous. I don't like her touching you. And kissing you. And pushing her boobs on you. And while we're on the subject, do you have to put your arm around her? It makes it look like you're enjoying it when she rubs herself all over you, which from what I've seen is pretty much every time you're together.

Yes, that's just a teeny bit jealous.

I ignored the laughter in my head to deliver a glare at him before turning my attention back to David.

"Benedikt said you weren't happy about that. I'm sorry, but Naomi is familiar with members of the European therion community," David explained. "We needed someone who could get into her confidence, and that required an unknown. Benedikt offered to do the job, and although I know you don't like it, he's been tremendously helpful to us by allowing Naomi to believe he's romantically interested in her. He found the group that we believe is organizing the abduction of therions across Europe."

"Agrippans?" I asked, remembering the word he'd used.

"Yes. Do you know what an Agrippa is?"

I shook my head.

"Originally, it was the name of a book of mystical spells. A few millennia ago, the word came to be applied to the people who created those books, the seekers of knowledge who spent their lives locating and learning magic, which they offered to wield for a price."

"Sort of walking encyclopedias of magic?"

"More or less. They hired themselves out to support their endless thirst for knowledge. Today, there are three Agrippan sets: one in North America, one here in Europe, and one in Africa."

"I don't see the connection between a seeker of knowledge and missing therions," I said.

"Neither do we. Yet," Ben said, his thumb sending little tendrils of heat up my hand with every stroke of it across my fingers.

"Benedikt's been pressed hard by Naomi to join the local tyro—that's a ceremonial meeting of Agrippans—so he can be inducted into the group, but he's resisted so far."

"Oh? Why?" I asked Ben.

He was silent, his eyes turning dark.

"Why?" I asked David instead.

He looked extremely uncomfortable. "Tyros are . . . The Agrippans tend to celebrate their baser natures, and that's especially true at their ceremonies."

He's talking about sex, isn't he?

Yes.

He wants you to have sex with Naomi? I asked, ignoring as best I could the cold wave of nausea that hit me with tidal force.

He wishes for me to participate in the tyro. Unfortunately, that would require me to be a part of the group sex that is conducted during the ceremonies.

You can guess how I feel about that.

Yes, I can. And just so you stop thinking lovingly about a serrated grapefruit knife in relationship to my testicles, I will point out that the reason I haven't at-

*tended a tyro is that I have no desire to engage in sex
with anyone but you.*

I will admit that both his words and the emotion behind them made me feel all warm inside, but David's
next words killed that.

"I know it's asking more from you than I should, but,
Fran, it's important that we find out as much information as he can before Naomi discovers the truth about
him. There's a tyro scheduled for tomorrow night.
Benedikt told Naomi he wouldn't go, but she's already
suspicious, and if he misses yet another one . . . Well,
it could make the last couple of years' work all for
nothing. Not to mention risking the lives of two of my
pride members who have gone missing in the last six
months."

I stared at him in horror. "You are not asking me to
sanction Ben having sex with a bunch of other people,
are you? Because that's what it sounds like to me, and if
you are, you're seriously in need of some mental coun-
seling."

"You have every right to be angry, and I completely
understand your reaction, but it would be for just one
night. You are Benedikt's Beloved—he would never
want to be with any woman but you."

"No," I said, wanting very much to punch David
again.

"If you understood just how close we are to getting
the names of the people involved, and how they are related to the disappearances of my pride members—"

"No!"

"If I can do it without the sex, would you agree?"
Ben asked.

I looked at him thoughtfully. "Could you do that?"

"It might be possible." He was silent for a moment. I

could feel him considering and discarding various options. "I might be able to use you as an excuse. Naomi knows you are my Beloved, but that we've had some relationship issues. If I told her that you being here is hampering my ability to make a final commitment to her, she might believe it."

And what if I wasn't here? What if I was back home where you thought I was? Would you be going ahead with this tyro and all it implies?

He didn't answer me for a good thirty seconds. When he did, his words were stark with honesty. *If you weren't here now, I would feel compelled to participate in the tyro, but in such a way that allowed me to keep my oath to help David at the same time it honored the bond between us.*

You'd have sex with strangers.

No. I'd pretend to have sex with strangers.

How do you pretend *to have sex?*

You get naked and roll around with a bunch of other naked people.

Fury unlike anything I'd ever felt burbled up inside me. *And you think that would be honoring me?*

No. I think that would be getting naked and rolling around with other people. That is not sex, Fran.

It's close enough to make no difference! I snapped.

You think not? Let me ask you this—you believed you had severed our relationship a year ago. How many men have you slept with since then?

You know full well I haven't been with any man, sexually or romantically. What's your point?

My point is that I did not believe our bond had been broken. I did not have then, nor do I have now, any desire to engage in sex with any woman but you.

I thought about that for a moment, strangely pleased

by the little tinge of outrage to his words. *But you would if you had to?*

He sighed. *There is no way I'm going to be able to continue this discussion without you becoming angry with me.*

I was going to point out that was a cop-out, when Inner Fran piped up once again with yet another dish of wisdom: What might have been was not important. It was the here and now that mattered. *You're right. I won't lambaste you for something you haven't done.*

I didn't think it would happen, but you have changed, Beloved.

Matured?

Not in the sense you mean. Before, you were fairly insular, very reticent to become involved with anything or anyone. Now you are more aware of others. You are more . . . earthy.

I hope being earthy is a good thing.

Oh, yes. He let me feel his emotions. The little spark that had always been between us shimmered into an electrical charge of attraction that skittered down my back. I could feel him considering me, as if he was seeing me with new eyes, and what he saw pleased him immensely.

I basked in that for a moment before I realized David was saying something to me.

"Fran? Benedikt has said he would not attend the tyro unless you agreed."

I looked from David to Ben, my emotions torn. On the one hand, I wanted to tell David to stuff the tyro where the sun doesn't shine. On the other hand, I knew from feeling the strength of Ben's emotions just how much this mattered to him, to them both. And while I didn't have any qualms about dissing Naomi, I hesitated at giving in to jealous anger if it meant that David's lion friends might suffer for it. "There will have to be conditions. I want to know exactly what is involved in the orgy part of the evening."

Ben's lips thinned. "I will escort Naomi to the tyro. She will name me as a new member. They will initiate me into the group."

"With sex."

"A group celebration of primal forces."

"Sex," I said, nodding. I held up a finger. "Condition one: no sex."

"Agreed," Ben said. David watched us warily.

"No getting naked and rolling around with other people."

Ben frowned. "That is not sex."

"I don't care. I don't like the idea of Naomi seeing you naked."

Ben said nothing.

I gasped, and socked him as hard as I could on the chest. "You didn't!"

"I have to take a shower sometime, Francesca. I try to do it when she's not around, but there are times when it is inevitable."

I seethed for a few minutes, and desperately tried to remember a curse I had learned when I was fourteen. When my mother found out that I was trying to practice what she called harmful magic, she grounded me for three straight months. "There will come a day, Ben, when I am going to settle things with Naomi."

To my surprise, he grinned. "I look forward to seeing that."

Don't be so happy—I have a few things to settle with you, too. "Can you at least try to limit the nudity in quantity and time? Maybe just take off your shirt and hope no one notices your pants?"

"Yes," he said gravely. I thought I heard David snort, but when I looked, his expression was blank.

"Condition two: no touching or kissing Naomi."

"Francesca," Ben said on another sigh.

"I don't want you kissing her," I said, realizing full well I sounded like a petulant child.

"She will be suspicious if I distance myself from her in that manner. I don't enjoy it, if that's what you're worried about," he said.

I ground off a layer or two of enamel. "Fine. You can kiss her. But I get to kiss other men. In fact, I think I'll start with David."

David's eyes widened as I leaned toward him, reaching for his shoulders. Before my mouth was even close to his, I was yanked backward, onto my feet, and spun around to face a Ben whose dark oak eyes fairly spat flames. "You will *not* kiss other men!"

I raised my eyebrows and tapped my fingers on his chest.

His jaw tightened as David laughed.

"Fine," Ben snarled, letting go of my arms. "I won't kiss Naomi. But I can't stop her from kissing me."

I thought about that for a minute. "Fair enough."

Once again, he looked surprised at my acquiescence. I made sure I kept hidden the thought that I'd just see to it that Naomi didn't have the chance to try any moves on him.

"Are those your only conditions?" he asked.

"For now," I said. "I reserve the right to include others at a later date."

"And I reserve the right to qualify any subsequent terms," he added.

I made a face, but stopped when David took my hand and shook it vigorously. "Thank you, Fran. I know that you must be anxious to Join with Benedikt, and I appreciate you putting it off on my behalf."

I glanced at Ben. *You're going to hell for all those lies you told him.*

I haven't lied. The Joining has been delayed until such time as you feel comfortable with it. His mind felt shuttered, as if he was trying to keep something from me.

And if that is never?

Then it will still be postponed.

This is because of Naomi, isn't it? I asked, trying to see what it was he wanted to keep hidden.

He didn't answer. The patented Ben silence . . . but I was no longer a teenager intimidated by that sort of tactic.

Let's say I was ready to Join with you right now. Why couldn't you use that as your excuse for not wanting to indulge in the orgy at the sex party?

Unfortunately, Naomi knows enough about Dark Ones to realize the difference between a Beloved who is not yet Joined and one who is. If we Joined, she would know that you would take precedence in my thoughts, and that she could never hold sway over me. That isn't the case now.

I didn't know what hurt worse: the thought that Ben was willing to continue with the farce, or that I didn't matter as much to him as David.

Francesca—

No, don't say it. I am ashamed of myself for even thinking that. I gave him a chagrined smile. *I'm going to have to get used to you seeing the real me, warty thoughts and all.*

There's nothing about your thoughts that are warty. I just wish—

I know, I interrupted. *I'm being selfish and self-centered, and you're only trying to help your friend. All right, we'll help him.*

David had been thanking me during that entire exchange, finally finishing with, "I can't tell you how much this means to my pride and me."

I was even more ashamed that I had put my own feelings so far ahead of his concern for his family. "There's no need to thank me. Is there anything I can do to help you?" I glanced at Ben. "I assume Ben told you about my abilities?"

David looked down at my black-laced hands. "Yes, he did. I don't know how psychometry can help us now, but I appreciate you offering your assistance, and I'm just desperate enough that I will ask for help should you be able to give it. I just hope you forgive me for . . . er . . . bringing you here as I did. Benedikt told me to bring you without causing you any distress, and it seemed easiest to simply drug you."

"I won't say I enjoyed it, but there's no harm done." I looked around us, trying to figure out just where we were. We seemed to be in some sort of thickly wooded area. A faint thrum of noise sounded in the distance. "Are we near the Faire?"

"About seven miles," Ben said. "This is a small wildlife preserve that David uses when he's in the area. No one ever comes out—"

He stopped speaking when three people, two men each wearing half a horse costume, and a woman clad in a nude-colored body stocking and knee-length blond wig, strolled past with polite greetings.

"—here," Ben finished, looking after the threesome.

"This is the weirdest town I've ever been in," I commented.

"I'll take you back to the Faire," Ben said, holding out his hand for me. I took it, smiling to myself when he peeled off both sets of gloves, handing them back to me before taking my hand again.

"Will David be all right out there by himself? Well, by himself and with whatever oddballs are walking through the woods in the middle of the night in stage costumes?" I asked, glancing over my shoulder to see David waving at us before disappearing into the shadows.

"Yes. His kind prefers solitude to intense contact with mortals. Would you have really kissed him?"

My secret smile grew a lot bigger. "What do you think?"

He helped me down a gravelly incline, holding back the branches of a scraggly fir tree. "I think you were deliberately trying to bait me."

"Then that must be the answer," I said complacently, greatly enjoying the irritated look he shot me as he lifted me over a fallen tree. I debated pointing out that I was perfectly able to clamber over obstacles on my own, but decided to enjoy his show of masculinity.

Ten minutes later we reached a narrow dirt track. Ben's lantern didn't cast much light, but there was enough for me to see no bulky shape of a car. "We're walking to the Faire?"

"No." He tugged me after him. A few hundred yards down the track, it curved. As we rounded it, a black shadow loomed up against the darker trees. I stopped, a strange joy filling me. "Your bike! You still have it?"

"Of course. It's a classic." His lips quirked for a moment. "No helmets, though. Do you think your mother will be angry?"

"No doubt, but I trust you not to kill me or leave me brain dead," I said, waiting for him to get onto the motorcycle before climbing on behind him. "At the risk of inflating your ego past bearable levels, I have to admit that I've often thought of the rides we took together. For some reason, they always left me . . ."

I hesitated, searching for the right word.

"Aroused?" he asked, looking back at me.

"Yes. I just didn't realize that's what it was."

He grinned. *I'm glad I wasn't alone in that. The last few times, I was afraid I'd scare you off forever with the natural consequence of you riding in front of me.*

Oh, I noticed you were in a very happy mood. I was flattered, to be honest. And more than a little intrigued.

He gave me an unreadable look before turning around to start the bike.

A little thrill ran through me at the combination of the motorcycle vibrating beneath me and the fact that I was plastered up against Ben's back. "I've missed this."

"As have I. If you want to drive, though, I'd prefer you wait until we get onto the road proper."

"Hang on a second." I wrapped my arms around him, made an unhappy noise, and slid my hands beneath the black leather jacket he'd donned. That wasn't enough, either. Ben looked down in surprise when I yanked the front of his shirt out of his pants, slipping my hands under it to his bare stomach. The muscles there contracted as I spread my fingers out across their warmth. "Perfect. Let's go."

I swear I heard him mutter, "You have no idea," but contented myself to rest my cheek against his shoulder, silky little wisps of his hair brushing against my face as he drove us through the night. I wondered if sex on a motorcycle was possible.

No, but it is on horseback if you have a very well-trained horse.

I pulled back from where I had my nose buried in his nape and pinched his belly. *Stop reading my wicked thoughts about you!*

He laughed in my mind, and I settled back against him, my heart and my mind, for the moment at least, at ease.

Chapter 10

The Faire was in full swing when we returned, the center aisle positively crammed with people. I could hear gasps of awe and applause coming from the main tent as Peter or Kurt and Karl did their magic acts.

"I suppose I should find Imogen and see if there's been any word on my Vikingahärta."

"She will no doubt be busy reading rune stones."

"True. I suppose it'll have to wait until later." I stopped next to my mother's stall, worry suddenly consuming me.

Ben, holding my hand, knew what I was thinking. His fingers tightened around mine now, offering comfort just by his touch. "Your mother is not only a woman *not* to be trifled with—she's also a powerful Wiccan. I know you are worried about Loki, but I can't see him wishing to engage in a battle with her for no reason other than to harm her."

"Imogen said the same thing."

"That is because Loki has no reason to harm Miranda, and every motivation to keep her safe so that he may use her to barter for the Vikingahärta."

"That's the only reason I could figure he'd be interested in seducing her. I mean, she's not really his type. But what if he already has it? What if it was he who stole it?"

Ben looked thoughtful for a moment, rubbing his chin as he mulled that idea over. Such an action never failed to make my legs go wobbly. "It's not beyond the realm of possibility that a god could control a lich, but I've never heard of it being done. To my mind, the lich indicates that there's someone else involved who wanted the valknut. Just who remains unclear. Regardless, I don't believe your mother is in physical danger."

Despite a tiny remaining worry, I agreed with what he said. I had a feeling I'd know if something truly horrible had happened to my mother. I had known when I was little and in school and her appendix burst. Surely I would know now if she was being tortured or worse?

Ben held tightly to me as he forged a path through the dense mass of bodies. As he came up to a booth painted in black and red, he dropped my hand.

I'm going to stop in a few feet. Please slap me when I do so.

I beg your pardon?

Slap me. If I am to convince Naomi that you have some sort of a hold over me, we must give her a show.

Don't get me wrong. I'm more than happy to slap you, but what on earth will that prove other than I'm pissed at you?

Just follow my lead. You're hurt and angry with me, but you aren't ready to walk away yet. All right?

I kept the thought to myself that it wouldn't take much, if any, acting to depict those emotions, following Ben as he stalked through the crowd, his jaw set.

Yell at me.

"Will you wait for me, you great big wart on the bottom of a slug?" I shouted, running after him.

He spun around and glowered at me. I noticed from the corner of my eye that he had stopped right in front of Naomi's booth, and that she, holding a tattoo gun, was watching us with a calculating glare. "I will not be spoken to in such a manner as that!"

I slapped him hard enough for him to feel it. He emphasized the slap by snapping his head to the side before slowly turning back to regard me with fiery eyes. "You will regret that."

"In your dreams!" I snarled, and shoved past him to storm my way through the crowds toward the trailers.

I assumed he would return to Naomi to make the most of the scene, but was surprised to feel his presence behind me as I stomped my way to my mother's trailer.

Uh . . . should you be here?

Probably not, but unless you order me to leave, it would take a monumental effort to remove me from your side tonight.

Heat swept up from my chest as I realized just what he was implying. I'd all but given him the go-ahead to jump into bed with me, but he really was going to do it? Excitement fluttered in my stomach. *Naomi won't like it.*

He thought something extremely rude about her that made me smile. I entered the trailer, waiting for him to close the door behind himself before I looked at him.

"I've wanted to have you alone for a long time," I said, every bit of me tingling at the nearness of him.

"Even when you thought I was trying to control your life?" he asked, one side of his mouth going up in a smile.

"Well . . . I won't say there weren't some fantasies

about decking you with a two-by-four mixed in there, but for the most part, even then. Ben, I know I sound like an inarticulate, confused twit—"

"No, you don't."

I raised my eyebrows.

"Perhaps you sound a little confused," he admitted with a grin. "But I understand that this is of vital importance to you. Which is why I'm prepared to give you the space you need should you require more of it."

"I appreciate that." I bit my lip, trying to figure out how best to get his clothes off him without looking like that's all I could think of. Which it was, but he didn't have to know that.

"Are you sure you wish for me to be here tonight, Francesca?" he asked, and the meaning behind his words was extremely clear.

"I'm sure of that. But, I'm . . . uh . . . it seems a little crude of me to just tell you to strip, and then pounce on you. Although right now, that really does sound good."

He laughed and gently pulled me into his arms. "We will do this slowly, all right? If you wish for me to stop at any time, I will."

"You will? Really?" I gazed up into his eyes, those beautiful eyes now the color of gold-bespecked honey oak. "What if we had been going at it for a bit, and you were about to"—I waved one hand around in a vague gesture—"blast off?"

He grimaced. "Then I would stop. I'd probably die in the process of stopping, but it would be a noble sacrifice to know that I gave my life making you happy."

"I never realized just what a big ham you are," I said and giggled, nipping his lower lip. "Oh, Ben. Even when I didn't want to be bound to you, I still couldn't stop thinking about you. You have no idea how long I've wanted to do this."

I know exactly how long, because I've endured each second of it wanting you, as well. And now, seeing you as a woman—my woman—so near to me, has almost pushed me beyond all bearing. His mouth was as hot as a furnace as he took charge of the kiss, making me squirm against him as his tongue twined around mine. I pulled off his shirt, my mind giddy with the sight and feel and taste of his bare chest.

I wrapped my arms around him, pressing little kisses to his bare shoulder. *You don't think I'm . . . um . . . You don't think I'm wrong for wanting to have sex with you, but not Join with you, do you? It's not against some sort of vampire code, is it? Because I haven't made up my mind yet about the Joining, and if this is going to be taken as a tacit acceptance of the idea that I'm your Beloved—*

If you do not wish for it to be an acceptance, then it will not be. His mouth moved on my skin, his hot breath making me shiver with pleasure as he pulled off my own top, his hands busy with my breasts.

It wasn't exactly the words I wanted to hear, but it was enough.

I shivered when he nibbled on my shoulder, his hands stroking my breasts, the satin of my bra rubbing sensuously against my nipples. "You know, if we'd done this all those years ago—oh, yes, please!" My fingers clutched the thick muscles of his shoulders as he dipped his head and licked the valley between my breasts.

He chuckled into my mind as my bra fell to the floor, his mouth instantly claiming one of the aching nipples that were waiting just for that touch. I arched my back, stroking and clutching and pulling his shoulders as little spirals of pleasure and heat sank low in my secret parts.

There is a reason we did not, Francesca. You were too young to understand what a physical commitment would mean. Imogen urged me to give you time. She wanted me to show you that you mattered beyond my own base needs, and it didn't take me long to realize that she was right. I wanted you to come to me without coercion. I wanted to know you were truly mine, and I was content to wait for that.

You think I was that much of a pushover, huh? I was a bit indignant about that. Until he kissed a path over to my other breast, his fingers and mouth working to bring me to a frenzy.

Right. I was. Thank god for your presence of mind. My nipple feels abandoned and unloved, could you please . . . Words flew out of my mind, replaced only by the sensation of Ben's mouth on my breast, nibbling, licking, and teasing me, my sensations mingling with the ones he was feeling.

I knew that you were ripe for seduction, yes. But that wouldn't have been what was best for you. You were simply too young, as I quickly realized.

I hope to the stars that you are over such a protective attitude, because it's very irritating. Would you like me to reciprocate?

Reciprocate making decisions for my welfare?

"No, do you want me to nibble on your nipples? I've heard that some men are into that, and others aren't. Are you go or no go in that respect?"

He lifted his head from where he was nuzzling the underside of my breast. "I've never been stimulated that way, no."

"Ah." I looked at his chest. "Maybe I should just give it a try and we'll verify that."

"If you wish, although I don't want you to be disappointed when I don't—" He froze when I gently, ever so gently, bit his nearer nipple.

His eyes rolled back into his head when I stroked one hand down his chest, to his crotch, feeling the hardness beneath the fly of his jeans.

He stopped breathing when I let him feel just how much enjoyment I was receiving from tasting him, kissing his chest, stroking his back, and running my thumb up and down his growing proof of arousal.

"Oh, no, you're not finding this stimulating at all," I cooed into his other nipple, licking it until Ben grabbed my shoulders and groaned with unadulterated pleasure. "I really like the taste of you, Ben. I had no idea men could taste . . . well, manly. Without being sweaty or musky or anything unpleasant like that. You taste kind of hot, kind of smoky, like you've been out by a campfire. You smell . . ." I took a deep breath, relishing the way his scent seemed to quicken my blood. "You smell wonderful."

He nuzzled my neck as I moved up to kiss his shoulder, silent for a few seconds. *Are you sure, Francesca? Absolutely sure? If we do all those things you are thinking of doing, assuming I survive them, and I may not because you have evidently become quite inventive during our five years apart, if we do them, it will mean we are just one step away from Joining.*

I gently bit the tendon of his neck, causing him to rear back with a startled flash in his eyes.

"I'm certain. Only . . . it sounds trite to say be gentle, but I'm new to all this, so I'd appreciate any pointers on what you give a green light to, and what leaves you cold."

"You had no trouble finding several new things I give the green light to," he said, his body trembling a little as I stroked down the front of his fly again.

"I didn't say I was naive, just new to—"

The door to the trailer opened. Imogen, out of breath and looking very worried, dashed in. "Fran? Are you here? When you disappeared, I was worried, but then I heard from Desdemona that you and Ben had the most appalling scene, and I knew you must be all—oh. You're here." Her eyes took in the fact that neither of us wore shirts. "I . . . uh . . ."

"Are *de trop*? Yes, you are. That was a scene put on for Naomi's sake," Ben answered, handing me my shirt, which I quickly slipped on. "And Francesca is just fine."

Her brilliant smile lit up the room. "I'm so glad. I worried . . . but I see I was worrying amiss."

I studied her for a moment. She didn't look any different, and yet . . . my gaze went from her to Ben, and seeing them together, I suddenly realized what it was. Although Imogen was older than Ben, suddenly she looked younger. The Ben I remembered appeared to be about nineteen or twenty; this Ben looked ten years older.

How did you do that?

He cocked the other eyebrow at me. *Do what?*

You look older. Which is good, I guess, because I wouldn't want to spend eternity bound to a guy who looks nineteen. But now you look more mature.

You aged, so I altered my appearance to what was appropriate for you.

You can change your appearance like that?

"I will leave so you two can . . . I will leave. Good night, Benedikt. Good night, Fran."

I'll explain the concept of Dark One aging to you later.

"Night, Imogen." *I'll hold you to that.* "I'll see you in the morning."

She hesitated at the door. "I just knew things would work out, and now they have, and I'm so happy for you both. But, Fran, where's your ring?"

She turned inquisitive eyes to her brother.

"Here." Ben pulled the ring from his pocket, taking my left hand, placing the ring first over my thumb, then forefinger, then middle finger, where he left it. I smiled.

Sorry I threw it at you.

There is no need for you to apologize. He pulled my hand to his mouth, placing a kiss on my palm. I shivered at the touch.

"There, you see? I just knew you couldn't have abandoned dear Fran," Imogen said, tears of happiness glittering in her blue eyes. "And now I really will leave."

As she opened the door, a whirlwind entered the trailer, or at least that's what it seemed like. The door was flung open and three large men charged in, all of them yelling at the same time. Ben turned to block my view, but the whirlwind didn't end until Imogen said one word.

"Finnvid!" she gasped, her expression mingling delight with chagrin.

One-third of the whirlwind stopped, staring at her in surprise for a second before he whooped and scooped her up, spinning her around. "Imogen!"

Ben said something that sounded remarkably like swearing, his eyes narrowed on the Vikings as Eirik and Isleif stopped in front of me. "What the hell are *they* doing here?"

"Didn't I mention they were here?" I asked with a lame smile before turning on the three men. "I thought you guys were going to spend the night in town?"

"Finnvid, I wasn't . . . I had no idea . . . Fran never said . . . ," Imogen sputtered, trying to slip out of Finnvid's hold, but not succeeding.

Eirik moved so he was between Ben and me, his frown matching Ben's as the two men glared at each other. "Do you think we would leave you unprotected, virgin goddess?"

Virgin goddess? Ben asked.

Don't even go there.

"You are ours to protect, and we hear how this Dark One abused you a little while ago. We have come to save you from him. Shall we cleave him in two?"

"I'd like to see you try," Ben said in a low, dangerous voice that had my eyes opening wide.

"Finnvid, you must set me down. Things have changed since I saw you last."

Eirik stood toe-to-toe with Ben, the Viking's eyes narrowed as he snarled, "I will be happy to meet you, Dark One."

"Break it up, boys," I said in a tone that I realized sounded just like my mother when she was annoyed. I cleared my throat and added, "Eirik, stop baiting Ben. He's not going to tolerate—"

Eirik flew past me, slamming against the wall.

"—that." I sighed and raised my hand when Isleif leaped forward, flinging himself on Ben. I spent a moment offering thanks that they hadn't found bullets for their guns, but as Finnvid, catching sight of the fight that was going on, unceremoniously dumped Imogen and joined the fray, I kind of wished I had a ladies' small beheading ax. I knew three Vikings who I'd use it on.

Eirik, recovering from being knocked silly against the wall, ran past me and leaped onto Ben, who was currently engaged in beating the crap out of Isleif and Finnvid. I was about to demand they stop fighting when Imogen put her hand on my arm. "Oh, let them, Fran."

"You can't seriously mean you want me to let the Vikings beat up Ben? I might not be ready to be his Beloved, but I really would prefer he not be hurt. I have plans for him tonight."

She smiled and tugged me a few feet away from where the three Vikings were pounding the bummocks out of Ben. "Does he look like he's being harmed?"

I stood on my tiptoes and tried to peer through the mass of whirling, punching, and swearing bodies. For one moment, I caught a glimpse of Ben. He didn't look any worse for wear—in fact, there was a remarkable look of satisfaction on his face as he landed a punch on Isleif that sent the much bigger man staggering backward.

"I swear I will never understand men," I said, sighing. "He's enjoying himself, isn't he?"

"Yes, he is. You don't know, but he's been keeping all of his emotions bottled up inside him ever since you left, and I knew he was aching for a good brawl to release some of the frustrations. Although I will say I hope he doesn't harm Finnvid too much."

I raised my eyebrows at her.

She smiled. "Well, Günter hasn't returned, and . . . I'm sure you understand."

"I do, and I am happy to have one less Viking underfoot." I looked at my watch. "How long do you think we should let them go at it?"

"Oh, I think it's been long enough for Benedikt to work through the worst of his anger."

I put my fingers to my mouth and let out a whistle that was effectively piercing in the closed confines of the trailer. "Vikings! Stop beating up Ben!"

Reluctantly, they did as I bid, Isleif stepping back rather than throwing himself onto the pig pile on Ben. Finnvid, with an elbow to Ben's nose, managed to rise and move off him. Eirik tried to get one last shot in, but Ben nailed him with a punch to the gut that left the Viking doubled over. Ben got to his feet, his breathing hard, a cut over his left eyebrow bleeding sluggishly, and a slight swelling on one side of his jaw. He flexed his fingers, absently rubbing them.

Are you okay?

Of course. Did you think I could be harmed by three ghosts? Arrogance was rich in his voice.

I kept my smile to myself. *I was a bit worried at first, but then I could see you were holding your own. Imogen says it was good for you, that you were holding in all sorts of emotions that needed to be released, and that only a good brawl could do that.*

Imogen doesn't know everything.

"Well, now that that's done, perhaps you can go back to town for the night," I said, giving each of the Vikings a good long look. "I have plans, and I'm sure you'll understand if I say they don't include you guys."

"But . . . that is the Dark One!" Finnvid said, pointing at Ben. "The one who has betrayed you!"

"Appearances can sometimes be deceiving," I said simply. "I'm fine. Thanks for the rescue attempt, but I don't need it. I'm sure Ben will understand that you were just doing what you thought best."

Isleif helped Eirik onto the couch. Both men were

bleeding. Finnvid escaped being bloodied, but he did walk with a distinct limp as he moved over to his buddies, his eyes wary as he looked from Ben to Imogen to me.

"I will not apologize to the Dark One," Eirik said when he could talk without wheezing. "The goddess Freya sent us to protect you, and we will do so until we are called back to Valhalla."

"Yes, well, the goddess Freya probably doesn't understand that we have a very complicated relationship, and Ben is my . . ." I paused and turned to him. "Is there some Dark One word for what you are to me? *Boyfriend* seems so lame."

He took the tissue Imogen handed him and wiped the blood off his forehead. The cut was already closing. "Yes. Dark One."

"No, I meant . . . oh, never mind." I faced the Vikings again. "I appreciate your concern, but I don't need protection from Ben, so there will be no more attacking him, all right?"

The looks the three of them gave me were not at all commensurate with a peaceful relationship.

I sighed, suddenly too tired to fight them anymore. "Oh, just go back to Brustwarze and have fun with your huge hordes of women. I'll see you in the morning."

Eirik's gaze slid suspiciously from me to Ben. "You wish to get rid of us. You wish to rut with the Dark One."

"Not that it's any of your business, but yes to both. Shoo."

"Come, my angel of the night," Finnvid said, scooping up Imogen and marching out of the trailer with her. "I will reacquaint you with my many manly charms."

Ben looked for a moment like he was going to go after them, but stopped himself in time.

You get bonus points for your restraint.

Good. I deserve them.

I turned to the two remaining Vikings.

"We wish to make plans with you," Eirik said stubbornly, his arms across his chest. "We do not wish to be sent off because you want to bed-sport with the Dark One. We are not trivial. We are Vikings, sons of Odin, the fiercest of all his warriors!"

"You are very fierce, and I'm truly grateful you want to help. But we will continue to work out what to do tomorrow. All right? Good. Off you go."

"I will leave you in the care of this one," Eirik said, breathing somewhat noisily as I shoved both him and Isleif to the door. "But I warn you, Dark One, if any harm comes to the virgin goddess, I will cut out your heart and make you eat it."

"Oh, for pity's sake, chill! If anyone cuts out Ben's heart and feeds it to him, it'll be me." Ben looked at me in surprise. I blinked. "And I would never do that, of course, because he would never do anything that would hurt me. Except maybe what he's thinking now, and I am not at all turned on by the thought of spankings, so you can just drop that idea."

Eirik considered me for a moment. "I'm told they can be very pleasurable for a woman. I, myself, like to position my hand so that when the blow lands on the arse cheeks, my fingers dip down between the woman's—"

"Okay, I'm adding spanking to the list of things we don't talk about," I interrupted quickly, making shooing motions. "Sheesh! Vikings!"

He left, but not without giving Ben one last look.

Chapter 11

"Thank the god and goddess and all the little sprites," I said, heaving a sigh of relief. "I really do like them, but sometimes they're a bit much."

You should have sent them to Valhalla, as I suggested.

I'm not sure that I would even if I could. I'm going to need help with Loki, and I have a feeling they will be important in that regard.

Nonsense. I will take care of Loki.

The second the words hit my brain, I felt Ben eye me warily. I slid him a glance out of the corner of my eye. *You did not just say that.*

He sighed. "Unfortunately, I did. Are you now going to lecture me again about how you can take care of yourself?"

I laughed. "No. Oh, don't get me wrong—I haven't changed into a wimpy woman who can't deal with her own problems, but even if I had the Vikingahärta, I am going to need help with Loki. And since you already said you would help me take care of him, there's nothing for me to be upset about, now, is there?"

"No, nothing at all," he said with a wry twist of his lips. "You have changed, though. Not into a feeble woman, but the Fran of five years ago would have fought me for weeks before she allowed me to help. I prefer you this way."

Oh, how I remembered the arguments we had in the past about Ben's insistence that he take care of my troubles for me. "Something Imogen told me right before I left stuck with me. She asked me if I had really wanted you to change into something you weren't. It took me a while to understand what she meant. You are who you are, and nothing I can do will change that. Not that I want you to be different. I never did," I added with a little quickening of my breath and pinkening of my cheeks. "I like you the way you are. And despite the fact that I'm far from helpless, I'm aware that you feel the need to protect me, and I appreciate that, so long as you don't go overboard."

His eyes widened slightly. "Who are you, and what have you done with my Beloved?"

I laughed. "I abused you terribly, didn't I?"

"I wouldn't go so far as to say abused, but you didn't seem to understand how I felt."

"No, I don't suppose I did," I said thoughtfully, remembering how overpowering Ben's protective instincts used to feel.

He grimaced and took my hand, stroking his fingers over mine. "That was my fault. You seemed so adult, I lost sight of the fact that emotionally you weren't ready for what I wanted from you."

"Ben . . ." I bit my lip, wanting badly to ask him something, but not sure how to phrase it without sounding like a total idiot.

"You can ask me anything you want." He leaned forward to kiss me, just a little kiss, but one that held such heat, I felt a blush of arousal start at my chest and wash upward.

"What have you been doing for the past five years?" The words blurted out of my mouth just as if I was still a gauche seventeen-year-old, leaving me flinching at both the bluntness and the fact that Ben knew exactly what it was I was asking.

He was silent for as long as it took me to count to twenty. "I have existed."

I put my hand on his chest, feeling again the blackness that dwelled within, a dense, unfathomable midnight that would have sent me screaming into madness had I borne it. But despite that, I knew there were tiny little pinpricks of light. I had felt one of them, the hope that I would return to him, that light now shining steadily in a corner of his soul. I smiled at it, smiled at him, and nipped his lower lip as I fed the hope until it shimmered like a star against the velvety black sky.

With a groan that started deep in his chest, his hands swept down my back, pulling my hips closer to him. "Fran, I will not be able to think if you do that again."

"Thinking is overrated. I've done enough of that for the last five years. Let's move past it, shall we?" I sucked in my breath when he pressed kisses to that sensitive spot behind my ear. With a moan, I slid my hands up his back, my fingers tracing out the swell of his muscles, my entire body tingling with anticipation.

"When I saw you again, it was as if the last five years had never been. I want you, Francesca. I want you in my life. I want you in my bed. I want to wake up knowing that no other man will touch you."

"That is seriously possessive. I don't know why it doesn't irritate me. Maybe it's because I know what you mean. It's like time just kind of stopped, although things between us have changed. It's as if now it's something . . . bigger."

He chuckled and pulled my hips against his. *I assure you* it *has not changed.*

Thank you for the obligatory smutty comment, you man, you. You know what I mean—our relationship feels bigger. More epic. Like . . . oh, I don't know, somehow grandiose and frightening at the same time. What if it's just our chemistry after all, Ben? What if everything we feel is out of our control?

"That is how life is. I think you are worrying unduly," he murmured in between kisses pressed to my neck. "We have both changed during the last few years. Can you not accept that? I have."

"I don't want you to simply accept me," I protested, pushing back from his chest. "I want us both to be more than just comfortable."

His mouth was hot on my flesh as he bit gently on my earlobe before moving over to my breastbone, trailing what felt like fire. "I am extremely *un*comfortable at this moment."

I clutched his shoulders, my breath already ragged and uneven, those parts of me that had anticipated his touch for so long becoming very aware of him. My breasts almost hurt they were suddenly so sensitive, and when he whisked off my shirt, burying his face in my cleavage, I thought I might pass out with the sheer pleasure of it all.

A loud clang outside the trailer had us both recalling where we were. Without speaking, I peeked out of the blinds, relieved to see that it was just Karl, Kurt's brother, moving past with a prop. "False alarm. Are you tired? How much sleep did you get in Naomi's bed?"

His gaze was steady on me. "You're never going to forget that, are you?"

"Not for a *very . . . long . . . time*," I answered pleasantly.

He looked like he was going to sigh again, but instead he smiled ruefully, his smile making everything inside me wobble like gelatin. "Naomi tiraded about you most of the day, so I did not get much sleep."

"Poor little sleepy vampire." I moved over to the door, locking it before turning to look at him. He watched me with hope in his eyes. I smiled and held out my arms. I didn't even see him move. One second he was standing a good twelve feet away, the next I was plastered against his chest, feeling every inch of him. I couldn't help myself. I melted into a giant puddle of Fran, my legs going just as wobbly as the rest of me.

Ben slid an arm behind my knees and stood holding me, indecision gripping him as he turned to face the door at the end of the trailer.

"Would you mind your mother's bed?"

"Under any other circumstances, yes. But I think she'd understand. And if she doesn't . . . well, we'll just deal with that."

Before I could blink, I was on my back on the bed, Ben's body pushing me into the mattress. His mouth and hands seemed to be everywhere at the same time, touching me, teasing me, stroking and tormenting my suddenly bared flesh in a way that was so overwhelming, I could do nothing more than writhe against him, trying to touch, tease, and torment him as well.

He reared back when I got both hands on his rear end. "How did you do that?" I managed to ask, noting with interest that his eyes were mahogany, shimmering with passion that left the little gold bits sparking as if they were made of flames.

He flexed his cheeks. "It's always been that way."

"No, not how did your butt get to be this way— although, I have to say, Ben, if I had known all those years ago that you had a butt this fabulous—well, that's beside the point. What was I asking?"

He leaned forward, and a shiver went down my body at the sensation of his chest hair on my breasts. His mouth took possession of mine long enough to leave me almost completely witless. "I don't know. You asked how I did something."

"How come you can think and I can't?" I demanded, sliding my hands up his spine, dragging my nails along his backbone. He groaned, his eyes closed for a few seconds. "I object to you being able to do that."

His head dipped and he sucked on the spot behind my ear that he knew full well turned me into mush. "Do what?"

"That thing. With your brain."

"Think?"

"Yes, that! I want to think, too, Ben. I want to be able to analyze what it is you're doing to me, and what I'm feeling, and what you're feeling, and what's going to happen next, and whether or not you're going to do the behind-the-ear thing on the other side of my head, because that ear is feeling a little left out."

He laughed in my head as he duly attended to the other shivery spot, making me quiver with arousal. *You are the most delightful woman I have ever met, Francesca. Am I overwhelming you?*

Yes, but that's okay. What are you going to do next?

I'm sorry, he said, moving off me. *I'm trying very hard not to rush this for you. I know this is your first*

*time, and I don't want you frightened by anything we
do.*

I blinked at him, pulling at his arms until his top part
was over me again. "Who says I'm frightened? And,
Ben, I'm not a virgin."

He froze for a moment, his face impassive. "You have
not been with another man. I would know if you had."

"No, of course I haven't. I explained that. But a girl
can have toys, you know."

His frozen expression relaxed, a wicked glint coming
into his beautiful, expressive eyes. "What sort of toys
gave you pleasure? Were they ones that touched you
here?"

Oooh, Mr. Naughty! I squealed as his head dipped
and his teeth scraped gently across the nipple nearer
him. I swear my eyes crossed when he followed that
with a long, wet lick of his tongue. *No, no boob toys.*

He moved slightly, so he could take care of my other
breast, the sensation of his hair and slightly stubble-
roughened cheek as they brushed against sensitized
flesh sending little zings of electricity down my skin,
where it pooled low and hot.

His hand followed the path of the electricity, sliding
down my stomach until his fingers curled into my
warmth. *Did your toys touch you here?*

Maybe. Oh, sweet stars and moon, do that again!

He did, kissing a wet trail down my breastbone and
stomach as his fingers, his clever, clever fingers, danced
among intimate parts of me, making my stomach
tighten, my hips twitch, and various bits that had previously possessed purely mundane functions suddenly
start clamoring for more Ben, much more Ben.

When his fingers sank into me, I saw not just stars but
entire constellations, and quite possibly a galaxy or two.

When he nudged my legs apart and settled himself there, his mouth returning to mine, I knew that all the years of waiting for him, all those lonely nights dreaming of him, all that time I had spent figuring out who I was so I could finally return to his arms where I belonged, all that had led me to this grand moment, this pinnacle of ecstasy, this joining of bodies and souls that I knew would be the most profound experience of my life.

Ben eased into my body, his mouth hot on my shoulder. Need roared within him, and was echoed in me.

I shifted my hips to better accommodate him, stroking his back as he gave one thrust, then suddenly moaned, *No! Bloody hell . . .*

What? What? What's wrong?

Aw, Fran, I'm sorry, he murmured, his face now buried in my neck as his hips gave tiny little convulsive twitches.

Sorry about what? Sorry that we're finally doing this? Sorry that I'm not a virgin? Sorry that I'm not good at it? Goddess! That's it, isn't it? I've disappointed you! I've failed at sex!

His body shook against mine, and I wanted to die right then and there. All those years waiting for this moment, and I was so awful at sex that Ben was shaking in repugnance?

He lifted his head, and I could see tears in his eyes, but the rolling laughter that poured out of him told me they weren't tears of horror. He kissed me loudly, smiling down at me. "As if I found anything about you repugnant. I'm sorry because I anticipated this moment a bit too much."

He slid out of me with a wet, squishy noise that startled me. We both peered down at the offending organ. "You mean you—"

"Yes. I'm sorry. I wanted your first time to be special. But the things you were feeling were too much for me, and . . ." He started laughing again.

I looked at his penis for a moment, then giggled. "I suppose I should take it as a compliment, but I have to admit, I'm feeling a bit . . . well, let down. I mean, all those years dreaming about this moment, Ben. All those hot, steamy daydreams about what it would be like. All that anticipation. Never once in my fantasies were you like this."

"Like what? Anticipatory?"

I touched his penis with the tip of one finger. "Floppy."

He rolled off me, laughing even harder, pulling me onto his chest. "Every second of every minute of every day since you left, I've thought about making love to you, and when I finally get the chance, this is what happens." He had to stop talking, he was laughing so hard. "I swear I will make it up to you, Fran. Just give me a minute to catch my breath, and we'll do this again, properly. I promise my floppiness is only a temporary situation."

"Well, I hope so, because frankly, at this point my toys have you beat."

He roared with laughter at that, and my heart did amazing little flip-flops. I'd seen Ben laugh before, but never had I seen him this way, so caught up in mirth that tears sneaked out of the corners of his eyes. I kissed the tears, then kissed his jaw, then kissed the spot behind *his* ear, breathing deeply of the scent of him. "You smell like a well-pleasured man," I told him, biting his ear.

His laughter slowed down to a chuckle, his hands sliding up my hips to my breasts. "You smell like my woman."

"Arrogant as ever, I see. Hey, I thought you were supposed to be catching your breath so you can do all the things to me that I've planned for you to do. And the ones you thought of that I had no idea we could do. Like that one. Seriously? With honey? I thought you didn't eat?"

The grin he gave me was pure devilishness. "Do you really want me to answer that?"

I blushed at the thoughts that went behind his words. "No. Yes. Oh, I don't care, but I would like you to do that bit with the honey."

"Later," he promised, pulling me over his body so my boobs were at his mouth. *Right now I have a gauntlet to pick up. You've challenged me, Francesca, and I intend on proving to you that I far exceed your toys.*

I squirmed with delight as he rubbed his face against my breasts, capturing an aching nipple in his mouth, where he laved his tongue over it. *All right, but I have my own challenge to take care of.*

What challenge is that?

I have to prove to you that I'm not horrible at sex.

He filled my head with laughter. *What happened was not because you are inexperienced, love. It's because I was not in control of myself as I should have been.*

"Good. I like you out of control," I said, sliding backward a little bit. "In fact, I think I should . . . um . . ." I looked down his body at his penis, taking a moment to admire the sights along the way. "I like your stomach."

"Thank you. I like yours as well." He tried to pull me up again, but I evaded his grasp, moving down to his hips, so I could press a kiss on his stomach. There was a thin trail of hair that led down from his chest to his belly button. I teased it with my fingers as I eyed his penis. It looked a bit different from I had expected. "Is something the matter? Why are you frowning at my cock?"

"It's . . . uh . . . is it supposed to look like that? The ones I've seen look different."

He sat up. "How many have you seen, Francesca?"

I grinned to myself at the outraged tone in his voice. For some reason, it warmed me to the tips of my toes when he used my full name. Not even my mother did that. "In person or on videos?"

"Both."

None and I'm not telling. You can just assume that I've seen porn, okay? And stop being outraged, because I'm sure you've seen it as well. Aha! See? I knew you have.

There are times when I regret the ability for a Beloved to share Dark Ones' thoughts, he muttered darkly.

Ha. You love it and you know it. Now lie down. You had your turn. I want to look at you. And . . . er . . . touch you.

He hrmphed again in my mind, but lay back down. "I'm not circumcised. That is the difference."

"Ooh, okay." I looked down at his penis again, trying to assess it.

"Now what are you doing?"

"Assessing. I think I want to . . . um . . ." I gestured toward the object in question.

A little smile curled his lips. "Do you at all see the irony in the fact that you are unable to say common phrases despite conducting the act itself?"

"It's not a matter of irony at all," I told him, sliding

down and pushing his legs open. I settled between his knees, eyeing his penis. "It's not just curse words that have power, you know, and I try to avoid the ones that might get me into trouble. I'm sorry if that sounds prissy or wimpy, but it's how I am."

It's not prissy or wimpy at all. I find it charming that language means so much to you. Does it offend you if I use words like "cock"?

I thought about it for a moment, reaching out to gently touch his thickening penis. *No. I did a paper once for an English class on the etymology of various profanities, and I know that word and others have a long history to them. Since you do, too, it doesn't bother me how you speak. Well, except the accent. I would hate it if you ever lost your accent.*

One eyebrow rose. *I have an accent? I thought my English was perfect.*

It is perfect, but you have a little bit of an accent. It's very sexy. Kind of a cross between English and Czech, I guess, since you're from there. It makes me feel . . . warm.

He was about to answer me, but I tipped my head at that moment, and took him into my mouth.

"Well, this is different," I said a moment later as I tried to analyze the taste and feel of him on my tongue.

Flurg.

"What?"

Flurg. I said flurg. Do that again.

I swirled my tongue along the very tip of him.

His hips bucked. "Flurg!"

"I take it by the fact that Mr. Floppy is gaining in stature that you're going to be willing to give this another try."

"Francesca," Ben said sternly, but his lips twitched

as I blinked innocently at him. "I am selfishly grateful that you have not had experience with other men to know this, but there is one term you never, ever use to your lover, and 'Mr. Floppy' is that term."

I looked at his penis. He was not unduly large, not *walk funny for a week* large, but judging by my rough estimation, he had Finnvid beat. "I'm sorry," I told his penis. "I will never again refer to you as Mr. Floppy, Mr. Overly Anticipatory, or even Mr. Leave Fran Wondering What All the Fuss Is About—"

"That impertinence, Beloved, is not something I am going to stand for." Ben was suddenly looming over me, the sheets of the bed cool beneath my back as he nipped my hip.

"I knew you were bossy, but I never knew you were this bossy. Oh merciful goddess! Are you going to . . . You are! Oral sex! I've been dying to try—" My eyes opened wide, almost crossing at the sensation of his hot breath on intimate parts of me that had not previously entertained anyone, my hands clutching at the sheets as my hips rose.

"You have to tell me what you like," Ben said somewhat indistinctly as he nipped the sensitive skin of my inner thighs.

"That! I like that!"

"So the swirl gets a thumbs-up. And what about this?"

"Oh, it's good, too," I moaned as my hips moved in a restless rhythm in response to the dance his fingers were doing.

"Hmm. Does this do anything for you?"

I tightened my legs around his head when his fingers sank into me as his tongue swirled across aroused flesh. "Flurg!"

He smiled into my mind. *I thought that might give you pleasure.*

Everything you do gives me pleasure, Ben, but please, please, finish it! I feel like I'm about to explode into a million bits of sexual ecstasy.

If you feel like that now, wait until I really get going, he promised, sliding up my body, bringing my legs with him until they rested on his arms.

"Um, Ben. This is . . . I mean, I'm kind of exposed," I said, feeling both vulnerable and yet at the same time desperate to have him where I wanted him most.

"Yes, I know. You're at my mercy. Like the feeling?"

"Imogen told me that you were naturally dominant. I didn't understand quite why she said that, but I guess now I know what she—Ben!"

He leaned forward to capture my gasp as he slid into my body with a movement that left me breathless.

It's a good thing I'm double-jointed, or I don't think this would be at all comfortable, I said, mentally moaning at the sensation of him moving within me. *The difference between you and my toys is . . . well, indescribable!*

"I begin to think I'm doing this wrong," he said, releasing my lower lip from where he had been sucking on it. His hips flexed, and this time my eyes did cross as he released my legs. I wrapped them around his hips and arched up against him.

I scraped my nails down his spine, enjoying the sensations he was mentally feeding me. I could feel his arousal building, which just fired mine to new heights. "I can't imagine that what you're doing is anything but absolutely perfect. Particularly that."

He gave another hard little thrust that had me digging my fingers into the thick muscles of his behind, trying to pull him in deeper. "If I was doing it correctly, you shouldn't be able to talk at all, let alone think."

I started to laugh. I couldn't help myself, it was just so funny that in the middle of all that thrusting and heaving and wet, slick noises that were slightly embarrassing since I knew they had their source with me, in all of the passion that wrapped us in its fire, he thought he wasn't doing it right.

I kissed him, savoring both the taste and feel of him as our bodies moved together in a rhythm that seemed wholly unique to us. I wanted to say something profound, something that would tell him what this moment meant to me, but all that came out was a plea. *Feed from me, Ben. I can feel your hunger. I'm offering my blood willingly. I want you to take it from me.*

His mouth moved to my neck and down to my shoulder, trailing burning kisses in its wake. I had spoken the truth—the desire to feed swamped him, filling his mind with a need that claimed me as well.

He licked a spot on my shoulder, his teeth scraping as he fought a war between need and self-control. I couldn't stand it, couldn't resist any more of the sensations of pleasure he was pouring into my mind. My body tightened around him as I was sent spiraling into a moment of pure, unadulterated rapture. Ben groaned, arching back to yell something in a language I didn't understand, his hips making a couple of short, fast thrusts before he collapsed down onto me.

I welcomed the weight of him, my breathing as ragged and rough as his. I held him tight as our hearts beat wildly, slowly calming until some minutes later, when Ben roused himself with a murmur about crushing me.

"Not in the least," I told him as he rolled over onto

his back, pulling me flush against his side. I was glad he did—I felt as boneless as a newborn baby.

Ben suddenly cracked an eye open. "Are you taking some sort of—"

"Yes," I answered, reading the question he was about to ask.

"Good. Not that I wouldn't have taken care of you if you weren't, but it's just easier this way. I assume you do not wish to have children yet."

"Not yet, no."

"I find it interesting that you are not seeing any men, did not wish to see me, and yet you are utilizing birth control."

"Are you implying I expected to have sex with you?" I asked, wanting to be annoyed, but as I've mentioned before, Inner Fran doesn't let me lie to myself very often.

He closed his eye again, his arm tightening around me until I was lying halfway on his body. "I would never presume anything so clearly out of the bounds of possibility."

I giggled into his damp chest, wanting to say something, but hesitant to ruin the lovely postcoital afterglow. "I'm sorry, Ben," I finally said.

"You're sorry you ever doubted I could bring you more pleasure than your toys?" he asked, his eyes still closed, but his fingers making lazy circles on my behind.

"No. Well, yes, although I think we both know that was never really in doubt." I snuggled into him, cherishing the sensations of my body plastered against his.

His eyes opened again. They held a certain sated look that made me feel extremely smug. Just let Naomi try to bring that look to his eyes, I thought cattily to myself.

"What is it? Why do you look so pleased with yourself, but there is apology in your mind? Did you wish to Join now?"

"No. I enjoyed this. I still am enjoying it. I think it brings our relationship to a new level of intimacy, but that doesn't mean I'm ready to sign away my life to you. I think we need to explore what it means to be us more, before either of us makes a decision."

He just looked at me, his eyes lightening as I spoke.

"What I meant is that I'm sorry that I asked you to feed off of me. It wasn't very nice of me to try to tempt you when you explained why you didn't want to take what I offered."

He sighed, a gesture that came from the depths of his being. "Francesca, there is nothing in this world that I want more than to conduct all the steps of Joining with you, including feeding from you. But you yourself set bounds, and I am trying to keep within them as best I can, and do my duty by David."

I was silent for a moment, stroking the thick line of his pectoral muscle. "I didn't set bounds to harm you, you know," I said finally. "Now that we've done this, are you going to be okay with them?"

"If it will make you happy, yes."

"Good. I imagine it's a lot harder for you than it is for me."

He grinned. It was a wicked grin, one that melted me. "It'll be hard for you again if you give me a little time to recover from your lusty demands."

I pinched his nipple. "That's not what I meant, and you know it, Mr. Mind Reader. It was hard for me to feel the need inside you, and not want to give you what you wanted."

He rolled onto his side, both arms around me as he kissed my eyes. "I promised to not ask you for more than you can give, and I appreciate that you have done the same for me."

An echo followed those words, so faint I wasn't sure I caught it. *You're mine. I could ask for nothing more.*

I kept my thoughts from him as he pulled up the blankets and settled me so I was more or less tucked under him, one of his heavy legs thrown over mine in a manner that left me feeling protected. Ben might not want to ask for anything more, but I could. The question was, did I want to?

Chapter 12

Some nine hours later I stared at a little beam of sunlight that had penetrated the blinds, falling with golden cheer onto the spot on the bed next to me. I leaned forward, unable to keep from sniffing the sunshine. It smelled like Ben. My toes curled happily.

Are you still awake? I asked softly, just in case he had gone to sleep. He'd woken me up a short time before to tell me he was returning to Naomi's trailer before the sun came fully up.

Yes. You're not still angry with me?

No. I was for a bit when you insisted you had to go back to Naomi, but I understand, Ben, I really do. I'm sorry I called you a ratty pustule on the buttocks of a slug.

Your apology is accepted.

And I'm sorry I threw that fire extinguisher at you. You're sure the lump on your forehead has gone down?

Yes. You have remarkably good aim considering the bulkiness of the weapon you wielded.

And I much regret telling you I never wanted to see you again, and that you could rot in the scummiest part of the underworld, eaten by plagued rats and cock-roaches. I didn't mean that.

I know you didn't. For which I am truly thankful.

I do miss you, though.

I miss you too, love.

I smiled at the word. Oh, I knew full well it was used as a term of endearment and not a declaration of his emotions, but it still made me feel cherished. *You sound kind of distracted. What are you doing?*

Waiting for Naomi to finish ranting at me so I can take a shower and go to bed.

She's yelling? I smiled with satisfaction. *Because you were out with me all night?*

I didn't tell her I was with you. I told her I was con-fused and conflicted by your presence. She just threat-ened to have you turned into a water vole.

I hope you discouraged that.

I haven't had the chance to say a word yet. She's too busy screaming at me.

Poor little Ben, I said with mock sympathy. *Left one pissed-off girlfriend, only to find your other girlfriend is just as angry. I feel for you.*

She's not my girlfriend, and that statement would carry a little more weight if you weren't thinking all sorts of smug thoughts about me getting my just deserts. Ah, at last.

At last?

She stormed off to go into town to pick up breakfast. Now I can have a shower and try to get some sleep be-fore she returns to harangue me again.

I sat up straight in bed. *You're going to take a shower? Right now?*

Yes.

I almost started drooling at the thought. An idea

popped into my head, one so audacious I almost couldn't believe it. I leaped from the bed and snatched up a pair of sweatpants and a T-shirt.

Why do you ask? Did you wish for me to touch myself again and allow you to see? He flooded my head with the sensations he was feeling as he stepped into the small shower in Naomi's trailer. Warm water cascaded down his naked self, his hands running down his chest and belly until he was cupping himself.

I was out of the trailer and across the common area before he could do more than ask, *Did you want me to do this?*

I moaned under my breath as he swirled soap around his chest.

"Good morning, Fran. Isn't it a lovely day?" Tallulah's voice wormed its way into the dense haze of lust that filled my mind at the feeling of Ben stroking his wet, soapy chest, bringing me to a halt. I whimpered.

"What was that, dear?" she frowned at me.

"Ben. Shower. *Soap*," I said, somewhat desperately.

"Ben needs soap? How very odd."

"No. He's in the shower. Right now." I clutched Tallulah's arms as Ben soaped up his rear. "Oh dear goddess. He's all wet. Completely and utterly wet!"

"One generally gets that way in the shower."

Do you wish it was your fingers touching me? Ben asked as he stroked soap onto his long legs.

"Calf muscles," I gasped, whimpering once again. "Thighs!"

She looked at me oddly for a moment, then gave a quick nod. "Yes, I see. Go to him, my dear. I believe you have made the right choice."

"Slick, soapy chest!" I babbled and then realized she'd given me her blessing. I grinned and ran to Naomi's door, opening it cautiously to make sure she really had left.

The room was empty, but the sound of running water had me stripping off my clothing and hurrying to the narrow door that led to the tiny shower.

Or perhaps you wish for me to do this? His fingers wrapped around his penis, partially erect, and growing more interested in every passing moment.

I'd rather you let me do that, I told him.

I'd rather you would, as well, but since you can't—

I jerked open the shower door, the warm mistiness of the environment enveloping me as Ben, startled, spun around to face me. "Oh, I think I can."

"What the hell are you doing here?" He gave a surprised jerk, his dark hair slicked back from his forehead, warm water and steam cascading around him. "Naomi could be back at any minute."

The shower wasn't large, but it was big enough for the two of us. Barely.

"I know. I figure it takes at least fifteen minutes to get to town and back." Joining him in the shower pretty much meant I was smashed up against him, a fact I wasn't going to protest at all. I closed the shower door, avoided hitting the showerhead, and wrapped my arms around the slippery, soapy Ben.

"This is not at all wise," he started to say, but I stopped him by kissing him, and rubbing my demanding breasts against his chest. "Naomi—"

"—isn't here, and I am, and we have fifteen minutes, so let's make the most of it. Are you a dirty boy? Do I need to soap you up?"

Ben frowned, annoyance and passion mingling in his eyes, which were darkening with each passing second. "I am not dirty, nor a boy—" He stiffened when I slid my hands from his chest to his penis. "Perhaps I am a little dirty. Would you like some soap?"

"Oh, yes," I purred, accepting the sea sponge that was lathered with a spicy-scented soap. With my back to the showerhead, I blocked most of the water, which allowed me to swirl the sponge down his chest and belly, to his groin. Although I wouldn't have minded soaping all of him up, I was conscious of the need to be quick, and went straight for pay dirt. So to speak.

Ben splayed against the back of the shower, his eyes closed as I lathered him up, spreading my fingers through the slick hair, exploring the length of his quickly growing penis and accompanying scenery. He groaned as I found a tempo that pleased him, his hips making little thrusts, sending his slippery length through my hands.

"This is so much better than you doing it," I said, water cascading down me. I watched him move in my grasp, gently rubbing the underside, as I understood men liked. "I've wanted to do this ever since you let me see you the first time."

Ben said something in another language, then gave a little head shake and returned to English. "That's an understatement. You said you're double-jointed?"

"Yes." I was fascinated by the feel and sight of his arousal, wanting to touch it in all sorts of ways, wanting to stroke and lick and kiss all the rest of him, too. Confined in a small space as we were, however, I would have to content myself with just indulging in some tactile pleasure.

"Good. Put your arms around my shoulders."

"Huh?" I looked up. "You don't want me to give you a soapy hand job?"

"Oh, I do, but I think if we're fast, there's time for more."

"More? You don't mean—"

He bent slightly, grasping me around the waist and hoisting me up. "Legs around mine," he said, slipping his hands down to my butt to pull me up a little higher before pressing me against the wall.

"Sun and stars, Ben! You don't mean—hoo!" He lunged forward, his penis sliding along my private parts. "In the shower? Standing? Oh, you missed, just a smidgen to the left. Merciful goddess, I didn't know we could do this. Am I too heavy for you? Am I hurting you? Should I maybe put one leg down to take some of my weight off your back? No, you missed again, a little higher, I think. Oh! No, not quite. Close but no banana."

"Francesca," Ben said through what seemed to be gritted teeth as he lunged somewhat wildly now, his aim, given the fact that we were now both soapy and wet, not as good as could be hoped for.

"What?"

"Too much talking, not enough helping me."

"Oh." I could help? I released one arm from where I'd been clutching his shoulders. He moved his hips back slightly so I could snake my hand down between us, positioning him where he would be assured success. "Sorry. I'm new to this."

"Believe me, I'm well aware of that," he said, groaning again as he sank into my welcoming flesh. "And no, not because you're doing it wrong. You're very tight, Francesca. So tight it makes my head spin. No, don't try to help. Just tilt your hips up slightly . . . Ahhh."

It was my turn to moan in pleasure as our bodies moved together despite the awkward position and confined space (and my concern that holding me up would give Ben a hernia).

"Dark Ones . . . don't get . . . hernias . . . ," he grunted, his voice and breath rasping in my ear as I gave myself up to the pleasure of his warm, wet body sliding against and inside mine. I felt the need in him for more, to take blood from me, to join us together in a way unique to his kind, and for a moment, I thought about just doing it.

His mouth burned on my wet shoulder.

If you want to— I started to say.

To do so would mean we were Joined forever. He turned his head, his jaw tightening as he leashed the almost overwhelming urge to drink from me. *I will not force it upon you.*

Inner Fran pointed out that there wasn't any force involved, but I said nothing, just gasped out his name as my climax claimed me.

"That may have been fast, but it will remain in my memories as a high point of my sexual experience," I said a few minutes later, as Ben let my legs go, his chest heaving against mine, the water, now tepid and heading for cold, pouring over us both. The need for him to feed from me still rode him hot and hard, but he controlled it with a desperation that touched me deeply.

He kissed me. "I think it's safe to say there will be many others to join that one." He turned off the water, which was now starting to get uncomfortably cold. "We must get you dressed quickly. I will take you back to your mother's—"

The shower vibrated with the noise and force of the trailer door banging. I widened my eyes as Ben swore.

"Stay here. I will get her out of the trailer," he growled.

He opened the door the bare minimum, stalking out of the shower. Stark naked, I couldn't help notice. Through the thin walls of the shower I could hear Naomi haranguing him. Or at least I assumed she was—she spoke in French, a language I didn't understand beyond a few tourist phrases.

I stood there for a moment, indecision gripping me as Ben's deep rumble danced around Naomi's higher, strident screech. Inner Fran opted to stay in the shower until the coast was clear, but as she should have known, I've never been one to be told what to do. At a particularly vicious-sounding tirade from Naomi, I opened up the shower door and calmly grabbed my sweatpants and T-shirt, pulling them on despite being wet.

Naomi had Ben backed almost to the bedroom. She spun around at the sound of my movements, her face going from irritated to furious at the sight of me. Ben glowered behind her. I was pleased to see that he'd managed to don a pair of jeans. "You!" Naomi screamed, her hands fisted.

"You have a really big capacity water tank. I'm going to tell my mother to get one. Makes taking a long shower really nice," I said before smiling over her head at Ben, blowing him a kiss. "Later."

I think Naomi might have tried to jump me as I left, because I heard her squawk as if Ben had grabbed her to keep her from attacking. She was clearly furious, but I didn't let that bother me.

"She has no idea about what a stupid idea it is to mess with a Beloved," I growled to myself as I returned to my mother's trailer, my fingernails once again digging into my palms.

"You have decided to Join with the Dark One?" a voice asked as I passed one of the chaise longues set out in the common area.

Isleif lay sunning himself in what looked like a garment better suited to a beach in Rio. It was more or less a pouch into which he'd stuffed his genitals. I gaped at him for a few seconds, wondering if there was anything on his backside, quickly deciding I really didn't want to know.

"No, I haven't decided what I'm going to do yet." I hesitated, then sat down on the lounge next to his. "Things are a bit confusing."

"You are wet." He handed me a towel, which I used to towel off my thankfully short hair. "And confused? That sounds like you need advice. We are most good with advice. We will counsel you. Eirik! Finnvid!" He gave a deep battle cry. "The goddess needs advice."

Eirik emerged from my mother's trailer, a bowl of granola in one hand, a half-eaten banana in the other. "Advice? Did you say advice?"

"Aye, the goddess is having man trouble."

"No, I'm not. I don't need advice. I can work things out on my own, although it is very considerate of you all to want to help me." I didn't point out that I noticed they'd dropped the title of virgin, feeling the least said about that, the better.

The door to Imogen's trailer was flung open, and a naked Finnvid stood in the doorway, grasping either side of the doorframe. "The goddess needs us?"

An arm reached across him, stroking his chest and the biceps of one arm. Finnvid looked to the side, grinned, and allowed the arm to pull him out of view, thankfully shutting the door behind him.

"There are just some sights that I really wish I could expunge from my memory," I said softly, watching with foreboding as Eirik set his breakfast on Isleif before pulling over a chair.

"What is it the goddess needs help with? The Dark One?" he asked, reclaiming his bowl, but losing his banana to Isleif's seemingly never-ending hunger. This morning, Eirik was clad in a pair of green and gold paisley men's silk boxer shorts, and a sleeveless T-shirt promoting the local opera competition.

"You're not planning on wearing that outfit in public, are you?" I asked, distracted by the thought of him wandering around in his underwear.

Eirik looked surprised. "Aye. I bought the short breeches yesterday. They're silk. The sales slave said that was most desired by women."

"They're also underwear, Eirik."

He blinked at me.

"I don't know the word for Viking underwear, but it's something you wear under your clothes, not in place of them. You can't wear them around town. It's too impolite."

"I am a Viking. I do not care for such things as politeness," he said scornfully. "Besides, my arse and rod are covered."

"Which is more than I can say for some people's outfits," I murmured, sliding Isleif a look. He grinned and adjusted his pouch. Hastily, I averted my eyes, only to have my gaze fall on Eirik.

"They may be covered when you're walking around, but when you sit, they . . . er . . . gape open."

Eirik looked down at his crotch. The fly of the shorts was indeed gaping open, allowing the casual passerby to get an eyeful. "Aye, so they do. Handy, that, don't you think?"

I ran my hands through my damp hair, trying to fluff it up so I wouldn't look like a wet seal. "Moving on, let's talk about today's plan. I'm not quite sure what we should be doing next to find—"

"First," Eirik interrupted, burping and setting down

his now empty bowl. "We will deal with your Dark One problems."

"I don't have problems—"

"Was he too rough with you when he bedded you? Were you concerned because you bled?"

"No, that's not it at all—"

"All virgins bleed, goddess. It is the way of things. One of my wives, the second, I think, was convinced I had torn her up inside, but it was just her maidenhead. Took her three weeks before she'd let me bed her again, and although I don't approve of you allowing the Dark One to rut with you, you have chosen to do so, and thus you should not keep him from your bed for three weeks because of a little maidenhead blood."

"No, she shouldn't," Isleif agreed. "It's hard on a man, that sort of a wait. Makes your stones ache."

"Honest, there's nothing I need advice about concerning sex—"

"Aye, it does." Eirik fixed me with a stern look. "A man's stones are not to be trifled with, goddess. If you insist on bedding the Dark One, then you must let him do so whenever he desires. Anything else would be cruel."

I sighed. They were going to advise me whether I wanted it or not. Going with the attitude of the quicker it was over, the faster we could move on to important things, I said, "Right. Let him have sex whenever he wants. Don't fuss over blood. Anything else?"

Isleif looked thoughtful. Eirik frowned at the empty bowl. "If he wishes to do unnatural things to you, allow it. It is not as unnatural as you think."

"What sort of unnatural things?" I asked, picturing Isleif's son-in-law with his sheep.

Eirik cleared his throat and leaned toward me,

speaking in a confidential tone. "He may wish to put his mouth on your woman's parts. Some men enjoy that. Others refuse. I, myself, find it entertaining to make a woman squirm with pleasure, so if your Dark One wishes to do so, you must allow him. It would wound his pride if you were to refuse."

I bit back the laughter that wanted desperately to burst forth. "Okay. I won't make a fuss if he wants to indulge in oral sex. Now, if you've—"

"And if he starts talking about how pretty a particular ewe is, call us. We know just what to do," Isleif added with dark meaning.

A little chirp of laughter escaped, but I managed to keep the rest of it contained. "I will definitely let you know if Ben suddenly falls in love with a barnyard animal. I hate to change this fascinating subject, but it's already almost noon, and we really need to get cracking."

Naomi chose that moment to storm out of her trailer, shooting me a glare that probably would have dropped a horse on the spot, before marching off to her car.

I thought about seeing if Ben was all right.

I am fine. Just tired. I am going to sleep for a bit. What are your plans for the next few hours?

I need to find the Vikingahärta. Any ideas of where I should look?

None, I'm afraid. I will help you if you like.

I was conscious of his hunger and exhaustion. Evidently Naomi hadn't fed him. That pleased me to no end until I realized that Ben was the one who would suffer for me pissing her off. *That's okay. You rest up for a bit. Imogen offered to help, and I have the Vikings.*

He thought something extremely unflattering to the

Vikings, then inquired in a cautious manner, *If I ask you if you will be all right without me, will you lecture me?*

Not now. Later, perhaps. I can feel how tired you are. Did Naomi rip you a new one?

Just about.

I'm sorry, Ben. I shouldn't have taunted her that way. Are you very hungry?

Not terribly. I can feed from Imogen if I must.

A little pain inside me burst into being at the thought of him feeding from others.

Naomi demanded that I attend the tyro tonight. I told her I would. That seemed to keep her from wanting to smite you on the spot.

I said nothing, but thought a great deal to myself. *Sleep well, Ben.*

I will dream of you. And the shower.

"Er . . . what were we saying?" I suddenly realized both Vikings were staring at me. "Oh! Today's plans." I slumped back against the lounge. "I'm at my wit's end what to do. We don't have the Vikingahärta, and I don't have the least idea of where to even start looking for it. Or the lich who might have taken it."

"You are a goddess," Eirik said, shrugging. "You will use your goddess powers and tell us what we must do to find the Vikingahärta."

"I'm not really a goddess, and I don't have any . . ." I stopped, a light dawning in what passed for my brain. I looked at my hands. They were bare because I'd been with Ben, which meant I had been very careful not to touch anything I didn't absolutely have to. I'd even used my T-shirt wrapped around my hand to open Naomi's trailer door. "I wonder if I could."

"Could what?" Isleif asked, flipping the long braids

of his beard over each shoulder before donning a pair of
sunglasses and squirting suntan oil on his belly.

"I wonder if I could touchy-feely my way to finding
the guy who took the Vikingahärta." I turned and
looked speculatively at Imogen's trailer.

"You are a goddess," Eirik repeated, shooing me off
the chaise so he could lie on it. He peeled off his shirt
and used Isleif's suntan lotion on his chest and arms.

"Eirik!" I said sternly.

"Aye?"

I pointed at his crotch, where the silk boxers were
once again gaping in a manner that let everyone see
clearly everything he'd been born with.

"Ah." He yanked the boxers down and applied suntan lotion to his penis before pulling them back up. "It
warms my heart to know you're so concerned for the
well-being of my rod, goddess. Are you sure you
wouldn't like to rut with me rather than the Dark
One?"

"Quite sure, and that's not what I meant for you to
do." His forehead wrinkled in confusion. "Oh, never
mind. You guys stay here while I go talk to Imogen."

"Finnvid is no doubt plowing her field, but he won't
mind if you watch," Isleif called after me, pulling out an
iPod. "He's always been fond of audiences."

Chapter 13

I knocked on Imogen's door, waited a few seconds, and was about to use my T-shirt to open the door when it struck me that whoever entered her trailer most likely had to touch the door to do so. Taking a deep breath to calm my thoughts, I wrapped my fingers around the doorknob, allowing the imprints of the people who'd touched it recently to fill my head.

"Imogen, giddy and excited," I murmured as I sorted through the images and emotions that were imbued on the metal. "Finnvid, filled with lust. Günter, annoyed and . . ." I tried to analyze the emotion that had been uppermost in Günter's mind when he had touched the door. "Dutiful? Huh. Karl. Peter. Ben, very, very annoyed at Naomi." I smiled at that before realizing there were no other traces that I could detect. Which either meant someone else had opened the door for the thief or he hadn't gone into the trailer.

"Imogen? You decent and not in the middle of having your field plowed?" I poked my head in through the open doorway. I didn't hear any sounds from her bedroom. "I'm really sorry to disturb you guys, but I kind of need to touch things in your trailer. You don't have to come out if you're busy."

"Fran!" Imogen emerged from the bedroom, tying a belt around her white satin bathrobe. "Of course you are always welcome here. What did you need?"

"I'm sorry to bother you in the middle of . . ." I waved my hand toward the bedroom.

"You are no bother. We were finished."

I looked beyond her, to where Finnvid stood naked, an irritated expression on his face. He looked anything but finished. I cleared my throat and turned so my back was to him. I heard the door slam behind me. "I thought it might help me figure out what's going on with the Vikingahärta if I was to touch a few things in the trailer."

"Oh!" She whirled around, the teakettle in her hand. "What an excellent idea! The lich must surely have touched things. You must start with the door."

"I did." I bit my lip, then listed the people who'd touched her door lately.

"That's odd." She frowned as she plugged in the teakettle. "There was no lich?"

"There was no one I didn't recognize, no."

Her clear blue gaze held mine. "Then how did the lich get in?"

"I think the question is more, who let him in? Or better, who took the Vikingahärta?"

"Fran!" she said in a shocked voice. "You can't mean to imply that one of us took it?"

"No, not you, obviously."

"But the only people who were here are our friends: Peter and Karl and Günter. And Ben! Surely you can't think—"

"No, I know it wasn't Ben. But . . . er . . . how well do you know Günter?"

She just stared at me for a minute. "You can't think Günter took your Vikingahärta? Fran, I've known him for, oh, it must be six months. We haven't dated that long, but we have been together for at least four months. Günter is a musician, so he is able to travel with me much of the time, although he does occasionally have to go off and record things."

"What sort of things?" I looked around the trailer. There were no musical instruments of any sort.

"Oh, you know, music," she said, her hand fluttering in a vague gesture.

"Ah." My first roommate had dated a guy in a band, and he was forever leaving all sorts of musical paraphernalia around our apartment—broken guitar strings, bits of scribbled music, and hundreds of picks. Although Imogen's trailer was spotless, and not at all the sort of place you'd fling your guitar strings, my experience with musicians was that they were never happy unless surrounded by the tricks of their trade. "I didn't mean to cast a vile aspersion on him. I just thought that perhaps if you hadn't known him for long . . ." I let the sentence trail off before starting again. "You don't mind if I touch a few things here?"

"No." A frown pulled her eyebrows together. "Although if the lich didn't open the door, I'm not sure what you'll find that could be useful."

"You never know." I stood up and glanced around, trying to figure out what someone might touch if he was creeping around the trailer looking for a valknut. That brought up a question. "Just how did whoever took the Vikingahärta know it was here?"

Her frown evened out. She looked thoughtful. "I don't know."

"If it was this lich guy who took it, then someone must have told him." I left the rest unspoken.

A faint blush colored her cheeks as she looked away, a mulish set to her jaw. I proceeded to walk down the aisle, my fingertips grazing surfaces that looked likely. I kept contact just long enough to absorb the emotions and thoughts that had been imbued on the surface, but not long enough to let them swamp me. There was nothing out of the ordinary, although I did find it interesting that the doorframe of Imogen's bedroom door held a distinct note of anger—from Imogen. At some point recently she had been downright furious, an emotion in which I'd seldom seen her indulge. It felt far too much like prying to keep my hand there long enough to see what it was that had made her so angry, so I moved on to the doorknob. That held only three impressions, all of which I expected: Imogen, Günter, and Finnvid.

The door jerked open as I stood there contemplating how someone could get into her bedroom without touching the doorknob. Finnvid glared at me until I moved aside. He strode past me, still stark naked, spreading his glare to Imogen before stepping into her tiny shower.

I pursed my lips as I admired his backside when it passed, then looked at Imogen.

She looked back at me. We kept that up for the count of three after the shower door closed, then both of us burst into laughter.

"Oh, boy, he's really pissed," I said, wiping at my eyes.

"He has no right to be. He definitely had a very good evening," she said, smiling demurely, but the wicked twinkle in her eyes reminded me of Ben at his most roguish. "But isn't his derriere delicious?"

"Very nice," I agreed, turning back to the bedroom.

"Not as nice as Benedikt's, naturally, but it's very close to being as nice."

I shot her a look over my shoulder. "Do I want to know how you know what Ben's butt looks like?"

"Fran!" she said in mock shock. "I'm his sister! If I checked out his derriere, it was only on your behalf, to ensure you would not be disappointed by it."

"Well, I'm not, so you can relax. Do you mind if I touch the nightstand?"

"No, go right ahead." She followed me into the room. "Touch whatever you like, although the sheets . . ."

"Yeah, I think I'll give those a pass."

She gave a little gurgle of choked laughter. I touched the curtains and window, just in case someone had come in that way, but got no sense of anyone but Imogen. It wasn't until my fingertips brushed against the top of the nightstand that the electric shock hit me.

"Oh," I gasped, my legs collapsing from under me as shimmers of pain and anguish skimmed along the surface of my skin, my palm flat against the nightstand as if it was glued there. I crumpled onto the bed, my eyes wide, the breath caught in my throat. I felt strangled, bound somehow, as if I was a slave to a strong presence, unable to break away from the endless torment that wrapped around me like invisible chains.

"Fran? Are you all right?"

"Pain," I gasped, trying to get air into my lungs. My entire chest felt compressed by my bondage, despair forcing me down to the floor on my knees. "Blessings of the goddess, the pain."

"Finnvid!" From a distance, I heard Imogen's voice, filled with panic.

Francesca? What's wrong?

Pain.

Where are you?

Can't breathe. Too much.

Ben's presence in my mind was a calming influence. *Do not panic, Beloved. I will help you. Is someone harming you?*

Lich.

I understand. Think of me, Francesca. Remember last night. Think of what you felt.

My mind was so overwhelmed with the blackness of anguish and panic, it was difficult for me to focus. *No air!*

There is air. Think about how you lay on my chest last night. Our hearts were beating together, do you remember? I felt every breath you took. Breathe now.

Slowly, the images he was projecting into my mind pushed back the fear and pain and sense of utter despair. I opened my mouth, wanting desperately to get some air into my lungs, little wavering dots starting to form in front of my eyes, but I couldn't do it.

"Goddess? What has happened to you?"

I felt someone kneel next to me and knew it must be Finnvid, knew that Imogen was fretting beyond him, but I couldn't see them. I couldn't see anything but a hazy redness that was slowly being eaten up by black.

Faintly, I heard Imogen cry in relief. Just as I thought I was going to fall into the inky redness, Ben was there, pulling me back from the edge. Fingers clamped painfully around my wrist, pulling my hand from the nightstand.

The second the contact was broken, the mist disappeared and my vision slowly cleared. I looked up to find myself cradled in Ben's arms, his face and naked torso as red as a boiled lobster, with tiny white blisters along one side.

"You're burned."

"What happened?" he asked, ignoring my statement.

I leaned against him, drawing comfort from the strength of him. I wanted badly to touch his burned face, but when I tried to lift my hand, I found it just hung there, as heavy as a lead weight. "My hand."

He frowned, lifting my hand, turning it slightly so the palm faced him.

Imogen gasped. "Oh, Fran!"

My palm was as black as if I had painted it. I stared in horror at it, then looked closer. It wasn't a true black; it was a blackish purple. "That's . . ."

"Blood," Ben said. "Does it hurt?"

"No. It's numb. I can't feel it at all. Why is my hand filled with black blood?" My skin crawled at the thought of some heinous disease.

"It's not a disease. It's like a bruise, a profound bruise. I believe I can heal it."

I watched with concern as he gently stroked my fingers and palm. It was true I didn't feel any pain; the hand was almost icy in its numbness. But the color was enough to freak me out. *What happened to me?*

You said it was a lich.

Yes, it was. A man named Ulfur. And oh, Ben, he's in so much pain, so much torment. It was different from what I feel when I touch you.

I startled him. He shot me a quizzical glance before returning his attention to my hand, his long fingers stroking my abused flesh. *You can feel my pain?*

Oh, yes.

I'm sorry. I had no idea you would feel the negative aspects of being a Dark One. I will take care to shield you from them.

No, you won't.

He looked even more startled.

Ben, I don't just want to see all the happy feelings inside you, although those are always nice to share. If we are to get to know each other, that includes all the less than flattering stuff as well, like the fact that you snore, and I am always grumpy in the morning until I've had coffee.

I do not snore! he said, outraged. *I am a Dark One. Mortals snore—we do not.*

Fine, you don't snore. You breathe heavily, in a rhythmical way that everyone else would assume was snoring.

You imagined it.

As Ben continued to stroke the flesh, I felt a faint sensation of warmth, not enough to make my hand feel normal, but a bit of the iciness left it. I looked away from my hand to where Imogen was hovering behind him, making little distressed noises. "Imogen, does Ben snore?"

She didn't even bat an eyelash at that question. "Yes, he does."

I won't say "I told you so" because that would be gloating. But I did tell you.

I can see I'm going to have to separate you two lest you continue to gang up on me, he grumbled, but I felt his amusement nonetheless.

Why would touching something that a lich touched do this to me? Are they evil like demons?

They are beings like any others—some good, some bad. The one who was in here, assumedly to take your valknut, must have been tainted with evil.

I thought for a moment about what it was I felt. *No, not evil,* I said slowly. *He was in pain, lots of pain. It was like he was wrapped so tightly in chains that he couldn't breathe, couldn't think.*

He is a lich—they are bound to necromancers much in the way demons are bound to demon lords.

That makes sense, then. I don't think he wanted to be here. I think he was being forced.

It doesn't matter much, Ben said, shrugging off the matter of the lich's bondage. *He carried out his master's orders regardless of his own wishes.*

But that doesn't explain why touching something he touched should have affected me so profoundly.

You weren't prepared for it. Now you know to shield yourself when coming into contact with items tainted by those who wield dark power.

That's an understatement if I ever heard one. I may never take off my gloves again.

He said nothing, focusing his concentration on my hand. After a few minutes of silence, he looked up. "I'm afraid this is as good as I can do."

My palm and the underside of my fingers were now a vivid shade of saffron. "It's better than it was. Thank you. It doesn't feel so cold, either."

He released my hand and it fell like an anvil. Ben picked it up again, frowning. "Is your arm affected?"

"A little, yes." I flexed my arm, my muscles trembling as if they'd been worked almost to the breaking point, but at last they responded and I managed to pull my arm up to my chest.

"She needs a doctor," Imogen said.

"Aye," agreed Finnvid, naked and wet. He stood behind Ben, looking down at us.

Ben glanced back, face to genitals with the Viking. "For god's sake, you randy ghost, put some clothes on. Imogen!"

"Fran needs—"

"I will take care of her," Ben interrupted.

Imogen looked like she wanted to argue with him, but backed down under his potent stare, murmuring something about helping Finnvid.

"I don't need a doctor," I said, leaning back against the side of the mattress, still cradling my arm. "It's nothing a normal doctor could deal with."

"No, it isn't. However, I will take you to Tallulah. She has some healing powers, and she will be able to determine if there is something needful to be done."

I smiled at him, feeling a warm glow in my belly at his concern. "Did you know that when you get stressed, your speech becomes more formal and old-fashioned?"

He raised his eyebrows, flinched, and reached up to rub his burned face. "What does that matter?"

"It doesn't matter; I just think it's kind of cute. Hey, wait a minute . . . You're not going out like that. You're all burned and blistered as is."

Dark Ones have amazing recuperative powers. I'd seen that in the past when Ben had been both burned by the sunlight and attacked by some force he hadn't explained. But despite knowing that, I still watched with amazement as he rubbed first the side of his face, then his chest and arms until the blisters disappeared, and the redness abated.

"You ought to become a doctor. Just think of the

people you could heal with those fabulous vamp powers."

He made a little face and held out a hand for me. Since I was still feeling a little wobbly from the episode, I allowed him to pull me to my feet. "Unfortunately, there are limits to both the amount of healing I can do and who it will work on. Individuals with a close blood tie and Beloveds can be healed; for others, I am powerless."

"That's a shame, although I suppose it makes sense. Otherwise the world would be full of vampire doctors."

He said nothing, just opened the door for me. Just as we left the room, Imogen came up the steps from outside, talking very fast. "It was truly frightening, and I had no idea what to do for her, but luckily, Ben is here, and he saved Fran. And there she is. Fran, my dear, you look so pale. Sit down, and I'll make you a cup of peppermint tea while Tallulah looks at your hand."

Go back to bed. You're tired and should sleep.

Francesca, if I were to tell you to spend the rest of the day resting in your mother's trailer, what would you say?

I'd say you are nuts for thinking you can give me orders like that.

Exactly.

I looked at him while Tallulah examined my hand. It took a minute or so before I understood what he meant. Inner Fran crossed her arms and smiled as I realized I was guilty of ordering Ben around in the manner that I myself hated. *Sorry. My relationship skills are a little underdeveloped.*

Your apology is accepted. I will return to bed just as soon as I know you don't need further care.

"She has had an injury, but it is one of a psychic na-

ture rather than the physical. The trauma to her hand
has been partially repaired," Tallulah said, pushing up
the sleeve of my shirt to press on the muscles of my arm.
"I am not an expert, of course, but I do not see any signs
of permanent damage."

I smiled weakly, relieved despite my attempt to put
on a brave face. "Thanks, Tallulah. I'm sorry to have
bothered you."

She was silent for a moment, looking at my arm with
a faint frown. At last she nodded and looked up at me.
"It is my proclivity to warn you against the sort of beings that could have such an effect on you, but Sir Edward tells me that in this, I am wrong. The being who
inadvertently did this to you needs you, Fran."

I groaned. "Oh, great, that's just what I want to
hear—someone else wants me to fight dragons for
them."

"Not dragons, no. Liches. Or rather, Ilargis."

"Well, whoever he is, he's going to have to get in line.
I have to find out exactly what's going on with my
mother, and take care of Loki, first."

Tallulah gave me an odd look, but said nothing behind the reassurance that my hand and arm would be
fine in a day or two, and that a sling wouldn't be amiss
if I desired.

I didn't. Nor did I wish for the fuss that Imogen made
over me, crafting a stylish sling out of a designer silk scarf,
but she meant well, and I was warmed by her concern. By
the time she had tied on the sling and gently tucked my
weak arm into it, Ben had unburdened himself of several
warnings about taxing myself when he wasn't around.

You're dangerously close to the line, I told him when
he left to get some sleep in Naomi's bed.

I know. He sighed. *It's difficult, Francesca. I wish to*

protect you, but I know that will only serve to drive you away.

I mused on that as I returned to my mother's trailer, changing into a pair of sage-colored linen walking shorts and sleeveless tunic that Inner Fran hoped Ben would find attractive. A memory returned to me, that of me angrily telling Imogen I was leaving Ben because all he wanted to do was to run my life, and that he was arrogant, stubborn, and inflexible.

"He is a Dark One," she had snapped back, her eyes flashing with ire. "Would you want him to change? Would you want him to become something he isn't?"

I didn't really want him to change. It wasn't Ben himself that was at the root of my quandary—he was quite obviously trying to adjust himself to my needs, and that, more than anything, touched me. But was he doing that because he had to, driven by the same forces that matched us up, or was his motivation something more promising?

To be honest, I'm a bit surprised you're not insisting on coming with me, I told Ben.

I thought about it, he answered, a sort of hesitant amazement tingeing the words. *But you are more capable now, not so heedless. The incident with Imogen's nightstand aside, I do not believe you will put yourself in danger.*

You've come a long way, baby, I laughed into his head.

As have you. Once again I had the sense of surprise from him, as if he was adjusting his mental image of me.

Did that include warmer feelings? Something beyond the physical attraction? I shook my head, unwilling to spend the day trying to figure out something that would surely be made clear in time.

"Right," I told the Vikings a little later, when I had assembled them in the trailer to organize the day's plan of attack. "First of all, you have to change your clothes, all of you. Isleif, if you turn around one more time, I will send you back to Valhalla. Sit down. Oh dear goddess . . . cross your legs or something! Thank you. I know you guys are enjoying wearing modern clothes, and heaven knows, I'm no couture snob, but there are levels of decency that I think are being ignored, and that's got to change. So you're all going to change your clothes before we go into Breast Warts."

"I told you she wouldn't like the rod sack," Finnvid said to Isleif. "I told him, goddess!"

I narrowed my eyes at him. "Indeed. And why, if you don't mind me asking, are you wearing a kilt?"

Finnvid looked down at his wool kilt, above which he wore a fishnet sleeveless shirt. "Imogen said women like men in a short skirt. She said they run after them and ogle them and try to see their rod."

"There are times when I truly feel like I'm in the Twilight Zone," I said to myself. "You're a Viking, Finnvid."

"Aye, I am."

"Scotsmen wear kilts. Vikings don't."

"Are you sure?" he asked.

I nodded.

"All right." Before I could do so much as blink, the kilt dropped to his feet with a *fwoop*.

"For pity's sake . . ." I turned around so I wasn't staring at his nakedness. "Put something on! Something decent! And you—" I pointed to Eirik, who was lounging against the wall, looking somewhat bored. "Put on a pair of pants. Yes, over the silk shorts."

I waited until all three men were dressed in their previously worn bizarre (but decent) ensembles. "I think we all agree that I can't go any further in locating my mother without the Vikingahärta."

The three of them nodded.

"What I propose doing today is to talk to the lich Ulfur to find out what he's done with it, and encourage him to return it to me."

"Encourage him?" Eirik asked with a puzzled look.

"That was my polite way of saying force him."

Pure joy lit up the faces of all three Vikings. Eagerly, Eirik stepped forward. "You'll let us kill this lich?"

"No. Not kill. Just scare the crap out of him. If he refuses to give it back . . ." I hesitated a moment. I wasn't a big fan of using violence, but I'd found in the past that some members of the Otherworld simply wouldn't respond to anything but a show of strength. "If he refuses, you can rough him up a little. Not enough to permanently harm him, but enough so he sees we're not pushovers."

The Vikings whooped at that, and were very busy for the next twenty minutes, gathering up not only their bullet-less Walther P38s, but anything else they could find that they felt would be useful in persuading the lich to do as I wanted.

By the time I rid them of most of their arsenal, including the fire extinguisher, a length of rope Finnvid had stolen from Peter's supplies, and what turned out to be Naomi's tattooing gun, I was ready to crawl back into bed and just let the world pass me by. But thoughts of my mother were enough to send me out, packed in a taxi Eirik had called, with three Vikings, a wonky arm, and a whole lot of determination.

Chapter 14

"Where will we find the lich?" Eirik asked as the taxi headed into town. He was in the process of honing the edge of a sword he'd acquired from Nils, the sword swallower.

"I hope you paid him for that," I told Eirik with a dark look as he stroked the whetstone lovingly down the blade, periodically pausing to test the sharpness on his thumb. The other two Vikings were similarly engaged: Finnvid with a pair of short swords and Isleif with a huge ax that I vaguely remembered Karl using to "decapitate" his brother in one of their showy magic acts.

"Aye. I knew you would not let us keep our weapons if we did not pay for them with weasel gold."

"Good. As for the lich, I know where he is. Or kind of know where he is. One of the images he imprinted into the table was that of a big old house overlooking the town. Kind of like a castle, but not quite as elaborate. I figured something that prominent shouldn't be hard to find. Finnvid, could you ask the driver if he knows of a house like that?"

He held a brief conversation with the driver (who

was dressed like a sea nymph, including seashell bra
and long green hair). "The taxi wench says she'd need
more information to say for sure which house it is."

I spent the trip into town trying to dig from my memory anything that would help pinpoint the house in
question. I didn't have much to go on, and it took some
time (and an ever-increasing meter total) before the
taxi driver finally hit pay dirt.

"I'd ask her to wait for us, but this has already been
the most expensive taxi ride of my life," I told Eirik as
the driver zapped my MasterCard.

He pulled out the sword, which he wore strapped to
his back. "I will take care of the taxi wench for you. You
save your weasel gold."

"No, you will not. You know the rules—no hurting
anyone unless I give explicit orders to the contrary."

"Like the lich," he said with an anticipatory smile,
the avid glint in his eyes making me a bit wary. As the
taxi zoomed off, all four of us turned to look at the
house. It was of gray stone, with a red tile roof that
flared upward into a variety of small turrets and spires.
The entrance of the house was flanked on one side by a
tall square tower attached to the house, with diagonally
slanted white-framed windows. The upper floors had
narrow arched windows. The side of the house that
faced the courtyard, comprised of a circular paved drive
around a small fountain, looked very familiar. Or rather,
the stone projections like miniature buttresses sprout-
ing off the side of the wall looked familiar. I looked up
at them, noting the runes that had been carved with
rough cuts into the stone. "For some reason, those give
me a bad case of the willies," I told the others as a little
shiver rippled down my arms and back.

The Vikings glanced at the runed arches, but said

nothing, just waited with obvious anticipation for me to give them the okay to storm the castle.

I gave them all a quelling glance and raised the huge cast iron knocker in the shape of a man hanging upside down by his feet, his hands tied behind his back. I was extremely grateful for the double layer of my gloves as I banged the knocker against the metal backing. The noise seemed as loud as a gunshot, making me jump and my heart race with unreasonable nervousness.

One of the heavy wood double doors creaked open with suitably atmospheric noise. I half expected to see someone in a full Dracula outfit answering the door, or at least a hunchbacked minion in a lab coat, but the man who stood at the door with a polite expression of query on his face was anything but standard monster movie fodder. He was a little taller than me, had sandy brown hair, freckles, and absolutely black eyes.

"Ja?" he asked.

It was the black eyes that gave him away. "You're the lich, aren't you? You're . . . Ulfur?"

He blinked at me a moment, then answered in a voice with a slight Scandinavian accent, "Who are you?"

"The lich!" Eirik yanked me aside, sending me crashing into a large planter as he lunged forward, the other Vikings giving bloodcurdling cries of happiness as they rushed with him, their weapons in hand.

"No! Wait, guys—" Painfully, I scrambled out of the planter, about to order the Vikings to stand down their attack, but the words left my mouth as I flung myself to the side to escape the path of a screaming, rampaging horse that suddenly burst out upon us.

Isleif yelled something and ran over to protect me, while the other two Vikings started hacking away at the horse. I had a moment of sheer unadulterated horror as

I imagined the worst had happened, but when I leaped out from behind Isleif's bulk to stop the carnage, there was nothing to stop. Oh, to be sure, Eirik and Finnvid were fighting the horse, and he was a mass of flashing hooves and teeth-gratingly loud, angered screams, but there was no blood, no gore, nothing. I stared with fascination for a moment at the sight of the Vikings and horse before turning to the man who calmly watched the scene from the doorway.

"You live with a ghost horse?" I asked.

"That's Ragnor. Yes, he is a ghost. My master refused to raise him when he had me raised."

"You *are* Ulfur, aren't you?" I asked, examining him for signs that he might be tainted by evil power.

"Yes, I am." He turned his attention to the three Vikings, who had by now realized that the horse was insubstantial. "Those are ghosts, too, aren't they?"

"We are Viking ninjas, lich," Eirik said as he swaggered over to Ulfur. "We are here to protect the goddess Fran, so do not think to attack her, for we will cut out your liver and eat it before your eyes."

Ulfur's eyebrows went up at that. "I have no intention of attacking anyone, let alone a woman. Did you say goddess?" He gave me a once-over. "You don't look like a goddess."

"I'm not. It's just a misunderstanding. I'm Fran. Francesca Ghetti. I believe you have something of mine, a valknut."

Ulfur's black eyes widened for a few seconds, then he glanced over his shoulder, hesitant, before stepping back and gesturing toward the inside of the house. "You may come in, but you must not stay long. My master isn't at home now, but he does not like visitors, especially unexpected ones."

The room he led us to was a surprise—I had expected that with a house this old, it would be filled with dark paneling and antiques. But this room, clearly one meant for entertaining, reminded me of something a hip, urbane Satan would have. The walls were rock, not wood paneled, the floor a glossy cream marble cut into diamond shapes, and the furniture was ultramodern, all scarlet in color, with uncomfortable-looking chairs, swooping, curved-seat love seats, and white, headless, armless statues of naked women dotted around the room.

I could see the Vikings appreciated the statues, but the room left me cold, literally and figuratively. Ragnor the ghostly horse followed us, his eyes narrowed, his ears back. It was vaguely disconcerting that his hooves made no sound on the marble floor, but I decided that was the least of my worries.

"We won't stay long. Assuming you give me back the Vikingahärta," I said, holding out a hand when Eirik, with a growl, started toward the lich. "Eirik, let's try our party manners first."

The outraged look Eirik shot me spoke volumes. "You said we could force the lich to do what we wanted. You promised us blood sport."

Ulfur's face paled, but he didn't back up. He looked like he knew he was overwhelmed, but was going to stand his ground, regardless.

"I said you could persuade Ulfur if he refused to give me back the Vikingahärta, but he's not going to refuse. Are you?" I kept my voice and expression sweet as I gave Ulfur an encouraging smile. I remembered well the unspeakable anguish that held him in an unbreakable grip.

His face tightened as if he was, in fact, going to refuse, but after what must have been an inner struggle, his shoulders slumped, and he shook his head. "No. I will not refuse to return to you the valknut, although it will mean serious trouble with my master. Wait here. I will get it for you."

"I think my friends and their extremely sharp weapons would really be happier if we were to come with you," I said, following him as he left the room and started up a flight of stairs, the Vikings collectively muttering under their breaths as they trailed behind.

He said nothing, but led us to a small room done in shades of olive and muted red. At a giant desk that dominated the room, he removed a small red box, holding it for a few seconds while he gave me a piercing look. "How do I know this is yours?"

"I know where you stole it from, and approximately when. I can also describe it to you. But more important, the valknut knows me. It doesn't like anyone else touching it, which you probably found out if you took it out of the velvet bag it's kept in."

He grimaced and held up one hand. Like mine, his fingers were marked, but his held an angry-looking burn. "Unfortunately, I did. If you don't mind, I'd like to see you hold it. Just to be sure, you understand."

"He will not give it to us," Eirik growled, stalking forward. "He intends to keep it for himself."

"I never wanted it in the first place," Ulfur said frankly.

Eirik suddenly halted, an indescribable look on his face. He spun around to face the now solid equine face of Ragnor, who I could swear was grinning as he munched on a piece of black leather, obviously nipped off of the baldric Eirik wore on his back.

"Your horse can ground himself?" I asked Ulfur.

"For short periods of time, yes. Ragnor, stop that. I'm sorry," Ulfur apologized to Eirik. "He has been moody ever since I told him the master wasn't going to have him returned to life, too."

"Wait a second . . . You're alive?" I asked, distracted by that idea. "I thought you were dead."

"I was." He sighed and sank down onto the edge of the desk, still holding the box with the Vikingahärta. "I was quite happy as a spirit, too. We had lots of tourists in our village, and although it was sometimes boring in the winter, the summers we all enjoyed greatly."

"We? Your family are all ghosts, too?"

"Yes. My village was destroyed by a mudslide about a hundred and fifty years ago. We were all trapped there until Pia rescued us."

"Is Pia your master?"

He looked appalled. "No! Pia is the Zorya who was sent to take us to Ostri, our heaven. But then she met Kristoff, and he didn't like us much, especially Ragnor, who admittedly bit him once or twice, but when the reapers tried to kill Kristoff, I was left behind, and so the Ilargi got me."

"It's kind of sad when my life needs a glossary," I said to no one in particular, then recalled where I was, and what I was doing, and held out my hand. "Could I have my Vikingahärta, please?"

He looked at my gloves. I *tsk*ed and peeled them off, then held out my hand again. He stared in horror at my hand.

"That's not from the Vikingahärta. It's from touching a table you touched," I told him, noting absently that the saffron was already starting to fade. "Which reminds me—if you could keep from touching my hands, I'd be grateful."

He withdrew the small gold velvet bag from the box, carefully undoing the strings, and just as carefully up-ending it over my open hand. The Vikingahärta hit my hand with a warm glow of familiarity. I smiled at it, holding it up to admire the runes so delicately carved into the three linked triangles that the old Norsemen referred to as a valknut. "Hello, Vikingahärta. Do you know what a valknut is, Ulfur?"

He shook his head, not looking particularly inter-ested. "My father would know, but he is in Ostri now."

I felt so adrift in the things he had told me, I figured it wouldn't hurt if he saw that I knew a few things, too, and traced along the three heavy gold triangles. "A valknut is the knot of the slain, a symbol of the afterlife. It has nine points, which represent the three Norns, who, centuries ago, the people in Scandinavia believed were weavers of fate. This one belonged to Loki, and is imbued with his power, but it's mine now."

"I can see that it is." He gave me an odd considering look for a moment, then added, "My master may well destroy me when he finds out what I've done, but I will let you take it if you promise to do something for me."

"I'm afraid I don't know anything about liches or their masters, so I wouldn't begin to know how to free you from him—"

"No, it's not that," he interrupted. "Or rather it is, but I don't expect you to help me. The Zorya I men-tioned, Pia, will help me. If you could get word to her and her Dark One, Kristoff, I would be very grateful."

"You know a Dark One?" I asked, surprised for some reason. "I didn't realize that liches and vampires mixed."

"So far as I know, they don't, but this is a special case. My master knows that I was under Pia's protection for a while, and he's forbidden me to have any contact with them. But you could tell them where I am, and explain what happened to me."

The lost look in his eyes tugged at my heart. I was silent for a minute, trying to sort through my thoughts. "I'll do what I can," I said at last.

"Goddess!" Eirik protested. "You are going to help the lich? You won't let us gut him if you want to help him!"

"I wasn't going to let you gut him in the first place. Honestly, Eirik, you'd think by now you would realize that I'm not going to just let you run around killing whoever you want to kill. From this moment on, you can assume that I'm not going to let you kill anyone. Got that?"

As the words left my lips, the door opened and a man walked in, but the acrid stench that clung to him told me that this was no mortal man. He was slight and dark, and the moment his eyes lit on me, they glittered with unholy light. "A Beloved? For me? How thoughtful of you! I haven't had a Beloved sacrificed to me in . . . oh, forever. I will enjoy ripping out her soul."

Eirik shot me a look.

"Fine," I said, glaring at the demon. "You can gut him. But no one else."

The Vikings were on the demon before it had time to do much damage to them. I moved back out of the way as they jumped the demon, blades slashing, black blood flying, and various oaths and demonic screeches piercing the still air of the room. The Vikings were whooping it up as well, and so far as I could tell, having the time of their lives pounding the demon to a pulp. After a good minute and a half of that, all that remained was a blob on the floor that disappeared in a blast of nasty, oily black smoke that stained the floor and covered the Vikings in a fine black ash.

"Don't tell me—your master keeps demons, too?" I asked Ulfur.

He shook his head, looking with curiosity at the spot on the sage carpet. "No. That was Verin, a demon in Asmodeus's legions. He was acting as courier between his demon lord and my master."

I pursed my lips. "Whops. The demon was just sent back to Asmodeus, right? Because you can't destroy a demon, just his form?"

"Correct." Ulfur looked a bit worried, which in turn made me think we'd overstayed our welcome and wonder if his master would seek retribution.

"That's all I need—someone else after my blood," I said on a sigh. "This necromancer master of yours . . . is he likely to be peeved to find out the courier was temporarily destroyed?"

"De Marco isn't a necromancer," Ulfur said, prodding at the black stain with the tip of his shoe. "He's an Ilargi."

"Ah." I tried to remember what it was that Imogen had told me about them. "Those are the guys who steal souls. So, what—" I paused, something Ulfur said chiming a warning bell in my head. "What did you say your master's name is?"

"De Marco. Alphonse de Marco."

My jaw dropped a tiny bit. I actually stood there blinking with my mouth hanging open in surprise. "Are you sure?" I asked, immediately realizing how idiotic that sounded.

"Quite sure."

I shook my head, trying to clear the confusion that clogged up my brain like so much sticky spiderweb. "It can't be the same person. It just can't be. It's coincidence, nothing more. You don't happen to know his birth date, do you? Or whether he was ever married, or had a daughter named Petra?"

Ulfur looked as confused as I felt. "I don't know his birth date or whether he was married, although I don't believe he was. He did have a daughter, but she was stolen from him when she was a baby."

"Stolen by who?" I couldn't help but ask.

"Gypsies."

"Oh, come on, that's a cliché! Real Gypsies don't do things like that," I protested.

He shrugged. "That's what de Marco told me. He has long sought to find his daughter, but says she's been hidden well. He did say something odd about her, though...."

"I don't know what could be much odder than being stolen by Gypsies," I said, feeling more and more like Alice in a really deranged version of Wonderland.

"He said that so long as he had her horn, the baby couldn't be used against him."

I just looked at him for a few seconds. His mild gray eyes held my gaze. "You know, I think it's going to be better for my sanity if I just move along, both figuratively and literally. If your master wants to have a hissy on my butt about destroying the demon's form, he can. Otherwise, it's time to leave. Where can I find your friend Pia and her vampire?"

He gave me the names of a couple of towns where he thought they might live, and escorted us to the door. The Vikings were still riding high on their adrenaline rush caused by destroying the demon's form, and were quite happy to walk the quarter mile into the town proper, reliving the (in their minds glorious) fight blow by blow.

Chapter 15

Ben was nowhere to be found when we made it back to the Faire. I considered calling him on my mental cell phone (it seemed so much easier than using a real one), but decided I wasn't such a wimp that I needed to keep tabs on him every second of the day. He was a big boy— I could trust him to go off and do things on his own without knowing exactly what it was he was doing.

The fact that Naomi was at her tattooing booth might have had something to do with my determination to give Ben his space, but I preferred to think of it as being comfortable with our blossoming relationship.

"Let's go find a quiet spot," I told the Vikings.

"You are going to summon Loki?" Isleif asked, hope in his eyes.

"Yes."

They cheered, and accompanied me to a corner of the field that held a couple of huge round cylinders made of up hay. I moved behind them, so they blocked the sight of anyone who might be arriving at the Faire, and pulled out the Vikingahärta. "I just hope I remember how to use this."

"You will," Eirik said, taking up a protective stance on my left. Finnvid did the same on my right, both swords in his hands, while behind me Isleif hefted his huge war ax. I didn't point out to them that Loki wasn't going to be as easy to destroy as the demon had been.

I held the Vikingahärta, closing my eyes for a few seconds to help calm my troubled thoughts, focusing on one image, as my mother had taught me to do whenever I was about to conduct an invocation.

That image was of her.

"By the fire that burns within thee." My words came out halting and stiff, reflecting how uncomfortable I was with this. I held the image of my mother in the forefront of my mind and tried again to calm my nerves. "By the earth that feeds thee. By the air that hides thee, by the Vikingahärta that holds thee."

The valknut grew warm in my unharmed hand, little pinpricks of light beginning to beam out from it. I slipped off the makeshift sling, not wanting Loki to see that I was anything but in the most tip-top shape.

"Deceiver."

The air around us crackled.

"Slayer."

Before us, motes of light started gathering together.

"Trickster."

The lights swirled faster and faster around each other, spinning and elongating into a long oval shape.

"Betrayer."

The shape shimmered, and darkened in the center as a human form began to resolve itself.

"I invoke thee and call upon thee to descend here!"

The man who stepped out of the light was not who I expected. We stared at each other for a few seconds—me utterly surprised, and he looking furious.

"Who are you?" he demanded, glaring first at me, then at the Vikings, who were just as taken aback as I was.

"I'm Fran. Er . . . you're not Loki, are you?"

He didn't look like Loki, whose appearance I remembered as an older man, rather thin, with very white hands and balding red hair. This man had dark brown hair, a goatee, and dark eyes that glittered with anger. I took an instinctive step back, raising my hand with the valknut in a protective gesture that attracted his attention.

"What do you have there?" He ignored my questions, casting his own out with a sharp bark that had a compulsion attached to it—a sort of magic spell that made you want to do whatever was asked of you.

"It's mine," I said, struggling against the need to answer him.

"Vikingahärta," Finnvid blurted out.

I glared at him.

"Sorry, goddess," he murmured, looking somewhat chagrined.

"Goddess?" The man's eyes narrowed on me. "Vikingahärta?"

I straightened myself up, holding the Vikingahärta firmly, drawing strength from the fact that it didn't like this man. "No to the first, yes to the second. Would you mind telling me who you are, and why, when I summoned Loki, you appeared instead?"

"Do not summon me again," he snapped, and while I stared at him in surprise, he spun around and walked back into the oval of light, which proceeded to dissolve until it was nothing.

"Bullfrogs! With warts on them!" I swore, wanting to do bodily harm to someone. "What was all that about? Who was that man? And why did he come when I called Loki?"

"Should we know the answer to that?" Isleif asked Eirik.

Eirik shrugged. "The goddess knows things. She tells us, not the other way around."

"This goddess hasn't a clue," I muttered, kicking at a clod of earth. "Now what do I do?"

The sudden hum of the generators as they were turned on, triggering the big lights that lined the Faire, was the answer to that question. I sighed, felt sorry for myself for sixteen seconds, then turned and marched back to the Faire, slipping the Vikingahärta's chain over my neck.

"What are you guys going to do this evening?" I asked Eirik later, as the three stood around my mother's booth, where I was selling off the last of her stock.

"Bed Imogen when she is done," Finnvid said immediately, casting a warm glance down the line of tents toward the one Imogen manned. "Until then, I will think about bedding Imogen."

"We shall wench," Eirik announced, nodding at Isleif. "There are many women in town who desire our rods. Then, after we have wenched our fill, we will pillage a McDonald's. We have not done so in five years, and we have missed the joy of plundering Chicken McBlobs and dipping sauces."

"And Big Macs."

"Aye, and the Big Macs."

"You would pillage without me?" Finnvid asked, looking hurt.

"You will be bedding Imogen," Eirik pointed out.

Finnvid thought for a moment. "Imogen would like

to pillage, too. We will do so after I have bedded her several times."

"It is important that a man regain his strength after repeated beddings," Eirik told me in the tone of one confiding a fact of great importance.

"Er . . . yeah." I gnawed on my lower lip for a bit, wondering if I should ask Eirik and Isleif to stay with me when I tracked down the orgy Ben was supposed to go to, but decided that there really wasn't any danger in what I planned to do—a little spying—and sent them all off with a happy wave, and a warning to Eirik and Isleif to use protection while wenching, and to be sure to pay for their pillaged goods.

I didn't have much time to worry about them for the next four hours, since the crowds around my mother's booth just about cleaned her out of all of her potions, charms, and spells. I waited until there was a lull, when the band started playing in the main tent, and tucked away the evening's proceeds, shut down the booth, and dropped off the money with Absinthe.

"Peter says he is not sure if you will join us again or not," she told me as she wrote up a receipt for Mom's takings. "He says you may wish to return to your job."

Absinthe and I never got along, at least we hadn't when I was young and didn't know how to protect myself against her mind-reading ability. Now I was an old hand at locking out people. I slid my mental barriers into place and gave her a placid smile. "That's true. My plans are uncertain at this point." Such as whether or not my future would involve a sexy vampire.

"Just so you do not forget your debt to me." She tucked the money away in the big safe that sat in the middle of her trailer.

"I'm not likely to. You haven't . . . uh . . . had any other visions of my mother, have you?"

One shoulder rose in a careless gesture. "I have not tried. It seemed clear to me that she was happy. I am not worried about her, although if she wishes to leave the Faire, I wish she would close her booth so that we may replace her. Peter says we must give her time, however."

I murmured something polite and made my escape before she could pin me down with pointed questions, wondering once again how she and easygoing Peter could be twins and yet be so different from each other.

The speculation of what form paying off the debt to Absinthe may take kept me occupied as I sat in a taxi at the edge of the Faire parking area, waiting for the small blue car that I knew was Naomi's to leave, praying to any and all gods and goddesses I could think of that they were actually taking Naomi's car, and not going on Ben's bike. I didn't want to know if he'd taken her on long rides, where she could smell his hair and feel the warmth of his body pressed against hers, and even if she tingled all over just thinking about the way his muscles stretched and contracted as he moved with the bike . . . I shook away the image that was building in my head, just in time to point at the car that was exiting the pasture parking lot, and say, "That's it. Could you follow that car, please, but don't let them see you?"

The driver, dressed like a monk (complete with tonsure) in rough brown robes, and a rope belt upon which was attached his cell phone, gave me a long look in the rearview mirror. "If you get me into trouble—"

"I won't. I promised you it was simply a little misunderstanding between me and my boyfriend, and that's all it really is. So if you could just follow them, please?"

The driver gave me another stern look, but obligingly pulled out after them. I was a little surprised to find that Naomi drove not into town but away from it. I guess I'd always connected orgies with nightclubs and sleazy motels, but she drove deep into the countryside, entering what I judged from a sign to be some sort of official park.

"Now this is odd. They're having an orgy outside?"

The driver, who had pulled up just outside the open gate, shot me an accusatory glance.

"Party, I mean. Not orgy. Er . . . here, will this cover it? Thanks. I'll just get out now."

"Yes, I think you should."

I slipped out of the taxi, waved politely as he pulled a U-turn and sped off into the night, then slipped into the shadows of some scraggly fir trees that dotted a tiny parking lot, and immediately stepped on something soft and squidgy that moved.

Before I could scream, a hand clamped over my mouth. I didn't wait to find out who it was—I brought my knee up, slammed the heel of my hand into his nose, and was about to gouge at his eyes with my other hand when a garbled, "Stop! It's me!" reached me. I peered in the darkness at the shape as he doubled over, breathing hard.

"Who's me?" I whispered.

"David. I think you broke my balls."

"Frogspawn! I'm so sorry, David. I didn't know it was you."

"I really am going to have to stop surprising you," he said softly, pain threading his voice as he lurched upright. Although the moon was almost full, we stood in the shadow cast by the trees, and all I could see of him was a silhouette. "One of these days you'll actually succeed in breaking something."

"Are you okay?"

"I'll be fine," he said, straightening up even more. "So long as you don't attack me again. Damn. You have a good right punch."

"Why on earth are you here lurking in the trees?"

He took my arm and steered me to the side, so that we skirted the edge of the parking lot, deep in the shadows. "For the same reason that I suspect you are here. Diego? How many?"

I stifled a squeak when another shadow loomed up next to me. "Five, counting the Dark One."

"Two more to come, then."

Even if I couldn't see him beyond a black outline, I could feel the other man examining me.

"Fran, this is Diego, one of the members of my pride. Fran is Benedikt's Beloved."

Diego murmured something polite. He had a Spanish accent that made me think of Antonio Banderas. "Is she staying here?"

"No, she's not," I answered firmly.

Diego gave a soft chuckle. "It's like that, is it?"

"On the nose."

"Don't mention noses," David said, obviously feeling his nose. "Ow. Benedikt would have my balls if I left you alone, Fran, so it's best if you come with me. Diego, you know what to do."

"I'll be on the south side. If he shows up, do you want me to take him?"

"No. It's important we see what they are doing. If things get out of hand . . . we'll deal with it."

"Agreed."

Diego moved off, as silent as the shadow he was.

"Who's the 'he' Diego was talking about?" I asked as I followed David around the edge of the parking lot and up a steep, forested hill.

"Luis, Diego's brother. He is the one the Agrippans have taken. We expect them to bring him here tonight."

"For what purpose?"

David was so hard to see in the dark, I grabbed the back of his black shirt and held tight to it as we climbed up and over a rocky hill covered with dried pine needles. "Most likely to kill him."

"They're going to orgy him to death?"

"Sex isn't the only thing they do at the tyro." His voice was grim.

At the top of the hill, he paused. To the south of us was an open area ringed with tall, narrow fir trees. A couple of rustic tables and fire pits indicated it was normally used as a picnic area, but the tables had been stacked to one side and several blankets had been laid out in the center of the ring. As we watched, torches were placed and lit in an outer ring, while the two fire pits on either end had been set ablaze. The light from the fires and the moonlight made it possible to see the people beyond just their shapes. I was suddenly nervous as I recognized Ben's form before he stepped into the firelight. I was sick at the thought that Naomi and her people might actually harm someone, but at the same time, I definitely did not want Ben there.

I'd gone and fallen in love with him, I chastised myself, while being very careful to keep my mental shields in place so Ben could not pick up on what I was thinking. All that talk about wanting to know if you were really meant for each other, or just programmed that way, and what do you do? You fall for him. Hard. Fran, you're a boob.

David turned toward me, still in shadow. "Did you say something?"

"No. Just yelling at myself."

"Ah. About what?"

"Ben."

He gave a ghostly laugh. "I won't say I'm glad you're yelling at yourself, but in fact, I am. It means you care about him."

"Yes, I do." My gaze shifted from David's shadow to the group in between the fires. I could see three women, including Naomi, as well as Ben, and another man, who looked to be arguing with Naomi. Every once in a while he gestured toward Ben. "Do you know who they are?" I leaned into David so I could whisper my question in his ear.

He did likewise. "We know their names. The two women are from Austria and Switzerland. One is related to Naomi, although we aren't sure how; the man is Micah, a biologist from England. The last one we're expecting is Isaak, a Dane. He's the leader of the set. We believe he's been holding Luis somewhere around here, but we haven't been able to locate him."

"Are you planning on rescuing your guy from them?"

"Of course. But after we see as much of the tyro as we can—even after almost a decade of trying to find out the truth, we have no idea *why* they are killing random members of the therion community."

I squatted down on my heels, making myself comfortable for what I feared would be a long wait. And I was right. I spent most of the time watching Ben, not because I distrusted him, but for the simple fact that my eyes were drawn to him. He sat on a cooler, somewhat separated from the others, most of whom lolled around on the blankets talking, laughing, and guzzling beer. Naomi, I was annoyed to see, had evidently forgiven Ben for the shower episode, and spent most of her time hovering around him, touching his shoulders or his arm or head. Twice she leaned down to kiss him, which just made me grind my teeth.

A spike of jealousy ran hot through me when she tugged him onto his feet, then plastered herself against him, both hands on his hair as she slapped her lips on his. Ben's arms went around her in a loose embrace, which sent me to my feet, my hands fisted, and fire in my eye.

"Steady," David said, one prohibitive hand on my arm. "I know it's difficult, Fran, but she's just kissing him, that's all."

"That's more than enough," I growled, somewhat surprised to find that I was holding the Vikingahärta. I narrowed my eyes on Naomi as she giggled up at Ben, wiggling herself against him. The Vikingahärta had a good deal of power . . . perhaps I could use that to deal with Naomi. Change her into something fitting, like a slug. Or a cesspool. Or a patch of mildew.

Instantly, I was ashamed of myself. One of the precepts my mother held strongly to, and one that I had absorbed from her teaching, was the threefold law that said whatever I did to others would be returned trebled to me. Although the desire to use the Vikingahärta to bring disaster to Naomi burned in me almost as hot as the anger at seeing her touch him and kiss him and all but jump his bones in front of everyone, despite that, I clung to the belief that to purposely do harm to others was wrong.

Satisfying as all get-out, but wrong.

It was almost an hour before we heard the distant sounds of a car. By that time, Naomi's group had donned long flowing robes, under which the women squirmed to remove their clothing. The men did likewise, but with much less gyrating.

"Why are they being so modest?" I asked David, standing for a few minutes to get the circulation going again in my legs. "I thought an orgy meant everyone stripped off all their clothes, not wore neck-to-ankle robes."

"I have a feeling those robes won't be in much evidence once the tyro commences," he answered drily.

I made a sour face, looking at the berobed Ben. I couldn't tell if he had taken off all of his clothes under the robe or left his pants on, and I was irked with myself that it mattered so much. I might have finally decided that I was in love with him, but that didn't mean I had to be all gaga over him, did it?

Naomi cooed something at him and brushed her hand against his groin.

The Vikingahärta grew hot in my hand as I imagined what she would look like as an octopus with a form of leprous sucker rot, but my lovely fantasy of her tentacles dropping off was interrupted by the arrival of two men, one of whom bore a halogen flashlight.

Naomi's group greeted them with happy cries, and it wasn't long before the two men were also clad in long robes.

"Is that your guy?" I asked David. We had shifted position slightly, moving a quarter way down the ring of trees so that we were downwind.

A thin shaft of light pierced the tree next to us, making it possible for me to see David's face. We both knelt behind a stump, in order to lessen the chances anyone would see a human shape lurking in the shadows. He lifted his chin as if smelling the air. "Yes, that's Luis."

"You can smell him?"

"Of course. All the members of my pride have a distinct scent."

I would have asked him what they smelled like, but at that moment, the new arrival, presumably Isaak, stood in the center of the group and raised his arms to the sky, calling down a general invocation. At the last word of it, he turned to where Naomi was smooshed up against Ben.

I leaned forward a bit, keeping low against the stump, intent on hearing what it was he said.

"We have a full agenda for tonight, so we will get started immediately. Tonight we welcome a new member to the set. Benedikt Czerny, step forward and receive the blessing of the tyro."

Ben moved into the center of the circle, and just like that, everyone tossed off their robes to reveal a whole lot of flesh in varying colors, covering forms that ranged from skinny to plentiful.

"Moon and stars above," I said, blinking a couple of times.

"You will welcome our new brother to the set, Naomi."

Naomi, stark naked, took Ben's hand and led him over to a central blanket. All the others stood around, evidently going to watch them go at it.

I was on my feet again, the Vikingahärta almost burning my hand, my heart beating so loud I thought Ben would hear it.

David held both my arms, whispering, "Wait and watch, Fran. Please. For Luis."

I ground off yet another layer of tooth enamel, looking away as Naomi pulled Ben's robe off. I couldn't stand not knowing the worst, however, so I looked back and found her gesturing to the jeans he still wore, laughing as she said, "Isn't that sweet! He's shy! Don't worry, my darling. By the end of the tyro, you won't have anything to be shy about."

Without further ado, she unzipped his pants and pulled them down.

"Revenge is bad, revenge is bad," I murmured to myself as Ben reluctantly lifted each foot so she could pull his pants completely off.

She reached for his penis, but Ben caught her by her arms and spun her around, whispering something in her ear. She laughed again, a shrill sound that made the hairs on my arms stand on end, and called out in a loud, clear voice, "Poor Ben hasn't eaten since yesterday. He doesn't think he can perform until he does so. Is there any objection to me feeding him first?"

"Make it fast," the man named Micah called out, fondling the boobs of one of the two other women.

"By all means, don't let my hunger keep you from celebrating the glory of the set," Ben said, moving with Naomi to the far end of the area. She twined an arm around him, offering her neck, but he took her hand instead, his head bent over her wrist.

"Clever Benedikt," David said softly. "He bought himself some time."

"He can't feed all night," I said, watching him and Naomi with many dark thoughts that would have shocked my mother. "Sooner or later he's going to have to stop, and then they'll want him to join in the orgy."

David was silent for a moment. "I can only imagine what you think of me for asking this of you, but I assure you that what Benedikt does tonight, he does for the welfare of my pride. He will not enjoy himself in the least."

"Do you have a wife? Girlfriend?" I asked him, noting that he was right—the others were on the blankets, rolling around in one big mass of writhing arms and legs. I avoided looking at just what it was they were doing, keeping my attention on Ben.

"No. Why?"

"Because if that was your girlfriend out there about to have sex with someone who wasn't you, I think you'd have a different perspective on the whole thing."

He said nothing, but shifted uncomfortably.

"They don't seem to be holding your buddy prisoner," I added, my eyes drawn to him when he arched up from where one of the women was bent over him, and howled in wordless ecstasy. "In fact, he seems to be having a pretty good time."

"So I've noticed," he answered, a hard, flinty edge to his voice.

"I see I've arrived a little early."

Both David and I ducked as two men strode within twenty yards of us, stopping at the edge of the ring of lights. I gaped in openmouthed surprise, then mentally chided myself for doing so yet again. I never used to be the sort of person who stood like an idiot with her mouth hanging open. It must have been Ben's influence on me. He made me fall in love with him, thereby causing me to become a mouth breather.

Or something like that. I stared in disbelief at the dark-haired man who had appeared when I tried to summon Loki. "What is he doing here?"

David shot me a quick questioning glance, and whispered, "You know them?"

"I know the one. Well, kind of. I summoned him by mistake, but I don't know who he is."

"We have had a late start, but you are welcome to join in the celebration of the set," Naomi said, stroking her hand through Ben's hair. He was still bent over her wrist, although now I could see he was kissing his way up her arm. A stall tactic, no doubt, I snarled to myself. "Come, my darling. We must initiate you properly."

She led Ben toward the mass of bodies. He stopped just at the edge of them, looking over at the two men who stood watching the scene. The man I'd summoned had a sneer on his lips. The other man, thin and anemic-looking, shot little darting glances around, as if he was looking for a way to escape. "I don't perform in front of strangers," Ben said. "Who are those people?"

"Just a friend of mine and his pet necromancer," Naomi cooed, sliding her hand down to his crotch. He tried to sidestep her, but she had hold of him so he couldn't. "Let us partake of the blessing of the set, lover."

Ben, his brows lowered, glared at the strangers. "I said I don't perform in front of strangers. Make them leave."

"They can't, darling. They are needed for what's to follow your initiation," she purred, pulling him down onto the blanket.

I clutched the trunk of the tree so hard my finger-nails broke through my gloves. With a snarl, I ripped them off, holding the Vikingahärta tight, sick to my stomach with indecision and anger. I wanted to help David, but not this way. There had to be another way.

"What is to follow? I thought my initiation into the set was the highlight of the tyro. Now you tell me it's not?" Ben's voice was filled with arrogance and hauteur, and for a moment I smiled at it. The arrogance, yes, that was him, but he was never haughty, and I knew he disliked being the center of attention as much as I did.

"No, lover, of course your ceremony is to be the highlight," Naomi said, trying to pull him back when he moved out of her reach. Beyond them, the others were fully engaged in their orgy, little cries and groans filling the night air. "We had an unexpected opportunity to further our experiments for de Marco, that's all. Just as soon as we're done with your ceremony, we'll get on with the experiment, and then he will leave and it will be just us again."

De Marco? The name rang in my head like a bell. What had he to do with this?

"I do not like how I have been shoved aside for another," Ben said, getting to his feet, and to my intense relief, snatching up his jeans and pulling them on. "I will not have it. I am a Dark One, not some mortal you can appease with a little sex and then set aside."

Naomi's eyes narrowed on him. "Benedikt, you are important to us. But you cannot be one of us unless you complete the ceremony."

He glared at the man I had summoned, and insight hit me with a flash. Was that de Marco? The man who'd had a baby with my mother?

"I will not be treated in this manner!" Ben snapped. "Obviously, you have some reservations about my involvement, or you would not delegate me to such a lowly status. Until such time as you realize my true value, I will find something else to occupy my time."

Ben's performance drove speculation about the mysterious de Marco from my mind. I wanted to cheer him, and kiss him, and lick every square inch of his delicious

body. And then I would make him fall in love with me,
so we could live together happily, and he would be safe
from the wiles of smut-mistresses like Naomi.

"I think, perhaps, it is you who have reservations,"
Naomi said slowly, getting to her feet. She had her back
to me as she faced Ben, so I couldn't see her face, but
her body language made it clear she was no longer in
sex kitten mode. "It is that damned Beloved of yours,
isn't it? She's leading you around by your cock. I knew I
should have taken care of her when I had the chance."

Ben gave her one of his haughtiest looks. "No woman
leads me, Naomi. *No* woman."

"Such a shame." She ran her hand down his bare
chest. He stepped back. "You had such potential, too.
Isaak?"

I had been ignoring the orgy in order to concentrate
on Ben, but when I glanced back, I was surprised to notice that everyone appeared to be finished with their
lechery. They lolled around in attitudes of limp exhaustion, their bodies draped over each other with apparent
abandon. At Naomi's call, Isaak pushed Luis's legs off
his stomach and got up.

"I believe in addition to our scheduled event, we have
an extraordinary opportunity at hand." She smiled at
Isaak before gesturing at Ben. "Our friend here seems
to prefer his Beloved to us. De Marco, have you ever
tried a Dark One?"

"Uh-oh," I whispered, my stomach tightening. "I
think things have gone wrong. Not that they were right
to begin with."

"Yes," David said slowly, his gaze moving from person to person. "I suspect you're correct. Are you
armed?"

I looked at him in surprise. "No. I don't . . . I'm not

big on guns and things. I have the Vikingahärta, but it's not a weapon. At least, I don't think it is. It protected me from Loki once, but that could be due to some other circumstance."

De Marco had strolled into the center of the ring by that point, followed by the slight man who reminded me of a nervous ferret. "I hadn't thought it was possible, but now that you bring it to mind, it would be a good experiment."

"Experiment on someone else," Ben growled, snatching up his shirt. "I am no one's guinea pig."

"Do you know what experiment they're talking about?" I asked David softly, holding on to his arm as we leaned forward to hear.

"No. But if that little man is a necromancer . . ." His voice trailed off as he eyed de Marco.

"They raise the dead, don't they?" I shivered at the implication.

"Yes."

"But Ben is immortal. They can't kill him."

"So is Luis, and yet they have destroyed countless therions over the last decade. Immortal simply means we're harder to kill than mortals. It can be accomplished."

"Not so fast," Isaak said, jerking a gun out of a backpack that lay beneath strewn clothing. The sight of a naked man holding a gun on Ben might have struck me as amusing in another circumstance, but I wasn't laughing.

Ben did, though. He gave a short, harsh laugh. "Do you really expect me to feel threatened by a gun? I've been shot more times than you can imagine, mortal."

The gun in Isaak's hand wavered.

"Oh, for god's sake . . ." Naomi stomped over to

where she'd left her clothing and bag, marching over to Ben with a glinting dagger about twelve inches long. She thrust it toward Isaak. "I swear, if I want something done, I have to do it myself. Here! Take this. You can slit his throat with it, or cut out his heart, or whatever, but just do it!"

"Right. That's enough for me. How good of an actor are you, David?"

He looked confused. I didn't waste time explaining, I just marched forward until I reached the lights, hauling a softly protesting David with me. The second we became visible, I switched my determined stride to a stumbling stagger, leaning heavily on David as if my legs couldn't hold me up. "That was the besh party I've ever sheen. Washn't it the besht? I gotta say, theshe Germans know how to throw a shindug. Digshug. You know what I mean. But man, I gotta pee. Back teeth are floating. Oh, look, a blanket."

I came to a stop near the sated orgyists, who quickly scrambled to their respective feet.

"David!" I said in a faux whisper, cupping my hand around his ear but not turning my head into it. "Peepsh! They're having a naked party! We should totally join in. Do you naked peoplesh have a Porta-Potti around here? Gotta pee." As the surprised faces of Naomi's group turned toward us, I staggered to the side, pointing. "David, look! It's that evil Naomi! And Ben! You bastard!"

"What the hell is she doing here?" Naomi demanded to know of Ben.

Fortunately, he looked as genuinely surprised as the rest of them, which gave me just enough time to do my best drunk walk over to him, waving my fist as I did so.

"I am sho gonna punch you! I'm your Beloved, bushter!" I unguarded my mind just as I reached him. *Hello. Would you duck, please?*

I drew back my arm and swung in a huge circle. Ben obligingly ducked, which left Naomi the only body in the way of my fist.

I'd also like to know what the hell you're doing here! he thought furiously at me. *This is no place for you, Francesca!*

She screamed and leaped toward me.

Did you honestly think I was going to let you go off and have sex with someone else?

Isaak and Micah jumped into the fray as Ben jerked Naomi to the side, roughly pushing her away from me.

No. I thought you would trust me to uphold my promise to you. There was pain behind his words.

David roared, actually roared as he shifted into lion form. He leaped onto Isaak, knocking the man to the ground.

I do trust you. It's Naomi that I have issues with. And I'm glad I did, because clearly, you need us.

"I want him!" de Marco said, pointing at David's lion form. "And the vampire. I want them both, along with the other therion."

Fran, get out of here!

No way, Jose.

The two women whose names I never did hear looked at each other, then turned and grabbed their clothing, disappearing into the night. Luis stood watching the men fighting, looking confused and unsure of himself.

"Are you Alphonse de Marco?" I asked the man who was now yelling at Isaak to hurry up with it. "And did you once know Miranda Benson?"

He stopped shouting long enough to shoot me a piercing look. "Just who are you? Why do you keep interfering in my plans?"

"I'm his Beloved," I said, pointing at Ben. "And you can't have him. He's mine."

Ben and Micah had been duking it out until Ben sent the latter flying a good twenty feet. He turned toward me, his face a picture of shock. *Did you just say what I think you said?*

Look out! Naomi, with a bloodcurdling shriek, threw herself at him, slashing at his torso with the knife.

It was my turn to scream, and scream I did. "You bitch!"

Ben twisted her arm just as I ran toward them, intending on pulling her off him, which sent the dagger flying. Naomi suddenly seemed to radiate a shock wave of light, knocking back everyone nearest her with a deep compression blast.

I stared in surprise as I got to my knees. She turned on me, a strange black and blue light glowing around her in a corona that filled me with dread. "Now I will be done with you!" she snarled, lifting her hand toward me.

"No!" Ben leaped forward to stop her, but he wasn't fast enough. A pulse of light shot out from her toward me. Without thinking, I raised the Vikingahärta, yelping when it glowed white for a moment as Naomi's dark power hit it.

It was her turn to stare in openmouthed amazement as I did a little dance, transferring the burning Vikingahärta from hand to hand until it cooled down enough to hold.

"You . . . What is that . . . ?"

"Luis!" David was back in human form now, Isaak

and Micah having been knocked out. Uncaring about his nudity, he jerked his pride member to the side, shaking him and speaking rapidly in an unfamiliar language.

I looked up from the Vikingahärta to Naomi, my eyes slits. "I have had enough of you." I raised the valknut, but rather than it blasting her with its power, it shifted in my hand, changing form, the three triangles rotating until they all slid into a new position.

"What in the name of all that's green and glorious . . ." *Did you see that? Did you see what it did?*

Are you all right? Ben was at my side in an instant, one arm around me as he looked not at the valknut but at my hand, before pushing me behind him as he faced Naomi. "Harm her, and you will die."

I looked up from where the Vikingahärta had settled into a new arrangement, surprised by the threat in Ben's voice.

"That goes for you, too," he added, looking at de Marco.

He looked furious. "Your woman matters little to me, vampire. Just keep her out of my way. You, however, I will see again." Without saying anything more, he spun around on his heel, shoved the slight man out of the way with a rude word, and strode off into the darkness. The second man shot us an unreadable look, and followed. Which left us with . . .

"Naomi," I said in a sickeningly sweet tone as I turned to face her. "I have a score to settle with you."

Francesca, do not, Ben warned me. *She is more powerful than you know.*

"It's not nearly so big as the one I have for you," she answered in similar style, smiling to boot. Her gaze dipped to the Vikingahärta for a few seconds, her jaw tightening as she lifted her chin and looked down her nose at Ben. "I am not done with you, either, lover."

I started toward her, but Ben wrapped an arm around me, pulling me into his side.

She laughed, and with sublime indifference to the fact that she was still naked, strolled casually over to her stuff, slipped on a discarded robe, and left with her clothing stuffed into her bag.

Chapter 16

I looked around at the remains of the orgy. Isaak was covered in blood oozing from deep claw marks and bites, and was half sitting up, groggily touching his chest. Micah was still out. David, who had left off shaking Luis, and had given him a couple of hard slaps, turned to face Ben. "He's drugged. He won't come out of it for a while. I don't know what they used on him, but it's effectively stripped him of his will."

I was filled with contrition. "I'm sorry I messed up the tyro," I said, leaning into Ben. *I feel horrible. Did I ruin everything?*

No. To my surprise, there was laughter in his mind. *On the contrary, I think you progressed us quite a bit.*

How so?

We now know that there is someone else working with the Agrippans. Who is this de Marco? You seemed to know him.

I'll tell you about him later.

"You didn't mess it up. Luis is safe, and although Ben has been outed, I believe that we should be able to learn what we wish to know from Luis once we can counteract the drugs he's been given. I might have wished for things to turn out a little differently, but no, you didn't ruin anything. On the contrary, I have much to thank you for, although Ben looks ready to hang me up by my intestines for letting you get involved."

"Not your intestines. Your balls," Ben answered with a dark look.

I nudged his side with my elbow. He made a big show of sighing. "When I was young, I used to dream of the day when I had a Beloved who would allow me to take care of her as I was born to do. I never imagined she'd be a woman who spurned that which I had to offer. You may stop looking daggers at me, Francesca. I know perfectly well that you are able to take care of yourself."

"Just as I know you can't help being overly protective. What are we going to do about them?" I nodded toward the two men.

"I'm sure David has plans for them." Ben lifted his head, his body language tense for a moment before he smiled and relaxed when Diego emerged from the trees.

"Oh, yes," David said, a note in his voice sounding remarkably like the low rumble of a lion. I edged closer to Ben. "I have plans." He said something to Diego in whatever language it was that therions spoke to each other, then tossed Ben a set of keys. "Take Fran home. We won't need you any more tonight."

Ben lifted an eyebrow. "Not even for the . . . interrogation?"

"You're not going to torture them!" I gasped.

"Torture? No." David shook his head.

"They will have to be questioned, though," Ben said.

"And they are bound to resist," Diego added, smiling as he nudged the still unconscious Micah.

David hauled Isaak to his feet and looped a nylon hand restraint around the latter's wrists. Isaak was aware enough to protest, but not to put up much of a fight. "Torture implies violence for no particular reason other than to cause pain. Our violence against Isaak and Micah will be for a completely different reason."

Isaak understood that well enough. His eyes widened and he started stammering out excuses as David, with a cheery wave at us, hauled him down the slope to the parking lot. Diego cuffed Isaak, and since he still wasn't conscious, simply grabbed his feet and hauled him naked after David.

I winced as Diego purposely dragged Isaak over a prickly looking bush. "I really don't want to know what they're going to do, do I?"

"No." Ben took my hand and led me on a diagonal line from the path the two shape-shifters had taken. "But David will not harm them if they tell him what they know. He's not a vindictive person." He stopped for a moment, making a little face. "Well, not normally."

David's car was parked a half mile away, hidden behind a ramshackle shed that was obviously used to store farm equipment. As we drove back to the Faire, I mused over what I'd seen.

Ben suddenly interrupted the silence that had filled David's car. "Francesca, I do not like this silent treatment. I know you are angry at me for what you saw, although in my defense, I would like to point out that you wouldn't have seen it if you hadn't insisted on spying on the tyro. I know you are angry about it, however, and I'd much prefer that you yell at me now rather than seething quietly."

I laughed at the outrageous picture he drew. "Since when have I ever seethed quietly?"

"You're not angry?" He shot me a quick look before negotiating a busy intersection in the middle of Brustwarze.

"Oh, I'm furious. But at Naomi, not you." I laughed again at the confused expression on his adorable face. "Ben, I'm well aware that you did everything humanly possible to keep from participating in the orgy. I don't like the fact that Naomi was all over your private parts with a familiarity that makes the hair on the back of my neck stand on end, but I do recognize the difference between her helping herself and you egging her on. You may rest your mind that I am not sitting here seething quietly, not that I think I could even if I wanted to. I'm not the quiet anger sort of person."

"I didn't remember you being so, but thought that, too, had changed."

I slid him a hesitant glance. He smiled. *No, I do not want you to change any more than you have. You more than please me the way you are, nonseething abilities and all. Did you mean what you said?*

Absolutely. I honestly don't know how to seethe.

His lips thinned for a few seconds. *You know what I mean. You said you were my Beloved, twice, before others. The first time I understand you were simply trying to establish your hold on me with Naomi. But you said the same thing to de Marco.*

"Your hearing is entirely too good," I told him, smiling to myself.

"I felt that!"

I looked down at where my hand rested possessively on his thigh, immediately pulling it into my own lap. "Oh, I'm sorry. I just . . . er . . . like to feel the muscles in your thigh move when you drive. I didn't mean to bother you when you're trying to concentrate."

"It's not bothering me at all." He placed my hand back on his leg, then shifted uncomfortably. I couldn't help but glance at his crotch when he gave a little wry laugh. "Not in the sense you mean. I was referring to the smug smile you tried to hide from me. You did mean it, didn't you?"

Inner Fran urged me to spill everything to him, every thought, every emotion, every intention, but I have not lived with her my entire life without having some ability to ignore her desires. Instead of yielding to her demands, I looked long and hard at what it would mean to say yes. My lifetime would be measured in centuries, not decades. My life would be bound to Ben's in ways that right now I had only the vaguest of understanding. It would be acknowledging that yes, in this case fate was right, and that rankled. I had fought so long and hard to make my own decisions and not do what people felt I should that it smacked of surrender to give in.

On the other hand, who's to say I didn't just decide that fate was right, and agreed to go along with it? There was the issue of Ben, too. I wanted him as in love with me as I was with him.

Ben waited patiently while I sorted through my thoughts, never once trying to touch me either mentally or physically. He was just there, a warm and comfortable presence who seemed to merge so well with me. I had a mental picture of the yin and yang symbol, with the two of us fitting together in a way that left us individuals, and yet greater as a sum total.

Did I mean what I said to de Marco?

Ben glanced at me, his expression wary.

Yes, I meant it. But I'm only one half of the equation, Ben. I think you need to make absolutely sure that your feelings—

I banged against the door as Ben jerked the wheel of the car and slammed on the brakes, the squeal of tires on cobblestones causing several people in the parade we'd almost plowed into to turn around and glare at us.

"Are you hurt?"

I was still shaking the stars from my eyes when Ben was out of the car and at my side, unbuckling the seat belt, running his hands quickly over my and shoulder. "No, not hurt, just kind of surprised. What on earth is going on?"

He closed my door and went around to the driver's side, backing up the car until he parked in front of a bakery. "I believe this is the Running of the Brunhildes. Francesca, I must have you."

"You must?"

"Yes. Right now." His jaw tightened, and I was immediately aware of a burning red need pulsing deep inside him.

"I thought you couldn't," I said, panting just a little at the instant arousal that inflamed my body at the thought of him touching me. *Tasting* me.

"I think Naomi trying to kill me is a sign that I can finally do what I've wanted to do for the last five years."

"Have sex in the middle of a parade?" I asked, looking around at the crowd packing the sidewalks in order to watch a race of people dressed in metal breastplates, winged helmets, and knee-length blond braids. The crowd cheered as a group of Brunhildes raced past, skirts hiked up, braids a-flying, each one bearing a fiery torch.

"Have sex *with you* in the middle of a parade," he corrected, turning first in one direction, then another. "Why aren't there any hotels in this damned town?"

"I don't know." I almost sobbed with the overwhelming need to have him feed from me. His compulsion to do so fed my desire, leaving my entire being tight and wanting and desperate for release. I looked around frantically, needing to be alone with him so he could feed, so we could complete all those things we'd started so many years ago.

Ben snarled something rude at the world in general. I didn't argue, just followed when he took my hand and wove his way through the throngs, avoiding a thundering herd of Brunhildes, moving in and out of the crowds, his eyes constantly searching for a potential spot.

"Whoever heard of a town without hotels?" I said, shivering when a fresh wave of desire washed from Ben to me. If I was desperate, he was nigh on frantic. We darted here and there, looking for a hotel, but it was slow going through the mass of people. It was as if the entire town had turned out to watch the race. "I'm seriously going to complain to the tourist board about this!"

Ben shoved past a group of men bearing spears and wearing long fur capes who were using the former to beat back the enthusiastic crowd as a fresh batch of Brunhildes took up the starting line, waiting for the starter to signal the beginning of this heat. Ben paused and pointed. "There. That's a hotel."

At his voice, one of the spear bearers turned from where he was poking at a businessman in a three-piece suit and horned helm. "Goddess!"

"Eirik?"

Ben pulled me after him to a red door with a small sign proclaiming it to be a hotel. Unfortunately, it was locked.

"Goddess Fran is here!" I heard Eirik cry over the noise of the cheering throng.

"Christos!" Ben swore, spinning around, his eyes burning with black light as they searched the street. "I am never coming to this town again!"

"Me neither! Ben . . . ," I whimpered. Just a little whimper, but it was a sign of how overwhelmed I was with his emotions, and my own need to Join with him. "There's got to be somewhere!"

"What is it you seek?" Eirik asked, looming up with Finnvid and Isleif. Eirik narrowed his eyes at Ben. Ben's jaw tightened at the sight of Eirik. The two men glared at each other for a minute, then I smacked Ben on the chest.

"A hotel. We want a hotel. Right now! Do you know where there is one that's not locked up for the race?"

Eirik gave Ben a long look. "You wish to rut with goddess Fran?"

"I wish to Join with her, not that it's any of your bloody business. Do you know of a hotel or don't you?"

"Joining is good," Isleif said, nodding. "Then the Dark One won't ever be able to leave the goddess. They should Join, Eirik."

Eirik was silent for a few seconds, then grudgingly nodded. "Aye, they should. But no hotels are open. The ale wench at the café told us that. Everyone is watching the race. We were helping."

"We were part of the elite Viking Brunhilde guard," Finnvid clarified.

"I thought you were going to spend the evening with Imogen?" I asked.

He scowled. "I was, but she told me she is having her woman's time, and unless I brought her sacrifices of chocolate and potato chips, I was not to go near her. I am a Viking! I do not fear a woman in her monthly time! I will spurn her until it is over and she has returned to desiring my rod."

"You should fear her," Ben said, momentarily distracted from his frantic search. "Imogen in that mood frightens even me."

"What are you boys doing here, though? In the parade?"

Eirik gestured toward the other two men. "We were given spears and fur capes, although the spears are not well made at all. The tip of mine fell off when I tried to thrust it through the chest of an interloper."

A wave of urgency washed over Ben and me. His body trembled as he fought with the hunger that overrode every other emotion. It filled both our minds until I thought I was going to scream.

"We have to find somewhere," I told the Vikings, clutching Ben. "He needs me."

"Turtle!" Eirik said decisively.

I gawked. "What?"

"Turtle. We will form a turtle. You will rut with the Dark One and Join. Our turtle will keep others from seeing you."

Immediately, all three men formed a semicircle around us, facing outward.

"You're crazy! I'm not going to have sex right here in front of a couple thousand people!"

Eirik glanced over his shoulder at me. "Why not?"

It says a lot about just how great Ben's need was that for a second I considered it.

"To hell with this," Ben snarled, and promptly kicked down the hotel door.

Naturally, there was no one in the lobby or at the reception desk. Ben leaned across the reception desk. This hotel's proprietors evidently favored the old ways, as evinced by the cubbyholes with keys for the rooms. Ben grabbed one of the keys, and with me in tow, hauled me up three flights of narrow stairs.

"Don't you think we should ask first?" I said as he unlocked the door, pushed me inside it, and locked it again, all without me having time to do more than blink. "What if the room you picked is occupied?"

He let me feel the emotions running rampant in him. His need was so overpowering, my knees buckled. He scooped me up in his arms, almost throwing me on the bed before following me down.

"We can ask later," I agreed, wrapping my legs around him as I kissed every available bit of exposed skin.

I managed to get his shirt off before a crash sounded at the door.

Ben was off me and at the door in an instant. Eirik stood at the door. "What the hell do you want?" Ben growled.

"We are guarding the door while you bed the goddess," Eirik said with much dignity.

"Aye, we're guarding." Finnvid belched as he held up a mammoth stein of ale. "You go right ahead and rut, Dark One."

"Guys—" I started to say, but didn't have a chance to finish when Ben slammed the door shut in their faces, quickly turning the lock and racing back to me, shedding his pants and shoes in the process.

"Ben! I can't do this with them outside listening to every squeak of the bed!" I protested.

Ben ripped my shirt off. He just ripped it right off my body, exposing my by now heated flesh to cooler air. As his head dipped into the curve between my breasts, his mouth a flame on my skin, I groaned and clutched his head. "Ignore me. I can do it just fine with them there. Please, Ben, do it. I feel like I'm going to shatter into a million pieces if you don't."

He didn't need any further urging. There was a brief sting, followed by a warm rush of pleasure as my blood flowed into Ben, satisfying a bone-deep craving in both of us. He let me feel just how profoundly he was shaken by the experience, and I knew to the very depths of my soul that I had made the right decision. We *were* meant to be together.

His tongue lapped at my breast as his hands busily removed the remainder of my clothes.

"That's it?" I asked, my body vibrating like a plucked string. I ran my hands up his arms, the velvety soft skin over hard muscles making me squirm almost as much as his hot breath on my now bared breasts. "You're full?"

"Oh, no," he said, his voice deep with wicked intent. "I've only begun."

"Good, because I don't want to have to invoke a comparison between you and my toys again."

His smile was both tender and incredibly arousing. "I can see I'm going to have to banish the ghost of your sex toys once and for all. But first . . ." An elongated canine tooth flashed in his mouth as he nipped his thumb. I stared at the welling drop of crimson on it. "Are you sure, Francesca? There will be no going back after this point."

I held his gaze for three seconds, then took his hand and sucked the tip of his thumb into my mouth.

He moaned and closed his eyes as I let my tongue swirl over his finger.

"Spicy," I said, releasing his thumb. His blood didn't taste at all like mine, which was coppery and unpleasant—his reminded me of a heavily mulled Christmas wine, filled with the rich notes of cinnamon and cloves. "Does this mean we're Joined? Do you have your soul back?"

"Yes, and not yet," he said, dipping his head down to claim my mouth. "My soul will be returned soon."

He made love to me slowly despite both our heightened sensitivity. I wanted him deep within me, but he resisted, using his hands and mouth and the incredible sensations he was feeling to push me to the edge three times before he finally let himself find pleasure. As his motions became more frantic, more wild, I arched up against him and demanded, *Do it again!*

He knew what I wanted. His teeth pierced the flesh of my shoulder as his hips pistoned into me, my body moving with him in a celebration of everything that we were together. I poured every ounce of love I had into him, wanting him to know that he meant the moon and stars to me. I knew he didn't love me, but at that moment, it didn't matter.

When did I ever say I didn't love you?

My body exploded into a supernova of rapture so intense it made little sparkles dance before my eyes. He groaned into my neck, his breath hot and hard and fast as he pumped wildly now, his hands fisted on the sheets beneath me, and at last his back arched and he surged his own form of life into me.

It took me a couple of minutes before I realized what he'd said. He lay heavy on me, our breathing erratic, his body crushing me into the soft mattress. I slid my legs along his, my hands stroking his back. Our bodies fit together so perfectly, I cherished the feeling of him lying on me, boneless and limp with satisfaction.

Am I too heavy?

No. I like it. It makes me feel like we're a whole.

We are a whole. He lifted his head from my neck. *Why do you think I don't love you?*

I touched his face, sliding my fingers through the slight stubble that was starting to darken his jaw. "Last year, I asked you if you loved me. You didn't answer. You can't lie to me, Ben, so I knew that meant you didn't want to answer in case it hurt my feelings. Have you . . . have your emotions changed?"

"No," he said, and my heart dropped into my gut.

His lips nibbled on mine, urging them to part. They did.

I've loved you for five years, Beloved. My feelings haven't changed, but they have grown deeper since you returned to me. You were beautiful and intelligent and strong before, but now there is a depth to you, a welcoming warmth and softness that draws me to you, binding me in ways I never imagined. You're everything to me, Francesca. You're my light and life and reason for being here. You bring me joy where there was only existence; hope when there was only despair. I loved you that first day when you wanted to kiss me, but were too nervous to try, and have continued to love you every day since.

Tears burned behind my eyes. *That is . . . oh, Ben. That's the most wonderful thing anyone has ever said to me. I love you, too. And I really messed up that first kiss, didn't I?*

He laughed, and slid out of me, rolling on his side, tucking me against him, his big hands warm and comforting on my hip and back. *Yes. But I greatly enjoyed your attempts.*

Chapter 17

"It's going to be dawn soon," Ben commented several hours later, as we approached the Faire.

"Then we'd better try summoning Loki now, before the sun comes up. I'd much rather do it when you're able to be with me."

I'm glad to know you don't shun my help.

I told you before—I've never shunned your help. I just don't like it when you try to take over things I'm supposed to do.

It's in my nature to do so, I'm afraid. I have to constantly remind myself that you wouldn't like it if I shielded you from trials.

My heart warmed at his admission, and by the fact that he was trying to accommodate himself to me just as I was to him.

When do you get your soul back?

I don't know. It will return at some point.

I glanced at him out of the corner of my eye. There was the faintest shadow of a thought behind those words, something he was keeping from me. I ran over the seven steps that Imogen had told me were needed for a successful Joining: all of them from the marking, protection, various bodily exchanges, and emotional trust had been completed. So why didn't Ben have his soul? I made a mental note to ask Imogen

"Goddess! Finnvid is sitting on my hot fried fish."

I turned around and looked in alarm at where Isleif was trying to dig something out from underneath Finnvid. "What hot fried fish?"

"The hot fried fish we pillaged from the hot fried fish shop." Isleif gave a mighty heave and held up a squashed blue and white box. "There, you see? It's squashed. The hot fried fish panini is as flat as a gelding's bollocks."

Finnvid looked guilty. "I didn't know that was there."

"By the gods, you didn't!" Isleif looked like he wanted to punch Finnvid, and since the three of them were crammed into the back of our borrowed car, I felt it best to quell any sort of squabble.

"I'm sure Finnvid didn't mean to sit on your late-night snack, although I would like to point out that you three managed to clean out that fast-food place's all-you-can-eat buffet, and shouldn't need late-night snacks to begin with. I thought the owner was going to call the cops on us until Ben handed over his hard-earned money to pay for the vast amount of fish and shrimp and strudel you three ate."

"You ate a lot, too," Finnvid pointed out.

I glared at him before turning to face the front again. "I was recovering my strength. And it's not polite to notice how much a woman eats. We get paranoid about that sort of thing."

"Aye, it does take a lot to recover from a three-hour rutting," Eirik allowed.

I sighed. "I told you guys to please move past that.

We weren't rutting the entire time. It just seems that way because you guys insisted on standing outside the door to our room."

"How many times did you hear the goddess yell?" Eirik asked Isleif, who was busily trying to reshape his squashed fish sandwich into something resembling the original form.

"Three."

"I heard four," Finnvid said, idly eating a potato wedge from Isleif's fish box.

"It wasn't anything like that!" I said, appalled and amused at the same time. I'd long since given up hope of ever having anything even remotely approaching privacy around the Vikings.

"It was four," Ben said.

I glared at him.

"Well, it was," he answered the glare.

"Possibly, but you don't have to encourage them."

"Four times?" Eirik pursed his lips and looked with new consideration at Ben, who I was annoyed to note had a remarkably smug air about him. "Just the goddess, or both of you?"

"Eirik!"

He raised his eyebrows at my outraged look. "If it was you who found pleasure four times, then that is nothing. But if the Dark One is able to rut with you four separate times in three hours, we wish to know how he does it. Even Finnvid can't empty his stones four times in three hours, and he's happy to rut with anything."

Finnvid adopted a modest expression.

I looked at Ben. "Do you think the Vikingahärta has enough power to zap them back to Valhalla?"

"I don't know, but it's definitely worth a try." Ben pulled up at the now empty parking field, smiled, then said something in what sounded to my nonlinguistic ears as Swedish.

What did you say? I asked as the Vikings piled out of the car, murmuring to themselves.

I said three.

Three?

Yes, three.

It took me a minute before I realized what he meant. I socked him on the arm, which just made him laugh and put the very same arm around me. *I'm sorry, Francesca. I assure you that I had no intention of kissing and telling. But there is a matter of my sexual prowess to be considered.*

Your sexual prowess is no one's business but ours, and to be honest, I'm amazed I can still walk.

He laughed again, and pulled me closer. *Shall we go to your mother's trailer and leave the summoning for tonight? I can't guarantee you that I'm up to another three times, but I believe I can at least make you yell out my name a couple of times.*

I really won't be able to walk if you do.

"Summons it is, then," he said, but he pinched my behind as he said it.

The sky was starting to tint rose by the time we assembled in the isolated spot in the far pasture. I held the Vikingahärta in both hands, ignoring the now faded yellowish smudges on the palm of my left hand.

I cleared my mind, focused on the image of Loki, and repeated the invocation.

At first, I thought nothing was going to happen. The air in front of us wavered a little, as if something might be resisting the summons, but after a half minute of anticipation, it finally shimmered into a swirly oval and parted to reveal the form of a man.

"What the hell do you think you're doing?" Alphonse de Marco snarled as his form solidified. "Why have you summoned me again, foolish mortal?"

"Bullfrogs!" *What is going on? Why do I keep getting him when I'm trying to summon Loki?*

I don't know, but I don't like it. "My Beloved is not mortal, nor did she summon you intentionally," Ben said, stepping in front of me. "What ties do you have to the god Loki?"

De Marco spat out a word that would shock a sailor, and dissolved into nothing.

"Houston, I think we have a problem," I said as I sat on a large rock and looked down at my hands. The Vikingahärta looked perfectly fine. I squinted at it in the light of Ben's lantern. Nothing seemed to be out of the ordinary. So why wasn't it working?

"Try it again," Ben suggested.

"What if we get Mr. Pissy again? I don't like him, Ben. He wanted to use you in all sorts of experiments, and I don't think they would be fun ones."

"I'm sure they wouldn't be, but you need have no fear. I will protect you from him."

I tipped my head to the side. "And I will protect you from him, right?"

He looked away.

"Right?"

"I am fully capable of taking care of myself, Francesca."

As am I, but we're a team now, remember? Partners. That means we watch out for each other's backs, and you can just stop thinking that you'll let me think I can protect you, but really will keep me out of any form of danger, because not only can I hear that, but it's cow cookies. Either we work together, Ben, or this just isn't going to be good for either of us.

He sighed. *I will do what I must to protect you—I can do no other. But I do appreciate you watching my back.*

That's not quite what I said, but it's a good enough start. I took a deep breath. "All right. Trying again. Everyone stand back."

The Vikings moved back a few paces, the three of them forming a semicircle in front of us. Ben moved closer behind me, his hand warm and reassuring on my back. *I have confidence in you, Beloved.*

A little glow of pleasure grew in me at his words. I used it to fuel my intentions, set the image of Loki foremost in my mind, and spoke the invocation. "By the fire that burns within thee, by the earth that feeds thee, by the air that hides thee, by the Vikingahärta that holds thee." As it did the other times, the valknut grew warm as I spoke the words. "Deceiver, slayer, trickster, betrayer. I invoke thee and call upon thee to descend here."

A spate of very irate Italian emerged from the air as a familiar figure formed in front of Ben and me. "I will not tolerate this again!" De Marco drew a symbol in the air that glowed blue black, then said as he disappeared, "Renata! Kill them!"

Ben shoved me hard to the side as from the depths of the shimmering air a woman's shape formed, then morphed into that of a russet-colored wolf. The wolf-woman leaped on Ben with a flurry of razor-sharp teeth and claws. I screamed as I flung myself onto her back, trying desperately to wrench her off him.

The Vikings' war cry startled me, giving Eirik the

break he needed to jerk me off of the wolf, his sword raised high in the air.

"Don't hurt Ben!" I shrieked, dancing around the battling pair. Renata the wolf had her jaws clamped on Ben's neck, clearly trying to rip out his jugular. Ben rolled them over, both hands on her massive wolf snout, trying desperately to pry off her slavering maw. Renata kicked out and they rolled over again, obviously hindering the Vikings' attempts to get at her. *Ben, stop! The Vikings will help you if you can hold her still!*

Easier said than done, he grunted, pain seeping into my head.

I yelled and clutched the Vikingahärta, willing it to blast the wolf to smithereens, but all it did was gently hum in my hands.

Now, Ben yelled as he rolled onto his back, a spray of blood arcing into the air, warning that she had hit an artery. I knew full well that Ben wouldn't die from just that, but if she managed to rip out his entire throat, he might not survive.

"Get her!" I shrieked to the Vikings.

They did, and with such efficiency that it was only a few seconds later that the bloodied corpse of a wolf lay crumpled next to Ben. I was on him in an instant, pulling back the remains of his tattered shirt to see how bad his injuries were.

The claw marks on his chest had a strangely familiar appearance, but it was the mangled and bloody flesh of his neck that kept my attention. I ripped off a piece of his shirt and held it to the arcing blood. *By the love of the goddess, Ben! You're hurt bad.*

No. I've lost some blood, but I'm all right. You can stop thinking all those morbid thoughts of spending the rest of your life mourning me, because it would take more than a therion in wolf form to kill me.

Do you want me to call Imogen?

No, but if you don't mind feeding me as soon as I'm done healing up the worst of these wounds, I would greatly appreciate it.

It took him almost a half hour to recover to the point where he could sit up. The wounds had long since closed, although he was weak from loss of blood.

"I'm sorry, Ben," I apologized as I sat on the ground with him, allowing him to lean on me as he fed from my upper arm. "If I hadn't tried summoning Loki, it wouldn't have gone all wrong, and we wouldn't have gotten de Marco again. It's my fault you were attacked."

"Mayhap you're cursed," Eirik said. The three Vikings had hauled off the corpse of Renata—who remained in wolf form, contrary to popular movie lore regarding shape-shifters—and returned to clean their weapons with handfuls of grass.

"Cursed? Me?"

"Aye. Why else would Loki refuse to come when you summoned him?"

I thought about that for a minute. "Could I be cursed?" I asked Ben.

He lifted his head from my arm, his tongue swirling across the bite mark. "I doubt it. I don't see a curse on you, and it would take a first-level demon or a demon lord to curse you and not leave some sign. Loki may have a grudge against you, but I doubt if a demon lord is after your blood as well."

"That's a relief, at least," I said, getting to my feet and holding on to him as he did the same. He had lost a lot of blood, but he didn't wobble at all.

Of course not. I'm a Dark One. We don't wobble.

I laughed at the outraged tone in the words.

"What the goddess needs to do is appease Loki," Isleif said.

"Get on his good side, you mean?" I shook my head. "He doesn't have a good side."

"He likes sacrifices," Eirik said as he replaced his sword in the baldric on his back. "He always has. A good sacrifice would bring him to you."

"What sort of a sacrifice?" I asked, thinking about the vast amounts of fast food the Vikings had once used to lure Loki into being summoned.

You can't seriously be considering that.

I wouldn't, but Ben, it worked before, when we were in Sweden, remember? The Vikings pillaged a McDonald's and brought all the stuff back and sacrificed it to Loki. Who knows, the man may have a fast-food addiction! It seemed to work before, so it can't hurt us to try it again.

"Let us think of people we would like to see sacrificed," Isleif suggested.

All three Vikings turned to look at Ben.

"Hey!" I glared at all of them. "Stop looking at him like that!"

Ben rolled his eyes.

"She's right," Isleif admitted. "Dark Ones are not easily sacrificed. It would take a decapitation at best, and the goddess would not be happy with us when we were done."

"The goddess isn't hideously happy right now, so if I were you, I'd think of something that isn't a living being to sacrifice. Maybe some of Isleif's squashed sandwiches would do the trick."

They perked up at that thought, and after asking for,

and being denied, the keys to David's rental car, they trooped off, making plans to find several packhorses so they could bring back enough sacrifices for both Loki and their own needs.

Ben and I walked slowly back to the trailer. He paused at the stairs, glancing across the common area to where Naomi's trailer sat. "I should get my things, but I believe I'll leave them until later."

"Good idea." Wearily, I unlocked the door and plodded my way up the three steps. "I know you don't want any, but I desperately need some coffee."

"You desperately need some sleep," he said, scooping me up effortlessly.

"Ben! I'm not a lightweight. Put me down before you hurt your owies."

He chuckled. It was a warm, intimate sound that made me feel all warm and fuzzy inside. "My owies are quite healed, thank you. And even if they weren't, I'd be capable of carrying you to a bedroom. I can feel how tired you are, Francesca. You've given me a lot of blood, and you need rest."

I protested only long enough to use the bathroom before allowing him to put us both to bed. "If you're going to want to—"

"We will not make love," he interrupted, pulling me over to him so I was half draped across him. "I wish for you to rest."

I slid my hand down his belly, encountering warm, hot skin that belied that statement. "You do, huh? What's this, then?"

"I didn't say I didn't want to, I said we would not indulge ourselves. Although I would greatly enjoy bringing you pleasure as many times as you could stand, you are tired, and it's better you rest."

"Now I know why Dark Ones and their Beloveds are immortal. Any man who can make love three times a day has to be."

A deep rumble of laughter formed in his chest as he kissed the top of my head, one hand caressing my back. "I admit that I was a bit enthusiastic earlier today, but I have waited for you for five years. It's going to take me a while to work through all that anticipation."

"You'll hear no complaints from me," I said, snuggling into his side. My eyes were drawn to the still faintly visible marks on his chest. I traced a claw mark. "Is this what happened to you in Sweden?"

"No. Your mother would have murdered me."

I pinched his nipple as he laughed in my head. "Were you attacked by a therion that time in Sweden when you were almost killed?"

"Yes." The laughter in him died, replaced by a great sadness. "The woman who attacked us was, for lack of a better word, feral. I suspect she was also under some sort of a compulsion placed on her by de Marco, although what kind I don't know. Perhaps it has something to do with the experiments Naomi mentioned. He may have found a way to bind therions to his will."

"Why didn't you tell me then?" I asked, my mind on the events in the past.

"Because it was one of David's pride who attacked me. I had to kill him, and notify David. There were many disappearances at the time, and all therions were suspicious, so I sent him word of what happened with a sign to know it was really from me."

"Your cross," I said, sitting up to examine the beautiful Celtic knot cross he wore.

"Yes. David recognized it, and knew the note was

from me. He came to Sweden immediately afterward. We searched for two months for the person who had turned his pride member feral, but were unsuccessful."

"I don't think I've ever heard of a religious vampire," I said.

"I'm not religious. The cross was my mother's. It has many good memories attached to it."

I touched the cross with one finger, allowing it to speak to me. Mostly it carried Ben's emotions—pain, frustration, and patience—but there was also a faint image of a woman, filled with happiness and love for her son. "Your mom loved you very much. She was proud of you. She was happy you weren't—" I stopped.

"Like my father?"

I frowned at his chest, trying to sort out the emotions. "Yes. But at the same time she loved him, too. But he didn't love her."

"No. My father is not a loving man."

"Is?" I sat up and looked at him. "He's still alive?"

Ben's eyes opened, surprised. "Yes, of course he is. I told you that Dark Ones are hard to kill."

"Oh. I just thought . . . accidents and such. Surely sometimes you guys are killed?"

"We are, both accidentally and intentionally. But both take some doing."

"Good. Where is your father?"

"South America. He prefers young, nubile women and has no problem finding them there."

I wanted to ask Ben a gazillion questions about his dad, but decided that would have to wait for another time. There was another, more pressing matter I was concerned with. "My mother. We don't seem to be getting any closer to figuring out what's going on with her.

Who is she in love with? Why hasn't she called me to tell me she's so gaga about this guy? And just where the Hottentots is she?"

He pulled me tight, both arms around me. "You torment yourself needlessly. She is as strong as you are, Beloved. We will work together to uncover the truth."

I fell asleep with that thought easing my worry, and Ben's comforting presence surrounding me.

Chapter 18

"Good afternoon, sleepy head. Can I just say how much good it does my ego to know that although you might be Mr. Three Times, such devotion to your duty caused you to sleep like a rock for seven solid hours?"

Ben, looking wonderfully sleepy with mussed hair and manly stubble upon his cheeks, blinked bleary-eyed at me and sat down across from me at the tiny table where I was having lunch. "I woke up and you weren't there."

"I woke up about an hour ago. Unlike you, I have to use the bathroom. And I've been thinking."

He ran a hand over his face, blinking at me. "Oh?"

"It's about Naomi."

He grimaced.

"Yeah, I feel the same way, but I think we need to talk about her."

"If it's about the tyro—"

"No, I told you that I thought you did everything you could to keep that situation under control. It's about Sweden. Or rather, the attack on you there five years ago. Was Naomi's group a part of that?"

Ben rubbed his stubbly chin thoughtfully. The sound of his fingers rasping against his whiskers sent little skitters of electricity down my back. "I assume they were. It is a chilling thought to imagine two such groups preying on the therion population of Europe."

"Right. And since de Marco is . . . Well, I don't know what he is, other than nasty and badass and he had sex with my mother thirty years ago. But since he's all that, I say we tackle Naomi."

Ben shot me a look that said I had orangutans in purple tutus dancing on my head. "Who had sex with your mother?"

"De Marco. Oh! I never told you about that, did I?" I got to my feet and hurried to the bedroom, filling him in on how Peter and I had found the birth certificate. "And you can see right there that his name is Alphonse de Marco."

Ben examined the birth certificate. "It appears genuine. But your mother?"

"I know. It means I have a half sister, too. Look at the dates, Ben. Mom was sixteen at the time, and this Petra person is nine years older than me, and yet I've never heard of her. My grandparents never mentioned her, and there're no family pictures or anything. Just this."

"Odd." Ben stared sightlessly at the paper, his fingers tapping absently on it as he thought. "I wonder if there's a connection between it and your mother's disappearance."

"I thought of that this morning, too," I said, leaning into him when he wrapped an arm around me. "But I don't see why he'd want to seduce her. Why now? She's been kicking around Europe for the last five years, so if he was just waiting for her to come around the area, that doesn't make sense. And she's been divorced from my dad for eight years, so if he was waiting for that, it doesn't fly, either. Not to mention the fact that Mom doesn't suffer fools gladly, and if she broke up with him once, she probably wants nothing more to do with him."

"I think we should consider the possibility that perhaps your mother has simply found a man she loves," Ben said gently, kissing my arm.

Instantly, a dull red throb woke up inside him.

"Hungry?" I asked in my best sex kitten voice.

"For you? Always."

I slid sideways onto his lap. "I had my breakfast, so I guess it's only fair you have yours."

The look in his eyes could have melted cement. "You know what will happen if I feed off you now."

"Lovemaking so incredibly hot, it'll banish further references to my toys?"

"Lovemaking so incredibly hot, it'll make you forget you ever had toys."

I squirmed delightedly at the thoughts he was sharing. "Oooh! But that sounds like it might take a while. Especially that one. The *entire* Kama Sutra?"

He smiled just before his teeth pierced the upper slopes of my breast. *I've always wanted to try all of them. But since you wish for us to locate your mother, I will content myself with simply doing this.*

"Do what . . . Holy Swiss on rye! Ben! You don't mean you're going to . . ." My entire body went up in a fireball of excitement as his fingers slid up underneath the midthigh-length skirt I wore (with the secret hope that he would admire my legs), and proceeded into restricted areas. I lolled back against him, my mind flooded with both the sensations of him feeding and the ecstasy that his fingers brought as they danced an illicit dance.

It took longer than he anticipated for us to leave the trailer, mostly because by the time I had recovered from the experience of his magic fingers I felt a little reciprocation was in order, and then we both wanted a shower, and that meant much soaping up of each other, with the inevitable conclusion.

"I am so glad you have strong back muscles," I murmured an hour later as I walked down the stairs of the trailer. "I never knew a shower could be so very satisfying. Ready to tackle your girlfriend?"

Ben angled one of my old baseball caps so it shaded his face from the midday sun and turned up the collar of his leather jacket. "You'll have to do better than that if you wish me to rise to your bait."

I know how to make you rise, I said with a little mind leer as we dashed across the common area to Naomi's trailer.

You do, and you're going to if you keep thinking about that shower. Francesca, I know you wish to help, but I really would prefer that you do not come with me to Naomi's.

If you think I'm going to go sit at Imogen's while you are locked up with that psychotic nympho, you're bonkers. I'll knock. You keep your hands in your pockets.

Naomi didn't answer when I knocked politely on her door. Nor did she when I pounded on it and yelled for her to open up. By the time Peter and Kurt appeared to see what all the noise was about, I was beginning to suspect that all was not right.

"Think she's gone to town?" I asked Ben as Peter approached with a spare set of keys.

"She might have." His gaze, as clear as honey, met mine. "Particularly if she wished to meet with someone in particular."

The question was made moot once we saw the trailer. Drawers had been yanked open and were tossed willy-nilly around the living area. Papers were strewn around in utter disarray. Cupboards spilled food onto the counters and floor, as if someone had carelessly knocked stuff aside in an attempt to snatch up a few desired items.

"She's gone," I said, looking around as Peter exclaimed in German. "Without telling anyone, I bet."

"Most likely. My things are in there," Ben said, heading for the bedroom. "I'll just get them and—"

"What a mess." I stepped carefully over spilled sugar, distastefully eyeing the chaos. "Just like her to go leaving as much trouble for people as possible. Does she own this trailer, Peter?"

"No, it is mine. I rent it to people when they do not have their own." He looked as dismayed by the prospect of losing a tattoo and piercing professional as he did at the task of cleaning up the debris.

I glanced toward the partly open bedroom door, slowly picking my way down the aisle to it. "Did she take your things, too, Ben?"

He stood just inside the door, not moving, looking across the bed at the wall.

"Ben?"

I stepped into the room and froze. Blood splattered the far wall in a fine spray at the top, with heavier smears lower down. Bloody handprints that dragged downward set up a chill in my gut.

Ben shifted, and I saw the body of a man lying half on the bed, the upper part of his torso having slid in the space between the bed and wall.

"Merciful goddess!" I gasped, starting forward. Ben caught me and pulled me back. "Who is it?"

"Luis."

I stared at the lower legs of the man, his brown corduroy pants soaked with blood. "David's Luis?"

"Yes."

"How horrible." It was horrible, too. Although I didn't know Luis, and what I had seen of him at the tyro hadn't been such to make me very sympathetic to him, he was a member of David's pride, and I liked David. Beyond that, no one deserved to die in such a violent way.

Ben pulled out his cell phone and started entering a text message, no doubt to David. Behind me, Kurt entered the room, his shocked intake of breath and murmured oaths bringing Peter.

"Who is it?" the latter asked after swearing in German.

"It's Ben's acquaintance," I told him before asking Ben, "Do you think Naomi killed him?"

"No." He finished texting and put the phone away in his jacket pocket before herding us all out of the room. "He was killed by another therion."

"Another therion?" Peter asked, looking extremely wary. "What is happening here? Are we in the middle of a therion territorial dispute?"

Ben briefly explained the circumstances regarding both Naomi and Luis, ending with, "I don't think this has anything to do with territory. It's my belief that this man de Marco has somehow enslaved some therions, and is using them to attack their own kind." He held Peter's gaze for several seconds before adding, "I don't think the mortal police should be informed of what's happened."

Peter released a long breath, shaking his head. "I don't like it, but no, I agree, that would mean much trouble for the Faire. It will mean calling in the watch, though, and they are almost as bad."

"At least they will understand about therions," Ben said. He thought for a moment, then went back into the bedroom, emerging with a small satchel. "There is no sense in having my clothing confiscated by the watch. You will call them?"

Peter nodded. Kurt asked, "Will we have to close the Faire for a few days?"

"Possibly." Peter rubbed his hand over his face. "And just as we were doing our best business. Ah, well, there is no help for it. I will call the watch. They will wish to talk to you, Benedikt."

"I'm sure they will. You can tell them we'll be here."

"Actually . . . no, we won't." Ben and the others looked at me in surprise. I gave a feeble little smile. "I was going to tell you about the epiphany I had this morning, but then you got up, and we . . . er . . . Never mind."

"Epiphany about what?" he asked as we left the trailer. I was only too happy to do so, the image of all those clutching bloody handprints on the wall one that would remain with me for a very long time. Peter and Kurt hurried off to call in the watch, the paranormal equivalent of a local police force, or so Imogen had once told me.

"The Vikings came back with their sacrificial offerings for Loki this morning." I stopped next to the side of the trailer, automatically shielding Ben with my body as he stepped into a narrow patch of shade.

"Where are your troublesome trio?" he asked, looking around.

"They're out where we tried summoning Loki, ostensibly to ready the area, but I heard Isleif telling Eirik that the woman he was with last night didn't like his thong tan lines, so I suspect they're really out there working on their all-over tans."

Ben's gaze was steady on mine. "Do I need to point out just how odd it is that you have three Viking ghosts who enjoy nude sunbathing?"

"Not at all. Nor do you have to mention the fact that their choice of sacrificial offerings is on the eccentric side."

He closed his eyes for a few seconds. "Do I want to know?"

"I have them right here." I pulled up onto a nearby table a small foam cooler that Eirik had presented me with a few hours earlier. "Sacrificial item number one: a pink bunny vibrator." I held up the adult toy, flicking it on. It buzzed loudly, the pink rabbit moving up and down against the shaft of the toy in a manner that could only be described as obscene.

Ben stared at it. "You're joking."

"Alas, no. Item number two: a magazine featuring breasts that could in no way have their origins in nature." I waved a bright red magazine with the title *Busen-Extra* in front of him. His eyes widened.

"Good god. No, they don't look natural at all."

I quickly tossed the magazine back into the cooler, straightening my shoulders as I did so. Ben didn't say anything about the fact that the move thrust my breasts out, but I did see a tiny little smile form. "The final sacrificial item is over there." I pointed to the end of the trailer, where a huge four-foot-tall triangular tube leaned against the hitch. The upper part of the package was torn, exposing shiny foil.

"A giant Toblerone?" Ben asked, squinting at it. "It looks partially eaten."

"It is. Evidently Finnvid got a bit peckish on the way back to the Faire."

Ben looked from the cooler to the chocolate to me. "They're insane."

"I admit that they seem that way, but they are Vikings, and to them, these are desirable things. Eirik and Finnvid had to wrestle the magazine away from Isleif."

Ben's eyes narrowed on me. "Why aren't you more upset about this?"

"Because of the epiphany I had."

"Ah, yes, that. What was it about?"

"Well, it was obvious to me that there's no way on this good green earth that Loki would want a vibrator and a porn magazine. The chocolate might sway him, but going on the assumption that he can get as much chocolate as he wants, I started thinking about what would actually tempt him to answer a summons. And then I hit on it, the one thing that would be sure to draw him out from wherever he's hiding."

Ben thought for a moment, enlightenment dawning in his eyes. "That might do it."

"I thought it would. Do you mind taking me there? I looked it up and it's about an hour's drive."

"I don't mind, but I had wanted to talk to David about de Marco." Ben pulled out his cell phone, frowning at it. "He hasn't answered my text message."

"I'm sure he will. I'd really like to talk to my mom, Ben. I need to know for sure if Loki is involved with her or not."

He pulled me against his chest and gave me a quick kiss. "Then we will go to find Tesla immediately. Let me get a different hat from Imogen's trailer, since mine is covered in blood, and then we will leave."

"Great. I'll go get the Vikings."

He paused halfway across the common area. "Do you have to?"

"They were sent to help me with Loki. I assume that Freya knew what she was doing, and they will help me somehow. I admit I can't quite see how yet, but I'm sure they'll be helpful. Kind of."

Ben rolled his eyes and proceeded on to Imogen's trailer. I toddled out to the far pasture, yelling from a few hundred yards away for the Vikings to put on some clothes so we could tackle Loki.

"You will offer him the sacrifices after all?" Eirik asked as he trotted up, clad in a pair of biker shorts that molded to his body in a way that had me averting my eyes.

"No, I really do think that you guys can enjoy the sacrifices yourselves." The vision of the obscene rabbit came immediately to mind. I banished it, along with any ideas of how the Vikings might care to use it. "We're going to a small horse farm about an hour away. Which means we're going to need to get you guys transport, since I noticed that David reclaimed his car sometime during the early hours of the morning. Perhaps Imogen would drive you. . . ."

"Not until Finnvid is done spurning her," Eirik interrupted, and then added loftily, "We will have our friends take us to this horse farm."

"Friends? What friends?" I asked, unable to keep from being a bit suspicious.

"Does it matter?" Eirik asked, pushing me toward the trailers. "Where is the town?"

I told him the name of it, and gave rough directions gleaned from a quick map search on my cell phone.

"We will be there, goddess. In an hour?"

"It'll take you that long to get there. Let's say two hours—I want to talk to Imogen before we leave."

"Remind her that I am spurning her woman's time," Finnvid said as he marched off with the others. I thought for a moment of pointing out that the towel he'd wrapped around his lower half wasn't exactly clothing, but given some of the bizarre costumes I'd seen in town, I figured no one would notice.

Ben was giving Imogen a rundown of all that had happened in the last twelve hours. She sat huddled over a cup of tea, a large bottle of painkillers next to her.

"Fran! Thank the goddess. Please tell Benedikt he may touch me."

I blinked at her. "I beg your pardon?"

"My belly. The cramps are very bad this time, and he can ease them, only he said he wouldn't without you saying it was all right, which is just silly because I am his sister! You can't mind if he rubs my belly."

"Of course I don't mind." I looked at Ben with a new appreciation. "You can make cramps go away?"

"I told you that I have some healing powers with people close to me." Imogen hurried over to a white leather couch, lying back on it with her hands on her upper stomach.

"If you had told me five years ago that I never had to have cramps again . . . well, things would have been different, that's all I'm saying." I watched with interest as Ben knelt next to Imogen, placing both hands on her abdomen, kneading gently. She tensed up for a moment, then sighed and relaxed.

"Oh, that is so much better than the medicine," she purred, a blissful look stealing over her face. "Thank you, Fran."

I laughed. "Don't thank me. Thank Mr. Magic Hands. You are totally on call for cramp duty with me, Ben. I always have a couple of hellish days."

He smiled, lifted Imogen's hand to kiss it, then rose and went to find his hat as Imogen chatted about the situation with Naomi.

"Do you wish for me to come with you?" she asked as she put away the pain meds and poured me a cup of tea.

"I would prefer you stay and talk to the watch for us," Ben told her, putting on a black leather fedora that matched his distressed jacket. "They will no doubt be here in the next hour."

"What do you want me to tell them?"

"Just that we'll be back later. We have to find where Miranda is staying, and then David will no doubt wish to locate Naomi."

"I think you should leave her to the watch," Imogen said, her face tight with worry as she reached out, like she was going to touch Ben's shoulder, but stopped, casting me a sidelong glance.

Why is she acting like I'm the queen of jealousy? She has to know I'm not going to get mad if she touches you.

You are my Beloved now, in deed as well as name. Moravian women do not, as a rule, touch Dark Ones who have a Beloved.

Why?

It is a sign of disrespect.

"Imogen," I said, interrupting Ben as he started to explain that David would not tolerate allowing the watch to mete out the justice David felt was his. "I am not jealous of your relationship with Ben. I am not a typical Beloved. If you want to pat him on the arm, or shoulder, or kiss him on the head like you always used to do, then you go right ahead and do it. We might be a couple, but that doesn't mean you can't be his big sister."

"Oh, Fran!" she cried, hugging me with a strength that belied her petite size. "Thank you for accepting Benedikt! You are the best thing that could ever have happened to him. To us. I'm so happy!"

"That's why you're crying?" I said, laughing as I hugged her back.

"I always get weepy at this time of the month," she answered, sniffling, then reached out to hug Ben. "I will stay here and handle the watch for you. Go and find Miranda. And you will call me if you need my help, yes?"

We promised to do just that. The drive to the farm where Tesla lived could be a bit hairy at times, since Ben didn't have a helmet to protect his face from the sun, although he did have leather gloves to keep his hands from being burned. But his face . . . I worried about that until Imogen bestowed on him a black silk scarf and pair of wraparound sunglasses. He wrapped the former around his lower face, slid the latter into place, and with my arms firmly around him, we headed off on his motorcycle to a farm region north of Munich.

Tesla was an elderly white horse, a Lipizzan I had saved from being turned into whatever it is people turn horses into these days—dog food, I presumed. Just how Tesla came to be with me is an odd story, and even odder is the mystery that surrounds him, a mystery I never did have time to fully investigate. But strangest of all is his relationship to Loki, one that I would never have imagined in a million years if Loki himself hadn't explained it to me.

"Mikaela!" I greeted the woman with short black hair as she emerged from a neat little house surrounded by pastureland. She was followed by two little girls, both of whom had inherited her husband Ramon's copper hair and quiet, studied demeanor.

"Fran! And Benedikt! What a surprise. Why didn't you tell me you were coming? What am I thinking—you must come out of the sun, Benedikt."

"It's been a long time since that summer when Circus of the Darned joined up with the Faire," I said, following her back into the house, picking up the littler of the girls and giving her a kiss on the head. "So this is my namesake?"

"Yes, that is our Fran. And this is Abigail, our older. You remember me telling you about Fran, don't you, girls?"

It took a bit to conduct all the greetings, admiration of Mikaela's girls, and exchanging of news, but at last Mikaela put little Fran down for a nap and ushered us out to a gently sloped pasture.

"Do you and Ramon still do the sword swallowing?" I couldn't help but ask, noting she was apparently early on in another pregnancy.

"Ramon does sometimes, for special events, but me . . ." She patted her tummy. "My sword-swallowing and chain-saw-juggling days are over. I don't regret the decision, though, so you needn't look so sympathetic. We are very happy here with the horses, and we are finally starting to make some money, so all is good."

"I'm glad to hear it. I certainly have been grateful you decided to run a horse farm, because I know Tesla is in good hands with you."

"He's been no trouble. He's quite the gentleman, and has even allowed Abigail to ride him a few times. Walking only, because he is so very old, but she loves him, as you can see."

Ahead of us was a pasture with a clutch of horses dozing in the sun. Abigail, who my mental arithmetic worked out to be almost five years in age, had clambered through the fence and was stroking the face of a dirty gray horse.

"I'm sure Tesla will be happy to see you, although Ramon will be annoyed he has missed you. He went into town to pick up feed. And oh, we have not had time to bathe Tesla so he would be clean for you!"

"That's okay," I said and laughed. "I don't demand cleanliness in horses."

Tesla seemed to remember me, although it had been many years since I had left him in Ramon and Mikaela's capable hands. He snuffled my chest, then my hips, evidently looking for treats, blowing out a sad breath when he found nothing.

"I'm sorry, old guy. I'll bring you something later," I murmured in his ear, stroking the still thick-muscled curve of his neck. *He looks the same, doesn't he? He looks like he hasn't aged at all. Just a little creakier, maybe.*

He is Loki's descendant. I suspect that gives him a bit more staying power than other horses.

True, although you know, I really do prefer not thinking about Loki going all wild and wacky and turning himself into a mare. It's bad enough that his descendant is a horse, but to know he was once a mare who got knocked up? Just a bit too freaky for comfort.

Ben laughed. *There are many things about Loki that are too freaky for comfort.*

Amen to that.

I'm surprised that you're not more ecstatic about see-

*ing Tesla. In fact, I assumed that would be the first thing
you did when you got here.*

I peered at Ben over Tesla's gently bobbing head as I
scratched the base of his ears. *I would have, if I wasn't
in weekly contact with Mikaela via e-mail. And she
sends me lots of pictures. And sometimes videos of Tesla
wandering around, or of the girls and Ramon with him.
Last year, she put a Christmas wreath over his head and
sent me an MP3 of the girls singing Christmas carols to
him.*

*There is something wrong with the fact that you are
more concerned about your horse than me,* he said in a
disgruntled tone as he walked around to stand at my
side.

I licked his lower lip.

"If you can wait, Ramon should be back in another
hour," Mikaela said. "I do not like the idea of you trying
to deal with Loki with just the two of you. He is the
trickster."

"We have backup coming. In fact . . ." I squinted
toward the house, where a large, colorfully painted bus
pulled up. "I believe they just arrived. Monkeys flinging
poo, does that say what I think it says?"

"Flying Maraschino Brothers," Ben read the psyche-
delic letters painted on the side of the bus, which was
covered in neon-bright peace symbols, flowers, and
strange, half-animal, half-people creatures.

"It's like a bad acid trip on wheels," I said, watching
with amazement when the door to the bus opened and
people poured out of it whooping and squealing and
turning somersaults and backflips all the way out to us.

"It's like a bad acid trip, period," Ben said, his eyes
wide as he took in the bright red and black costumes the
people wore, some sort of odd Gypsy-belly-dancer-

Cossack hybrid with voluminous trousers that were tucked into boots that ended at the knee, gold sashes around their waists, and little red bolero jackets edged in black fringe that spun and whirled as the acrobats—they couldn't be anything but acrobats—whooped their way out to us.

I eyed three of the booted, trousered, boleroed people as the entire group stopped in front of us with a yell and dramatic pose.

"Goddess! We have come. And these are our friends, mummers who are here to help us."

Chapter 19

"Eduardo Maraschino," one of the acrobats said, with a deep bow. "These are my brothers, Herve, Manuel, and Itzik."

As he spoke each name, the men bowed. I raised an eyebrow at the last one. He was black, and wore a yarmulke. He grinned, and said in a heavy Bronx accent, "The others were adopted."

"Gotcha. You guys are performing in Brustwarze for the big celebrations?"

"Yes, we have three shows a day," Eduardo said, twirling the big mustache that curled up in dramatic fashion from either side of his upper lip. "We are the acrobats most popular, and many womens crave our bodies."

"Not as many as want our rods," Finnvid said with an insouciant little smile.

"Aye, we won the wager," Eirik said. "We had eight lusty wenches, and you only had five."

Eduardo's smile slipped a notch. "That is because Itzik was sick. If we had had him with us, he would have brought in many more womens."

"Ahh, so that's how you guys met Eirik and his men," I said, nodding when Mikaela, with a long look at the acrobats, took her daughter and returned to the house. "Well, I really appreciate you bringing them up here, but I wouldn't want you to miss any of your performances. Or attentions of the many women who apparently lust after you."

"No, no, we have made the wager most profound with the Eirik Redblood, and we always pay our wagers—do we not, my brothers?"

Herve and Manuel mumbled something in Spanish. Itzik grinned again. "Taking out this Loki sounds like fun. Let's have at him."

I looked from Itzik to the other three men. "You guys know about Loki? You're not wigged out by the idea of an ancient Norse god?"

"We know of him," Eduardo said with a little head toss. "We had dealings with his son, Nori, a few years ago."

"It will be a pleasure taking care of him," Itzik added as he cracked his knuckles.

What do you think? I asked Ben.

He gave a mental head shake. *I don't suppose they will provide any assistance against Loki, but they can't hurt, either.*

Loki can be unpleasant, though. And I hate to involve innocent people in something that could be dangerous to them. I think we should do this with just the five of us.

It is your decision, Beloved.

It took some doing to convince the acrobats that Loki posed too much of a threat for them to remain, but once Ben pointed out that they wouldn't be able to perform—acrobatically or sexually—if Loki injured them, they gracefully withdrew, waving farewell and wishing us luck.

"What odd sorts of people you know," I told the Vikings as the eye-popping bus drove off.

"Odd how?" Eirik asked, genuinely puzzled.

"It doesn't matter. Let's get going."

Ben led Tesla over to a section of the pasture where we would be alone.

You'll watch over him while I do this?

No. I'll watch over you.

I let him feel just how much that irritated me. *I want him protected from Loki. I love Tesla!*

Not as much as I love you.

Irritation vanished in an instant, its place taken by the warm glow of Ben's love. *That is not playing fair at all.*

Perhaps not, but it's the truth. Tesla will be fine, Francesca, so long as you are safe.

He had a point, drat him. "Everyone ready? Good. Here we go."

Ben stood beside me, not touching me, but the tense air about him, and the watchful look around his eyes, told me he was ready to spring into action should the need arise. Behind us stood the three Vikings, their weapons in hand.

I placed one hand on Tesla's neck, the warm solidness of him giving me a measure of comfort, while Ben's presence provided me with confidence. "Fire burns thee, earth feeds thee, air hides thee, Vikingahärta holds thee. Deceiver, slayer, trickster, bet—"

I didn't even get the last word out before Loki was suddenly there, in front of us.

"Loki Laufeyiarson!"

The tall, thin man with fading red hair turned astonished brown eyes on me as I spoke. The astonishment quickly turned into calculation as his gaze flickered to Tesla.

"I bind you to the honor of the Vikingahärta, which you yourself created."

"You!" he said in a manner that made me think of a cat hissing. "Why do you torment me so?"

"I am tormenting *you*?" I gawked at him in an outraged sort of way that he totally missed.

"You taunt me with the presence of my own descendant! That is a torment which I cannot tolerate! Begone, Beloved!"

His image started to fade. *Ben! What do I do? He's leaving!*

You have the power to summon him, Francesca. You have the power to keep him here. Use the valknut.

I clutched the Vikingahärta in a hand that was still slightly numb and pulled hard on its power, willing Loki to remain.

"You think you have power over me, little human?" he said, laughing, but an indescribable look crept over his face as he stopped fading. He looked like he was standing in a dense patch of fog, his figure kind of wispy and indistinct, but after a few seconds of that he solidified again and marched toward me, his jaw tense and his hands fisted. "The Vikingahärta has the power to summon me, not keep me. What have you done to it?"

I held it up. "I did nothing to it. But it got zapped by an Agrippan and the triangles shifted."

He stared at it for a moment, then turned a haughty scorn-filled gaze upon me. "I begin to regret my leniency on you earlier. Very well, since you have summoned me, what sacrifices have you made in my name?"

"Er . . ." I tried to think of what I had with me at the moment—other than the Vikingahärta and Tesla—that Loki might be willing to accept as a sacrifice. "I didn't know I was supposed to bring one. That is, I know we've used them in the past, but I wasn't aware they were mandatory."

"No sacrifices?" His red eyebrows rose.

"Don't have any on me at the moment, no."

"No boons meant to sweeten my favor?"

"Er . . . sorry."

"No gifts to honor me as the greatest of all the Aesir?" His hair stood on end as he spoke.

Tesla suddenly flicked his head up and snorted at him.

"I'm afraid I don't have—"

"We have the sacrifices, goddess!"

Loki sniffed in an irritated manner, his jaw set pugnaciously as Eirik stepped forward, pulling out of his voluminous shirt a purple plastic object. "O father of lies, O bale-smith, O Loki the sly, in the name of the goddess Fran, the goddess Freya, and Odin All-Father, we bring to you these highly valuable sacrifices, which we gladly make in your name that you might bestow your favor upon us." Eirik lovingly caressed the purple vibrator, then laid it at Loki's feet, bowing three times as he backed up to where the other Vikings stood.

Oh dear goddess. Not the sex toy! Loki is going to go ballistic!

Loki spared it a brief glance. "Have one. What else have you brought me?"

He has one? I asked Ben, astonished.

I really think it's best you don't ask.

Agreed. But still . . . Loki has girl toys? Who'd have thought?

You are speaking of a man who was a pregnant mare at one point in his life.

Point taken.

"I bring unto you captured images of many large-breasted women," Isleif said, presenting the magazine.

"Bah," Loki said, looking down his long narrow nose at Isleif. "I have many such magazines."

"This one has twin double-D cups in the centerfold," Isleif pointed out.

Loki's lips pursed as he took the magazine. "I accept this gift. What else have you brought me?"

Okay, that's it. I'm just going to stop being surprised by anything he says from here on out.

Ben laughed in my head.

"We have the chocolate most fine, hewn by many peasants in the Toblerone province," Finnvid said as he offered up the now yard-high stick of chocolate.

Loki looked at it, then at Finnvid. "Someone has eaten half of my chocolate sacrifice."

"Turks," Finnvid said without batting so much as one single eyelash. "Turks tried to take your fine sacrifice, many Turks, clad in the finest steel, riding elephants, and with legions of bowmen, but we slayed them and retrieved your sacrifice before they could completely consume it."

"Turks love chocolate," Loki said darkly, taking the giant candy bar. "All right, I accept your offerings. Since it is clearly your wish to humiliate me before my descendant, you will tell me now what it is that you desire of me."

"I'm not humiliating you before Tesla!" I objected. "He's not even awake! He's dozing!"

We all looked at the horse. It was true his eyes were half open, but he had that dreamy look that told me he was enjoying a little horsey nap.

"It is true that my descendant looks well," Loki admitted. "But I expected nothing else when I arranged for him to be taken into the care of a high priestess of Ashtar."

"Mikaela?" I asked. "You arranged for it? I don't think so. I had her and Ramon take Tesla when they decided to leave Circus of the Darned to become farmers."

"Who do you think urged them to do so?" Loki asked with a self-satisfied smirk. "I did not trust you, a mere child, to see to the welfare of my descendant. But a priestess of the Asatru is a different matter. Tesla is well. I am content to have him remain here."

"Good, because that's what *I* arranged," I snapped, then remembered that it wasn't good to lose one's temper with a god. "We've gotten off track. You asked what I want of you, and I'll tell you—I want my mother back, so you can just stop seducing her now." I straightened my shoulders in an attempt to look like the sort of person who routinely summoned gods to do her bidding. "And don't tell me you haven't done so, because I know for a fact you've been stirring up all sorts of trouble, like trying to kidnap me, but getting my roommate, Geoff, instead."

What was that?

I'll tell you later.

You'll tell me now, Ben answered in an inflexible tone that would have rankled if I wasn't trying to keep control of a pissed-off Norse god.

It's just like I said—he tried to kidnap me, but got my roomie instead.

Loki continued to look speculatively at me, his gaze sharp and calculating. "I swore to take from you that which you most valued, and I did so. You suffered much—that I know—and it pleased me. If you have continued to suffer, it is not by my doing, although that, too, pleases me. It is interesting, however, that the Vikingahärta did not protect you as you believed it must. Perhaps it has tired of you and is willing to return to me. You will give it to me now."

"Whoa, hold on there," I said as Loki took a step forward. Ben did likewise until the two men were just a foot apart, glaring at each other. *He already took something from me? What does he mean? What did he take?*

I don't know for certain, but I am beginning to suspect. "Do not approach my Beloved without her permission."

Loki gave him a jaded look. "Do you think you can stop me, Dark One?"

"I think I can make a damned good attempt, yes," Ben said calmly, although there was an underlying note of steel in his voice that made Loki hesitate.

"What did you take from me?" I asked, letting go of Tesla to stand next to Ben, my fingers brushing his until he took my hand. "How did you make me suffer?"

He gave me a look that mocked my questions. "I am Loki the Trickster, brother of Odin, and member of the Aesir. I do not need to explain anything to a mere human."

"Well, I think you're going to have to explain to this human, because I don't know what it is you took from me. I don't recall losing anything I valued except my backpack, and I haven't so much suffered because of that as I have been annoyed."

"It is not material things that he stole from you," Ben

said slowly, his eyes a lightish oak color as they considered Loki.

"Then what?" I asked, puzzled.

Have you been happy since you left the GothFaire, Beloved?

I was about to answer that he knew full well I hadn't been, when it struck me what he was implying.

"You took love from me." Enlightenment flooded my poor excuse for a brain. "You took the love of my mother and Ben from me by driving me from them, didn't you? You made me miserable for five whole years!"

Loki smiled a smug smile that I wanted to smack off his face. "I told you that I would have my revenge. Watching you suffer for the last few years has been worth all it has cost me to keep a glamour on you for an entire year."

"It was a glamour that made everyone drive me crazy?" I asked, stunned by the depths of his machinations. "Is that why everyone—Ben and Imogen and even my mother—was insisting I do what they wanted?"

Is that possible? Casting a glamour on someone for a year, I mean.

For a god of Loki's power? Absolutely.

So it wasn't you being bossy, and Imogen being pushy, and my mom being my mom? It was the glamour that made us all miserable?

It seems so. Although I doubt if your mother would have changed her mind about me until you were older.

Still . . . I took a deep breath and lifted my chin. "Where is my mother, Loki Laufeyiarson?"

"That you would have to ask Frigga, for I do not know your mother's fate," he said with a return of his haughtiness. "Give me the Vikingahärta, and I will let you live in peace."

I don't know what to believe. He doesn't seem to be lying, does he?

No, but he is the trickster.

I sighed. *I'm going to have to touch him, aren't I?*

It would probably be the easiest way to determine whether or not he is lying, Ben agreed, his fingers tightening around mine when my stomach clenched at the thought of opening myself up to Loki. *I am here, Francesca. I will not allow any harm to come to you.*

I know. But I feel obligated to tell you that I love you nonetheless. Would you mind—

You should know by now that you are my earth and stars, Beloved.

It is always nice to hear it, I said as I pulled off my gloves. *No sun in there?*

The sun and I do not get along, he said with a wry little smile.

"You want the Vikingahärta? You got it." I held it out, and when he reached for it, I shoved it into his hand, allowing my fingertips to brush his palm. For the space between seconds, I was in the world of Loki. It was a scary place, and left me with the feeling that my hair was standing on end, but one thing was made absolutely clear to me—he wasn't lying about my mother. He truly did not know where she was.

"Ah, it is as I thought," Loki said with a fat smile as he beheld the Vikingahärta lying on his hand. "It has returned to me of its own will. I knew the day—" He stopped, frowning. The Vikingahärta didn't burst into a bright light as it had the last time he touched it, but I felt a slight vibration inside me that seemed to come from it. To our collective amazement, the triangles that made up the valknut shifted for a second time, causing Loki to yelp as he dropped it.

He glared at it for a few seconds before transferring the glare to me. "Perhaps I am not finished with you as I thought to have been."

Instantly four big, bulky men blocked my view of him.

"Ben! Eirik! Move!" I protested as they and Finnvid and Isleif put themselves between Loki and me.

He is threatening you. I will not stand for that. "You heard her—move," Ben told the Vikings, scowling at them. "I will protect Francesca."

"She is our goddess," Eirik told him with a matching scowl.

"She's my Beloved. That trumps your goddess."

"Oh, for Pete's sake . . ." I shoved aside Eirik, glared at Isleif until he stepped back, and shot Ben a look that he chose to ignore. The field in front of him was empty of all but the Vikingahärta lying on the grass. "Great. Now Loki's gone, and I didn't get to ask him who would want to seduce my mother, not to mention banish him like Freya wanted, not that I think I could."

"I doubt if he would have told you the truth, assuming he knew it," Ben answered as I picked up the Vikingahärta, touching the three triangles with the tip of a finger. They felt just the same to me, and yet different somehow, as if the power it possessed had shifted when its physical form did.

"He didn't know where Mom was—that I know," I said, lifting my gaze to his. "Ben, what are we going to do? If he isn't behind my mother running off, who is? And how are we going to find her?

"I think we're going to have to consult a source that has been hidden to you," he answered, the words portentous.

"What source?" The image of a black-haired man

came to mind. "Alphonse de Marco, you mean? I thought we decided that he couldn't have anything to do with Mom?"

"Not him," Ben said thoughtfully, rubbing his chin.

I looked into his mind, my eyes widening as I saw what it was thinking. "Petra?"

His arm was warm around me as he steered me out of the pasture, toward Mikaela's house, the Vikings falling into step behind us. "I think it's time we locate your half sister."

Chapter 20

"You know, for a man who used to ride around in carriages, and probably wondered at the amazing technology of gunpowder and steam engines, you are awfully Internet-savvy," I remarked an hour later as we sat at Mikaela's kitchen table, hunkered over Ramon's laptop. "It didn't take you very long at all to find her. But what's Mom's other daughter doing in Paris? Her birth certificate says she was born in California just like me."

"Evidently she's living on rue de la Grande Pest."

"Street of the big plague?" I asked, my French being rather limited.

"Yes." His eyebrows rose. "Odd."

"What is?"

"That's where G and T is located."

"What's G and T?"

"Goety and Theurgy," Ramon answered as he took a seat with little Fran. He'd arrived home about twenty minutes before, surprised but pleased to see Ben and me . . . and a little less enthusiastic to find the three Vikings raiding his kitchen.

"Black and white magic? Is it some sort of school or something?"

"Nightclub," Ben said, tapping on the keyboard. "A very popular one. Everyone who's anyone goes there. I'm surprised Imogen didn't take you there when you were traveling with the Faire."

"Are you kidding? My mother barely let me go to museums on my own. She never let me go out with Imogen at night. She thought Imogen would try to hook me up with guys." I gave Ben a twisted smile. "As if."

"She is going by the name Petra Valentine, not de Marco," Ben remarked as he continued to poke around in an online database of personal information. "That's what took me so long to find her. Evidently she's living with some relatives by the name of Valentine. They have a business, Valentine and Company, located on rue de la Grande Pest, but I can't ascertain just what sort of a business it is."

"If her father is an Ilargi, maybe she's one, too," Mikaela suggested, watching with dismay as the Vikings stuffed a variety of bowls into a small microwave.

"I'll pay for whatever it is they eat," I told her in an undertone.

"Don't be ridiculous—you pay us very generously for Tesla's board. It's just that I will have nothing to give you for dinner if they eat everything."

"The position of Ilargi isn't a hereditary one," her husband told her, peering over Ben's shoulder as best he could with little Fran demanding he read her a story from the book she held.

"Maybe she's normal, like me," I said.

Everyone looked at me, including the Vikings.

"Perhaps *normal* wasn't the best term," I said somewhat lamely.

"She has a Wiccan mother and an <u>Ilargi</u> father," Ben said in a dry tone. "I suspect she is anything but mundane."

Mundane, I remembered from my time with the Faire, was the Otherworld term for normal mortal beings. It was a word I once cherished, wishing with my whole being that I could be perfectly ordinary, just like everyone else. My gaze slid to Ben, caressing the hard planes of his face, softened now as he focused on the laptop, the sweet curve of his lower lip curling a little as Ramon made a joke about mundane folk. I was filled with a profound sense of rightness, a warm glow of love that made me wonder how I could ever believe life would exist without Ben.

His gaze flashed to mine, a question in it.

Just thinking about what I'd like to do to Loki for making me miss all those years with you.

He returned his attention to the laptop. *I suspect, Francesca, that although the glamour had much to do with our unhappiness, you would not have been so quick to Join yourself to me regardless.*

Possibly. I am awfully stubborn, and I really do hate being told I have no choice in my own life decisions, but still, it was very cruel of Loki to do that.

He believed himself justified. I am just relieved that you no longer have his threat hanging over you. "Ah. And here is an e-mail address for her, and I think . . . yes, a cell phone number." He looked up. "Shall we call her?"

"Do I want to know how you got her private information like that?" I asked.

"No." He closed the screen, which looked like it belonged to a mobile phone service, and handed me a piece of paper with a phone number. "I assume you wish to do the honors?"

"Yes." I stared at the paper for a second or two, feeling my palms go damp.

If you would prefer me to do it—

No, I should be the one to call her. She is my half sister. It's just that . . . Well, it's all still a bit weird, partly because my mother kept the fact from me that I have an older sister, and also because Mom's who-knows-where, and what if this Petra is responsible for her disappearing?

You won't know unless you talk to her.

The Vikings, in the process of eating Mikaela and Ramon out of every morsel of food they possessed, gathered around to watch.

Ben offered me his cell phone. I took it and punched in the number, hesitating a second before I hit the TALK button.

After a couple of rings, a somewhat breathless voice answered. *"Bonjour."*

"Um . . . *bonjour.* Do you speak English?"

"Like a native," the woman answered with laughter in her voice. She had a slightly English accent—not truly English, but a little hint of it that made it sound like she watched way too much BBC America. "Who's this?"

"My name is Fran Ghetti. You are Petra Valentine de Marco, aren't you?"

The woman hesitated. "I'm Petra Valentine, yes. But not de Marco."

Odd. Is she trying to distance herself from Alphonse?

Possibly.

"Hello, Petra. This is going to sound extremely strange, and I apologize in advance for saying it to you this way, but is your mother's name Miranda Benson?"

"Who did you say you were?" Petra's voice turned as flinty as a quarry.

"Francesca Ghetti. And I'm sorry. I know I'd freak out if someone called and asked me questions about my mother, but I assure you it's really important that I do so. Is your mother Miranda Benson?"

"My birth mother, yes, but she died when I was born."

I felt like a sledgehammer walloped me in my chest. "She died?" I repeated, staring at Ben with wide eyes.

Mikaela, who had been trying to find something left in the kitchen to fix for dinner, raised her brows. The Vikings, not finding anything of interest in a phone call, moved off to the living room, where they were squabbling over which TV channel to watch.

"Yes. Now, would you mind telling me why it's of vital importance that you know about my birth mother?"

I took a deep breath. "Because she's my mother, too, and she's very much alive. Or at least she was the last time she was seen. She's . . . uh . . . kind of missing. I was hoping you'd know something about what happened to her."

The silence from the other side was heavy with surprise. "I think . . . I think you better start this from the very beginning," Petra said slowly.

And so I did. With Ben leaning his head against mine to hear Petra's side of the conversation, which admittedly consisted of mostly exclamations of surprise and disbelief, I gave her a brief synopsis of my mother's life, her work with the GothFaire, how I found she had disappeared, and my subsequent discovery of Petra's birth certificate.

"This is absolutely mind-boggling," she said when I was finished. "I've never heard of an Alphonse de

Marco. My father's name was Albert Valentine. At least . . . that's what my family told me. Then again, they told me my birth mother was dead."

"And you don't know anything about the where-abouts of my mother? Er . . . our mother?"

"No, I'm sorry. I don't."

I glanced at Ben. *She sounds like she's telling the truth.*

I agree. There is genuine shock in her voice. She could be faking it, but I suspect not.

"Well, then, I guess this phone call was unnecessary. Except . . . this is all a bit strange to me, too, but it's nice to talk to you. I had no idea until a few days ago that I had an older sister."

"You said you were in Germany—where, exactly?"

I gave her the name of the town. "I'm staying at the GothFaire with my . . . er . . . boyfriend."

Ben sighed into my mind. *You're going to have to marry me.*

I am?

Yes. The term "boyfriend" is starting to irritate me. Husband, while not nearly as binding as Dark One, at least sounds a bit more formal.

I laughed. *Look, I just finally wrapped my mind around the whole Joining thing. Let's not rush anything else.*

Petra was silent for a few seconds, then said, "Lucy is going to kill me, but there's no help for that. I'm going to go out to help you find Miranda."

"You are?" I realized how rude that sounded and hurried to smooth over the faux pas. "We'd love to have your help, of course, not to mention have the chance to meet you, but . . . oh, man, this is my day for sounding like a lunatic. Petra, what exactly are you?"

"What *am* I?" she repeated.

"Yes. Our mother is a witch. She's very well respected in Wiccan circles. I wondered if you inherited any of her skills."

She gave a short little bark of laughter. "No, I have my own set of skills. My family—my adopted family, I should say—are necromancers. I'm a fourth-class necromancer, which in case you aren't familiar with the classifications of necromancy, means I am able to raise deceased animals as liches."

I sighed with relief. "I'm so glad you're not normal."

She laughed in a way that made me think I would like her, promised we would have a long conversation when she got here, and hung up.

I made a couple of quick calls after that, then finally turned to Ben. "Now what? We've exhausted every avenue—Loki is innocent of involvement with Mom, Petra doesn't know anything about her, and Peter says she's still not back."

"We will return to the GothFaire," he answered, glancing at a text message that burbled at him when I handed him back his phone. "Imogen says the watch wish to see us, and . . ." He frowned.

"What is it?" I asked.

"David sent me a message saying he was following a trail, but didn't say what or whose. Damn."

"What do we do about Loki?" I asked, suddenly feeling exhausted and overwhelmed. "I'm supposed to banish him, and I have no idea how to do that, or even if the Vikingahärta will let me. It seems to be a bit wonky right now."

You are tired, Beloved. You need food and rest.

What I need is lots of steamy vampire lovin', I corrected him.

That, too.

"It seems to me that Loki is the least of your worries right now," Mikaela said, holding a package of ramen soup and a soggy potato covered with scraggly eyes. "My biggest concern is what I'm going to feed you. This is all your plague of locusts left."

I laughed, and after a bit of polite wrangling over who would foot the bill (Ben won), we agreed to go into the nearest town and replenish our energy at an Italian bistro.

Three hours later the sun had set and Ben and I arrived back at the GothFaire to find it in full swing.

"You know, I could have rented a car and driven Eirik and his men back here, rather than making them take the train," I told Ben as I took his hand to avoid being separated from him in the crowd of Faire-goers. "It seems kind of ungrateful to just shove train tickets in their hands when they were sent out to help me."

"After what it cost me to feed them, the word 'ungrateful' can hardly apply," he said drily. "I reiterate what I said before: They are not living with us. I couldn't afford their upkeep."

I laughed and squeezed his hand, feeling a rush of joy despite my worries. "Do you think the watch is going to be difficult?"

"I don't know, but I think we're about to find out."

I looked in the direction he nodded. Three men in long dark coats and with grim looks about their eyes were bearing down on us. *Oy. Anything I should avoid mentioning to them?*

It's never wise to lie to the watch, Francesca.

I didn't mean lie so much as perhaps sticking strictly to the questions asked and not offering any other information.

That has frequently been my modus operandi.

So I've noticed. I greeted the watch members as they stopped before us, one of them speaking rapidly in French to Ben. At their request, we followed them to Naomi's trailer, and spent the next forty minutes explaining how it was we had come across the body of Luis.

"I take it that it is your contention," said the tallest and grimmest of the three men to Ben, "that the death was due to a therion attack?"

"It bears all the signs of being such," Ben said, nodding to where Luis's covered body lay. "If those weren't claw marks on his chest, then I do not know much about therions."

"Indeed," said the watch man smoothly, giving Ben a curious look. "I find it surprising that a Dark One is so conversant with therion lifestyles."

"As I explained, my blood brother is the leader of his pride. Naturally, I have learned some things from him."

"Naturally," the man said, his lips compressed as he turned to me. "And you have nothing else to add to your statement?"

"Nothing. I do, however, have a question for you."

Not one single flicker of emotion crossed his face. "We are the watch, demoiselle. We do not answer questions; we ask them."

"I'm going to go ahead and ask nonetheless. My mother has been missing for almost a week. She works here, at the GothFaire, and no one has seen her since she went to Heidelberg for a long weekend. How do I file an official missing persons report with you watch guys?"

"You do not. We 'watch guys' "—he made a face as

he spoke the two words—"do not investigate missing persons. There are other resources available to members of the L'au-dela for that."

"But what if she's mixed up in Luis's murder?" I asked, waving a hand toward the door to Naomi's bedroom.

One of his eyebrows rose a fraction of an inch. "Do you have reason to believe that? If so, you have withheld that information."

"No," I admitted. "I don't have a reason other than it's a pretty big coincidence that my mother should go off with some guy no one knows anything about right before a mysterious lich comes sniffing around the Faire, and a dead shape-shifter is found in the trailer of a woman who has ties to my mother's ex-lover."

The man turned a stony look on me. "You will explain this ex-lover and his ties to the woman named Naomi."

Oh, dear. He looks pissed.

I cautioned you about involving them too much, Ben said, putting an arm around me as we sat on Naomi's small couch and explained about de Marco and my mother. *Now you will have them poking into everything.*

Yes, but they might be able to help find Mom.

True.

After another fifty minutes, it became apparent that the watch wasn't, however, going to do anything.

"We will keep our eyes open, as the mortals say, for signs of your mother, but there is insufficient evidence to convince us of her involvement with the death we are investigating," was the watch's final pronouncement.

"They are not very smart," Imogen said shortly after we were released and had gone to her tent to tell her we were back. "Those watch! They asked me all sorts of impertinent questions about Benedikt's involvement with the therions, as if he had something to do with the death. It was ridiculous, and I told that marble-faced creature that. Yes? Both of you? Excellent!"

Ben and I moved aside as Imogen smiled at a couple who had come to have their rune stones read.

What did the watch guy mean when he said there were other resources open to members of the L'au-dela? I asked as we fought our way through the dense crowd of people, stopping briefly to check that Mom's stand hadn't been tampered with. Since I'd sold most of her stock, there wasn't much of value left in it, but I didn't want her coming back to a trashed stand.

A little pain squeezed my heart at the thought that she might not be coming back.

We will find her, Francesca, Ben said, pulling me into his arms as he stood at the side of the stand. He kissed my temple, then my eyes, and just like that the hunger was on him, pouring out of him to wrap itself around me.

Goddess! I clutched his shoulders as I planted my mouth on his, suddenly needing him more than anything. *I don't think I can make it all the way to Mom's trailer.*

Beloved, you must not. I won't be able to resist you. Ben moaned as I moved my hand between our bodies, stroking him in a way intended to inflame his passion even higher.

You don't need to. The booth is empty. . . .

Ben twisted to jerk aside the canvas strapped to one of the wood struts. I ignored the sound of rending canvas, my mouth still glued to his as he moved us into the dark confines of the booth. The noise and lights and dense pack of humanity flowed around our little hidden paradise, which was a good thing, because if anyone had bothered to lift that torn side of the booth, he would have been given an eyeful.

Feed from me! Love me! Now! I demanded, my fingers desperately trying to undo both his belt and his zipper, while at the same time trying to get out of my own jeans.

Ben, with a snarl, ripped my pants off, just ripped them right off my body. I stood for a moment, astonished by the fact that he could do so without hurting me, but as the warm, close air of the closed booth caressed my naked flesh, other, more primal thoughts claimed my mind.

I need you right now, I moaned, trying to help him get out of his pants. *This second! You're not fast enough!*

You're not making things any easier on me by thinking things like that. And that. Christ, Francesca! I'm not going to make it if you think about using your mouth on me like that! He swore into my mind, grabbed my behind with both hands, and hoisted me up onto the sales table. There was a tiny little tinkle of glass, no doubt from the couple of remaining bottles of understanding (the least popular item that Mom sold), spread my thighs, and surged into me with a strength that left me breathless.

For about three seconds. Then I pulled his head down to my shoulder, dug my fingers into the thick, tense muscles of his behind, and pulled my knees up to clutch his hips.

The sharp, hot pain of him biting me made me moan, but it was the sense of our spirits joining together, of our beings bonded as he both took life from me and returned it, that sent my soul spinning toward a climax I knew would rock my world.

Dimly, as if from a very long distance, I heard a familiar voice calling, "Goddess Fran! We have returned!"

"Bullfrogs! They're back! Hurry, Ben, hurry!"

His mouth was hot on my flesh as he drank from me, his hips pistoning as I urged him on with thrusts of my own, wanting the physical completion but also that shining moment when we were truly one entity.

"Goddess? Didn't Imogen say she was headed this way?"

The voice was louder. I sobbed my wordless plea into Ben's mind as our bodies raced.

Bite me, he ordered.

What?

Bite me!

I didn't stop to question that command. I nuzzled aside his hair until the tense cord of his neck was exposed, then gently bit.

A surge of ecstasy shot through Ben that was instantly translated to me, sending both of us over the edge. He lunged into me, his back arched, his mind and mine filled with an exquisite sense of rightness.

It wasn't until we had managed to separate that I realized something was wrong.

Chapter 21

"Ow. I think . . . Ow!" Ben stood with the shredded remains of my jeans in his hands, his eyebrows raised when I reached behind me. "My butt hurts. I must have sat on something."

"Goddess Fran!" The voice that bellowed was sufficiently loud to stop the nearby hum of conversation for a good thirty seconds.

"Oh, for the love of the moon and stars . . ." I stuck my head out of the torn side of the booth. "I'm right here, Eirik. And no, you can't come in. Go to my mother's trailer. We'll be there in a couple of minutes." I pulled my head back in, and glared at Ben, who stood laughing. "What is so funny?"

"Turn around, Francesca," he said, making a twirling motion with his finger.

"Why? What did I sit on?" I turned my back to him, trying to peer over my shoulder at my own butt. "Whatever it is, it stings like the dickens."

I felt the soft brush of Ben's fingers, then a painful pinch.

"Hey!"

"It says 'rstandi,' whatever that is." He held out a small piece of curved glass with a hand-printed paper label.

"Oh, goddess! I sat on one of the bottles of understanding. Ow! Ben!"

He chuckled again as he picked out the remaining bits of glass. "You aren't injured badly, Beloved. Besides, there are benefits to having wounded yourself in such a manner."

"Benefits? Are you nuts? You try sitting on glass and then we'll talk about the bene—jumping Jeremiah!" His mouth was hot on my poor, abused flesh. "Ben! That's my butt! You're *licking* my butt cheeks!"

"I'm healing you," he murmured against the swell of one cheek. "I would take my time over the job, but duty is pressing, so I will make this quick."

I was torn between the pleasure of his mouth on flesh that was surprised to receive such attentions and shock that he wouldn't mind at all healing me in such a fashion, but didn't have time to dwell on such considerations. It took him only a minute to fetch a pair of pants for me, and by the time I returned with him to my mother's trailer, the Vikings were lounging around telling stories about how many women they had on the train ride down.

"You are the lustiest ghosts I've ever met," I said as I eyed the couch. A little smile hovered around Ben's lips when I gingerly eased myself onto the cushions.

"We have had nothing but ale wenches since you sent us to Valhalla," Finnvid pointed out. "Having mortal women who do not smell of hops is a pleasant change."

"Change-of-subject time," I said, relaxing when I realized my butt didn't hurt at all.

As if I would let you go out with a sore ass.

"I'm at a loss as to what we should do to find my mother. You didn't answer me before, Ben, because we were . . . er . . . distracted, but the watch said something about there being other resources—do you know what those are?"

"Yes. A professional diviner like Absinthe's mentor would probably help, but diviners are dangerous, and I would not wish for you to consult one."

"I consulted Absinthe," I pointed out.

"Yes, but she is just an apprentice."

"Still, I'm having a hard time seeing diviners as people to fear."

He made a little half shrug. "Nonetheless, you should be wary. They demand too much in payment. There is another resource closer to you, however, and one that will think kindly about helping you."

"Who's that?"

"Tallulah. Or rather, her mate, Sir Edward."

"Hmm." I thought about that. Tallulah was a renowned medium, although mostly people consulted her in order to talk to their deceased relatives. Despite the constant, nagging worry that seemed to grow daily, I refused to consider the idea that my mother might be in that class. "My mother isn't dead, though."

Ben noted my stubbornly raised chin, but simply said, "Sir Edward's abilities, and those of Tallulah, are not limited to conversation with the dead. We will consult them as soon as possible."

"You go with the Dark One, goddess," Eirik said, waving a hand containing the remote to my mother's tiny portable TV. "We do not care for mediums."

"You don't? Why?"

"Archaeologists are always using them to contact us in Valhalla. They wish to know the location of our villages, and where we buried our dead. It is most annoying."

There wasn't much I could say to that, so after warning them to stay out of trouble, we went to see Tallulah and her ghostly boyfriend. She had only one person with her, so it only took ten minutes before we were shown into the small booth containing a table, her scrying bowl, a crystal ball, and three chairs.

"Fran!" She looked up in surprise as we took the chairs opposite hers. Ben placed some euros in the small stand to the side, where payment was made. "What are you doing here?"

"We wish to talk to you and Sir Edward."

"You can do that any time," she said, frowning toward the stand. "I do not require payment for that."

"This is a professional consultation. We want you and Sir Edward to find my mom."

Her eyebrows rose, her dark eyes speculative, first on me, then on Ben. "I am not a diviner. I do not have the power to locate your mother, Fran. If I had, I would have offered to do so when you told me she was missing."

"Sir Edward—"

"He is limited in what he can see from the Akasha," she said, shaking her head.

"But the two of you together . . ." Ben let the sentence trail off, his gaze just as speculative as hers had been. "You helped Fran once before, when her horse was stolen."

"We did," she admitted slowly, her gaze now on the table before her. Her fingers twitched as if she wished to touch the scrying bowl or the baseball-sized glass orb that sat in a mound of midnight blue velvet. "This is more difficult, however. Someone has gone to much trouble to hide Miranda's whereabouts. If that person should discover that we sought to uncover his actions, it could be dangerous not just to me but to Sir Edward and Fran and you, as well. Are you willing to risk your Beloved's safety for that?"

"Yes," Ben said without hesitation, and I was comforted by the fact that despite his past differences with my mother, he would do everything possible to locate her. It didn't escape me that he was also determined to move heaven and hell to keep me safe, but that was fine by me. I had the same plan with regards to his safety.

"Very well," Tallulah said, rising from her chair. "Remain here. What you ask will take both Sir Edward and myself a little time to prepare."

I didn't have time to do more than envision three different types of grim deaths for Ben, my mother, and myself before she returned. I smiled my thanks when Tallulah returned, carrying, much to my surprise, Davide, my mother's fat black-and-white cat. She plopped him in my lap before retaking her chair, hesitating between the glass ball and the scrying bowl, but eventually settling on the highly polished black metal bowl.

Davide looked at me with profound disdain.

"You smell like tuna fish, cat," I told him. His whiskers twitched, and he dug his claws into my arm when I asked Tallulah, "Is he giving you trouble? If he is, I'll put him in Mom's trailer. Stop it, cat, or I'll see to it you don't *have* any claws."

"I told you before that he is no trouble to me."

"Er . . ." I looked back at the cat. He flattened his ears and hissed silently at me, but at least he stopped digging his claws into the flesh of my arm. "Then why did you bring him out here?"

She smoothed the cloth over the table and poured a

little water into the scrying bowl. "He is your mother's familiar. He will provide a bridge to her."

"That's just an old wives' tale. Or more accurately, I guess, an old witches' tale, because my mother never used a familiar, and if she did, she would have hardly chosen a fat, grumpy cat to be one." Davide's lips thinned, his whiskers held flush with his face, his eyes shooting lasers at me. Or they would have if he could have managed it.

"You are mistaken," was all she said.

I looked back at Davide. He squinted back at me, and farted on my leg. "For the love of—"

"Silence."

At Tallulah's softly spoken command, I stopped glaring at Davide, shooting a quick glance at Ben out of the corner of my eye. He had adopted a mildly interested expression as Tallulah invoked a trance, but as I watched, one corner of his mouth tipped up.

You are entirely too sexy for your own good. How am I going to spend the rest of my life with you if all you have to do is quirk one side of your mouth to have me imagining the most lewd things?

You will enjoy yourself greatly, both in chastising me for my appearance, about which I can do little, and in being pleasured as only a Beloved can be pleasured. Yes, including more tongue swirls in that particular spot, although I object to you including in your fantasies that object, and I would like to know, since you've had no other men, how you learned about devices intended to prolong erections?

The Internet, baby, the Internet.

"Sir Edward is with us," Tallulah said, interrupting my mental review of all the toys I thought might be fun to use on Ben. She sounded brisk and businesslike as usual, not at all adopting the dreamy tone my mother did whenever she communed with the goddess. "I have told him of your request, Fran, and he has agreed to help you, although he warns that he is limited in what he can see."

I was expecting the session with Tallulah to take a long time, what with all the looking around Sir Edward had to do from the Akashic Plain, referred to by people in the Otherworld as Akasha, and by normal people as limbo. But to my surprise, it took Tallulah and Sir Edward only three minutes to tell us what we wanted to know.

"There is a man, swarthy and bull-chested," Tallulah said, gazing intently into her scrying bowl. "I see him clearly. Sir Edward says he has much dark power, although he disguises it well. He was a servant, but has been freed. It is he who holds your mother, bound by love."

"A swarthy man?" I glanced at Ben.

"De Marco," he said.

"That's what I was thinking. But why? Because he knew Mom in the past?"

"Perhaps the issues of their relationship were not resolved in the past."

"Possibly. But that doesn't sound like her."

Ben admitted it didn't.

"And is she really in love with de Marco, or did he magic her somehow?"

Ben asked Tallulah, "Is he nearby? Is Miranda with him?"

"Yes. And yes," she said, her gaze still locked on the smooth surface of the water in the bowl. She was silent for a moment, then added, shaking her head, "He has too much power for Sir Edward to see more details. He says that this man is gathering forces to him, dark forces."

The therions? His experiments, do you think?

It's possible, but therions are not beings of dark power.

Tallulah suddenly took a big gasp of air, then sat back, her eyes once again on us. "That is all we could see. The man sensed Sir Edward's interest, and would have attacked him had Sir Edward not retreated back to the Akasha."

"De Marco can attack ghosts?" I asked, incredulous at the idea. I knew ghosts in corporeal form, such as the Vikings and those that had been grounded, could be interacted with physically, but Sir Edward had never, in the time I had known Tallulah, had a solid form.

"Yes. He is an Ilargi, a reaper of souls." Her eyes held sympathy as she reached across the table and tapped Ben on his wrist. "You must guard well, Benedikt. He desires to add you to his forces."

"Well, he can just desire all he wants, Ben is mine," I snorted, immediately regretting the show of possession.

Why? I enjoyed it, Ben said with a smile.

Yes, and you're going to be absolutely unbearable after a few years of that, and I have to spend . . . what, a thousand years with you?

Possibly. Possibly more.

All of which means I need to start deflating your ego now, before it's too late.

Ben laughed in my head, and took my hand. We thanked Tallulah and Sir Edward for their time, after which I took Davide back to Tallulah's trailer, making sure to pat the cat on his head since I knew he disliked it. Kindlier instincts prompted me to pull out a little bowl of chopped chicken that Tallulah said she was saving for him. He looked like he wanted to bite me as I gave it to him, but decided instead to adopt a righteously indignant expression meant to put me in my place.

"I don't see the Vikings," I said some twenty minutes later, as I arrived at where Ben sat on the corner of a portable picnic table in the common area. I waved the sausage roll I'd bought just before the food stall closed down, adding, "Normally I wouldn't worry, but with the Faire closing down early for the big finale of the opera shindig in town, I suspect they've gone in to pick up women, and with them, that could be trouble. Did you get hold of David?"

"Yes." Ben put his phone away in an inner pocket of his leather jacket and slipped on the latter. "He says he'll meet us at de Marco's house as soon as he can. Do you have your valknut?"

I touched my T-shirt. "I do, but the Vikingahärta is Loki's valknut. Why do you think it will help us with de Marco?"

"It had its origins with Loki, but it's yours now, and it's you who is powering it. It protected you against Naomi's attack earlier, so it's my belief that it will do the same should de Marco try to harm you."

"Aren't we going to add Imogen to our posse? And shouldn't we have the Vikings? I can call Eirik and find out where they are. I'm sure they'd be happy to help us make de Marco hand over my mother. They love a good fight."

"I would like to avoid bringing a full-fledged attack force, since we simply intend to locate your mother. And I'd prefer Imogen to remain here. She's vulnerable right now."

"Vulnerable how?" I almost had to run to keep up

with Ben as he hurried toward the parking lot, where he'd left his bike. There were a few stragglers left at the Faire, but most had left in the last hour, and the Faire employees were happily shutting up shop in order to watch the festivities. "Is Imogen okay? Is something wrong with her? And why are you running? I'm going to get a stitch in my side if you keep up this pace."

"Nothing is wrong with Imogen, no. I'm hurrying because I just saw the time. It's going to be a nightmare trying to get through the town to de Marco's house."

"Why? Oh, the parade." The grand finale of the weeklong opera competition was a parade filled with floats, artists, and other performers.

"The sooner we get through the town, the better."

I waited until he got on the bike, then slid on behind him, happily burying my face in the nape of his neck and wrapping my arms around him.

Not going to fondle my belly tonight? he asked as we bumped over the lumpy pasture ground and up onto the smooth asphalt of the road.

My hand moved downward in a bold gesture that surprised even me. *How about I fondle you somewhere else, instead?*

We almost crashed. By the time Ben righted us, brushed the gravel off his boots, and delivered to me a lecture about the follies of groping the driver of a motorcycle going fifty miles an hour on an unlit road, I was alternating between remorse and amusement.

You can't tell me that you never had a woman grope you while you were riding a horse, I said.

What? He sounded confused.

If you remember, you told me it's possible to have sex on horseback. I assume that meant you had practical experience in the matter.

A little blush of embarrassment touched his mind. *Er . . . yes. And yes to your question, although I will point out that falling off a horse isn't nearly as painful as falling off a moving motorcycle.*

I said I was sorry. Are we going to do it?

Have sex on a horse?

Yes.

If you really want to, then someday, yes, I'll show you how it's done. Francesca . . .

Hmm?

I know you're worried, but I will take care of you.

I hadn't thought he could see into the hidden kernel of worry that poisoned my general sense of well-being. *I know you will. It's just . . . this is my mother we're talking about, Ben. If de Marco is as powerful as Sir Edward says he is, how on earth are we going to convince him to de-thrall her, or reverse whatever it is that he's done to her? We don't even know* why *he's done it in the first place.*

We will find out. All will be well, Beloved.

I spent the rest of the ride into town silently contemplating Ben's calm assurance, and my own worries that even he might meet his match in de Marco.

Chapter 22

The town was, as Ben predicted, a gridlocked night-mare, the huge parade of floats and costumed perform-ers that would wind through town and end up at an open-air amphitheater already under way, which meant much of the town was blocked off by both barricades and dense streams of people.

Ben had to resort to driving up on sidewalks a couple of times, scattering people as he slowly made his way around the edges until he was clear of the town proper, and into the neighborhood that looked down on the town.

The parade must be running through here, too, I commented as we zipped along the winding road that led to de Marco's house. Barricades lined the street, and people were already gathering outside their houses, setting up coolers and portable chairs.

That's just what we need. Hopefully we'll have your mother and be able to leave before it gets to us, Ben said, skillfully zipping around obstructions, barriers, and the occasional traffic cop directing neighborhood residents. *Is that it?*

Yes. I don't see David's car.

He wouldn't park here where de Marco could see.
Ben stopped next to the square fountain.

My eyes strayed to the gargoyle-like projections from
the side of the house. I shivered at the glint of the runes
emphasized by the light pouring out of the windows. It
was as if they glowed slightly in the thick night air, giving a sinister feel to an already charged atmosphere.

In the distance, coming from the valley below, the
faint sounds of music and drums could be heard as the
parade started to wind its way through the neighbor-
hoods. I looked up at the house as I got off the bike and
wondered if my mother was in it, or if de Marco had his
hidden love nest elsewhere.

"Do we wait for David?" I asked in a whisper, feeling
the Vikingahärta grow warm beneath my shirt.

Ben cocked his head for a second as if he was listening, then shook it. "I would prefer to get Miranda out of
de Marco's keeping before David arrives to deal with
him."

"Deal with him how?" I caught a sense of concern in
Ben that had me opening my eyes in surprise. *David is
going to attack de Marco?*

*So he says. He hasn't explained to me all his reasoning
yet, but I believe he's found a link between Luis's death
and de Marco. It will be safer for you and your mother to
be out of the way before David rallies his pride members.*

A vision of Luis's mangled body rose before my unwilling eyes, and I shuddered at the thought of what the
entire pride could do to a person, immortal or not. *I
agree with the sentiment, but are we going to be able to
get to Mom without any help?*

We won't know unless we try, he said with what I had
to admit was wisdom.

Before I could do so much as offer up a prayer to the god and goddess, Ben banged the huge hanged-man door knocker, the sound of it reverberating through the night, a deep, mournful sound that was counterpointed by the livelier noise of the parade as it progressed up the hill.

The door opened quickly. Ben tensed, then relaxed when he saw who answered the knock.

"Hello, Ulfur. This is Benedikt Czerny, my . . . er . . . Dark One. Ben, this is Ulfur, the lich who took the Vikingahärta. We'd like to see Alphonse de Marco."

Ulfur's lips formed a thin line, his eyes going flat. "He isn't here."

"That makes things easier," I told Ben.

"Perhaps," was all he said.

I trained a razor-edged gaze on Ulfur. "Since your boss isn't present, I'd like my mother, if you don't mind."

Ulfur blinked at me in a way that expressed utter confusion. "Your mother?"

"Miranda Ghetti. She's being kept here, isn't she?"

His face went completely blank.

"Ulfur?"

He just stared at me with wide, unblinking eyes.

What just happened? I asked Ben.

I think that's confirmation that your mother is here, and not somewhere else.

Oh, you mean he can't lie the way you can't lie to me?

Not quite the same thing, but probably it's along the same line. Do you know his surname?

Um. I searched my memory. *Hallursson, I think. Why?*

"Ulfur Hallursson," Ben said in a deep, intimidating

voice, putting his hand on Ulfur's head, as Ulfur's eyes grew big. "You will tell us what we want to know. Where is the witch named Miranda?"

What on earth are you doing? Magicking him?

Kind of. I'm laying a compulsion on him.

You can do that?

Only with certain types of beings. Liches, luckily, are one of those who are susceptible.

Ulfur opened and closed his mouth a couple of times, then awkwardly pointed behind him, toward the staircase.

"That's all I need to know," I said, pulling out the Vikingahärta and holding it in my hand as I pushed past him into the hall. "There may be a demon around, Ben. There was earlier, but the Vikings sent him back to Abaddon."

Ben didn't wait to examine the hallway; he took the stairs three at a time. I ran after him, stopping at the top of the stairs to bellow, "Mom? Are you here?"

My voice echoing down the hallway was all the response we got.

"Miranda?" Ben yelled, even louder than me.

We both listened intently, but heard nothing.

I looked down the stairs to where Ulfur stood silently watching us. "Is she on this floor?"

He just looked at me.

Ben asked him the same question. Evidently the compulsion was still strong enough to cause Ulfur to shake his head.

"Up another flight." We hurried up the flight to the third floor, repeating the process of calling for my mother. Again we were met with silence.

"There's only the attic left," I told Ben as we stood at the foot of a narrow flight of stairs.

"Up we go."

The door to the attic was locked, but Ben resolved that situation by simply kicking down the door.

"Mom? Are you here?" I asked as I brushed past Ben, coughing slightly on the dusty air that met his assault.

The attic, too, was empty of life.

"I don't get it," I said, slapping my hands on my legs in irritation. "Ulfur pointed this way, didn't he?"

Ben rubbed his chin, looking thoughtful, his eyes narrowed on nothing. "Use the Vikingahärta."

"Huh?"

"You said it's changed twice since you reclaimed it. Perhaps it has been doing that to reflect your needs."

"Since when does it change itself to suit me?" I asked.

"It represents the Fates. No doubt it's changing itself to be what you need it to be. Try using it to find your mother."

I looked down at the three metal intertwined triangles that lay in my hand. "Find my mom," I told it.

It did nothing, just lay inert on my palm.

"Use it, Francesca. Make it do what you want it to do."

I focused my thoughts on my mother, then grabbed Ben's hand as I willed the Vikingahärta to find my mother.

It glowed with an amber light for a moment, then suddenly I was running down three flights of stairs to the ground floor.

Where is she?

There, I said, stopping at the side of the stairs. A faint outline of a door built into the staircase was visible.

Ulfur did nothing as Ben broke it down. Before the last piece of shattered wood hit the ground, I stuck my head through the remains of the door and called out, "Mom? Are you there?"

"Franny?"

Relief swept over me like a warm blanket, tears pricking painfully behind my eyes as, heedless of the sharp bits of wood, I pushed into the recess. It turned out to be a landing of a flight of narrow stone stairs that led downward. "Are you decent? Is de Marco there? Are you hurt? Ben is here, so if you need healing, he'll take care of you."

"Am I hurt? Franny, what are you talking about?"

I skidded to a stop at the bottom of the stairs, Ben right behind me. I had half expected some sort of a honeymoon suite, with a heart-shaped bed and mirror on the ceiling, but what met my eyes was a beautifully tiled floor covered with expensive-looking cream and old rose rugs, matching cream furniture, a grand piano, a large-screen plasma TV, and floor-to-ceiling windows that gave a breathtaking view of the town below. My mother sat on the couch with a couple of books, a glass of wine dangling from one hand.

"You're not brainwashed?" I asked without thinking.

"Brainwashed? Of course I'm not." Her gaze slid past me to Ben, a frown pulling down her brows. "I would ask you what you are doing in Heidelberg, but I see the answer. Good evening, Benedikt."

"Miranda." Ben made one of his polished bows, the kind that never failed to make me want to jump him. "We are glad to see you are not harmed."

"Mom, what are you doing here? Are you a prisoner?" I looked around the room. Subdued lighting emphasized various paintings and works of art. The whole place reeked of good taste and money.

"You aren't making the least bit of sense, Fran." She set down her glass of wine. "I think perhaps you are upset. Why don't you sit down and tell me what has you in such a fidget? And why is Benedikt here, when you told me you'd cut all ties with him?"

Ben? What's going on?

I have no idea. But she mentioned Heidelberg.

So?

I wonder . . . He didn't complete the thought, and I didn't have the mental agility to follow what my mother was saying and try to pry into his hidden thoughts to see exactly what it was he was wondering.

I sat across from her on an overstuffed love seat, Ben beside me. "I don't quite know where to start."

Her gaze flickered to Ben. "I think you should start with what you're doing here in Germany."

"I came to find you when I realized that you had disappeared and no one knew where you were."

"Nonsense. I told Peter and Imogen and Absinthe that I was going into Heidelberg for a long weekend, and would be back on Tuesday."

"Yes, but that was a week ago."

"A week ago? It's only Sunday," she said, shaking her head and giving me a worried look. "Franny, where is your mind? Has Benedikt done something to you? Has he put some sort of a glamour on you?"

"No, but I'm beginning to think someone has placed one on you," I said slowly. "You think we're in Heidelberg?"

"We are in Heidelberg," she corrected, nodding toward the window. "You can see that for yourself."

"Er . . . yeah." *What has de Marco done to her?*

Obviously put some sort of glamour on her to keep her unaware of both her surroundings and the time that's passed.

Why would he do that?

I don't know, but I'd prefer we figure it out away from this house. David will no doubt be here soon, he answered, glancing at his watch.

Gotcha. "Mom, we have to go."

"Go? Go where?" she asked as I stood up and urged her to her feet. She was wearing some sort of silk amber-colored lounging pajamas, but I couldn't wait to collect her things. "Fran, what do you think you're doing? Stop pushing me!"

Can you do the mind thing on her?

Not on mortals, no.

That's a shame. "We have to get out of here. There's . . . uh . . . a terrorist attack going to happen," I improvised.

"Terrorists!"

"Yeah. Really nasty ones with bombs. We have to scoot now."

She argued with us all the way up the stairs, managing to stop us at the top. "Francesca Marie! I insist that you stop this! Before I go another single step, I want him to leave. I don't trust him, and I know he's behind all of your strange notions." She pointed at Ben.

I sighed. "You'd better learn to trust him, because I'm really and truly his Beloved now."

She gasped. "You didn't—"

"Yes, I Joined with him. We're bound together for eternity now, Mom. I love him with every ounce of my being, and none of the things I see you are about to say are going to change that. Now can we please leave? You can yell at both of us later, once we're out of here."

"Oh, Fran," she said, disappointment dripping from her voice as she shook her head at me. "I've lost you. I've truly lost you."

"Oh, for the love of the goddess . . . Vikingahärta! Do something!"

I had no idea what it was I expected it to do, but the second I lifted it, Mom gave a little sigh and slumped toward the floor. Ben caught her before she hit it.

"Bullfrogs! Is she okay?" I asked, reaching for her pulse.

"Yes. Just unconscious." His lips quirked. "I'd say it's for the best, but I doubt if you'd see it that way."

"On the contrary, it's exactly what we need. Can you carry her?"

He hefted her limp form in his arms, starting toward the front door. Ulfur stood at it, watching us with his eerily black eyes.

"Move, please, Ulfur," I said, trying to open the door for Ben. *Oh, goddess! How are we going to get her out of here on your bike?*

I'll hold her. You drive.

I didn't like the idea much, but didn't see any other answer to the situation. "Ulfur, move."

"He's not here," Ulfur said in a loud voice, then looked over his shoulder at the door.

"Huh?"

"The master." Ulfur held my gaze. "He's not here." He turned and looked at the door again.

What . . . ?

He's telling us something, Beloved.

"Great. Just great. How are we going to get out of here if de Marco is lurking outside just waiting for us to leave?"

"We are going to have to face him." He set Mom

down onto a wooden bench next to the door, pausing for a second before adding, "You will need to guard her."

"I will, but don't for one minute think I have forgotten the fact that de Marco wants you for his experiments. I'm not going to let you take him on by yourself."

Ben grinned as he opened the door. "I won't be alone."

A blast of noise hit us, my jaw dropping as I looked in astonishment at the sight of the battle that was going on in the courtyard. It was as if an all-out war had broken out at a zoo—wolves in every sort of color were pouring into the courtyard, attacking anything that moved.

"Are those real wolves or therion wolves?"

"Feral therions."

"Holy jumping saints! It's Eirik and the Vikings! And lions! And . . . is that the parade?"

"Goddess! Dark One!" Eirik, covered in blood and grinning madly, stopped hacking a gray blob on the ground. "We are here! Just in time for the battle, yes? You wish a sword, Dark One?"

"If you have one to spare," Ben said, and to Inner Fran's secret delight, Ben took up the bloody sword Eirik tossed him.

"If you get hurt using that—" I started to say, but at that moment, Ben leaped forward when a brown and gray wolf, spotting us in the doorway, lunged at me.

I love you too, Beloved.

"Goddess! It's a good thing we bought you a beheading ax in town," Isleif said, panting as he stopped before me, brandishing a small camping ax. "The Dark One said you would need it."

I took the ax he shoved in my hands. "Ben said that? When did he say that?"

"This evening, while you were having your supper. He sent us on ahead to get our weapons and lay in wait for the evil one to show."

"Oh, he did, did he?" *I thought you didn't want an all-out attack force?*

I didn't, but felt it would be wise to have one in reserve, should they become necessary. I believe this qualifies as necessary.

Yeah, well, you could have told me that. I'm going to have a few things to say to you once this is over, buster.

Stop talking to your Vikings and protect your mother.

I knew full well that what he really meant was to stay out of harm's way, but since someone did have to keep an eye on Mom, I decided it wasn't worth arguing about. Besides, I had to admit that the sight of Ben in black jeans and a plum-colored shirt battling what appeared to be ravaging wolves was a sight to make any woman melt with girlish admiration. Four members of David's pride were also in full attack mode, their roars and snarls as they fought the wolves adding to the general sense of chaos. But it was when the first of the parade floats came level to the circular drive of de Marco's house that things really got weird.

The float was supposed to depict some sort of scene on a river, with girls in scanty mermaid costumes bearing gold tridents, perched on papier-mâché rocks around a glittery river made up of sparkly blue sequins. A man with a huge sword and horned helm stood at the top of a waterfall that consisted of streamers of blue and white crepe paper. A sign made out of painted violet pebbles spelled out "San Francisco Queer Opera Co. Supports Brustwarze." As they started past the drive, one of the mermaids pointed and yelled in a deep bass voice, "Look, girls! PR opportunity! Let's join the fun!"

"Someone get the digital camcorder! We'll be the hit of YouTube!" another mermaid yelled, and in a couple of seconds all eight of the hairy-chested mermaids clambered off the float and had joined the fray, yelling and shouting happily to one another, walloping both wolves and lions indiscriminately with their tridents, as all the while the helmed guy stood on his float stomping his feet and screaming for them to come back and not leave him alone.

Do you see de Marco anywhere? Ben asked me, distracting me from the dazzling sight of the attacking mermaids.

No. Are we sure he's here? Watch out!

Ben ducked as a wolf leaped over the back of what looked like David, almost knocking Ben down at the same time. *Your lich friend said he was.*

Ulfur! I turned from where I was guarding the door and confronted him. "Ulfur, where's your boss?"

He said nothing, his eyes sad.

"Please, Ulfur. I know that he's put some sort of compulsion on you not to tell us anything, but this is important. He's done something to my mom and I have to know what, so I can reverse it. Please tell me."

Ulfur shook his head.

"Please, Ulfur. Please help me. I swear to you that we will do our best to get you released from him, but in order to do that, you have to help us now."

He shuddered, closing his eyes for a second, his face twisted in agony as he pointed to the left. "Chapel."

"Thank you." Impulsively, I leaned forward to hug him. "Thank you. Isleif! Come and guard my mother!"

"Goddess?"

Isleif paused in the act of hacking off the head of a dead therion in wolf form. I yelled for Eirik and Finnvid, likewise in the heat of the battle, and then sent out a call to Ben. *Ulfur says he's in the chapel. That must be the creepy building that the gargoyles sprout from.*

Francesca! You must stay with your mother!

Isleif is with her. Hurry up! I need you!

Ben muttered to himself as he fought his way over to me, his sword flashing silver and red in the light from the windows.

I can hear that, you know! And you aren't going to have *a next Beloved, so just buck up and come help me get a little payback before David finds out where de Marco is.*

The four of us raced around the side of the stone building that had evidently been added on to the main house at a later date, since the stone was a darker color. Several wolfy therions followed us, but Ben and the Vikings took care of them quickly. I couldn't bring myself to harm them, knowing that even though they were happily trying to kill us, somewhere in their furry form, a human being resided.

They aren't human anymore, Beloved. Their minds are now in de Marco's control.

All that much more payback he has coming to him, then.

Agreed.

Ben and Eirik broke down the door to the chapel. The darkness inside was lit only by candles, the flames of which jumped and danced with the swirl of air as we rushed in. At the far end, a man stood with a familiar-looking woman.

"Naomi," I said, clutching the Vikingahärta in one hand and my axe in the other. "Why am I not surprised."

She spat out something I took to be not at all complimentary. De Marco spun around, his face black with anger.

"You have interfered with me for the last time!" he bellowed, his voice making dust fall from the chapel rafters. He lifted his hand just as Ben jumped forward to protect me, but it wasn't de Marco that worried me. Naomi, her eyes spitting fury, stood silent and still for a moment, obviously gathering power. A silvery white glow formed between her hands, and I knew without a single doubt in my mind that she was going to blast Ben with it, completely destroying him.

I couldn't live without him. Not now. Not ever, really. I might have fooled myself into thinking I could, but I knew now that our lives were too tightly bound to ever be separated.

I don't remember moving at all. One minute I was at the door with Eirik and Finnvid; the next I threw myself forward, knocking Ben aside, but leaving myself standing where he had been. Naomi shrieked and the silver light pulsed forward, slamming into me with a force that sent me flying backward six feet into the chapel wall.

Ben called out my name, but as the light enveloped me, I was content I'd saved him.

Chapter 23

"How is she?"

Quietly, I closed the door to my mother's bedroom and turned to face the people crowded into her trailer. Ben was nearest the door, his mere presence bringing me joy and comfort and love in a way that I had never imagined.

Beyond him, Imogen and Finnvid sat, Imogen's face puckered with worry. Finnvid was eating sardines, occasionally offering a bit to Davide, whom Tallulah had brought back to comfort my mother. To my surprise, Davide seemed to have no issue with the Viking. Perhaps it was the sardines.

"She's sleeping."

"Is she still confused?" Tallulah asked, sitting at the table with Peter. Beyond them, Kurt, Karl, and Absinthe hovered around the tiny kitchen area, obviously handing out cups of coffee and tea. Eirik sat on the sink, while Isleif lounged in the chair opposite Tallulah.

"Yes. She doesn't understand why I've made her come home early from Heidelberg, nor does she seem to be aware of de Marco. When I ask her about him, she keeps telling me that's in the past, and best not mentioned. So who, exactly, is she in love with?"

"We won't know until she can tell us," Ben pointed out.

"She will be better in time," Imogen said, squeezing my hand. "The glamour will fade now that the Ilargi does not have her in his thrall."

"I hope so." I slumped tiredly against the door, my hand automatically seeking out Ben's, smiling at him when he pulled me down onto his lap, kissing the side of my neck. "I don't know what else I can do."

"Maybe there's a way I can help."

I looked up to see who spoke, not recognizing the voice, and for the umpteenth time in the last week, stared in complete surprise. Kurt, Karl, and Absinthe moved aside to let a woman pass. She was tall, like me, but not so sturdily built. Her hair was also dark and short like mine, but where I had gone for a carefree style, hers was pure urchin. She had big brown eyes, a heart-shaped face, and a hesitant smile, as if she wasn't sure of a welcome.

"Fran, right? Or do you prefer Francesca? Your Dark One said the latter, but it's kind of a mouthful, isn't it?"

"Petra," I said, goose bumps running up and down my arms.

We stared at each other for a minute; then Ben gave me a little push. And in the next second, we were hugging and laughing and even crying a little.

It took us a little time to calm down, but once Petra had gone in to sit with Mom for a few minutes, the others had left.

"All will be well now," Imogen said as she hugged me at the door. Ben stood to the side since the sun was starting to come up, sending rosy tendrils of light snaking across the floor. "I'm so happy, Fran, I can't begin to tell you. You and Benedikt are finally truly together, and he has his soul back, and now I can stop worrying about you both because I know you will be so happy together."

I glanced at Ben, too tired to feel surprise anymore. "You have your soul back? When did that happen?"

"You sacrificed yourself for him," Imogen answered before he could. "It is that act which redeems the soul. Didn't Benedikt tell you?"

"No," I said, just enjoying the sight of him. He was so handsome he took my breath away, but it was more than just the pretty package that made my soul sing—it was the Ben inside who completed me and made me more than I was when I'd started out. "No, he didn't."

You're going to yell at me about that later, aren't you?

Oh, yes.

"How are you doing?" I asked Imogen, concerned by Ben's comment that she was vulnerable. "Have you heard from Günter?"

Her expression darkened. "No, and I must admit I'm concerned about his welfare, despite Benedikt's assertion that he was only using me to get at the Viking-ahärta."

Ben snorted. "Why else would he disappear the moment Francesca appeared?"

"Regardless of that, I'm sorry you lost him," I told her.

She smiled, blushing a little. "Don't be too sorry on my behalf. Finnvid has been most attentive in consoling me."

"About him—" Ben started to say.

"Another time," I interrupted.

He hrrmphed in my head.

"I can't wait for you to have daughters, so you can worry about them for a change," Imogen told him, then turned back to me with an exclamation. "You were busy with your new sister, so Eirik wished for me to tell you that he and Isleif have gone into town to search for someone named Nori. Evidently they caught sight of him earlier today."

"Again? I wish I knew what Loki's son is doing in Brustwarze. I wonder if he was who Mom . . . hmmm."

"Who knows? I will be by later to sit with Miranda," Imogen said with a kiss to each of us.

I closed the door, thought about lecturing Ben, and decided to take a different tactic.

"What was that for?" he asked when I was finished mapping the inside of his mouth.

"You have your soul back. I'm happy for you, Ben."

Petra came out of my mother's room at that moment, her eyes red. "I never knew. I just never knew she was alive." She sat down at the table as if her legs were about to give out. "Of course, now I'm going to have to see this man you say is my father. He's in town here, isn't he? Can you give me his address?"

I sat in a slump at the table, Ben making a more graceful appearance. I was too tired to care. I leaned against him, my fingers twined through his as they rested on his thigh.

"I'm afraid that's not possible," Ben said, pain lancing him. "The house is destroyed."

"Destroyed? How? Why? When?"

Ben briefly told her about our evening's activities at de Marco's house.

"The light, or whatever it is that Naomi blasted me

with, set the chapel on fire. Although the exterior of it and the house itself were made of stone, the interiors were wood, and the whole thing went up in a blaze. I only vaguely remember it because I was a little rummy from the blast, but luckily the Vikingahärta took the brunt of most of it, saving both Ben and me from annihilation."

"What's a Vikingahärta?" she asked, her eyes huge.

I pulled from my pocket three twisted metal bits. "This is all that remains of it. I just hope to the skies that Loki never finds out about it. As it is, I'm going to have to explain to Freya that I'm now helpless against him, and won't be able to banish him like she and Frigga expected."

"That's sad," she said, prodding one of the broken triangles with the tip of a finger. "And de Marco? What happened to him and the woman who attacked you?"

Ben's fingers tightened.

I know it looks bad, my love, but you have to think positive. We will save him.

"Both disappeared in the confusion of the fire," Ben answered in a flat voice that said so much about his emotions. "As did David."

"Your therion brother?" She frowned. "Was he burned in the fire?"

"No." Ben's jaw tightened. "De Marco took him."

"I'm sorry," she said. "If there's anything I can do . . . I know we just met, and things are a bit weird and all, but . . . well, I guess we're family now."

"Yes, we are."

Ben's grief and guilt swamped me. Petra must have sensed it, because after a few more minutes of questions about recent events, she excused herself, saying she had a room in town, and would be back later that day to see if Mom had woken up.

"Assuming I'm able to sleep, that is," she added as she collected her purse. "There was some sort of celebration going on when I checked in, with fireworks and people in the most amazing costumes dancing in the street. I gather the town won some sort of a civic award?"

"Something like that, yes." I saw her to the door, then returned to sit with Ben, wrapping my arms around him.

"Wasn't it just yesterday you were telling me that my mother would be okay because she was strong and a fighter? Well, David is strong and a fighter, too. And he knows we're not going to rest until we free him. So stop feeling guilty because you were resuscitating me and couldn't stop de Marco from taking him."

"That's not why I feel guilty," Ben said, pulling me onto his lap again, this time so he could nibble at my neck. "You must come first in all things. You are my Beloved, my life, my sunshine."

I laughed, nipping on his ear until he looked up. Despite his pain, he smiled, love shining in his dark oak eyes, the gold bits glittering with a heat that shimmered along my skin. "You get bonus points for including the sun in that statement. I love you, too, my bossy vampire, and we're going to get your buddy away from that maniac and his whacked-out chick. Okay?"

"Okay," he said, and kissed me with enough steam to make my toes curl. *There is a problem, though.*

What? Finding David? I know the Vikingahärta is broken, but maybe there's a way to get it fixed, and then I can use it to find out where de Marco has gone.

No, not that.

What we're going to say to the watch when they're done tallying up all the dead therions?

I don't care about the watch.

Then what we're going to do with the Vikings? Eirik told me they are enjoying themselves way too much to go to Valhalla, and Finnvid claims he's madly in love with Imogen, although you'd think that would stop him from sleeping with every big-breasted woman he can sweet-talk into bed. I hope Imogen finds out he's been sleeping around, because he seriously needs to be whacked upside his head.

He laughed, and slid his hands under my T-shirt. *I shall make sure she finds out. The problem I was referencing is one of practicality. We have nowhere to sleep, and if you wish for me to do all the things you're thinking about—ice cubes, Francesca? Are you sure?—then we will need some privacy, and I don't fancy this couch with your mother in the next room.*

I laughed, kissed him again, then helped him put on his coat and hat so we could hit Peter up for the keys to Naomi's trailer.

Life is looking up, don't you think? Oh, there are still clouds on the horizon—David is the biggest, naturally, and my mother's mental state is another major concern. But you and I are a team, Ben, and together, there isn't anything we can't do.

Even the ice cubes? That sounds rather chilly.

Definitely the ice cubes. I have plans for them. Very big plans . . .

For a peek at how Ben and Fran met,
read on for a preview of

CONFESSIONS OF A
VAMPIRE'S GIRLFRIEND

a special omnibus edition of *Got Fangs?*
and *Circus of the Darned,*
two of Katie MacAlister's best-loved novels,
originally published under the pseudonym
Katie Maxwell.

Available in trade paperback from New
American Library.

"Narng."

Darkness swirled through my head, but it wasn't the familiar darkness of the inside of my eyelids, or even the twice-experienced darkness of anesthesia, but a really black darkness that was filled with sorrow . . . and concern.

Are you injured? Does anything hurt?

"Gark," I said. At least I think it was me, I felt my lips move and all, but I don't think I've ever said the word "gark" before in my life, so really, why would I be saying it now, to this sad blackness that talked directly into my head?

Gark. I'm not familiar with that word. Is it something new?

"Mmrfm." Yep, that was me speaking, I recognized the "mmrfm." I said that every morning when the clock radio went off. I'm a heavy sleeper. I hate being woken up.

You don't look injured. Did you strike your head?

The motorcycle! I had been run over. I was probably dead. Or dying. Or delirious.

You stepped directly in front of me. I had no time to avoid you. You really should learn to look before you walk out from behind trucks.

You shouldn't have been driving so freakin' fast, I thought back to the voice that rubbed like the softest velvet against my brain, not in the least bit surprised or shocked or even weirded out that someone could talk to me without using words. I'd been with the GothFaire for a whole month. I've seen stranger things.

The voice smiled. I know that sounds stupid, because how can a voice smile, but it did. I felt the smile in my head just as clearly as I felt the hands running down my arms, obviously checking me over for injury.

Eeek! Someone was touching me! The second my hands were touched . . .

My brain was flooded with images, like a slide show of strange, unconnected moments in time. There was a man in one of those long, ornately embroidered coats like Revolutionary guys wore. This guy was waving his arms around and looking really smug about something, but just as soon as I got a good look at him, he dissolved into mud and rain, and blood dripping from a dead guy in World War I clothes. He was sprawled backward in a ditch, his eyes open, unseeing as the rain ran down from his cheeks into his hair. It was night, and the air was full of the smell of sulfur and urine and other stuff that I didn't want to identify. That dissolved, too (thank goodness), this time into a lady with a *huge*—and I mean huge, like a yard high—powdered white wig and a giganto-hipped dress with her boobs almost popping out of it. She was lifting up the bottom of her skirt, peeling it back slowly, exposing her leg as if it were something special (it wasn't), saying something in French about pleasure.

I jerked my hand back from the man touching it at the same time I opened my eyes. Vampire. Moravian. Nosferatu. Dark One. Call him what you want; this man was a bloodsucker.

His eyes met mine and I sucked in my breath.

He was also the cutest guy I had ever seen in my whole entire life. We're talking open-your-mouth-and-let-the-drool-flow-out cute. We're talking hottie. Major hottie. The hottest of all hotties. He wasn't just good-looking; he was fall-to-the-ground-dead gorgeous. He had brown-black hair pulled back into a ponytail, black eyes with lashes so long it made him look like he was wearing mascara, a fashionable amount of manly stubble, and he was young, or at least he looked young, maybe nineteen. Twenty at the most. Earrings in both ears. Black leather jacket. Black tee. Silver chain with an ornate Celtic cross hanging on his chest. Oh, yes, this was one droolworthy guy bending over me, and just my luck, he was one of the undead.

"Some days I just can't win," I said, pushing myself into a sitting position.

"Some days I don't even try," he answered, his voice the same as the one that had brushed my mind. It was faintly foreign, not German, like Soren's and Peter's, but something else, maybe Slavic? I haven't been in Eastern Europe long enough to be able to tell accents very well, and since everyone in the Faire speaks English, I haven't really had to learn much. "You are unhurt."

"Was that a question or a comment?" I asked, ignoring his hand as I got to my feet, brushing off my jeans and testing my legs for any possible compound fractures or dismemberment or anything like that.

"Both." He stood up and flicked the dirt and grass off my back.

"Oh, lucky me, I got to be run over by a comedian," I growled. "Hey! Hands to yourself, buster!"

His hand, in the act of brushing grass off my legs, paused. Both of his eyebrows went up. "My apology."

I tugged down my T-shirt and gave him a look to let him know that he might be a vamp, but I was on to him. That was when it struck me that I had to look up to glare at him. Up. As in . . . up. "You're taller than me."

"I'm glad to see that you aren't suffering any brain damage. What is your name?"

"Fran. Uh . . . Francesca. My dad's parents are Italian. I was named for my grandma. She's in Italy." God, could I sound any more stupid? Babbling, I was positively babbling like an idiot, to a man who at some point in his life had a big-haired French Revolution babe baring her legs at him. *Oh, brilliant, Fran. Make him think you're a raving lunatic.*

"That's a very pretty name. I like it." He smiled when he said that last bit, showing very white teeth. Nonpointy teeth. As in no fangs. I wanted to ask him what happened to his fangs, but Soren and some of the band guys had just noticed us standing with the cable spilled all over, and the motorcycle lying on its side.

"Fran, are you all right?" Soren asked, jumping off the truck and limping toward me. One leg is shorter than the other, but he's really touchy about his limp, so we don't say anything about it.

The vamp glanced at Soren, then back at me. "Boyfriend?"

I snorted, then wished I hadn't. I mean, how uncool is snorting in front of a vamp? "Not! He's younger than me."

"Is something wrong, Fran?" Soren said, limping up really quickly, giving the dark-haired guy a look like he was trying to take a favorite toy away. To tell you the truth, I was kind of touched by the squinty-eyed, suspicious look Soren was giving the guy.

"It's okay, I was just run over. The cable isn't hurt, though."

"Run over?" Two of the band guys hurried around Soren and grabbed the cable, examining the ends of it.

"Joke, Soren. I'm not hurt. This is Imogen's brother."

The dark-haired vamp gave me a curious look before holding out his hand to Soren. He didn't deny it, so I gathered my guess was right. It was no surprise, though. I mean, how many authentic Dark Ones were going to be hanging around the Faire on the very same evening Imogen was expecting her brother? "Benedikt Czerny."

"Chairnee?" I asked.

"It's spelled C-Z-E-R-N-Y. It's Czech."

"Oh. That's right. Imogen said she's from the CR. How come her last name is Slovik?"

"Females in my family take their mother's surname," Benedikt said smoothly, then pulled his bike upright. He was talking about Moravians. I wondered if anyone else knew what he really was. Imogen said only Absinthe knew about her—I had discovered it by accident one night when we both reached for the same piece of berry cobbler and my hand brushed hers.

"I'm Soren Sauber. My father and aunt own the Goth-Faire."

Soren had puffed himself up, his normally nice blue eyes all hard as he glared at Benedikt. I'd never seen him like that; usually he was all smiley and friendly, kind of like a giant blond puppy who wants to tag along.

"It is a pleasure to meet you," Benedikt said politely. He turned to me and offered his hand.

I stuck mine behind my back. "Sorry, I have this thing about touching people. It's . . . uh . . . a skin problem." A skin problem. *A skin problem!* Great, now he'd think I had leprosy or something.

His left eyebrow bobbled for a moment before it settled down. He looked back at Soren. "Is there somewhere I can park . . . ? Yes, I see. Thank you." His black eyes flickered over to me. I sucked in my cheeks and tried to look like I wasn't the sort of leprosy-riddled babbling idiot who walks out in front of motorcycles. "I look forward to seeing you both again."

"Wow," I said as he walked his bike over to where a horse trailer was parked next to Peter and Soren's bus. "Is he, like, major cool, or what?"

"Major cool?" Soren looked after Benedikt. The guy had a really nice walk. I mean, *niiiiiiice.* 'Course, his skintight black jeans didn't hurt any. "I suppose so."

I hugged my arms around my ribs, vaguely surprised that they didn't hurt despite my being slammed to the ground. Nothing on me hurt. To tell the truth, I felt kind of . . . tingly.

"You should stay away from him," Soren said. I dug the latex gloves out of my pocket and put them on, then pulled the black lace gloves from my back pockets. I had bought them from one of the vendors because they looked suitably Goth. No one would look twice at someone wearing black lace gloves, but experience taught me that if you go around wearing latex doctor's gloves, people start to give you strange looks. Soren watched me put on the gloves without saying anything. I told him I had hypersensitive skin (not terribly far from the truth) the first day we met, and he's never said anything about my gloves since. I guess what with his limp, he figured it wasn't kosher to comment on my gloves.

"Why? He seemed okay to me."

"I don't like him. You should stay away from him. He could be . . . dangerous."

I grinned and socked him on the shoulder in a friendly buddy sort of way. "Yeah, right, I know the truth; you're jealous."

His eyes got all startled-looking. "What?"

"His bike. You're jealous 'cause he came roaring up on a big Harley or whatever it is, and your dad won't let you get a Vespa until you're sixteen."

He just stared at me for a second, then turned back to the truck. "Are you going to help unload or not?"

KATIE MACALISTER

The Dark Ones Novels

Even Vampires Get the Blues
Paen Scott is a Dark One: a vampire without a soul. And his mother is about to lose hers too if Paen can't repay a debt to a demon by finding a relic known as the Jilin God in five days.

The Last of the Red-Hot Vampires
Portia Harding is stalked by the heart-stoppingly handsome Theondre North—who's also the son of a fallen angel. Portia's down-to-earth attitude frustrates beings from both heavenly and hellish realms—and gets Theo turned into a vampire.

Zen and the Art of Vampires
Pushing forty and alone, Pia Thomason heads to Europe on a singles tour, hoping to find romance. What she finds are two very handsome, very mysterious, and very undead men.

Crouching Vampire, Hidden Fang
Pia Thomason is torn between two Dark Ones: her husband Kristoff—who doesn't trust her—and his best friend, Alec, who is MIA. So Pia goes back to her humdrum Seattle life—but fate has other plans.

Available wherever books are sold or at
penguin.com